£2·00

"These then are not
tricksters, but stories of people burning like djinn,
and djinn as fiery people. Nearly all of the stories are
haunting, reflective and firelight-beautiful...
Exquisite and audacious, and highly recommended."
N. K. Jemisin, *The New York Times*

"The authors weave the magical beings into their own
cultures, some taking heavy hints from *The Arabian
Nights*, others using djinn as an abstract, heavy longing
to belong or as a haunting presence on Mars. The djinn
is used to explore topics such as women's sexuality and
the disconnect between modern warfare and human
lives... Together, these fantasy stories offer a rich and
illuminating cultural experience."
Everdeen Mason, *The Washington Post*

"Their love for this work shines through in the care with
which they've selected and arranged the stories...
It is—here's that word again—gorgeous.
This thematic coherence adds an extra element to the
anthology as a whole: the individual stories, and their
relation to each other, have something to say."
Liz Bourke, *Tor.com*

"Readers looking for stories set in a variety of locales
(even outer space) and arrayed over various cultures
and religions will find much to like."
Publishers Weekly

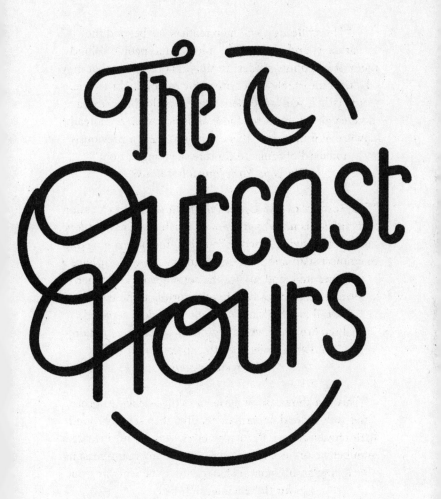

"We like to think we live in daylight,
but half the world is always dark;
and fantasy, like poetry,
speaks the language of the night."
Ursula K. Le Guin

First published 2019 by Solaris
an imprint of Rebellion Publishing Ltd,
Riverside House, Osney Mead, Oxford, OX2 0ES, UK

www.solarisbooks.com

ISBN 978-1-78108-594-3

Designed & typeset by Rebellion Publishing

Printed in Denmark by Nørhaven

CONTENTS

INTRODUCTION
Mahvesh Murad and Jared Shurin

One of the commonalities of human existence—something we all share—is the fundamental, inescapable presence of time. Night comes for us all: wherever we are, whoever we are, however we delay it—or, indeed, embrace it—there is an inevitability to the darkness that has framed the entirety of human existence.

That's no small theme, and, as you can imagine, the idea of 'night' prompted a free-ranging discussion with contributors. The stories, accordingly, are diverse: not only in how, and why, and where the 'night' falls, but in the authors themselves. *The Outcast Hours* includes contributions from authors and artists and screenwriters and illustrators; creators drawn from crime, fantasy, young adult fiction, historical fiction, romance and literature. The night comes to all of us; everyone has a say in how we embrace it.

Night is inevitable, but it is also paradoxical: it is private but shared; beautiful but terrifying; soothing but scary. It is where we are free from social gaze, or when we are most daring. It is when we hide, or when we venture forth. It is when we are most exposed; most hidden and most vulnerable. The night is simply—illogically, ironically, however you take it—a reflection of ourselves. It is an opportunity to be who you are, to do what you want, under the cover of darkness. It is the security of

9

secrecy, and the knowledge of the hidden. The night is what we make of it.

The night is when we are able to imagine everything and anything without bounds. It is when we can explore not just the shadows, but ourselves—our limits and possibilities.

The Outcast Hours is about those people who make the very most of it. It is about lovers and lurkers and thieves and trolls and police and predators and so many more. It is about those people who seek what the night has to offer, whether in a moment of passion or as a lifetime's pursuit. Whether it is dreams or *a* dream, they are glimpsing the truth buried in the darkness. These are the night-people: the seekers, the dreamers, and the outcasts.

As Le Guin notes, "half the world is always dark", and *The Outcast Hours* is a tour of this forgotten half of the world. In the following stories, the night is a border, an experience, an excuse, a home, a battlefield, even a character in its own right. Ultimately, the night is about possibilities. It is about that chance to be who we want to be—who we desperately long to be—and to rediscover or reinvent ourselves.

When the sun goes down, our imagination runs free. In the dark, we let go of our inhibitions and free our inner selves, be they monstrous or magical. The night is when even the best of us can live our worst lives... and the worst of us our best.

(You've long had this belief that this is what will happen when you're at last to descend. It will take your sphere a long time to go down. At first, at the surface, it'll snap and pitch, ungainly, and every wave will fuss it. But when the pumps start and the whirr of engines begin it'll move urgently down, out of the light. The window will sweat condensation as visibility diminishes.

You've long felt that, in a fashion, you will be met. That is to say this:

If you're lucky or have a say the journey will be close enough to the flank of some submerged cliff, that with the occasional blast of cold arc lights you'll see the face of earth and the corals close to you. Perhaps the attentions of cold unstartled animals. So you'll go down into this notional trench whispering into your recorder so you can later hear what a voice sounds like half a mile down. Descending beyond the level of the seafloor thereabouts towards a crack. But what will happen is something other than that swell behind the ribs occasioned by first arrival that you'd have thought you'd be expecting, your heart soon to stir instead because of *having been preempted*.

At the limits of your light, a few metres before the journey ends, you'll glimpse a figure on a ledge. A dark-glassed helmet and segmented limbs. Armour, metal and rubber and thick glass, of antique design. Tubs of old air, or airlessness now, strapped to a barrel-broad chest. Complex filigree of decorative details on the porthole. A style of which you recognise nothing but its age. Legs sitting straight-kneed looking out into the black like a child at rest after a game. It will have been thus for many lifetimes.

You'll see it below your window on your way and then beside you and then above, quickly, but you'll still be sure of what you saw. Without a word, so as not to alert your companion in the craft—this being a communion you'll claim for yourself—you'll salute that vanguardist who in their death has made you a promise and told you a secret. You and only you will know of a prehistory of women and men committed to the descent.

Maybe what you'll have seen is empty, dropped and fallen to rest in a chance attitude of placidness. But there'll more likely be bones within, pioneer bones. You'll know that.

More: you'll know without proof that the person stopped at their overlooking point not on the way down but the way back up again. Surely that was perhaps a grappling hook beside them? Rope and chains on their shoulder, already worn? When you watch the hagfish worry at the base of the world, they'll do so on striae of slime and silt themselves layered above the print of a caulked hobnailed boot.)

THIS BOOK WILL FIND YOU
Sam Beckbessinger, Lauren Beukes and Dale Halvorsen

I reach over for my phone to cut the alarm, knocking over an empty wine bottle in the process. I was awake anyway. Or, as much as someone can be if they haven't actually slept in five days.

Twenty minutes to three. Nearly time. It has to start at three, that's what the book says. I've read the words so many times they play in my head.

3AM is the witching hour. The dreaming souls around you build a bridge to the demon world. Start your ritual then. If you call for your lover, they might hear you, even in hell.

What's the point, even? I should just stay in bed. I should just keep staring at the ceiling. I have become intimate with its pits and contours, the mould that's established a colony in the corner, slowly expanding its territory. If I lie still enough, perhaps it will float down spores that can take root in my pores, dissolve my flesh, melt me away. *R v. Stone and Dobinson*—if you rot to death in a bed of your own filth, the person responsible for you is guilty of culpable homicide through negligence.

But the person responsible for me is already dead.

And she needs me.

I grope the bedside table, my fingers reading an assortment of variously shaped items. Adderall. Xanax. Trazodone. Grief salad. I stop when my fingers reach a round Adderall tablet and chug it down with a mouthful of wine from an open bottle next to the bed. It's like flooring the accelerator in a car that's out of petrol, but it's all I've got. I feel my heart flutter weakly as the drug hits my system. *Come on, buddy.* I drag myself out of bed, grab the wine and stumble through to the kitchen.

I climb out of the Pikachu onesie I'm wearing. There is a major practical drawback to the onesie as a mourning garment, compared to your traditional black dress and veil: you can't pee without getting totally naked. I step out of it, crouch over a bucket in the corner of the room and empty my bladder. I tip the bucket into the sink and run the tap. The whole house stinks of shit, but I barely smell it any more. It's been me and the bucket for a week, now. I haven't been able to confront the bathroom, where...

(Shanaaz is lying on the tiles, blood pooling around the side of her face. Her eyes lock on mine, and they're huge in panic. I lift her up and prop her sitting against the edge of the bath. "Ssh, baby, ssh, it's okay." She splutters, her mouth and chin covered in bloody foam. Her cheek is swelling up like a sack; the broken bones have become a one-way valve and she's trying to breathe, but every time she inhales, her cheek swells more and she's gasping and...)

I shove the memory down. Climb back into the onesie, ignore the smell of sweat and the various other body fluids that are making it so crusty. I make my way to the living room, stepping over empty take-away cartons as I go. Really keeping it together, aren't you, Kara.

The book is there. Perched on the edge of the tea crate used as a coffee table. A plain black hardcover, A4, the pages dog-eared. The stupid title written on the cover in permanent marker. *The Demon's Knock: A spell to bring back a dead lover.* Like a school exercise book. The kind of thing teenage girls would use to dare each other at a sleepover. And yet here I am, 30 goddamned years old, staring at it like it's got teeth.

I have no idea how I got this book. Is it possible that it just appeared, that night? Didn't I just find it...

(in the drawer in the kitchen crammed full of probiotics and vitamins, and I'm digging through frantically, calling to her, "hold tight baby, I'm coming, hold tight," but what am I looking for, a fucking plaster? Aspirin? Maybe if we had some bandages, if I could get the blood to stop I could fix it, but we don't have bandages because I'm useless and never buy the right things, I'm not prepared for this, and suddenly there's the book, right at the bottom of the drawer, like it's always been there...)

lying there innocently. I crouch in front of the tea chest and pick it up. It's heavier than it should be. Or maybe my whole body is just tired. I reach for the bottle, gulp a slug of wine and open to the first page, where someone has handwritten the rules in a cramped black script:

The rules
Only love can raise the dead.
You may not make a copy of this book. This will ruin the magick.
This book will find you when you need it. It has found you for a reason, and it will find someone else who is ready for it after you are done.
3AM is the witching hour. The dreaming souls around you build a bridge to the demon world. Start your ritual then. If you call for your lover, they might hear you, even in hell.
You have 66 minutes to complete the spell. Do not tarry. Demons get impatient. They get angry. They are devious.
There are six steps. Each one is a way for you to prove your love is true.
Wait for the knock on the door. You'll know if you failed, because something will come to find you, but it won't be your lover.

The book reads like a 'Six Ways to Know if They Really Love

You' article ripped from *Teen Vogue: Hell Edition*. But fine: sixty-six minutes overall, six steps. Eleven minutes per step. I set the timer on my phone. It's nearly three. Showtime.

I turn the page to Step One.

Step 1: Set the Mood
Music connects souls. Play their favourite song, loud enough to wake the dead. Put it on repeat.

Their favourite song. Easy enough.

(We're tangled in blankets on the single bed in Shanaaz's dorm room. We've just started dating, and everything stinks of sex. Her laptop is perched on the bookshelf, playing one of her carefully curated playlists filled with early-2010s emo. That song comes on—"Death" by White Lies. She leans over to turn up the volume: "I love this song! It's from *Vampire Diaries*." I keep forgetting how young she is.

I look at her incredulously. "You mean, from *A Girl Walks Home Alone at Night.*"

She shrugs, looking sheepish.

"Oh my god. Three words: Iranian Vampire Western. We're watching it tonight. No buts." I pull her towards me, sliding my hand into the curve of her waist. "Well, maybe some butts, after."

"You can't be serious. I'm writing my exam tomorrow. The one you were supposed to help me study for, remember? As my actual lecturer?"

"Please. You already know it all," I say, letting my hand slip down and under the elastic of her panties. "*Actus reus:* the guilty act." I bring my lips to her collarbone and taste her. "*Mens rea:* the guilty mind."

She tangles her fingers in my hair, pulling my lips to hers. "And when I fail first-year law..." she mumbles, through breathless kisses.

"I plead intoxication," I say, as I stroke my thumb over her.

Harry McVeigh breaks into the chorus. And she wraps her fingers in my hair and pulls me down where we are all touch and skin and wetness. And from that moment, "Death" is our song.)

Seems pretty ironic now, really.

I bring the song up on my phone, casting it through the Bluetooth speakers, *loud enough to wake the dead*. I tap the 'repeat' icon. Sorry, neighbours.

There's a crash from the other side of the flat. I nearly fall over. It's three in the morning and I'm trying to resurrect the dead and there's a crash in our fucking kitchen. What is happening to me?

I creep into the kitchen. A pair of reflective predator eyes stare at me from the sink. I flick the lights on to reveal Squirtle, Shanaaz's geriatric Persian, crouching on the microwave, licking one of the matted knots out of his fur. I make a move towards him, bring my bare foot down onto a shard of ceramic from the mug he's knocked onto the floor. I yelp and he hisses at me, drops onto the floor and zooms past my legs.

"Come here, you little shit!"

I hobble after him, trying to keep my weight on the side of my foot. He's crouched in front of the bathroom, hackles raised, growling at the door.

"Oi! Get away from there."

I rush at him, and he spits at me, racing back to the kitchen and out the window, into the balmy Cape Town night. It's the first time I've seen the little bastard in weeks. I wonder where he's sleeping now. In an open sewer somewhere, by the smell of him. I don't smell much better, so who's to judge. I pull the window closed but I can't fasten it because the lock's broken. Another thing on the list of boring domestic chores that never got done.

I pick the shard out my foot and go back into the living room just as my alarm goes off, marking the end of the first twelve minutes. Harry McVeigh is starting to sing about the safety of the clouds out his window for the third time tonight.

Christ. I'm really starting to hate this song.

I restart the alarm, and turn the page.

Step 2: Light their way home
   *Dim the lights. Draw a circle on the ground in chalk
or paint. As you draw the circle, whisper the words,
"vinces diligunt mortem" three times. Place a candle in
the centre, to guide your lover back to you.*

I don't have a dimmer. So I grab the heavy throw from the
couch, still rumpled up, and drape it over the floor lamp in the
corner of the lounge. I turn off the overhead lights. The lamp is
a glowing spectre in the darkness, watching me from the corner
of the room. I should be used to this by now.

I reach into the box of candles I've set aside. It's empty. Fuck.

All I want to do is lie down on the floor and sleep. Sleep until
it's all over. Because I can't do this. Shanaaz needs me, and I
can't even get my shit together enough to make sure there are
(bandages) candles. Here's Kara fucking things up as usual. I
can practically hear my father's voice in my head, telling me
how useless I am.

Pull yourself together, girl. You can wallow in self-pity later.

Trusty phone to the rescue, I guess. I open YouTube and
search 'one hour candle flickering' and open the first of the
apparently six thousand hour-long videos of flickering candles.
Thank god for the Internet. Let's hope that demons aren't
sticklers for tradition.

I take a stick of red chalk from the bowl, assume the position
kneeling on the carpet, and make my best attempt at drawing
a circle around myself. It's hard to make out the shape of it on
the scuffed parquet floor.

"Vinces diligunt mortem. Vinces diligunt mortem. Vinces
diligunt mortem."

This is another thing lawyers have in common with demons.
We're both way too into Latin.

(She always sits in the front of the classroom. I can't actually remember her name. I've been drinking too much to avoid thinking about the fact that I'm broke and two years late with my PhD and my funding is about to run out and I'm still just a temp lecturer and they could fire me whenever they want and my fiancé left me last year for a fucking boy named Johannes and all my friends who got real jobs at law firms are buying houses and having babies... and to be honest, all the first years have blurred into each other by now. She's a mid-blur smear. There's nothing remotely special about her. If I thought about her for a second, which I haven't, I'd describe her as idealistic, a people-pleaser, always moving in a pack, probably one of those girls who'll join a legal aid clinic in the townships and get too emotionally invested in her clients until she retreats into the soft comforts of suburbia and motherhood.

She comes to my office one afternoon to discuss one of her essays. "I just want to understand where I went wrong," she says, taking a notepad and a pen shaped like a banana out her bag. I worry that she's going to cry. They always cry. But she's got a smile on her face, ready to take notes, eager to learn.

"I felt like I was reading a sociology essay," I begin, my words clipped, hoping to hurt her enough that she'll just leave. "You missed the most basic difference between crime and delict. Criminal law doesn't give a shit about justice for the victim. The law sees crime as a harm against society as a whole."

She smiles at me. I note that she's got a chipped tooth, product of the public healthcare system. "A crime offends the natural order of things."

"Less esoteric than that, but yes, basically. The criminal must be punished even if the victim forgives them. *Nullum crimen sine poena*. There can be no crime without punishment."

"But what about restorative justice?"

I pause, caught off-guard. "Someone's been reading ahead."

She shrugs. "I'm the third sibling to do this degree. My

parents only know about two university professions and I faint when I see blood, so medicine wasn't an option."

"Well then, I'd have even more reason to expect a better essay from you." That was unkind. I feel my face flushing. I stand to cover my awkwardness. "If you'll excuse me. Office hours ended ten minutes ago and I didn't eat lunch."

"Can I keep asking questions if I buy you dinner?" She stands too. Shorter than me, still smiling, not at all fussed by my prickliness.

I'm completely bewildered now. "What?"

"Well, a cheap dinner." She laughs, loose and easy, like water. "My cousin's having a *braai*. They're making kebabs."

I'm so surprised that I agree before I know why. I steal glances at her as I drive us through to the Bo-Kaap. There are some signs. Short nails. Button shirt. Lip-ring. But I'm thrown off by her head-scarf, the little diamante S around her neck. Is this a date?

We're mobbed by family the moment we walk in the house. Everyone seems to be a cousin, or an in-law of a cousin. Someone puts a cider in my hand the moment I walk through the door and fifteen friendly strangers start asking me about my life. Weirdly, they even seem to care about my answers. Before I know it, I'm telling stories about growing up in Cradock, my *verkrampte* parents and their failing goose farm. They laugh at my bitter complaints like they are hilarious jokes.

People hover around Shanaaz like she's a brazier. She embraces everyone, holds their hands while she talks to them, cackles at their jokes. Already I feel a pang of jealousy. I have never seen anyone more loved by so many people. My eyes follow her everywhere, this girl I had dismissed as a blur, and I catch my breath and think: 'oh'.)

The alarm goes off. Another twelve minutes gone. I've just been kneeling here, trapped in my memories, running out of time. I can make it up to her. I swear I will. I can tell her how remarkable this warmth of hers is. How she banished my loneliness. How much I love her. But I've got to do this first.

I silence the alarm. There are 52 unread messages on my phone. But who would I talk to, now? What could they possibly have to say? More wine. That's what I need. I swallow several mouthfuls, relishing the sourness. Drink, you useless bitch. Drink until you can focus.

I turn the page.

Step 3: Invoke their memory
   Your lover has swallowed the waters of Lethe, they
   have already forgotten you. You're going to have to
   remember them back into flesh. Re-member them.
   Embody them. Put on their favourite clothes. Look
   into the mirror. Tell it the best memories you have.

Shanaaz loved this Pikachu onesie. Her brother bought it for her when he went to Japan. It was cleaner then. Sorry, baby. I'll get you a new one. Let's get you back, and then I'll buy you five.

She'd find any excuse to wear it.

(Dress-up parties that Shanaaz wore the fucking Pikachu onesie to, and her explanation for each:

Movie Stars: "There are six Pokemon movies, not even counting the TV specials."

Teenage You: "Pikachu fan since 1997, yo!"

PJ party: "You know better than anyone that this is literally the only thing I ever wear in bed."

Swingin' 60s: "No but listen—Satoshi Tajiri was born in the 60s.")

I bury my nose in the fur on my arm. It smelled like her for the first day or two, but now it smells like everything else in this flat. It smells like grief and feces.

There's a hand mirror propped up against the couch. I stare into it. I look like a vampire, all clammy skin and hollow eyes. But vampires don't have reflections, I guess. At least some people are spared the sight of the monster they've become.

Tell it the best memories you have.

I stare at her, this demon in the mirror. Memories. The good ones. Okay.

My voice is hoarse. "I took you to the Bollywood festival at the Labia theatre. You never stopped finding the name funny, even though I explained I don't know how many times that it was named for the Venetian countess."

("But I mean come on, did they *mos* have to paint the building pink also? You're telling me that's not on purpose?")

"We bought vodka slushies and you got drunk and kept talking about how you loved every single movie. Each film was four hours long, but you made us watch three in one day."

(I tease you about this for weeks. Every time you come in for a kiss, I make a big show of touching the tips of our fingers together and then faking an orgasm. "Bollywood sex!" I laugh.)

"You loved to sing," my voice cracks. "You *love* to sing. You sing everywhere, you don't care who can hear you. You dragged me to karaoke on Long Street on your birthday and I was a grumpy bitch about it, and I stood up on the stage and said the lyrics to 'Love Will Tear Us Apart' in a deadpan monotone in protest, but then you got up and sang 'Love on Top', smiling at me while you did your best Beyoncé impression, and every single person in that club fell in love with you, and I was so proud that you were mine."

("Shan, I'm sorry I'm such a grumpy bitch sometimes.")

You smile and you take my hand. "You are. But you're *my* grumpy bitch.")

"And I said I would sing with you but only if we were alone, and it became our thing to sing in the car together, and you called it Kara-oke."

The face in the mirror stares back at me. She still looks monstrous. But maybe there's some softness there, somewhere. Maybe there's something in that creature that can still feel. Maybe it's Shan, looking through my eyes.

"White Lies" is reaching the chorus again. Christ, I really,

really fucking hate this song by now. Trembling stars and tears dragged from cold eyes.

I glance at my phone. Okay. More. The demons want more. Bare your soul. Sell them your memories. Whatever you've given them so far isn't enough.

Memories, Kara. The good memories, but all I can see is...

(she's lying there, still propped up against the bathtub where I left her. The book is in my hand, and I'm not sure where it came from, and I didn't find any bandages but I found this book instead, and there's something not right about her eyes, and I realise that they're open but not blinking any more, they're not blinking because...)

...Shanaaz's body on the floor of the bathroom...

(she's cold, and she's so still, and it's like at that moment a video clip starts playing, and it's not real, because it can't be, but I can't stop it, or skip or rewind...)

...things happening one after the other, increasingly impossible things. I remember teaching my students about the automatism defence, *S v Stellmacher*, the times when the natural logic of consequence is so powerful that the very concept of choice looks like madness. Extreme drunkenness, extreme emotions, moments when the interruption of consciousness vanishes and your limbs act on their own, like you are a machine.

I shake my head. Grab the mirror. Get a grip, girl. You don't have much time. Happier memories.

"We'd sneak off to corners of the law building and make out in classrooms. Prof Higgins walked in on us and we tried to convince him you'd slipped and I was helping you up."

(The smell of you. The all-encompassing smell of you.)

"You were out in Manenberg in the heart of the gangland, running those community workshops about the constitution. You went missing and they called your sister, and she phoned me in a panic asking if I knew where you were. I was in my car driving out to the township, ready to bring the army to come look for you, and they called to say you'd just wandered back to the town hall, you were having tea with some auntie you met and your phone died and you didn't get why anyone was worried."

The phone alarm goes off. I silence it. This is going to take as long as it's going to take.

"And when you met my parents. I thought it was the worst day of my life."

(It's 42 degrees in Cradock, and my parents haven't stopped bickering since we arrived. They make little digs about you being a Muslim, and less subtle digs about their only daughter having turned into a rug-muncher and they should have known this would happen when they let me go off to an English university. My mom drops the potato bake and my dad shouts at her and my brother keeps turning the conversation to those awful terror attacks in Europe, nê, and this is the problem with letting refugees in who have different *morals* to *decent folk*. I make some excuse to leave early. The geese chase us on the way back to the car, flapping their wings, and I'm shaking as I pull off. I can't bear to look at you, I'm so ashamed. And then there's a noise from the passenger seat like you're crying, but I look around and...)

"You laughed and launched into an impression of the geese and my parents quacking with all their racist bullshit. 'Flap attack!' you said. 'Although, hang on, that's what they think we do to each other. Lesbian come-ons. Flap attack!' I had to pull over, I was laughing so hard and it was like that for the rest of the drive down. All you had to do was link your thumbs and flap your hands and we'd be helpless with laughter. But you also held my knee as I drove and told me that you loved me more because I came from a place of so much anger and defied all that to be me."

My reflection looks the same as always. Except for the glassiness in my eyes.

("Shan," I say, and I touch your cheek, but it's cold, and I realise that you're sitting in a puddle of your own shit, and

I remember how some injuries mean people shit themselves when they die, but it never occurred to me before that it would smell.)

It's no good. I scrub my palms over my eyes. Turn the page.

Step 4: Say their name
  Blood is passion, it connects you to others. Love is empathy. When you empathise, we say that your heart bleeds for them.
  So bleed for them. Bleed and write their name in your blood, in the centre of the circle.

I'm out of wine. I stumble back to the kitchen and grab a fresh bottle from the cupboard, unlabelled plonk, tucked behind the dregs of the sherry. It's the last one. I'd better nail it this time. Squirtle's eyes glow at me through the window. I hiss at him and he slinks back into the night. Persistent fucker. We have that in common.

I come back into the living room and hear the scuffles of tiny claws from the shoe box in the corner by the lamp. The mice are awake. But it's not time for them yet. I remember the man at the pet store when I bought them, the strange smile when I asked for pinkies. "A girl who plays with snakes is a girl with a taste for danger," he'd leered. I took the box without making eye contact with him and hurried out of the store.

Over the past week, I've spent a lot of time thinking about how the whole body is a map of blood vessels. There are the obvious places one could cut. Arms, hands. But arms and hands have so many nerves. Tendons. Bone. So easy to slip and slice too deep. My arms are already a mess of scars and scabs. Never thought I'd be a cutter. Who says people can't change.

I once read a case where some teenager talked his girlfriend into committing suicide over the phone. She'd cut into her femoral artery. The expert witness said it was the fastest way to die, but only if you could get to it. It takes a lot of determination

to keep going, he said, to hack through all that flesh, pulling
the strands of muscle apart, peeling back the skin...

(her eyes are empty, they stare at nothing through a mask of
blood, no baby, no baby don't be dead, don't be dead baby I'll
fix it...)

I'm not going to accidentally kill myself slicing my leg.
Probably the safest place. I stand up and pop open the buttons
on Pikachu, peeling it off.

There's already blood on my thigh. I touch it with my fingers,
confused, wondering whether somehow just thinking about it
made it happen already.

Oh. Stupid girl. It's your period. I hadn't even noticed.

Well, I guess that's convenient.

I slide my fingers into my panties and coat them with blood.
They come out slick, warm.

("You're my honeypot," I whisper, face in her cunt.)

I squat over the circle and start to write her name.

(She's curled up on our bed, groaning. I place a mug of tea on
the side table and sit down on the bed. She snuggles into me. I
tuck her hair behind her ear and kiss her forehead.

"Aren't our magical womxnly wombs supposed to
synchronise or something?" she says, muffled into my boob.

"Poor little love."

"I want you to be suffering with me."

"I've queued up *Vampire Diaries* for us. That's plenty
suffering."

She sighs happily. "I love being in pain. It brings out the best
in you.")

Her name, a thick red and brown smear on the floor. It looks
like I've written over it a hundred times, like I'm trying to etch
it into the floor. Shanaaz. Shanaaz. Shanaaz. Shanaaz.

Someone knocks on the door.

I bolt to my feet, heart galloping. It's too soon. *Wait for the
knock on the door. You'll know if you failed, because something
will come to find you, but it won't be your lover.*

There's another knock. Then three quick raps. Someone is at the door. Someone who is not my lover.

I reach down silently and pull the onesie back up around my hips, clutching it closed in the front. Something is moving out there. The floorboards creak slightly under the weight of something heavy. Heavier than Shanaaz.

I take another sip of wine. Dutch courage. Walk slowly to the door, trying to be as quiet as I can. I peep through the doorhole, but all I can see is a dark shape in the hallway.

"Kara?" a quavering man's voice, heavy on the Italian accent. "Kara, you there?" My downstairs neighbour.

"Sorry, just a minute." I click the buttons closed down the front of the onesie. Glance over my shoulder at the dim room, the mess, the demon circle and the blood on the floor. Fuck. Not exactly a paragon of good housekeeping.

I pull the sleeves over my hands to cover up my gory hands, open the door, slip out and shut it behind me as quickly as I can. Mr Russo is wearing green tracksuit pants, a white vest and a look of irritated concern.

"Hi Mr Russo." I go for sprightly. Nothing to see here.

"Kara *ragazza*, it is nearly four in the morning." His eyes flick over my onesie, my knotted hair.

"Oh, the music."

"Always this same song. Over and over."

"I know. I'm sorry, Mr Russo. I'll turn it down."

I see his nostrils flare, picking up the smell. He considers me, with a flicker of sympathy at my obvious patheticness. "She left you?"

"What?"

"The girl, the nice one. She left, no?"

Left me. Left me alone. Left me to fall apart.

"I'll turn the music down Mr Russo, sorry," I close the door against the horrible pity in his face with a firm, "Good night."

He knocks again, but I don't answer. After a moment, I hear him sigh through the door, and shuffle back towards the stairs. About time. I can't afford another interruption. My phone has buzzed its way to the edge of the circle. I lean over to turn off the alarm, and don't bother resetting it. What's the point of any of this? She's gone. She's gone and no demon spell is ever going to bring her back.

(We've been nested on the couch all weekend. I'm marking essays, feeling cooped up and hot and irritated. It's summer and I want to be doing something. Driving somewhere. Fucking someone. She's been watching *Buffy the Vampire Slayer* for ten hours straight, because bloodsuckers are her thing. Insert lawyer joke here. She gets so emotionally invested in everything. She cries in every episode. She cries when she watches fucking movie trailers, or when we drive past beggars, or when the southeaster blows, or every time we have the smallest fight. It drives me nuts.

Did she always cry this much, or just since she met me?

"I hate season six," she tells me, stroking Squirtle, who's purring unnecessarily loudly on her lap.

"Don't watch it then," I barely look up.

"It's the 'Bury Your Gays' episode."

"I know. I was a queer teen in the 2000s, Shan." I'm absorbed in writing an angry comment to some third year who somehow still hasn't grasped how legal intention works. *Dolus eventualis exists where the accused doesn't* intend *the unlawful consequence which follows her conduct, but foresees the possibility that it* might *and nonetheless proceeds to do it. It is to be reckless as to the possibility of the consequence.* Idiot, I don't write. Because that's unprofessional. Like fucking your student is unprofessional, falling in love with her, asking her and her wretched cat to move in with you.

Shanaaz's phone buzzes with a message. She reads it and blushes. Tilts her hand away from me so that I can't see her screen.

"Who's texting you?" I ask, as casually as possible, putting the paper down, glancing at her face. She's deadpan.

"My sister."

"Bullshit." I think about how much Shan loves people. She'll think the best of anyone, never wants anyone to feel uncomfortable. If someone hit on her, she'd be too kind to turn them down. She'd cheat on me out of politeness.

She frowns at me. "Who else ever texts me, since you hate all my friends?"

She's lying. She's lashing out to distract me. But she is mine and I have a right to know.

My mind races as I catalogue everywhere she's been. Everyone she might have met. Someone in her class? A professor? Some friendly stranger at the library? Someone more appropriate.

I lunge at her to grab her phone out of her hand. She pulls, away, startled, dislodging the cat, who swipes out with his claws, catching my arm. Without thinking, I whack him back. I can't help it, it's instinctual. He thuds off the couch and tears out the room, his tail puffy as a toilet brush. "Kara!" yells Shanaaz, as I shove past her and chase after him, into the kitchen. Little shit. Little shit must learn a lesson. This is how you train cats. My dad always said.

He's trying to get out the window, but I corner him. He hisses at me.

"Kara!" I hear Shan sobbing.

I aim a kick at the cat, but it's only a glancing blow and he escapes and takes off through the window. "Stay gone, you piece of shit!" I yell after him and latch the window.

Shanaaz is on the floor, weeping silently. There's a big red mark on her arm where I may have pushed her. There will be a bruise tomorrow.

I deflate like a balloon. What have I done? I sink down onto the floor with her, and hold the side of her face.

"Baby, I'm sorry. I didn't mean it." She won't look at me. "You just make me so mad. I hate losing my temper, but you make me so mad, hiding things from me."

She grabs her phone and hands it to me, still not meeting

my eyes. There's a message from her sister. It says, *U okay? Worried abt u.*)

Actus reus: the guilty act. *Mens rea:* the guilty mind.

Shanaaz, her name rattles through me. Shanaaz. Shanaaz. The one good thing I had and I broke it.

Barely in control of my own movements, I flip over the page to Step Five.

> *Step 5: Pay the price*
>
> *Your beloved is the most important person in your world. You would do anything for them. There's no line you wouldn't cross.*
>
> *True love requires sacrifice.*
>
> *You must have known this was coming. This is the first and last rule of magick: a life for a life.*

Determinism. It's one of those classic first-year questions. It's inevitable: at some point during the first semester, some kid who's also doing Philosophy 101 will put their hand up and talk about free will. If lecturers made bingo cards, this question would get you an instant win.

If everything in the universe is determined by something else, if the whole universe is God's overly complex Rube Goldberg machine, then why do we draw the line of causation back to the perpetrator and no further? Do we blame the bullet, do we blame the gunmaker, do we blame the woman who shot the gun? And if we blame her, do we blame the parents who raised her? Do we blame whoever hurt her first, who made her like this? Do we blame society, the patriarchy, the universe? Do we blame God?

Conditio sine qua non—but for this, that would not have happened. But that's true of every butterfly flapping its wings to cause a hurricane. So you find the proximate cause. The closest cause.

The intimate partner is always the most likely murderer.

But it wasn't on purpose, she…

(is in our bedroom, folding jeans into her backpack. Her face is blank and she's not crying anymore.

"My sister will come get my other things tomorrow."

She can try. Fuck you if you think I'm going to let that interfering bitch dismantle our home.

But I say nothing, just keep sitting on the bed, watching her pack.

She glances at me, like she's about to ask me to give her a hand, then she shakes her head, crams her last hoodie into the bag and zips it up. She gets up and starts sweeping hairbands and knickknacks off her bedside table into the front compartment. She leaves the framed selfie that we took on the Sea Point promenade, ice cream all over our faces, grinning into the sun. I framed it and gave it to her as a gift when she passed her second year exams.

An object she has no use for now. This is the thing that undoes me.

"Baby, I said I'm sorry," my voice breaks. She picks up the bag and carries it into the bathroom, starts zipping away her creams and makeup. I follow, begging now. Begging like a hungry dog.

"Shan I didn't mean it. Shan please. Shan. Baby, I'll be better. Shan…" and she doesn't even look at me, just keeps folding herself up, zipping herself up in pouches and compartments, cramming herself away in a backpack. And my blood starts pumping so hard in me that I can feel my pulse, I can feel it in my own neck.

"Shanaaz!" I grab her wrist and it's clear now. If she won't listen to me then I'll make her listen. I'll just make her stay here for long enough that she'll listen. Everything is too clear. The shock in her eyes as she tries to pull herself away from me. The fear in her eyes. The disgust in her eyes.)

I taught my students that character evidence is seldom admissible in a criminal trial. It doesn't matter what someone might have done in the past. Focus on the evidence, because everyone thinks they couldn't be the kind of person who could commit a murder, until they do.

Are any of us really who we think we are?

I get up, staring at the shambles in front of me like I'm seeing it all for the first time. This Sisyphean task. The red chalk circle, redrawn over and over and over again on the wood. My phone in the middle, a digital candle flame still flickering away, casting a glow on the blobs of candle wax, on the repeated word in red and brown, her name. I breathe deep and smell the air: shit, and sweat, and worse underneath it all: rot.

What a mess you've made, Kara. What a mess.

True love requires sacrifice.

I look up to see Squirtle nosing at the gap in the kitchen window. He freezes when he notices me looking at him. Time for you and I to say goodbye, cat.

I walk over to the cardboard box in the corner of the room, and tip it over. Six little mice rush out, fleeing to the corners of the room. My little "sacri-mice". They were blind and pink when I bought them, but already covered in thin pelts of white fur. Squirtle darts into the room and corners one under the TV stand.

There you go, Squirtle. Consider this a peace offering. Restorative justice, Shan would say.

(There's a thud as her head hits the corner of the bathtub. Her face is plastered to the floor. Her eyes roll up in panic. Her mouth is filled with blood. She can't speak, opens and shuts her jaw like a fish gasping for oxygen. Ohbabyohnonono...)

I bend down and pick up the knife. *Lex talionis.* The most ancient principle of justice: an eye for an eye. *This is the first and last rule of magick. A life for a life.*

But Squirtle won't do it. The mice won't do it, and the cat won't do it. Not this time.

I slowly approach the door to the bathroom. Impossibly huge in the dark, like a portal to the underworld. Did Orpheus feel it, the dark pull of death? My hands are shaking. I don't want to go in there. I know what is in there and I don't want to see.

I flick on the light switch and swing open the door.

And there is Shanaaz.

And Shanaaz.

And Shanaaz.

And Shanaaz.

And Shanaaz.

Shanaaz, still propped up against the bathtub with her bulbous cheek, dried blood a black half-mask on her face.

Shanaaz, on the floor under the window, from the first time. I couldn't believe it worked...

(The knock on the door. Open it and she's there, shaking and naked and confused, and I bring her inside and I'm sobbing, touching her face, telling her it will all be different now, but as she sits there her memories come back and she remembers, she remembers it all, and she backs away from me, she tries to run from me, her eyes are filled with fear and she falls back, hitting her head again. I am Prometheus, doomed to relive the same agony again and again.)

Shanaaz from the second time, leaning against the bath next to the original, the stab wounds, big and ugly, all down her chest, because by then I knew how duplicitous the demons could be...

("Baby please, okay I'll stay, just put it down...")

And Shanaaz III, draped face-down over the toilet seat.

(She sees her own body, and she stumbles away from me, "Kara, Kara what did you do, what did you do Kara...")

...the back of her head a mess of blood and bone. Shanaaz IV, crammed into a corner...

(this time I'm ready for her, I grab her the moment she walks in the door, gag her, explain to her that she can't leave me, I've brought her back so she can't just keep trying to leave me, and I keep her there for hours tied to the chair, but the clever girl manages to twist herself loose, she nearly escapes this time but I catch her before she reaches the door. I push the knife against her throat as I explain it to her calmly, "You think you can just come in here wearing her face, but I know what you are, demon, because the real Shanaaz wouldn't leave me, she always forgives me, but I'll do it again, I'll get it right.")

I think I even managed to convince myself that they weren't her, those first few times. But of course they were her. Kara, the demon slayer. Ha! What a fucking joke. The only demon in this room is me.

The departmental receptionist used to have this poster above her desk featuring a kitten sitting on top of a comically huge pile of paper. It said, "The definition of insanity is doing the same thing over and over again and expecting different results." I have a PhD and I haven't been as smart as motivational cat poster.

But I see it now. I can bring her back as many times as I want, and it won't matter. Because I'm the monster who can't let her live if she tries to leave me. And who wants to stay with a murderer? Not someone like Shan. Someone like Shan deserves better.

Step 6: Wait for the knock
Was your love pure enough? They'll be at your door. But maybe you lied to yourself, and you brought back something else...

I squeeze myself in between the two Shanaazes on the side of the bath, and I pull back the arm of the Pikachu onesie. My forearm is a mess of scabs and barely healed wounds. All the times I'd bled myself to write her name. I know how to cut. This time I just need to cut a little deeper.

There's no line you wouldn't cross.

"White Lies" singing, could it pull a tear from my eyes?

I lean against both of her as I pull the knife in. I think of all those infomercials I watched during depressed summer holidays back at my parents' farm. *It cuts through cans like a hot knife through butter!* But flesh isn't butter. The knife catches on sinews and tendons and scar tissue. I have to hack through. But it feels good, like cutting the truth out of me.

It takes longer than I think before my consciousness starts to ebb. But the room starts to swim away from me, at last. The knife clatters to the floor. Is that the sound of someone knocking on the door, or is it my own heart hammering its last urgent beat?

(Shanaaz, tangled in the blankets on her dorm room bed, her face flushed, that smile that says, I see you, I know you, I want you, I forgive you, her fingers brushing my bottom lip...)

Baby, I'm doing my best.

IT WAS A DIFFERENT TIME
Will Hill

People fucking love the rooftop pool.

It doesn't matter what time of the year, or what the weather is like. It does sometimes get cold in LA, despite what the movies and the tourist adverts want you to think: cold enough that you need to put on a sweater, or even a sweater *and* a coat. One day last January I saw a guy walking down La Brea with a wool scarf looped round his neck, although he looked like the kind of guy who would loop a wool scarf around his neck because he read somewhere that it was cool. To me, it mostly looked like he was sweating.

In the summer, when it gets hot enough that old people start dropping dead and the local news warns everyone not to leave their dogs and children in their cars, people are in the pool or lying on the beds that surround it by nine-thirty in the morning. They sip Bloody Mary's and mimosas and they talk loudly about how hard they partied the night before, about how they really need to start taking it easy, even though the guys all look like someone carved them out of wood and none of the girls look like they've eaten a carb in the last decade. Not without puking it back up five minutes later, anyway.

In the winter, when the sun drops into the Pacific in the late afternoon and the nights are that little bit colder, the pool is less busy. People wrap themselves in towels and order coffees instead of beers, and sometimes they shiver and hope that nobody noticed. But there's never *nobody* there, even on those rare occasions when it hammers down with rain or it gets so cold you can see your breath in front of you.

It's only actually empty after I turn on the big patio lights and tell everyone to get the fuck out. I mean, that's obviously not what I actually say, because I like this job and telling everyone to get the fuck out would be a definite violation of the Associate Pledge that everyone who works here has to sign on their first day, but I like to think that the message I'm transmitting is pretty clear.

The pool itself is just a rectangle with a sloping floor, six feet at the deepest end. There are strip lights along the walls and criss-crossing the bottom that glow red and purple and pink and orange and the water is kept really warm, so warm that it steams when the air is cold, but in the end, it's just a pool. The beds are just beds, the orange cabanas are just orange curtains and orange cushions and orange mattresses. The furniture is carved wood that looks old but isn't. I know because Stef told me she got them at a place in the Valley that mostly makes things for Pottery Barn. Sometimes people ask me where they can buy a side table or a twisted lounge chair, because OH MY GOD THEY ARE JUST SO CUTE, and I try not to smile when I say they're bespoke pieces that were specially made for the hotel, and I'm really sorry but there's nowhere they can be bought. So yeah. It's fair to say I don't really get the pool.

The view, though? That's different.

That I get.

I've been up here at least once a day since I started work eleven months ago and I don't think I ever haven't stopped to take a look, even if only for a few seconds. The hotel itself looks a lot like a filing cabinet; a tall, narrow rectangle of white walls and grey carpets and floor-to-ceiling windows with a digital screen that takes up the whole eastern side and is usually showing a motion poster for a comic book movie or the new *Star Wars*.

But from where it stands, rising up above a gentle curve on the north side of Sunset Boulevard, you can see almost all the way to the ocean. LA sprawls out beneath it, the endless grid of surface streets and the thick, twisting ribbons of freeway, and the thing that always strikes me is how green the city actually is. Not green like New York or London, where huge parks sit in the middle of the city, but just street by street, block by block. Trees loom over cottages and spring up between apartment buildings, and gardens squeeze into whatever space they can find.

Way over to the south you can see the cluster of skyscrapers that make up downtown, where every second building is a hotel and every fourth or fifth is a soft-serve ice cream store. People actually live down there now, in lofts with newly exposed brick walls that have been made to look old and full of character, because so much money has been thrown at making the case that it's a cool neighbourhood that some people have actually started to believe it. It's a pretty awesome deception, even by the standards of a city that's built on them.

At night, the city is a million dots of light of every conceivable colour. The endless parallel lines of red and white on the interstates, the grids of yellow in the apartment buildings, the orange glow of the streetlights. On a really clear night you can see the red and blue and green of the Santa Monica pier in the distance, all the way down by the beach. Right below the hotel there is the pink neon of strip bars and the white neon of hotels and restaurants and the red neon of the clubs where the paparazzi wait outside on their scooters, ready to give chase to some minor celebrity who just wants to get home and take their makeup off without ending up on TMZ.

The hotel itself used to be down and dirty, the kind of place where rock bands rode motorbikes along its corridors and threw TVs out of its windows, and every couple of days some grungy-looking couple with long hair will ask someone to take their photo in front of it, because this is *that* place where *that thing* happened thirty years ago. Then they'll walk along to the Strip and take the same photos outside Whiskey A Go Go and the Rainbow and they'll talk loudly about how Guns N' Roses used to play there, and how Lemmy used to live in the building across the road, and literally nobody will give a fuck.

I come up to the pool once an hour when I'm on the night shift, even though they close it at midnight. People sneak up here sometimes, and if they're just hanging out on the beds and drinking a nightcap or two, I usually leave them to it. It's sort of a grey area, in that the pool *is* officially closed but the hotel is the kind of place that prides itself on getting its guests whatever they want, so if they're quiet and they're not actually in the water, I'm probably going to let it slide. As much as anything, because it really isn't worth the shit that usually gets thrown your way if you try to get them to leave. The kind of people who stay here aren't used to being told what to do, and to say they don't much like it would be a really fucking massive understatement.

Sometimes I don't have a choice, though. I came up once at about five in the morning and found two people fucking in the pool, which actually doesn't happen as often as you probably think. Their clothes were on one of the beds and there was about five hundred dollars' worth of coke piled on the screen of an iPad next to the water and the dude kept ducking his head under the water for a really long time, coming up red faced and gasping for air, then just absolutely going to town on the girl while she yelled in his face, calling him a pussy and a little fucking bitch. There was water flying everywhere and I'm not going to lie to you: I watched for about five minutes before I finally went over and told them to get their shit together and go downstairs.

It was just too funny not to.

I get out of the elevator and walk past the little bar trolley that gets wheeled poolside during the day and step outside.

It's never all that dark on the deck—the pool lights get

dimmed at night, rather than actually turned off—and I can see that the beds are all neat and the marble table where people collect their towels is empty and sparkling clean. I look around, and my heart sinks.

There's nobody fucking in the pool. Not this time. But there *is* someone sat on the side, dangling their feet in the water.

It's an old guy, with grey hair and the kind of tan that looks like it's going to need chemotherapy one day. He's wearing a dark blue suit and he's rolled his pant legs up so they don't get wet. His shoes and socks are lined up neatly next to him and he's staring into the water. He doesn't look up as I walk out onto the deck.

My first thought is that he doesn't look like he's going to be trouble, but I'm still pissed that I have to deal with him. Even if he turns out to be the nicest man in the world, who genuinely didn't realise the pool is closed and apologises over and over when I tell him, I'm still going to have to stand there and make small talk—*he's a small talker, I know it just by looking at him*—while he dries his feet and puts his socks back on and laces up his shoes and then I'm going to have to walk him back to the elevator because I'm not allowed to just trust him to leave and carry on with my rounds.

I once asked Philippe why they don't just lock the door that leads out to the pool at night, and he told me that locked doors aren't compatible with the hotel's core values. I didn't reply because, seriously, what the fuck was I supposed to say in response to that?

My sneakers squeak on the wooden deck as I walk towards him. He finally looks up when I'm almost by his side, and his face looks vaguely familiar, which is pretty standard for this place. The really big stars don't stay here—the ones who don't live in town rent houses in the hills or stay in the super-luxury hotels in the Valley that look like shitty warehouses or office buildings from the outside, the places where you have to arrive in a car that doesn't attract attention—but it's still an industry place. Actors on their way up, writers and directors, producers. They fill the bar in the evening and take breakfast meetings in the restaurant, talking as loudly as they can get away with about all the projects they're juggling right now. This guy could be one of them. Or wants me to think he is, maybe.

"Hey," I say. "Pool's closed."

The old guy smiles at me. His face wrinkles up into a mass of deep ridges and furrows, and I see that he's older than I first thought. In his seventies, at least. Maybe older than that.

"I know," he says. "I saw the sign. It's quiet out here, though."

I shrug. "I guess so," I say, because I really don't want to encourage conversation. I want to get this old guy into the elevator then I want to walk the corridor on the twelfth floor, like I should already be doing.

"Have you worked here long?" the old guy asks.

Small talker. I fucking knew it.

"A while," I say. "Almost a year."

"It's a nice place."

"Sure."

He nods, and kicks his feet gently back and forth. Little waves roll away towards the sides of the pool.

"We've got a problem, you and me," he says. "I was hoping not to be interrupted. But here you are."

I shake my head. "There's no problem," I say. "I just need you to get your stuff together and go inside. It's not a big deal."

"I disagree," says the old guy. Then he brings his hand up from his side, and he shows me the gun.

The things that happen in movies don't happen. I don't freeze, my heart doesn't stop beating in my chest, and I don't forget to breathe. I just look at the gun. It's a black pistol, and I sort of distantly wonder how I didn't see it until now but it was hidden at the side of his leg and—to be perfectly honest—it never occurred to me that I should be looking out for a fucking gun when I approached this old guy with his feet in the water.

He doesn't point it at me. It's just resting on his thigh. But he smiles. "Yeah," he says. "Didn't see that coming did you?"

"No," I say.

"Sit down," he says, and waves the gun towards one of the orange beds. "Go on now."

I don't move right away because I'm still just staring at the gun and part of me is wondering what the fuck I did in a past life to deserve this shit. I must have been a real fucking dick to somebody.

"Didn't you hear me?" he asks, and now he does point the gun at me. The barrel is pitch black. "Sit down."

I make myself move, and slowly lower myself onto the edge of the bed.

"All right," says the old guy. His feet are still dangling in the pool, like he doesn't have a care in the world. "Now we can have a civilised conversation."

I take a deep breath. "What do you want to talk about?"

"Death," he says, and his smile widens into a grin. "Mine was the plan when I came up here. But now I'm not so sure. Maybe we'll do two for the price of one. What do you say?"

"I don't know what you're talking about," I say. I'm trying to keep my voice calm, keep it nice and level. The old guy doesn't look like the kind of person who is about to commit a murder-suicide next to a fucking hotel pool, but I guess if people looked like what they're capable of then avoiding the assholes and psychos in the world would be a lot easier than it is.

"Sure you do," he says. "You recognise me?"

I shake my head.

He rolls his eyes. "Fucking Millennials," he spits. "They did a retrospective on me at LACMA last year. Five of my pictures are in the Criterion Collection, for fuck's sake. Take a good look."

I stare at the guy for what seems like an appropriate amount of time, then shake my head again. "Sorry."

He sighs. "Fuck it," he says. "John Barker. That ring any bells?"

It actually does. I don't watch that many movies—*which is a thing that most people in this town just straight up refuse to believe is possible*—but I feel like I've seen the old guy's name, maybe on the credits of something, or on a billboard. I have this vague memory of a movie about a killer dolphin.

"Maybe," I say. "I'm not a big movie fan."

"Wash your mouth out," he says, but his smile returns as he speaks and it's really weird because it looks like a genuine smile but he's still pointing the gun in my direction. He kicks his feet again, sending new ripples out across the water. "What's your name?"

"Alex," I say.

"Good name," he says. "That's a real name. Alexander, right?"

"Yeah."

"Proper name," he says. "Not like the names they give kids now. Do you like basketball?"

"Not especially."

"About one in ten of them has a proper name," he says. "The rest of them are just made up. They're just noise. Do you know what I'm talking about?"

"You're saying you don't like black people's names."

His face darkens. "Who said anything about black people?"

I shrug.

"Did you hear me say anything about black people?" he asks. "That's where *your* mind went, son. Not mine. Are you prejudiced?"

I fight back the urge to laugh. "No," I say. "I'm not prejudiced."

"Are you sure?"

"Pretty sure."

He narrows his eyes. "Do you think I am?"

"I don't have the slightest idea."

"That's right," he says. "You don't know shit about me. Don't assume I'm some kind of fucking racist just because I'm old. *That's* prejudice right there."

"You just said—"

"I just said what?" he asks. "That basketball players have made-up names? You said you're not a fan, so you don't know shit about what I'm talking about. I didn't say shit about black people. I'm fucking *furious* you went there on me."

My eyes drift back to the gun. "I'm sorry," I say. "I guess I misunderstood."

"Yeah," he says. "You got that right."

He kicks the water again, harder than before.

"What are we going to do about this situation, Alex?" he asks.

"What situation?"

"This one," he says. "Where you interrupted a man who was about to kill himself and then called him a racist. How do we move on from that?"

I stare at him. A single thought has appeared in my mind, as loud and bright as a police siren.

Don't ask him why he was going to kill himself.

"Why were you going to kill yourself?" I ask.

I couldn't help it.

I just couldn't.

"You think that's any of your business?" he asks.

I shake my head.

"You're right," he says. "It isn't. But I'm here and you're here and we're both in this thing now. So I'll tell you. If you really want me to?"

"I do," I say. And it's the truth. I don't know why, but it suddenly feels like something I *have* to know.

"I killed someone," he says. "What do you make of that?"

"I don't know," I say. "Who did you kill?"

"My assistant. Little fucking prick."

"Why did you kill him?"

"He turned on me."

"What?"

The old guy—*Barker, he said his name was John Barker*—

45

grimaces. "Some people have been saying shit about me," he says. "Things they say I did, from years back. Actresses. A different assistant. A producer I used to work with."

"Female assistant?" I ask. "Female producer?"

"Don't be a fucking smartass," he says. "I've been letting my assistant deal with it. I mean, I don't even remember half the things they're saying I did. And some of them are lies, just outright fucking lies. But that's the world now. So I wrote a couple of checks, spread a little cash around. As far as I knew it was over."

"And?"

"My fucking cocksucker of an assistant has given the whole thing to the press," he says. "To the fucking *trades*. It'll be all over them tomorrow. And then that's it. All over."

"Why did he do that?"

"Because he hates me," says Barker. "The feeling is absolutely fucking mutual, believe me, but still. I never thought he'd fuck me like this."

"He must have had a reason."

Barker rolls his eyes. "He tried to shake me down," he says. "A few months back. He said I harassed him, and he wanted a raise or he was going to go public with all the shit he knew. I told him to get fucked, that he could quit if he wanted to. He didn't, so I thought that was the end of it."

"What did you do?" I ask.

"What?"

"What did you do that made him accuse you of harassing him?"

"Nothing," he says. "Called him a fag a couple of times. Maybe half a dozen."

"OK."

"I didn't mean anything by it," he says. "I don't have anything against him, against any of them. But seriously. I can't say the word fag in my own fucking house?"

"You pretty much can't say it anywhere."

"Why the fuck not?" he asks. "It's just a word."

I shake my head. "I don't have the slightest idea how to explain that to you."

"Right," he says. "Because I'm some fucking old dinosaur and all you fucking smart kids know everything about everything."

"I didn't say that."

"You were thinking it, though. Don't deny it."

I don't say anything.

"He told me what he'd done," he says. "After he'd sent all that shit to the magazines. He came and told me. What else was I supposed to do?"

"Hire a lawyer?" I suggest.

"Fucking bloodsuckers."

"Or a PR firm?"

"You got a hundred grand you want to lend me?"

"No."

"Well then."

"So what did you do?"

Barker smiles. "I hit him," he says. "With this statue they gave me once. Twice, or maybe three times. He wasn't breathing."

Jesus.

I feel sick. And I look at the pistol and it looks more threatening than it did when I first saw it. A *lot* more. And just like that, I realise I'm scared. I'm scared of this old man and the gun in his hand and the horrible things that won't stop coming out of his mouth.

"Where did this happen?" I ask.

"In my office. At my house."

"You just left him there?"

He grunts with laughter. "What was I supposed to do? Call fucking animal control?"

I shake my head.

"It wouldn't have mattered if you hadn't come out here and interrupted me," he says. "Because he'd be dead and I'd be dead and I wouldn't have to read all the shit people are going to say about me tomorrow. Wouldn't have to watch people who did worse shit than me line up to call me a monster. But you came and now I don't know if I feel like going through with it anymore, which means you're responsible for all this shit. This is all on you now."

"I didn't do anything."

"You know what you did," he says.

Barker shuffles backward and lifts his feet out of the pool. He keeps the pistol pointed at me while he dries them off and pulls his socks and shoes on. It takes a long time because he's only using one hand and he looks about as flexible as steel girders but eventually he's fully dressed and he gets unsteadily to his feet.

"All right," he says. "Come on. Let's go."

"Go where?" I ask.

He motions with the pistol. "Over there. Grab yourself that chair in the corner."

I look across the deck. There's a little glass table in the corner with two armchairs set around it. The last six feet of the walls leading to the corner are glass, so you can look out across the city from where you're sitting. It's always the most popular table.

I walk towards it, trying not to let my legs shake as I go. At least not badly enough that he can see. He follows behind me, and I sort of half-wonder what would happen if I spun around and made a grab for the gun. The guy is old, and I've got to assume his reflexes aren't what they used to be. But if the gun is pointing right at me, he only needs to pull the trigger before I reach him. So it doesn't seem like a smart play. Not yet, anyway.

I walk around the glass table and sit down. The sounds of Sunset Boulevard at midnight float up from far below as the old guy slowly lowers himself into the armchair opposite me. Engines, and car horns, and the thudding drone of a hundred basslines from a hundred clubs and bars. Laughter, and shrieks of delight. Running footsteps. Squealing tires.

But up here it's quiet.

I wonder how long it will take someone to notice I'm not where I'm supposed to be and come looking for me. Julia is in reception and Jason and Luis are somewhere between here and there, but everyone has their own schedule and nobody really checks on you on night shift. If you fuck up and forget to do something you'll hear about it, but not normally until the next morning.

So for now, at least, it's just me and him up here.

We're alone.

Barker settles the pistol on the arm of his chair. His finger isn't on the trigger, but it's close. The barrel is pointing at my chest and I feel a tightness there, like it's projecting some kind of weight against my skin.

Stay calm.

"What's your deal?" he asks.

I shake my head. "My deal?"

"Your story, son. Your fucking narrative."

"I work in a hotel," I say.

"I see that, you fucking smartass," he says. "What do you *really* do?"

I smile, despite myself, because I realise what he's getting at. It's a really common question in this town, where everybody wishes they were doing something other than what they're doing, wishes they were somebody other than who they are. I don't know if every cliché comes from something true if you go back far enough, but the ones about people who work in Los Angeles definitely do, in my experience, at least. It genuinely feels like every waitress is an aspiring actress, every barista has a screenplay in the trunk of their car, every bartender is just *this* close to getting a beat on Kendrick Lamar's new mixtape.

I've never taken an acting class, I've never written a screenplay, and I wouldn't have the slightest idea how to work a mixing desk. I sometimes meet people at parties and when they ask me what I do they look totally incredulous when I tell them I work in a hotel. Then they ask me the same question Barker asked me. "Yeah, but what do you really do?" And I tell them the same thing I'm about to tell him.

"I work in a hotel."

He smiles at me. "You've got a pretty wide fuck-you streak running through you, don't you?"

Yeah. Too wide.

"I don't know," I say. "Maybe. I guess."

"Yeah, I see it right there in your face," he says. "I could see it from *fucking space*. It ain't a criticism, so we're clear. There are worse things to have. Especially in this shithole town."

He fiddles with the cuffs of his shirt. For a second, his hand is maybe a foot away from the pistol and I imagine myself leaping across the table, grabbing it from the chair arm and rolling away out of his reach. But I don't move.

Of course I don't.

Barker looks back up at me, and replaces his hand on the gun. "You have to understand," he says. "It was a different time."

"When?" I ask.

"Before," he says. "Things were simpler then. Better."

"OK."

"People were civilised," he says. "They knew how to act. How to behave. Things were straightforward."

I shrug. I have no idea what he wants me to say, and I'm pretty sure he's going to keep talking anyway.

"Don't get them pregnant," he says. "Actresses, I'm talking about. That was the golden rule. And if you did, then you had to do the right thing. Pay for the scrape. Send a car. You know?"

"A friend of mine is an actress," I say.

He nods. "Working?"

"Sometimes. Commercials mostly."

"Good money in commercials."

"She was up for a movie once. The casting director told her the part was hers if she blew him."

"Did she?"

"No."

"Did she get the part?"

"No."

He shrugs. "There you go, then."

"What?"

"You make your choices," he says, "and you live with the consequences."

I frown at him. "You don't think that's a fucked-up way to behave?"

"I think it's how the world works," he says. "Or used to be, anyway."

"You know what a power imbalance is?"

"Get the fuck out of here with that shit," he says. "I get enough of that woke crap from my assistant."

I can't help myself. "You mean you did, right? Before you killed him?"

He grimaces. "Watch your mouth, son," he says. His voice is suddenly low. "You want to know what a *real* power imbalance is? When one man's got a gun and the other one doesn't. So just watch your fucking mouth."

He turns his head and stares out across the city for a long time. I don't say anything. I just watch him. His eyes have clouded over, like he's not really here anymore. Like he's somewhere else. Or some *time* else, maybe.

"I never hurt anyone," he says, eventually. "That's the honest truth."

"Maybe you don't think so," I say. "But that's not a thing you can know for certain."

He grunts. "So fucking smart. Smart enough to be working dead shift in a hotel. You think you're hot shit or something?"

"I don't think that," I say, honestly.

"There was a time when you'd have known my face soon as you saw me," he says. "When I wouldn't have even made it up to this fucking pool because the manager of this shitbox would have grabbed me in the lobby and given me the best suite in the place for nothing. You believe that?"

"Sure."

"Yeah, sure. You don't know your history, son. That's your problem. You don't know the men who built this fucking town."

"Jack Warner?" I suggest. "Louis Mayer?"

"Smartass," he says. He smiles at me and I almost smile back but then I look at the pistol and reality punches me in the gut, hard.

I'd sort of let myself start to think that this was just like one of those times some asshole stops me on my rounds at some godforsaken hour of the morning and decides he really, urgently *needs* to have a conversation with me, right then. It happens pretty often, and my heart always sinks because they're *never* the people you would ever actually choose to talk to: they're the people who want to complain about how the Jews still run all of Hollywood, or how social justice warriors are castrating America, or who mention George Soros within about thirty seconds.

Assholes, like I said.

But inside the hotel, down in one of the long corridors, I can listen and nod and if I'm really not feeling their bullshit I can kind of tease them on it because I know that if shit turns south, if they suddenly decide that actually they don't want some uppity minimum wage kid giving them mild shit, then management will have my back because their tolerance for assholes is not a whole lot higher than mine. Unless they're famous, of course, but that pretty much goes without saying in this town.

Here, though? Right now, in this moment?

This is different.

This is *fucked*.

Barker takes a phone out of his pocket and starts tapping at its screen with fingers that don't look like they bend anymore.

And again, his hand is away from the gun, and again, I don't move a muscle. I instantly rationalise it to myself: it's a dumb play, he's not going to shoot me anyway, better to just let this play out, you don't provoke people who are clearly in the middle of a crisis.

But it's all bullshit.

I'm too scared to make a move.

I'm fucking *terrified*.

"What's your email address?" he asks, and despite everything, I have to fight back the urge to burst out laughing. Because he asks the question so casually, like we've just met at a party and had a cool conversation and he has to head home but wants to connect with me later.

"Why?" I ask.

"I want to send you something," he says. "Bear in mind that when a man holding a gun asks you a question, you can assume it's pretty fucking rhetorical. So just tell me your email address."

I tell him. He types one-fingered into his phone, then I feel the familiar buzz of a notification in my pocket.

"Read that," says Barker. He sits back in his armchair as I take my phone out, his hand resting back on the pistol. I open Mail and expand what he sent me. It's a forward of an email that was sent to him this morning. I don't recognise the name of the sender, but her address is from one of the trade newspapers that everyone in this town pretends to read every day.

Dear Mr. Barker,

I wanted to give you a heads-up about a story we're going to be running on Friday. It concerns a number of allegations that have been made to me about you over the last month or so. If you'd like to make an on the record response, I'll include it in both the print and online versions of the story.

Best,
Jenna Walker

I glance up at the old man.

"Go on," he says. "Read it. The whole fucking thing."

There's a PDF attached to the email. I click it open and start reading. When I'm done, I barely even feel disgusted. Because I've read this story so many times over the last year or so. The details change, but the underlying shit is almost always the same.

"Is it true?" I ask. I know the answer, but I want him to tell me.

"I don't know," he says. "Some of it, probably. I don't remember."

"This woman," I say, pointing at my phone. "The one whose mom acted in your movie. She says she was fourteen."

"What was I supposed to do?" he snarls. "Ask to see her fucking ID? She came onto me, son. It was her fucking idea, and you fucking bet her mom was cool with it. I just went along."

I stare at him. "Fourteen," I repeat.

"Hey," he says. "Don't you fucking take that tone with me. It was a different time."

"A better time," I say. "That's what you said?"

"Goddamn right."

Barker's face is flushed with anger, and the gun is trembling in his hand. But all of a sudden, the fear that started creeping through me when he first showed me the pistol seeps away. Because just like that, I see him clearly. It's like someone turned a spotlight on and shined it right at him. His anger is real, I don't doubt if for a single second, but it's not the righteous anger of the innocent: it's the anger that comes from being caught, and it's not even really what's driving any of this. What's driving it all is fear.

He's scared.

I don't know of what, whether it's going to jail or the end of his career or just what people are going to say about him tomorrow, but he's *so fucking scared*. I can see it.

And he knows I can.

"Did you really kill your assistant?" I ask him.

"Who the fuck knows?" he growls. "Her head was pissing blood when I left her. She looked dead enough to me."

Her head. *She* looked dead.

I stand up. I don't even know I'm going to do it, I'm just suddenly on my feet.

"Hey!" he says. "Where the fuck do you think you're going?"

"I'm going to walk back inside," I say, "and I'm going to carry on with my rounds and if anyone asks me I'm going to say that I lost track of time looking at the view."

"You aren't going to do shit unless I say so," he says. "I thought you understood the way this works?"

"I understand," I say. "I get it."

I stand in front of him. His hand is still on the gun, but now I don't believe he's going to use it. I don't believe he ever was.

"I was in line for a lifetime achievement award," he says. His eyes are locked on mine, and his voice has dropped to barely more than a whisper. "From my guild. Do you think they'll change their mind?"

I shrug. He stares at me for a long moment, then nods. It's barely more than the tiniest dip of his head.

"Go on," he says. "Get the fuck out of here."

I walk slowly past him, and along the edge of the pool. My sneakers squeak on the tiles. The lights at the bottom of the pool are blue and purple. Somewhere far below I hear the squeal of tires and a chorus of horns. The doors that will take me back inside, that will take me away from John Barker, are right in front of me. Maybe ten more steps. A dozen at most.

I take one, then another, then another. Then I stop, and turn back, because there's something I have to know. Something I won't ever be OK with not knowing.

"Are there even any bullets in that gun?" I ask.

He's slumped in the chair in the corner, his gaze fixed on the horizon. But he looks round at me, and nods. "One."

I don't say a word. He smiles at me, a wide reptilian smile, and in it I see something of the man he used to be, the man who did the things I just read about, and a shiver races up my spine.

"Aren't you going to try and talk me out of it?" he asks.

"Why would I do that?"

He shakes his head. The smile disappears, and he looks down at the floor. "You have to understand," he says. "It was a different—"

I turn away and head for the doors. Part of my brain is screaming that I should run, that I should already be screaming for help or calling the police, but I force myself to walk, and I don't make a sound.

I'm still waiting for the shot when I step into the elevator.

AMBULANCE SERVICE
Sami Shah

Nazeem counted down the seconds. His shift started at nine and for over two decades he made it a point to never pass through the entrance until the watch hands were exactly at the hour. It was a personal victory, meaningless to everyone else, and perhaps never even noticed by the others. But to him it mattered. The night, and all it wrought, wouldn't begin until it absolutely had to. So he stood on the sidewalk, looking at his watch.

"Thirty-four Mashallah, thirty-three Mashallah, thirty-two Mashallah…"

There were no Mississippis in Karachi. The street buzzed around him—people passing as they walked in and out of the chai shop next door; a legless beggar cruising in a trolley at knee level, propelled by the power of knuckles-on-concrete; a fat one-eyed dog proudly carrying a tikka bone; a juice vendor balancing pint glasses of neon-green sugarcane juice to a family of six that had arrived on a single motorcycle; and suffusing it all, an ether of mosquitos and flies.

"Twelve Mashallah, eleven Mashallah…"

He had been leaning against the shoulder-high cot just outside the building entrance. A bare steel crib, containing a thin mattress, suspended under a bright blue tin roof. Painted in bold letters across the roof was

DO NOT KILL INNOCENT BABIES
PUT THEM IN OUR CRADLE
(DO NOT GIVE IN HAND OF ANY BODY)
BEGUM BILQUIS EDHI

In winter that cot stayed empty for weeks at a time, but on a stinking, fuming summer night like this, it was rare to find it so—Nazeem had long ago theorized it was harder to tolerate an unwanted child when its wailing was accompanied by the droning of mosquito hordes and sweat-soaked clothing. If he hung around a few hours, the cot would have an occupant again, maybe one still alive.

"Three Mashallah, two Mashallah, one Mashallah," Nazeem said. Then, "Bismillah ir Rahman ir Rahim."

He pushed through the saloon doors. Anjana Bibi sat just past the entrance to the Edhi Ambulance Center, lit more by hysterical splashes of color emitted by the small television mounted on the wall than by the humming tubelight. Rumor had it she was older than Allah himself, and her face certainly looked it; calcified folds of wrinkled flesh all converging to a point where a small mouth was anointed with enough red lipstick to resemble a raw wound. She whispered a greeting, Nazeem was sure of it. Even if the television wasn't blaring some breaking news that was never really breaking news, she was impossible to understand, speaking as she did with the hint of a shadow of a glance of a whisper. Her job was to take donations when they were brought in, and write out a receipt, the legibility of which was remarkable given that it took her several tries to even get pen nib to find paper.

"Walaikum-asalam Bibi," Nazeem guessed.

The betel nut face tightened for a second in acknowledgement, which was the signal for him to continue inwards, through the next set of doors and into the back room. White tiled floors and walls—or rather they had once perhaps been white, now each tile was the color of whatever had splashed, accrued, or settled on it over the years. Against the wall was a desk and a chair, the desk missing a drawer and the chair missing a leg. Pushed in next to them was a bed that Nazeem always said was the least comfortable bed on earth, given that its frame wobbled with every deep breath, and the mattress was so worn through his back pressed against the steel ribs beneath. Yet every time he'd needed a nap during the 12-hour shifts, that bed had carried him into the deepest of sleeps more effortlessly than his bed at home ever could. A fan spinning overhead was too close to the light next to it, shadows strobing across the room. Above the entrance he had just come through were eight framed photos of drivers who had been killed, a pleasingly small number. Standing between him and the desk, looking up at the pictures, was the kid. Barely eighteen, dressed in a crisp white shalwar kameez already with the red high-visibility jacket worn over it, and hair parted precisely down the middle. Were it not for the mustache, he would have looked to Nazeem like a toddler in grown-up clothes.

"Bilal, right?" asked Nazeem.

The boy startled, realizing he wasn't alone in the room. *Those nerves will loosen quicker than he thinks*, Nazeem thought.

"Nazeem sahib," he said, straightening and practically spearing Nazeem with his open hand.

Nazeem took it with a laugh. "Forget the 'sahib' stuff, yaar. I'm Nazeem. You all set to start?"

"Yes," Bilal said, and while he tried his best to sound eager, Nazeem could tell there was fear beneath it.

"You'll be fine," Nazeem said, squeezing the hand that was still pumping his up and down. "You're riding with the best."

Behind the center, parked in a lane just wide enough to contain it, was the ambulance. A small Suzuki minivan, it might once have been white as well but like the tiles, that too had been encroached upon. Large rust patches and splashes of mud and dirt had left the original paint limited to small Vitiligo patches.

The only consistently maintained color was the red EDHI and 115 emblazoned in large letters along the sides.

They checked first the van itself: tire pressure, oil, petrol, spare tire, siren, lights, battery. Then the interior contents: bottles of water, an oxygen tank, a stretcher, a small box of white gloves, a locket containing a single strand of the Prophet's hair, a pair of long, heavy sticks, and in the dashboard a Quran. Nazeem smiled as he watched Bilal consult a handwritten list before checking each one, then ticking them off with a pen that he placed primly back in his front pocket. He had never been that careful himself; he hoped the boy's diligence wasn't going to be a hindrance. The things they had to face were, in his experience, best confronted with an improvisational attitude.

"How many days did you train?" Nazeem asked.

"Three," answered Bilal. "They said that's all I'd need."

"Two more than necessary. Still, the first aid stuff helps I suppose. Just remember, once we start, instinct over education, okay?"

"Yes, of course, yes," said Bilal, now starting to pull at the edges of his mustache. "How much training did you get?"

Nazeem counted on his fingers, going through all ten twice, paused to consider with his eyes closed, then grinned and curled two fingers into a zero.

"I started this division. I had to convince Edhi sahib twenty years ago to let me. The stuff I go through is what you new kids are taught. But I had to figure it out myself."

Bilal didn't look suitably awestruck, just kept tugging at his mustache.

"And that's all we'll need," he asked, jerking a thumb at the van. "Not even a gun?"

"You can't save lives with a gun," Nazeem said. "Let's go."

They climbed into the van, Nazeem on the driver's seat while Bilal settled into the shell behind him. The van gasped and coughed awake, headlights flaring in the alley, and as Nazeem eased it out onto the street, Bilal begin to recite the Ayat al-

Kursi loudly, asking Allah for protection on their hours and hours of journey ahead.

They had barely left the Edhi center and the radio began crackling urgently. Nazeem pulled the microphone to his face with one hand, twisting the steering around with another so they could swing past a slow moving rickshaw.

"Nazeem to base. Go ahead. Over."

"Salaam Nazeem bhai." This was followed by an address. Then, "Family says it's a Churail. Over."

Nazeem heard Bilal stifle a yelp behind him. He grinned. A Churail was perfect to blood the boy with. He flipped a switch and the siren blast leapt ahead of them, pushing traffic out of their way. It was still too early in the night for Karachi streets to afford much space. Every flattish surface was congested with cars, bullied out of the way by kamikaze buses, and trucks so overladen they were given a wide berth only in case they toppled over. In the gaps between, filling spaces with a diligence that can be attributed to natural law, were motorcyclists and rickshaws. Even on a clear night, the moon was obscured by the haze of dust and exhaust. Despite this continuous battle for forward motion, every traveller maintained a respect for the authority of every Edhi ambulance. Each person knew one day it would be them riding in the back, and so space was afforded for Nazeem to plummet ahead. And those that delayed in giving way were shamed loudly through the megaphone on the ambulance's roof.

"Red car, move you bastard!"

"Sufi sahib, your beard is bigger than your sense, move it!"

"I'll shove that motorcycle up your ass idiot, move!"

An elderly man was sitting on the sidewalk outside the house when they reached, dressed in a shalwaar and white T-shirt, fanning his face with a newspaper, a dirty cloud of mosquitos drifting over his bald pate.

"My grandson is inside," he said. "The Churail appeared in his window every night and we prayed for her to keep away but it didn't work. Now she's got him." The old man conveyed all this with a tone of disappointment, as though he were informing them of a dessert he had been hoping to eat but found the insects got to it before he could.

Bilal began to ask for more details, but Nazeem cut him short. Instead he asked if there were any women of the house who needed informing of their arrival. The old man said the siren would have alerted them, pointed them towards the entrance, then sat back down on the sidewalk and resumed his observation of the night sky.

"Let's not waste time," Nazeem instructed. "Do you smoke?"

"No," said Bilal.

"There's a box of matches in the dashboard. Get them. Once we're inside, don't look in its eyes. Just do what I say. I don't want to be here too long, I haven't had my chai yet."

The small house was crammed with too-large furniture, and every wall had a framed painting of the Kaaba, or a Quranic prayer in swooping calligraphy. There were two women, the old man's wife and a younger one in her teens. Both had covered their heads with shawls, the older not bothering to hide her face. She was the one who led them to the door near the back. Nazeem thanked her and stepped into the room, followed by Bilal. The door was hurriedly pulled shut behind them.

Afterwards, seated across from each other at a wobbly plastic table, gently swirling steaming chai that was poured onto a saucer to cool, Bilal interrogated Nazeem over what they had just done.

"I didn't look at her, like you said, but I caught glimpses," he said. Sitting at the cafe, bathed in the undeniable reality of electric lighting, news blasting behind them from a wall-mounted TV, rotating fans swiveling their heads from side to side with arthritic squeals—all this had taken the hysterical edge from his voice. In the first moments after they had dealt with the Churail, Nazeem had even considered slapping Bilal, but was pleased to discover the boy recovered fast, faster than the last half dozen apprentices who'd served under him.

"What did you see?" asked Nazeem, waving over the small boy wiping down tables with a cloth dirtier than the surfaces it was supposed to clean and asking him for some paratha to dip in their tea.

Bilal turned over his memories.

"I saw an old woman. Her skin was like… like the concrete here." He pointed at a bare pillar next to them. "I looked down quickly, so I can't be sure, but I think she had a mouth. I saw teeth, long teeth like a picture I once saw of a man who had never cut his fingernails, and they were curled round and round. Her teeth were like that, I think. So long they were curled round and round. All the darkness around her, was that her hair?"

Nazeem appreciatively slurped some more tea, then refilled his saucer. "Yes, they have thick black hair all around them. I've never looked at them directly either. Then what did you see?"

The parathas came, piled high on a plate like stacks of pancakes. Bilal tore a bite and tossed it in his mouth, not even noticing how it was still too hot to barely even touch.

"She was standing over the man. Touching his face. Then the door closed behind us and she was gone. Just gone. The room was brighter."

The room had indeed brightened as suddenly as a switch being flipped. When they walked in it had been submerged in blue shadows, the only color being the Churail's pallid skin. Then she was gone, and it was as though she had never been there. The only evidence being the skinny, naked man, barely in his twenties, curled up on the ground. As Nazeem and Bilal watched, the color bleached from his hair, and it turned as white as *skin*

paper. His eyes were open, staring up as tears brimmed inside, then spilled over. Most trailed down to his ears, but some followed the curves of his gaunt face all the way to his mouth, where they dripped into the rictus scream. Nazeem had motioned to Bilal and they walked to either side of him, lifting the man off the ground by his arms and placing him on the bed at the end of the room. It was placed right under an open window, through which the tips of finger-thin branches grasped, their leaves whispering to each other.

Nazeem wrapped a blanket around the man, then reached under his pillow. Not finding what he wanted there, he rolled the man away from the edge, lifted the mattress as much as he could and peeked underneath.

"Ask him where it is," he'd said to Bilal. Realizing the boy was staring at the man's hair, Nazeem repeated the question loudly, snapping his attention back.

"Where what is Bhai?"

"Where her keepsake is. Ask him. He'll know."

Bilal had to gently slap the man several times just to get his eyes to focus away from the ceiling. When he repeated the question, the man emitted a wire-thin wail, then slowly shifted his gaze at the window sill. Nazeem reached over and pulled at the base of the sill. The wood pulled forward just a few inches, revealing a small compartment, inside which was a lock of black hair bound by a fraying pink ribbon. Nazeem prayed softly, then picked it up, laid it on the ground, and lit it with a burning match. The hair curled, then writhed like a salted slug until the small flame swallowed it whole. Nazeem stamped it out then, spreading the ashes across the floor with his foot. The man had been able to walk after that, although not without support, and they led him to the ambulance, laying him on the stretcher. The old man had climbed in the back with Bilal and both were deposited to a hospital close by. Then Nazeem and Bilal had gone for their chai.

"There's usually one or two a week. It's always the same too, as long as you can find the keepsake and burn it."

"What if you can't?" asked Bilal.

"Then you tell the family to keep searching until they find it. Or the Churail wins and you don't need to search anymore."

Bilal considered this. They finished the last of the paratha, dipping it directly into the tea, the glistening skin of milk floating on the surface wrapping around it.

Their next job, an hour later, was a man standing in the middle of a busy road. Cars were mostly swerving around him, but some had been coming too fast and it was only after those passed through him that they had gotten the call. The man was dressed in the same white shroud he must have been buried in, though it was soaked and thus transparent in places. Even his long grey beard was a knotted wad of sponge, and a puddle of water trailed him as he was led to the side of the road by Nazeem. He walked away only once Nazeem had assured him they would inform the graveyard owners of the water pipe that must have burst next to the grave.

And so the night went. They sped back and forth across the city, the siren always heralding their arrival. The streets of Karachi emptied as the hours passed, even the skies clearing of filth enough to show the moon, a curve of bone caught in the night's throat.

A woman with her feet twisted backwards had been seen feasting on a little girl, they'd found only the child's remains and wrapped all the bits in a cloth, taking the bundle to the morgue. A grown man had been pulled up a tree by something with claws and a lion's roar. Negotiating his release had involved raw meat and poetry. From the beach they'd pulled a woman's bloated corpse, thick blue veins marbling her skin. Someone had heard her yowling like a baby, even though her drowned eyes had sunken away. Bilal almost dropped her corpse when a baby's face peered out from inside her mouth. He and Nazeem carried her back to the water, letting whatever crawled up from her throat thrash its way back into the ocean. They would finish one job, and the radio would crackle, sending them hurtling to the next.

Nazeem would glance at Bilal when he was sure the younger man wasn't aware, assessing his resilience. There was exhaustion more than shock, eyelids drooping when the van's gentle rocking would soothe him. Nazeem had seen the opposite happen to others before, when by this time of the night they were staring unblinkingly ahead, whispering words of reassurance to themselves in increasingly unconvinced tones.

With only a couple hours left before dawn, they arrived at the apartment entrance. It was the kind that sat on the outskirts of the city, with spotlights syringing the sky around it, and a moat of private security guards needing to be crossed to get past the high walls. Within its borders were enough resources to ignore the Day of Judgment if its residents wished, with entertainment options. The police van parked in front of the apartment tower they had been summoned to looked even more incongruous than they did. Ambulances were still seen here from time to time; even rich people, when dying, had to contend with the same bare resources as the poor. The police, however, had no authority here, and would have had to request permission even to enter the compound.

Nazeem recognized the Superintendent, smoking a cigarette with a cluster of his officers. They were sheltered under the caramel glow of a sodium light. They exchanged pleasantries. The Superintendent's hands were shaking, Nazeem noticed. He knew the man had survived two Taliban attacks and attended to almost as many bomb blasts and gang-war aftermaths as someone with a lifelong career policing Karachi's streets could accumulate.

"So what happened?" asked Nazeem.

The cop pointed at the tower behind them. "We were asked

to come here two hours ago. I came myself, just in case. The building manager said the man in one of the apartments hadn't come out in a month. Went up myself and could hear him moving around behind the door. I sent two of my boys in. One never came out, the other one did but charged at me. I had no choice but to shoot him just to save myself." At this he pointed next to the police van. Nazeem and Bilal hadn't seen it when they pulled up because they had been on the other side, but on the ground next to it was a cop's body, the face covered by a bloodied shirt. Over his heart was a single bullet wound, still leaking.

"Did you shoot him in the face, why is it covered?" asked Bilal, looking back at the Superintendent, who had motioned to one of this subordinates to light him another cigarette, his hands being inept to the task.

"No, in the chest. One shot. You can see it. We covered his face because it was too hard to look it. He came out of the apartment that way you see. With his face turned."

"Turned," asked Nazeem.

"Inside out," said a younger cop. He tried to smile when he said it, then burped once, ran away from them, and vomited on the black tarmac.

"How long were they inside?" asked Nazeem.

The senior cop pulled hard on the cigarette, then indented the air with muddy grey smoke.

"Less than a minute," he said.

Every apartment was serviced by a single private elevator. As they rode up, Bilal turned to Nazeem. "Do you know what this is?"

Nazeem shook his head.

The elevator rose so silently the only way they even knew it was travelling upwards were the numbers changing in the digital display overhead. "Why did you volunteer for this?" Nazeem asked, after a second had passed.

"Edhi sahib told me to," Bilal said. "I grew up in one of the orphanages. I was a cot kid. I met him a year before he died, and he asked me what I wanted to do. I told him I wanted to help him, so he said when I was ready, to come to you. Do you… do you think I can handle it?"

"You've been good so far, child," said Nazeem, squeezing Bilal's shoulder. "Now let's see what this is."

The doors opened with a floral chime, and they exited into a small hallway. Just a few steps in front of them was the front door to their destination apartment. It was antiseptic white, the entire hall was, in contrast to the stink that suffused it.

Nazeem knew that stink well. He'd spent most of his adult life dealing with rotten corpses, especially in his early years as a regular ambulance driver tasked with collecting bodies wherever they were found. The first one had been blocking a sewer, left there for days before they had been sent to collect it. He was riding with Edhi himself that time, and the old man hadn't even flinched at the syrupy stench. He rolled up his sleeves, lifted the corpse as gently as possible to stop it from pulling apart, and laid it onto a white blanket. "We'll all smell the same one day," he told Nazeem, who had been unable to even approach the body. "It's a smell more common than the smell of a rose." Eventually, Nazeem had learned to dull himself to it, registering but never reacting to the stink anymore. Since then he had seen bodies blown apart by bombs, dead of all ages being abandoned by poverty and neglect, and countless others who were found only when they had alerted the living through olfactory signals.

Bilal gagged next to him. Three days' training. Two of them would have been basic first aid. The third telling him of the kinds of creatures he'd face working with Karachi's only exorcist.

Nazeem turned the handle and the door opened. In the center of the room sat a man in his underwear, his body glistening with sweat. Arranged in a circle around him were half a dozen bodies. They were recognizably human, but barely so, twisted and stripped of almost all skin and muscle. And then emanating outwards, all over the floor, all along the walls, on every surface of the cavernous space, were neatly spaced words, daubed in gleaming black strokes.

"Come in," hissed the man.

Nazeem and Bilal exchanged a glance, then entered. Nazeem felt it right away. The room exerted a pressure that was immediate: it began as an uncoiling of pain in his guts and the throb of something barbed pressing against his brain. His eyes hurt and he felt food and bile rising up in his throat.

"What have you done?" Nazeem choked out.

The man grinned lecherously at them. He had a few wisps of neatly combed hair, a long drooping nose, and no discernable chin. Sweat had puddled in the folds of his belly, and yet he was so clean, even the soles of his feet were pale.

Nazeem closed his eyes, felt the room swirling around them, and opened them right away.

"What is this?" he gasped.

The man laughed. It was a simple laugh, not menacing or evil, not even hungry with malice. It was the laugh of someone who had very sincerely just experienced joy.

"I created a new language," the man said. Nazeem noticed his eyes were sickly yellow, like the skin of a jaundiced child. "I have lived in this room for a year and every day of that year I've murdered in here. I've brought in children and men and women and the elderly. I've brought them in from the streets where they slept and no one even noticed or cared. And I've killed all of them. And with their blood I've written new words. Words that have never existed before. I am an author and this is my book."

"The room," Nazeem managed, as he staggered and landed on his hands and knees. "The room is the book?" The black words smudged under his touch.

"Yes," said the man. He began unfolding his limbs, starting to rise. "I've killed so many in here, that now all it knows is death. And all it causes is death. All it creates is death."

Nazeem was lying on the floor now, foam bubbling across his lips, limbs twitching.

The man stood up, watching Nazeem with hungry satisfaction. Then he turned to the only other occupant of the room still standing as well.

"Are you feeling the death of this room calling to you too?" the man asked Bilal.

Bilal had been utterly still, not sure of his own ability to move until just then. He took a deep breath, then another one.

"Actually, I feel fine," he said.

The man cocked his head and stared at Bilal.

"With blood I have written these words. They are words I conjured from my imagination, new words that have never existed. They are words of hate and anger, murder and pain. Since they've taken effect, every man or woman who has come here has either killed themselves, or anyone else they have seen. So you cannot be *fine*." This last was spat out in contempt.

"But I am fine," said Bilal. "I promise."

The man charged, running at Bilal with a howl, blood-inked text smearing under his feet. His hands were curled like claws, but Bilal had time to see that they were not claws, just hands. He leapt to the side and the man thundered past him, slipping and sliding as he tried to come to a stop. The man hit the wall, bounced off it, and spun towards Bilal again, this time managing to scrape at Bilal's face with his nails. Bilal yelped in surprise and shoved at the man, who fell backwards, tripping over Nazeem's prone form and sprawling on the ground.

"What are you," shrieked the man.

Bilal was standing over him now, looking down. The man had scratched at Bilal's left eye, managing a deep gash at the corner. From inside the wound a single curl of flame rose out, tasting the air with a smokeless red tongue. Bilal reached up, and the flame receded, skin sealing itself over it.

"I don't know," said Bilal. "But I know your cursed room works on the children of Adam, and I am not one of those."

He kicked out, connecting with the man's chin. There was the crunch of a jaw breaking, and the man fell back, unconscious.

Bilal knelt down and felt for Nazeem's pulse, grateful to feel it fluttering still. Then he heaved his mentor onto his shoulder and retreated to the entrance. Turning to survey the room, he said a prayer loudly for all those that had died there to find safe passage to Allah and forgiveness for their sins. Then Bilal spat. A glob of lava hit the floor and the room erupted in flames. They unrolled across the floor and walls, carpeting over the words with fire. The man was consumed by them so fast, he didn't even wake to scream in pain.

Bilal retreated back to the elevator and punched the button for the ground floor, the flames staying obediently in the apartment behind him.

Outside, the police had been joined by other sightseers, all looking up at the flames billowing out of the apartment windows, then staring in astonishment at Bilal and his burden as they emerged through the lobby. Bilal ignored them, laying Nazeem down on the stretcher inside the ambulance. He emptied a bottle of water over his face, then sat back in relief as the older man came up with a gasp.

"What happened?" Nazeem said, once he had collected enough breaths to speak again.

"The man killed himself. Set himself on fire. So I quickly got you out before we all died with him," Bilal said.

They stayed a bit longer, talking with the police, both Nazeem and Bilal saying they were unable to remember what they saw up there, only one of them being truthful. Then the radio crackled again.

"Why don't you rest in the back for a while. I can take over," offered Bilal. Nazeem considered him for a few seconds, then assented. As the ambulance sped back into the maw of the city, the emerging talons of sunrise bloodied the sky.

(The rise in the otherwise flat stretch of lowlands is not pronounced enough to be called a hill by most people, but the woman who lives there is herself so small that when she uses the term, no one quibbles. They even find themselves repeating it. 'How long have you lived by the wee hill?' they say.

The woman is small enough that people double-take to see her. It's not dwarfism. It's that she looks as if she is both smaller than and faded from an original, as if someone photocopied a more usual-looking woman at 70% scale and opacity. Her voice sounds similarly reduced.

'I was quite the dancer once,' she says in the post office queue, abruptly, and no one knows how to take it. 'I was bigger another time,' she claims when she is in the bus stop, and the look of memory that takes her over is unsettling. 'But not in this.' She jiggles her arms.

'That's a lot for your tea,' says the butcher, and the woman laughs in a tired way. That evening a tiny figure bundled under scarves comes off the bus and walks the short distance to the woman's house. People notice, as they do in any town of such size. The guest is another woman, hidden in her clothes.

The unlikely quantity of meat turns out to be a new norm. 'She's shrinking,' the butcher claims, 'no matter how much she's eating. She came in, I could barely see her over the counter.'

Sometimes when they glimpse her in the streets it seems to some locals that he's right, that she's smaller than she was, and even harder to focus on than before. Others beg for an end to such foolishness.

'She talks to herself now,' the publican says. 'That I will say. I heard her when I went past her house. Asking things in a whispery voice, and answering herself in one even whisperier.'

BLIND EYE
Frances Hardinge

"Twenty pounds an hour?" The man on the other end of the line covered his phone, but not well enough. "Bloody rip-off," Erin heard him mutter in the background.

"Jesus wept, Nathan!" hissed a female voice in answer. "Just tell her yes, okay? What else are we going to do? We can't exactly call an agency, can we?"

"But we'll be gone hours! That could cost—"

"Oh, for God's sake!" There was a crackle and click, and the female voice became clearer. "Pepper Donovan gave us your number. She says you're... trustworthy. Is that right?"

Erin knew what 'trustworthy' meant here. No questions asked, no talk afterwards.

"Yes," she said quickly. "It's like doctors. Confidentiality."

"Right, then. We're at the Harmony Inn in west Willbrook, just off the ring road. And you can have an extra thirty quid if you make it here in half an hour. We'll talk properly when you get here."

Erin didn't like heading out to meet people she knew nothing about, but the mention of Pepper was reassuring. Pepper was a bouncer, and a regular customer who would probably be annoyed if Erin went missing. If these people knew Pepper, they probably wouldn't want to annoy her.

As a rule, Erin liked to find out as much as possible before accepting a job. However, personal rules were like guy ropes. Whenever one of them snapped, it put more strain on the others. This evening, a week after an expensive MOT, her remaining rules were looking dangerously optional.

In the hotel's pocket-sized lobby, next to the empty reception desk, a man, a woman and a small girl stood waiting for Erin. They all had a defeated, exhausted air, as if there had been a raging argument that nobody had won.

The child had a narrow, wan face and hair the colour of dishwater. Unlike her companions, she did not look up as Erin entered.

"You the babysitter?" asked the woman. "Oh, thank bloody God. I'm Kim. This is Mia." She held the girl's hand high, as though she were apprehending a criminal rather than making an introduction.

Kim and her male companion were both dark-haired and in their thirties, with the same jowly, sullen look. Brother and sister, Erin guessed, not a couple. Both looked sick, purple shadows lurking beneath their eyes. Neither bore any obvious family resemblance to Mia.

Erin had a secret dread that one day she would be called out to guard a kidnap victim, and that fear now flitted across her mind. She dismissed it, however. Abductors would have spirited their stolen child into a hotel room quickly, instead of waiting around in a brightly-lit lobby in full view of the car park.

"Here." Nathan slapped a room key into Erin's hand. "There's food and tea in the room. And you've got my number." He started doing up his anorak.

"Wait—anything I need to know before you go?" asked Erin, startled. "Anything medical? Diet? Any rules I should know about?"

Nathan handed her a pill bottle.

"She doesn't sleep," he said.

Erin's hackles rose. She didn't like dosing kids, particularly with sleeping pills. Even prescribed melatonin made her uncomfortable.

"I might see if I can get her to sleep without them, first," she said, in what she hoped was a non-confrontational tone. "I have a few tricks that sometimes work. What have you tried?"

"No," said the man. "You don't understand. She *mustn't* sleep. You *can't let her sleep*. Not even for a moment."

"What?" Erin looked down at the bottle, and spotted the word 'caffeine'. "Why?"

"It's medical," Kim replied sharply. "She mustn't sleep while we're away. Health reasons. Look, we need to go *right now*. Is this going to be a problem?"

"No," said Erin, and tried to sound like she meant it. "We'll manage."

Of course it was a problem. Caffeine pills weren't safe for kids, let alone six-year-olds. If Erin walked away, however, Mia might be left with someone else—someone willing to chuck pills down her throat.

Erin had always wondered what she would do if she found herself in charge of a child suffering real abuse or neglect. She hoped that she was not about to find out.

She had known, of course, that her new customers would be dubious. These days they always were.

Erin had never been a morning person, or even an afternoon person. Day's tedious glare made her sleepy, and she only seemed to wake up properly after dark. So when her smattering of temp jobs didn't meet her rising rent costs, a friend suggested that she become a childminder and work evenings. For the first year or two, her babysitting was underpaid but mostly unchallenging.

When everything changed, it was the fault of Pepper

Donovan's daughter Lily. She was ten years old, with a craven, ingenious, furious hunger for attention. When she didn't get it, she set fires. Being dumped with a babysitter counted as being ignored.

In the dead of night, after she had been put to bed, Lily climbed out of the window and set fire to some rubbish in a corner of the garage. Erin smelt smoke and rushed into the garage to put out the fire. That was when she discovered the four damaged cash machines stacked against the wall, wires trailing from where they had been ripped from their bases.

She should have called the police, but instead she phoned Pepper to report the fire.

"You went into the garage?" Pepper's voice suddenly became tense.

"Yes."

Above her, Erin could see Lily leaning over the bannister in her sequinned top, white-faced and shocked by the success of her arson. Lily was smart, hard-eyed and frenetic. Erin imagined her kicked from care home to care home, her crazy fire fizzling under a cold, steady drizzle of rejection and neglect.

"Yes, but it's OK," Erin heard herself say. "No harm done. I don't think we need to… bother anybody with this."

Pepper had a lot of friends. Word got round that there was a babysitter who was 'trustworthy', and who would babysit all night at short notice.

There was the burglar who kept getting arrested because of his 'trademark' of baking a cake in any house he robbed, and whose twelve-year-old son seemed relieved to have actual help with his homework. A white-van-man needed somebody to look after his twins whenever he was out stealing charity bags of clothes from doorsteps, or raiding allotment sheds for their tools. And there were a lot of other parents with strange schedules and suspiciously nice cars…

Gradually, the normal agency work was squeezed out by Erin's new customers. Erin could not have explained quite how it happened. The work for her respectable clients was less well paid, of course, but it also started to seem less important, less rewarding.

Erin had already read up on child-minding and taken first aid courses. Now she took self-defence classes and Aikido lessons. She changed her dress style to something less cosy, a 'mafioso PA on casual Friday' look.

How bad would a crime need to be before she reported it? She didn't know, and felt uneasy every time she compromised a little further. *I'm doing this for the kids, not the parents,* she told herself. *I've got my foot in the door. I can make a difference.* It was Vichy logic, but she clung to the hope that she could be a lifeline for the children.

She remembered her own childhood, and what it was like when people gave up on you. That broken, defeated look when they made their final goodbye, as if you were abandoning them, not the other way round. And the cars, all the cars, when they dropped you off for the last time, their smells of pine and mud and dogs and feet rolled into one. All the same car, blurrily pulling away from you, and melting back into the world.

Reporting the parents and passing the kids to social services felt like giving up.

As soon as they entered the hotel room, Mia ran off and locked herself in the bathroom.

"Mia?" called Erin, after allowing her a few minutes. "Are you OK in there?"

Silence.

"I'm sorry we didn't get introduced properly. I'm Erin. I'm going to watch TV, okay? Come and join me if you feel like it."

She didn't waste time hammering on the door. Who could blame Mia, dumped in a dingy hotel room with some black-clad stranger?

Erin channel-surfed until she found cartoons. Sure enough, a little later she heard the bathroom door open. Without looking round, Erin shifted along the sofa to make room. When Mia perched on the very far end of the sofa, Erin put her crisp packet on the cushion between them, within reach of both. She didn't usually resort to TV and snacks from the very start, but the runaway adults hadn't given her much to work with.

Mia was silent, but Erin could respect silence. A different type of adult would have crouched in front of Mia, bringing their huge hot face level with hers, and talked to her in a loud, cheery voice. They would have wanted to 'bring her out of her shell'. As if it were that easy. As if shells were always bad.

"You don't have to make me like you, you know." Mia's voice was small but waspish.

"OK," said Erin calmly, taking another crisp. "What do you do to people you don't like? Do you stick forks in their feet?"

Crunch, crunch, crunch.

"Yeah," said Mia, with quiet bravado, and snuffled a laugh. She reached over and took the remote, flipped a couple of channels then stopped on a blue-tinted, moonlit scene.

"Oh." Erin recognised the show. "Maybe not that one—it'll give you nightmares."

"I watch it at home." Mia shrugged. "He's a werewolf," she added helpfully, pointing at the screen.

"Nathan and Kim let you watch *Bloodrise*?" asked Erin, aghast.

"They're only there in the day," Mia answered promptly. "At night I watch what I like."

It could easily be a lie. Kids often tested Erin's gullibility to see what they could get away with. *I'm allowed to stay up till midnight! Mum always gives me three biscuits. Dad said I could use his drill.*

"What, you're alone in the house at night? Every night?"

Small nod. Crisp packet rustle. Crunch.

Erin pursed her lips, and let out her breath slowly. Could it be true? Mia's offhand manner was oddly convincing. Then again, if Nathan and Kim usually left Mia alone at night, why would they pay over the odds for a babysitter now?

She was still troubled by the idea of forcibly depriving a young child of sleep, but perhaps there were good reasons. *Medical*, Kim had said. Wasn't there some weird kind of narcolepsy where people stopped breathing? Or perhaps Mia was suffering from concussion? Erin nursed a guilty hope that Nathan and Kim would return before she had to make hard decisions.

"Are you OK with TV, or do you want to play something?"

Mia had brought her favourite board game with her, and won the first six games by refusing to explain the rules to Erin. After sandwiches, they spent the next two hours playing the games that Erin had brought in her backpack. Mia forgot to be wary, and became excitable and aggressively competitive. As they played, Erin threw in more questions about Mia's home life, and was quietly appalled by the answers.

Mia didn't know where her home was, but it sounded like it was on an island. She said that from her bedroom window she could see Scotland 'over the sea'. She didn't go to school or know any other children. People came during the day— mostly Nathan and Kim—then 'went away on the boat'. Mia could play outside if someone was with her, but at night she was left alone in the house, the doors locked.

At one-thirty, there was still no sign of Nathan and Kim. Mia's moods were now zigging and zagging, her hilarity fierce and high-pitched. Eventually she tipped into tantrum.

"Noooo! You can't put your piece there! I want you do *that*, so I can do *this*! I want Nathan and Kim!"

"They'll be back in a bit."

"But *when*? They've been *hours*." The gale of distress ebbed, but only a little. "Is my mother coming here?"

"Did Nathan and Kim say she would?" Erin asked, surprised.

"No, but they've gone to talk to her. *I* wanted to go! *I* wanted to meet her!"

'Mother', not 'mum'. 'Meet', not 'see'. Hasn't she even met her own mother?

Mia threw herself on the carpet, and howled herself red-faced, with the inconsolable anguish of the very tired.

This is ridiculous, thought Erin. *This is cruel. I'm torturing this poor kid.*

What kind of abusive weirdos leave a little kid alone every night? I can't believe I've been following their instructions blindly.

"You should be in bed," she muttered aloud.

"Nooooo! Nonono! I need to stay awaaaake!" Mia thumped a cushion.

"Why?"

"Because I'm not meant to sleep! Because if I do... everyone screams at me." Mia gave a shuddering sob, her mouth rubbery and miserable. "*You're* going to scream at me!"

"No, I won't," said Erin firmly. "If you did something really wrong we'd have a talk about it, and maybe I'd tell Nathan and Kim when they got back, but I won't ever scream at you. I promise."

In Mia's wary gaze, Erin saw a tiny star of hope flare then die.

"Yes, you will," Mia mumbled sullenly into her cushion. "Everybody always screams."

Erin changed tack.

"Why don't we make a nest here on the sofa?" If Mia napped there, with the light on, Erin could watch over her and make sure she was OK. They buried themselves under cushions and blankets, and Mia calmed down. Her head sank to the cushion. Her eyelids drooped, then closed.

And in that instant, the world broke open like an egg.

*   *   *

No room. No hotel. No world. Such ideas were forgotten utterly. Even the words had no meaning.

There was a wintry yellow light, which ached in Erin's head and showed her nothing. The light got in her mouth, and was cold in her lungs, and then she couldn't breathe any more.

And she barely noticed because of the arches all around that went up and up and up into the shadows, till she couldn't see them any more, but could still feel them rising and rising to a sky of bone, stretching her mind until she begged it to snap.

Black things with dog-faces crawled around her, lashing their scorpion-words and trying to re-speak her into new shapes. And next to her pulsed the dark-light, a great and blinding mouth with teeth made for tearing horizons like crusts.

It was the heart of everything. It was sublime in its tragic, incurable hunger. And it was screaming...

There was a deafening smash.

The bright hotel room seemed to rush out of the darkness and surround Erin, then spun around her as she tried to remember where she was. She was on her knees on the floor, and for a confused moment she thought something was physically hitting her in the chest. It was her heart, banging around like a bird in a net. In one of her fists, Erin saw a tugged-out handful of her own hair.

Mia was still in the sofa nest, white-faced and aghast.

"You promised!" she squeaked hoarsely. "You promised you wouldn't scream at me! But you did! Just like everyone else!"

The murmur of voices from other rooms had been replaced by yells and panicky gabbling. There were shouts outside as well. Erin staggered to the window, and saw that a van had careered into the car park and hit a tree. Lights were going on in the distant high rises. On the tarmac walkway near the hotel, a dying bat flexed and twitched.

It didn't just happen to me.

"What..." Erin could barely speak, her throat raw. She was

afraid that she might start coughing up gouts of unholy light.

"I have bad dreams," said Mia in a small voice.

"What the *hell!*" Erin rasped into the phone.

"You let her fall sleep, didn't you!" Nathan exclaimed on the other end. "The one thing we asked—we *told* you—"

"You didn't tell me everything would go *Event Horizon*!" hissed Erin.

"No, course I didn't! 'Here, look after this kid, she's only half-human and her dreams drag everyone to hell.' Just... make sure it doesn't happen again!"

"I've given Mia some strong tea, but she's dead on her feet. How long has she been awake? I know you drove down from Scotland. She's been up since the early hours, hasn't she?"

"Oh bloody hell," muttered Nathan distractedly, "it's coming up as 'breaking news' on the *Post's* website. Chaos all over west Willbrook. They're sending helicopters!"

"Why did you bring her here?" Erin was starting to understand why Mia was housed somewhere far from other people, but the new mystery was why she had been so dangerously relocated.

"Because Mia's mother is local, and we need to talk to her. For the last three years she's been paying us to look after Mia, but she's not paying enough. The dreams get worse and worse. She won't answer our emails, so we thought bringing her daughter back here might focus her mind."

"You took Mia from her home and drove her several hundred miles without her mother's permission?" said Erin, aghast. "That's kidnapping! I can't be a part of that! I want to talk to Mia's mother."

"You really don't. Ever heard of Gail Delaney?"

Nobody with a sensible, well-lived life would have known that name. Even Erin's usual clients stayed well away from her. Delaney's name was shrouded in a sour fug of rumours—murmurs of narcotics networks, human trafficking and mutilations. Her enemies had a habit of vanishing without a trace.

"You're *joking*," whispered Erin.

"If you contact her, she'll know you know about her daughter. She keeps her kid a secret, so nobody can use Mia to get to her. Don't go thinking that she'll be grateful if she hears from you. She's a psycho—and you don't even want to know about Mia's father. Just keep Mia safe. We'll pick her up in a few hours, and Gail won't ever know you were involved."

"I'll keep her safe, but I can't keep her here." Erin's shell-shocked brain was still struggling with the new revelations. "There's an old people's home just down the road! And a dual carriageway five minutes' drive away! I need to take Mia somewhere where her dreams might not kill anybody."

"You were right, Mia, and I should have listened to you. OK, new game—'Let's Stay Awake.'"

Loaded down with her own rucksack and some blankets, Erin hustled Mia out to the car. Once they were strapped in, she put on a CD of comedy songs with sing-a-long choruses. Erin sang as she drove with all the gusto she could manage. Mia remained hunched and despondent.

"Come on, Mia! Join in! You can't fall asleep if you're singing."

Mia made some hollow-eyed attempts to mouth the lyrics, while Erin drove away from Willbrook. She had to steer up onto the pavement to get past two cars that had hit each other head on, and a few lanes were cordoned off by the emergency services, but further from Willbrook the lanes became clearer.

Erin still felt queasy and unglued. There was a tingle in her joints, and a faint, nagging feeling that she had been dismantled and then reassembled slightly wrong. Her headlights hypnotised her. There they were, forcing little scoops of reality to exist. All around them lay the void.

What was 'seeing', anyway? Energy bounced off things, and entered holes in the front of her head, and then her brain told her stories about what was in front of her. It didn't mean the stories were true.

The headlights abruptly sallowed, and everything tipped so that the road ahead was a helpless plummet into darkness. The steering wheel became a snake in her hands...

...and then she was back in the world again, her heart jumping. She swerved desperately, just in time to avoid a looming hedge.

"Mia!"

Mia's forehead had been resting against the window, her eyes half-closed. She jerked fully awake as Erin called out.

"You shouted at me!" she wailed, her eyes glossy with tears.

"I know—I'm sorry! Do you want to shout back at me?" Erin turned off the radio. "Let's shout our favourite things, shall we? Favourite dinosaurs—go!"

They yelled their favourite pizzas, vampire films, and animals beginning with S. It was too dark for 'I Spy' or 'First One to See', so they took turns to tell instalments of a story. But Mia grew sullen, and kept killing characters, so Erin was relieved when the estuary came into view. She turned onto a narrow tarmac lane along a slender promontory, and pulled up outside the stone hut that was the Ferry Museum.

Mia stared at the unlit building and car park, and burst into angry tears.

"I don't want to be here! I want to go back!"

"It's just for a bit, till Nathan and Kim get here—"

"They won't! They said they'd come back to the hotel! And if they bring my mother there I won't see her!"

Erin had temped at the museum for a while, and as she suspected the door code had not been changed. Most of the building was taken up by the exhibition hall, the big skylights letting in the grey-ish, pre-dawn light to reveal the info boards and 18th century rowboat. Erin led a fretful Mia into the tiny staff kitchen beyond, where she risked turning on the light and boiling a kettle for coffee.

"I *hate* you! I want to meet her! You're all just scared I'll tell her things! Like all the times they didn't play with me, and things Kim called me, and when nobody came! I'll tell her, and she'll stab you all! And … and… eat your eyes!"

"Eyes don't have much nutritional value," said Erin as calmly as she could. Clearly Mia knew enough to guess that her mother could be used as a threat. "She ought to eat them with some nice peas. Or Brussel sprouts."

I could leave, thought Erin. *I've brought Mia somewhere safe and warm, far from any houses. If I go, she can get the sleep she needs, and it probably won't hurt anyone.*

But I'd be abandoning a six-year-old in a strange building by a river. I can't. I just can't. She needs me.

At 4.30 am Erin's phone rang. It was Nathan, and he sounded surprisingly chipper.

"Everything's sorted. Where are you? OK, we'll be there soon."

As the next hour crawled by, Erin feared that 'soon' would not be soon enough. Mia was groggy and wobbly, and her head kept drooping dangerously. Erin wanted to shake her, out of sheer, craven fear.

"Mia, look at me! Mia, eyes open!"

The eyelids sank again, and for a sickening instant everything tumbled back into the abyss. Then Mia's dropped mug smashed, splashing her leg with hot coffee and waking her. Erin treated the scald, while trying not to throw up.

At last a car pulled up outside, and Nathan and Kim got out. To Mia's obvious disappointment they were alone. Both seemed in better humour.

Kim paid Erin without complaint. Nathan asked for the caffeine pills, and Erin felt a guilty pang as she handed them over. Nothing was solved. Mia would still be prevented from sleeping. It just wouldn't be Erin's responsibility any more.

Nathan opened the external door to leave, then hesitated, frowning.

"A car's stopped out on the main road," he said. "It's just turned its engine and lights off."

Kim scowled at Erin. "Did you tell anyone else you were here?"

Erin shook her head.

"Take Mia into the kitchen!" Kim hissed at Erin. "Turn that light off!"

Erin obeyed. In the darkened kitchen, Mia's breathing sounded frightened, so Erin crouched and put her arms around her. The door was open a little crack, giving Erin a view of the exhibition hall, and the tensed figures of Nathan and Kim.

There was a crunch of gravel outside, and then a loud, sharp knock at the door. Everyone stayed motionless.

"Stop messing around!" called a woman's voice. "I know you're in there! Your car's outside."

"It's her!" whispered Nathan, peering through the window. "Alone." Kim gave a reluctant nod, and Nathan opened the door.

The woman that entered was taller and more athletic-looking than Erin had expected. Despite the cold, she wore only combat trousers and a dark sleeveless top. Her dark hair was drawn back in a short plait. It looked girlish, in a way that her strong, hard face did not. Even in the dim light, Erin could see that the woman's muscular arms and shoulders were criss-crossed by lines that were too dark for scars, and could only be tattoos. They looked like fractures in ceramic.

"What can we do for you?" asked Nathan, failing to sound confident.

"I want to see her." Gail Delaney had a local accent, but it was tempered with something else Erin could not place. "If she's going to be used to threaten me, I'd like to see if she's worth it."

"She's not here," Kim said quickly, to Erin's relief. A mother-daughter reunion suddenly seemed a chilling prospect. Mia made no attempt to burst from Erin's arms and sprint to Gail. Perhaps her mental image of her mother did not match this hard-featured stranger.

"Really?" asked Gail, and her tone of menace was unmistakable.

"Don't try to scare us," Kim said bluntly. "You need us, and you know it. Anyone else you got to look after her would freak out in a day. They'd call an ambulance, or have a breakdown, or blub on the internet. We know *everything*. And we don't care.

"You told us Mia was half-human. You didn't tell us what her dad was, but we joined the dots. We heard about the mess the police found on Strapper's Hill eight years ago. Ritual stuff, severed fingers, the rest. And that was just before you and your boyfriend started making a name for yourselves, and kicking the hell out of anyone in your way.

"So... we reckon you did some occult shit and summoned something to help your 'business' along. And you told it to be your boyfriend, and together you took everything you wanted. And then the magic wore off or whatever, and it buggered off to where it came from, leaving you pregnant. That's about it, isn't it?"

Erin held on to Mia, wondering how much she understood.

"No," said Gail. "That wasn't it at all."

Despite the queasy, grey light from the skylights, the darkness in the hall was becoming more oppressive. Gail's eyes and her fracture-like tattoos grew blacker by the moment.

"The summoning wore off very quickly," Gail continued. "Within a couple of days. He didn't really know what he was doing with that book. But I decided to stay. I liked his ambition... and something about his bones. I suppose I loved him. That's probably why I ate him in the end. I did warn him I might, but I think it still surprised him. I regretted it afterwards, which is why I stayed on in this form, to find out what our offspring would be like.

"I didn't mind the pain of childbirth, but afterwards they handed me this... *thing*. A little, leaking wobble-headed cripple that couldn't even stand or find its own food. It was too weak—a waste of good flesh and bones. I wanted to eat it too, to return its flesh to mine. And I knew that I would, sooner or later, when I wasn't concentrating.

"But that little blob was all that was left of him in the world. If I ate it, I thought I might regret that too. So instead I sent it away, and paid people to look after it."

"You're..." Nathan looked flabbergasted.

Gail smiled. The cracks in her skin darkened and deepened, and then broke open, with a dry splitting sound. Clots of shadow leapt out of the fractures, and landed around her on dozens of knife-pointed legs.

The shadow-clots swarmed across the floor towards the siblings. They didn't move like spiders, but the motion triggered the same primal panic in Erin's hindbrain.

Nathan tried to smash at the shadows with a chair. Kim, perhaps remembering some childhood lesson, sprinted over and slammed her palm on the light switch, flooding the hall with light. It didn't help.

"Don't look!" whispered Erin, shielding Mia's eyes. Mia didn't need to see Nathan's skin spiralling off him like orange peel, or Kim being folded, and folded, and folded...

At last there was silence in the exhibition hall. There was no blood. Brown-pink ribbons of something scattered the floor, and hung from the lamp and the display stands. They did not drip. Sometimes they twitched.

A few moments later Gail walked into the kitchen. The shadows at her heels were the size of Great Danes now, but full of insectile angles. The black crevasses in her skin still gaped wide. Erin tensed, but Gail only had eyes for her daughter.

Mia scrambled to her feet, eyes and mouth soup-plate wide. But she did not whimper or try to hide behind Erin. Instead, she reached out one small hand.

"Mia, don't—" began Erin, but Mia was already gently stroking the mandibles of the nearest shadow-thing. She looked at her mother, eyes bright with excited appeal, as if she had been presented with a puppy. *Is it mine? Can I keep it?*

Gail let out a small, surprised 'huff' of a laugh. Her expression fogged, as if she were unsure whether to feel pained, pleased or confused.

Perhaps this was the mother Mia had dreamed of after all. A mother who would stab her enemies and eat their eyes. A monstrous mother, who would make sense of Mia's own monstrosity. In Mia's eyes, Erin saw recognition and hope. She was no longer the only freak in a fragile world.

"You should see this," Erin said, trying to keep her voice level as she held up her phone.

"Let me guess. You filmed everything, and I'm supposed to be scared."

"No. I'm not an idiot." Erin swallowed hard. "It's my CV. You've got a vacancy for a child-minder."

Erin felt her heart hammer as Gail peered at the little screen. Yet at the same time her mind had a strange, cold clarity. She felt as though every step she had taken for the last few years had led to this. Her destiny. The hole in the world where she fitted.

Who else would look after Mia? Who else *could*?

Gail raised her gaze, and her stare seemed to cut through Erin, right to the soft, tangled mess of her doubts and needs.

"Mia needs—" began Erin.

"Needs what? You?" Gail shook her head. "Don't kid yourself. You don't know what she needs. *She isn't yours.*" She gave a mirthless smile. "Are you trying to save her from me? What did you see tonight?"

Erin felt her spirits sink. There was only one answer.

"Nothing," she said huskily.

"Good girl. Keep it that way."

Gail lifted Mia, and placed her astride the shadow-fiend as if it were a Shetland pony. She walked out of the room, followed by the beasts and Mia on her indistinct steed. Mia did not look back at Erin, not even once.

Erin let them go.

She had survived, somehow. And without having to throw aside her entire life, and work for a demon. She felt vertigo at the thought, as though she had halted at the edge of a dark precipice. Just for a moment, that step off the edge had seemed so right, so perfect.

What was I thinking? Erin had accepted questionable jobs, but she had always thought—hoped—that some internal brakes would stop her going too far

Perhaps tomorrow she would feel relieved at her escape. Perhaps she would start to retreat, inch by inch, from the precipice. Right now, however, she felt a tearing sense of loss, as if something had been snatched away from her. Her martyrdom had been rejected. And the girl that should have needed her had left without a backwards glance.

Outside a faint roar revved, then receded. A car pulling away.

She's not mine, Erin thought. *None of them are. I want them to need me. But they don't.*

SLEEP WALKER
Silvia Moreno-Garcia

Only one out of every two streetlights was working, but that was better than many other parts of town where the lights were permanently off. Luxury condo buildings which had been halted mid-construction stood like pyramids to lost gods and every wall and every door, on certain blocks, were defaced with crude graffiti.

But this street, these few blocks of town, still supported some scant commercial activity and the diner, aglow with neon, was a beacon against the darkness.

She went there out of boredom, but also to seek business opportunities. She found them that day in the shape of an expensive car with tinted windows parked right by the front of the diner.

Inside there were a couple of regulars, sitting in a booth. They were none of her concern. But the stranger sitting at the bar interested her. She eyed him quickly. Nice shirt, fancy shoes, stylish hair. He didn't look like he cut out coupons from the circulars and his credit was maxed, no sir, and when she leaned against the bar, next to him, she caught a whiff of cologne.

Very nice.

"Hey, Annie, can I have a coffee and a slice of cherry pie?" she asked.

Annie turned around and gave her a big frown. Fucking old,

ugly, bitch Annie. The girl already knew the answer was going to be no. "I'm not putting anything on your tab. You have some nerve hanging out around here."

"It's a free country."

Annie frowned, but she was busy and turned around to head back into the kitchen. There was no dishwasher boy anymore, and Annie had to help with that and other stuff. The girl knew this and smiled.

She peeled off her jacket and tossed it carelessly on the bar, then she just as carelessly walked towards the beat-up green juke box sitting in a corner. She flipped through the song catalogue, picked an oldie, tossed a coin, then she walked back to where she'd left her jacket, right by the stranger while the strings of "Sleep Walk" played.

She didn't have to waste a coin on it, she had the same song on her music player, but she did it for the effect.

An effect it did have, the stranger turning his head to look at her and she could already see the questions forming in his head, the appraising look as he took in her bare midriff and the chains hanging from her neck, the torn jeans, the hair piled up and the eyeliner laid thick. He was wondering how old she was, and if he'd get in trouble if he put a hand down her pants, although no one gave any sort of importance to that shit around here. Not with the way things were.

She could look anything from fifteen to twenty-five, and it drove men crazy, that ambiguity. She did nothing to reassure them one way or another. Let him look and wonder, it helped with the mystique. *Who's that girl?* That's one thing you could still cultivate, even in a shit place like this.

"You wouldn't be able to buy me a coffee and a pie, would you?" she asked, sitting down and resting both of her elbows on the counter, asking without looking at him as she took out a cigarette from the back pocket of her jeans.

"I suppose I could," he said.

"Good."

She waved to Annie and Annie grumbled, but she brought the pie and coffee. The girl lit her cigarette, smiling at the guy. He looked twenty-something, going on the later part of the twenties rather than the early, but she didn't give a fuck if he was seventy and geriatric if he bought her a meal.

"Are those your wheels outside?"

"That's me," he said, sipping his coffee.

"Nice. Are you making a pit stop?" she asked, because there was only two reasons anyone ever stopped in this town, and she wanted to know what category of guy he was.

"Sightseeing," he declared, stiffly.

Ah. Well. The girl reached for the ash tray and tapped her cigarette against it one hand, while she pushed a fork-full of pie into her mouth with the other.

"Not much to see around here," she said. "You must be looking for the show."

He coughed, like a bit of pie crust had lodged in his throat. He washed it away with more coffee and then looked at her again, now more intently.

"How do you know about that?" he asked.

She shrugged. "Everyone knows. Do you need help finding it?"

He unfolded the camel coat he had set on a stool beside him, as if he were about to fish for his wallet. She knew he was trying to make a quick exit and she needed to make an even quicker pitch.

"I bet you're going to go check into the one hotel in town and you are going to ask the clerk there for directions, and hope they'll draw it on a napkin and make your way there. Right? But it's dark and lonely, and you'll get lost in two seconds flat. It would be better if I guided you. You can't even see the street signs at night, there's no lights."

He frowned. No doubt he'd noticed that and had made his way to the diner drawn by the glow of its sign. He had stepped out and looked around the ghostly town, chin up, determined, and realized life here was restricted to a thin strip of three blocks. Beyond that, the night swallowed you.

"I can get you there and back here," she said. "It's no big deal. And you don't even have to spend an arm and a leg on it. You'll never find it on your own."

"How much?" he asked.

They haggled briefly. Once the deal was struck she ordered a milkshake and another slice of pie on his dime. When she was done, the girl wiped away the crumbs off her jeans, spun around and walked with him back to the car.

It was a very nice car and she sank into the seat, comfy, as he started the engine and they drove across town. They passed the hotel and the pharmacy, then came empty store windows, buildings that looked like maybe they hadn't been pissholes ten years before, and eventually empty lots with chain-mail fences, blackberry bushes poking through them. In the summer she picked baskets full of blackberries, but it was the end of autumn now.

"Do you do this kind of thing often?" she asked.

"What kind of thing?"

"Look for odd attractions. Go to see the biggest ball of twine in the world or the clown motel?"

"There's such things?"

"Of course. There's a paper museum with doll houses made of paper and there's a spoon museum, and I'm sure there's other sights."

"No. I don't look for that stuff. This was a whim."

It couldn't be. She knew better. No one who came to town, who came to see the show, came just on a whim. It was greater than that.

"Can I smoke?" she asked.

"No. You'll stink up the car."

"I can open the window."

"You'll let all the heat out."

He did have a point there, although she didn't mind when the wind nipped at her fingers as long as she had a good cigarette between her lips. It cut down on the hunger, too, best damn diet in the world. Alright, so she smoked way too much and ciggies weren't free, but they did their thing, and on a night like this she had to chain-smoke to survive it.

The moon looked as if it was sliced cleanly in half and the girl observed it, putting a finger in her mouth and nibbling at the nail without chewing on it; she simply placed the nail between her teeth, feeling the bitter taste of dirt on her tongue.

"How did you hear about the show?" he asked.

"Everyone in town knows about it. You can't keep secrets here."

"Hmmm."

"We don't talk about it, though," she said. "It's just a thing we know, like we know where the creek is or where the old schoolhouse used to be."

She was going to have a good time with the money he would pay her. They'd agreed on half up front, half when they returned to the diner. She felt the cash tucked neatly against her breast pocket and thought she'd buy everyone a round at the bar. That's what she did when she returned from trips like this, walked into the bar and bought a round. The warmth of the crowd, the friendliness of them all, was like a ritual. Didn't matter none that she shouldn't have been out drinking at a bar at her age or that her grandma got angry when she came home late.

There'd be money left, for sure. Enough to pay the tabs she owed around town, enough to tide them up for a few weeks. When it was all said and done, Grandma complained about her nights out but she took the money all the same.

"How did you find about the show?" she asked, turning her head to look at the guy.

He had a fine profile. Grecian, Grandma would have said. Like those white, carved heads that served as book ends at the library, 'til they closed that down.

"A friend of a friend told me about it at a party. I looked for information on this town, but couldn't find much. But, then, somehow, I... heard a bit more and made my way here."

It was like that with the show. It was always people talking about it, you couldn't find it in no guidebook, in no webpage, despite nothing being hidden anymore. It was part of its mystique, the feeling of being invited into a select circle.

"When did you first hear about it?"

"Last winter," he said, quickly, eagerly.

"You took your time."

"I wasn't sure about it. I'm not sure now," he chuckled. "Is it real? I mean... you've seen it right? You must have. You say everyone knows about it."

"I haven't seen it," she said. "You have to pay for the show and we don't have money to spare. It's a tourist attraction; it's not for the locals."

"But then how do you know it's real?" he asked, frowning.

"It is. Like the creek and the old schoolhouse."

"I don't want to waste my money on something ridiculous," he said and he rested, for a moment, his right hand on his camel coat which he'd tossed in the space between them. It must be stuffed with cash.

He'd paid with cash at the diner. She could picture his money clip, the city where he came from, the girlfriend he'd lied to. Told her he was going on a business trip because the show was a secret. It was not something to be blurted out and if he'd told her, she would have convinced him to cancel the adventure.

"Everyone who watches the show says it's an experience. That's what you are looking for, no? An experience."

Boys like this one. They tried to climb Mount Everest or did a tour of the Antartica. They had to live, had to do something, had to experience. She knew the type. And others, too. Women with brilliant careers who secretly dreamt of stabbing their firm's director in the throat, bored housewives who didn't want to push the baby pram around the block any more, wealthy men who had two mistresses and resented both.

An experience.

Everyone wants one.

"Yeah," he said. "That's exactly right."

The streets had dissolved into nothingness and the road was bordered by pines. It really was dark and it really was confusing. He could have never found his way there on his own, he would have spun around seven times in circles and then another seven times more. He must have known it, too, by the way he squinted and tried to make out the road and she just said "keep going, ahead, now a wide left." On and on. Until she said "stop," and they were there.

A fence which had been white lay half hidden under dead blackberry bushes, much like the ones in town, and the trees by the road had lost all their leafs. A dirt path zig-zagged onto the doorsteps of a two-storey house.

It wasn't anything special, the house. Just like the fence, it had once been painted white. But it was now gray. All the windows were boarded up, graffiti lavishly spread upon them. The only thing in decent shape was the front door, which had been painted with two coats of vivid yellow paint, and did not have a nick or scratch to show, its brass knocker carefully polished; as if the door had been transported from another location and affixed to the old house as a joke.

There was light on the second floor, it trickled out through the boards, making the house glow like a dim ember. Above it the half-moon was bright and clear, not a cloud in the sky to hide its face.

It was a sad sight, but not a frightening one. Merely a derelict house with nothing to show.

"Are you coming with me?" the man asked.

"Of course not," she said. "I told you, the tourists are the ones who pay for the show."

"If you want, I can pay for your admission."

"No. I'll wait for you in the car."

"In the car?" he said, frowning.

"You're not going to make me wait outside, are you?" she replied. "I'd freeze to death. It's not like I can drive it away. Plus, you owe me my other half."

"Yeah, alright," he muttered.

He grabbed his coat, put it on and after lingering for a few minutes by the car he finally set off, following the path and knocking at the door. The door opened, he went in, and she leaned back, closing her eyes as she pressed play.

It was always good to bring music. Audio books could do too, but music was better. It made the time flow, it was louder. She didn't play her special melody, saving that one as she always did, instead circling through other tunes.

Her Grandma, she'd be asleep by now, but come midnight she'd wake up, grab her cane and wake up her brother, tell him to go find her. The bleary-eyed boy would protest, but he'd get up just the same and go to the bar to drag the girl home. She'd be there, eventually, and he knew to wait for her. Wait for the round she'd buy. Then they'd drink several beers, the two of them, until at closing time they'd walk back home.

But she didn't mind rituals none, it would have been silly to mind them. Spiders spin silk, salmon leap up stream, and people, they have their rituals. Don't step on a crack, break your mother's back.

It was time for a cigarette.

The girl opened the door, unfolded her legs and stood up, scratching the back of her head before she lit one. The smoke rose before her face and she turned off the music because she didn't need the music when she was smoking. That was another one of the benefits of the cigarettes.

You couldn't see much in the night, not even with that sickly light coming from the house. From this distance, it looked like the outline of a house, and the yellow door was a pale rectangle floating up.

In spring, if you stopped by this place during the middle of the day, the grass was speckled with dandelions and you could take out a can of spray paint and vandalize the outside at your leisure. Write "cock sucker" and "eat my pussy" on the boarded windows, taking your time, without any hurry. At night it was a different thing. At night you had to be careful. You smoked your cigarette and you looked at the house and you kept your distance.

In the day it was good, with all those dandelions. In the day the place was deserted, but friendly.

Nevertheless, not even in the day, would you damage the door. That was off limits. Everyone knew that.

She looked at the house, her cigarette between her fingers, cocked her head to the left. The earth under her feet was hard. The first snow should come soon enough.

It was peaceful and nice here, with the moon keeping her company.

She went back into the car and put her hands in her jacket's pockets, fiddling with a coin. Bored, she opened the glove box. She found a pack of gum, the car's registration, a pair of sunglasses which she put on, modeling them in the rear view mirror. She took the sunglasses off.

When she turned her head she saw the guy was walking back to the car. A cloud had obscured the moon. She couldn't see his face in the dark, he was just a shadow, walking slowly. But eventually he got there, opened the door, and sat in the driver's seat.

"Ready to go?" she asked.

He had his hands on the steering wheel, but he did not make a motion to start the car. He simply sat there, staring straight ahead. She gave him a couple of minutes before speaking again.

"Hey, we need to drive back. It's late."

He didn't reply. It was colder now than it had been before and her breath came out in a puff. The lights inside the house seemed to have dimmed and she heard a noise, like a bird flying above. An owl, hooting, only it didn't hoot. It was the motion of wings.

From the corner of her eye she could see the dead blackberry bushes which looked like they had been painted with ink, the tracery of the path.

"Buddy, you need to drive us back," she said.

There had been no wind outside, but now the wind began to blow, rattling the dead trees. The owl which was flying near them must have settled upon one of the trees because she caught a flicker of motion, but she did not look to confirm it.

She didn't look at the house, either, with its boarded windows and its yellow door. It was there. She could feel it. The house, the door, the night outside, the icy cold, and the both of them tucked like snails in a shell. She could feel it and she could feel the deadness of the soil upon which they stood and the half-moon, perfectly ordinary.

But not for all the gold in the world would she have stepped outside the car in that moment. Because the night was yawning.

That's how Grandma put it to her, *"the night was yawning,"* the time she told her and her brother about the house where the show took place, and how she'd come there, and the radio played Santo and Johnny while Grandma waited in the car.

"Dude," she said grabbing his chin with one hand and turning it so he would look at her.

His eyes were open wide. He looked young. She thought he wasn't late twenties, but much closer to her age. It didn't matter. Didn't matter if he was 70 or 20, he needed to drive them away.

"Dude, drive. *Now*," she ordered him, her voice firm.

She thought she was going to have to punch him, but the guy snapped out of it. He turned on the car and they drove. She saw a shifting silhouette in the rear-view mirror, but didn't pay attention to it, her gaze fixing back on him.

"You alright?" she asked him.

"I'm... yeah," he said.

He looked pale, beads of sweat on his forehead.

Tourists, she thought. *Idiots*.

She turned on the heat and the car warmed up quick. The guy was still holding real tight to the wheel, and if you looked close you'd notice his eyes were very bright. Like he wanted to cry and couldn't.

Fools, all of them. Looking for experiences.

"I'm gonna play a song, alright?" she said.

She took off the headphones and pressed play, and the old music swept around them. That slow steel guitar, chirping high, moaning of a lost love. No lyrics, but a love song. Ain't no need for words all the time.

He relaxed his hands. The girl lit a cigarette and placed it on his lips, and he didn't complain none about it, he took a drag, and then she took one.

Now she looked in the rear-view mirror, a hand tangling with one of the chains around her neck. Behind them there were pines, a narrow road, the night with pin-prickles of stars. Nothing else.

The diner was open late. They parked, and were greeted by its welcoming glow. The light, like the music that had played in the car, was soothing. The girl opened the door and stepped out. He did too, although more slowly.

"Here's your other half," he said as they both stood in front of the car.

"Thanks."

He had put on the camel coat and placed his hands in his pockets. She noticed he'd gotten the coat dirty, it had stains on it, as if he'd dragged the hem through the mud or dirt.

"I didn't think... the show, I didn't think..." he said, trailing off.

"Nobody does," she said.

"What now?" he asked.

"Get some rest. You have a long drive back home tomorrow," she said.

"I feel like I have to tell someone," he said.

"Not me."

"But—"

The girl took out her pack of cigarettes. She had two left. She handed both to him. He grabbed the crumpled box and looked at it in astonishment, as if he didn't know what it was. He nodded, slowly.

No need for words. Words didn't do.

She bid him goodbye with a quick wave of the hand and crossed the street, heading to the bar. She was going to buy everyone a round.

BAG MAN
Lavie Tidhar

1

"How come you never got married, Max?"

He was sitting on the edge of the bed putting on his socks and shoes. Marina reclined on the mattress. The street light outside the window cast her face in a yellow glow.

"Who says I didn't?"

He pulled up his trousers and buckled his belt and smoothed the crease in his trousers and put on his gun. He had one strapped to his leg and another under the coat and he also had a knife, just in case. The briefcase was on the floor beside the bed.

"I never figured you for the marrying kind."

Marina had been a working girl in the past but now she ran a flower shop and she and Max had an understanding. And he didn't normally say any damn thing, so why was he being chatty tonight? He thought of Sylvie in Marseilles and the boy, who might even have grown-up children of his own by now. It had been nearly forty years since he'd gone and left them. When he came to Israel he joined the army, full of enthusiasm, a patriotism he'd never quite lost. Never quite lost the accent, either.

These days he barely remembered what she had looked like,

even her smell. He wondered vaguely if she was still alive. But he'd done what was best.

"It wouldn't be fair," he said. "Considering."

You can't lose what you never had, he thought. Put on his wristwatch. Sat down again and ran his hand along Marina's smooth leg, fondly. "I have to go," he said.

"You always have to go," she said.

Max shrugged. Picked up the briefcase and went to the door. "A man's got to work," he said.

"And you're more honest than most," she said, and laughed, showing small white teeth. "What's in the case, Max? Guns? Money? Pills?"

"I don't know," he said. He really didn't, and he didn't care. "I just know where to pick it up and where to drop it off."

Truth was Benny was keeping him mostly on ice after that job in the Negev went bad. A Bedouin clan had been muscling in on some of Benny's southern territory and he'd sent Max to take care of things, and Max did, he'd left two bodies behind him in Rahat but they caught up with him as he was driving back along the lonely desert road and they filled his rented car with bullets. He was lucky to still be alive, he'd run into one of the dry wadis, and before they could come after him a border police patrol showed up and the Bedouins made themselves scarce. But it had been close and he wasn't getting any younger, sixty was coming up on him like a brick wall.

He tried to remember what it felt like, the pursuit and running through the dry riverbed, thinking they were coming behind with their AKs. For a moment it felt like being a kid again, playing cowboys and Indians. It should have been horrifying: instead it was a rush.

He smiled at Marina as he left. Went down the stairs with the briefcase in his hand. A kiddie job. He hummed a song, something even older than himself. Opened the door to the street and stepped outside still humming.

*   *   *

2

"On the *ground*, motherfucker," Pinky said. Pinky was hopped up on speed and he felt like he was flying. He perched on the seat of his bicycle and aimed the gun at the old man with the briefcase.

There were four of them on bicycles, all training guns on the old dude. They'd waited outside in the shadows until the light came on in the upstairs apartment where that old Russian whore lived. It was so easy it was laughable. He wanted to laugh. His teeth were chattering from the speed and he couldn't make them stop. "Hand over the briefcase, slowly."

The old man didn't put up a fight. He looked very calm, which annoyed Pinky. Pinky was seventeen and he didn't like old people, with the exception of his grandmother, who let him stay with her and sometimes cooked him roast chicken with paprika in the oven, which he loved, but who most of the time just sat by the window with a sad, resigned look on her face.

Apart from old people, Pinky didn't like African refugees, Filipino workers, Russian immigrants, beggars, teachers, fat people, stuck-up girls who wouldn't talk to him, Arabs (obviously), Orthodox Jews (obviously), social workers and, of course, the police.

He hefted the briefcase in his hand wondering what was in it. It felt light but not too light. He grinned like a maniac and his teeth chattered. "That's it," he said. "Stay on the ground, old man."

The old man didn't say anything, just lay there, looking up at Pinky like he was memorising his face.

"Did I say you can look at me!" Pinky screamed. The window overhead opened and the Russian whore stuck her ugly face out and Pinky raised the gun and she quickly withdrew.

"Come on, Pinky, let's go," Bilbo said. They called him

Bilbo because he was small and hairy. It was either that or, sometimes, Toilet Brush.

"Shut up!" Pinky said. "I said no names!"

"Sorry, Pinky. I mean—"

"You want me to shoot you myself?" Pinky waved the gun at Bilbo.

"I'm sorry, I'm sorry," Bilbo said. His real name was Chaim, which was even worse than Toilet Brush, or at least that's what Pinky always figured.

"Take the case and go," the old man said. His tone annoyed Pinky. He climbed off the bike.

"I already did," he said.

"Good for you," the old man said.

"Fuck you!" Pinky said, and he kicked the old man viciously in the ribs. The old man grunted but didn't say a thing.

"Come on, man!" Rambo said. Rambo was big and stupid but he was loyal. Pinky hawked up phlegm and spat on the old man but missed him and the spit landed on the pavement near the old man's face. Pinky got back on the bike and then, just to prove he could, he aimed the gun up at the sky and squeezed off a shot. It inadvertently hit the street light, which exploded loudly, startling all of them and scattering glass on the ground.

"Shit!" Rambo said. Pinky's heart was beating to a drum and bass track. They got on their bikes and pedalled away as quickly as they could, whooping into the night.

3

Max got up and brushed glass shards off his trousers. Marina stuck her head out of the window, and he could see her in silhouette against the light of the moon. "Get back inside," he said, gently.

For a moment there he thought that punk kid was going to shoot him. What a way to go, he thought. Shot by some kid on a dirty street in the old bus station area. They didn't even pat him down for his guns.

He didn't really care who they were, but he wanted to know who had employed them to rob him.

He began to walk, humming softly to himself. At this time of night the old bus station area was coming alive as its residents, mostly foreign migrant workers and refugees, returned home to their slum-like apartments. The bars and shebeens, always open, became busier. The junkies, who came from all over the city, congregated on the burnt remains of the old terminal building, and the sex shops and what was left of the brothels welcomed their furtive johns with tired indifference.

But there was beauty here, too, Max thought, passing a stall selling flowers, roses and chrysanthemums, anemones, poppies. They scented the air, joining the smells from the nearby shawarma stand where suicide bombers twice blew themselves up, the smell of cumin and garlic and lamb fat. Two Filipino kids, up late, played football by a butcher stall, where a man in a stained apron methodically cut chops out of the carcass of a pig, using the cleaver with a proficiency Max admired.

He wove his way deeper into the maze of narrow streets, crumbling building fronts, faded shop signs. A young white girl with needle marks on her arms tried to entice him into a dark hallway, lethargically. He waved her away. The night was still young and boys will be boys, but he had a feeling it wouldn't be as easy as that. He reached the front of a store that said *Bookshop* overhead. Dusty textbooks in the window, geography books by the long-deceased Y. Paporish with maps that showed countries which no longer existed. Max let himself in.

A bell dinged as he stepped through. The shop was dark and dusty, with books piled everywhere, paperbacks in English and French, forgotten Hebrew novels and ancient comics hung up by a string, their pages fluttering sadly like the wings of dead butterflies.

Hanging on the wall was a detailed artist's illustration of the imagined future of Tel Aviv's central bus station. It showed a graceful tower rising into the sky, a sort of 1950s retrofuturistic construction decorated with spiral bridgeways and floating flower gardens, and showed happy, well-fed, well-dressed residents, the men in suits and ties and the women in floral dresses, all smiling and holding hands as they beheld this miracle of engineering.

"Makes you cry, doesn't it?" a voice said. Max turned and saw Mr Bentovich, the ancient proprietor, a small pale man who always seemed to Max to resemble a particularly inedible and quite likely poisonous mushroom.

"Didn't see you there, Bento."

"You're being familiar again, Max. I don't like people being familiar."

"Sorry, Mr Bentovich."

They shook hands. Bento's was moist and cold. His touch made Max shudder. They stood there and admired the artist's impression of what the future most decidedly did not look like.

"To what do I owe the pleasure, Max? You're not here to do me in, are you?" Bento laughed, the sound a dry cough in the dusty air of the bookshop. "Don't get me wrong," he said. "If anyone's to do it, I'd rather it was you, Max."

"I'm flattered."

"What do you want?" Bento said. "I'm up on my payments to Benny." He went behind the counter and when Max looked at him he knew Bento had his hand, under the desk, on the butt of a gun.

He shook his head, raised his hands. "I come in peace," he said.

"I hate this place," Bento said. His little wizened face looked like it would cry. "I used to sell books, Max. Books!"

"I know, Bent—Mr Bentovich. I know. How's business, though?"

Bento shrugged. "Alright," he said. He pushed a hidden

button on the desk and the top sprung open and he swept his hand majestically as if to say, take your pick.

The desk was divided into compartments and in each one Max saw dried fungus, cubes of hashish, pre-rolled joints, moist cannabis sativa, pills, more pills, even more pills, and a bag of mints—"For my throat," Bento said when he saw Max's look.

"Sell to kids, much?"

"From where I'm standing," Bento said, morosely, "everyone's a kid, Max. Even you."

"I'm looking for one kid in particular," Max said. "About seventeen, pre-army. A little shit."

"They're *all* little shits, Max. Can I offer you anything? On the house. You need some Viagra? Cialis? Something to keep your pecker up?"

"I need what you know, Bento," Max said, and the friendliness was gone from his voice, and this time Bento didn't correct him on the use of his name. "About a little shit called Pinky, who has three friends even stupider than he is."

"Pinky, Pinky," the old bookseller said, "now, why would I know a Pinky?"

"Because he was as high as a kite the last time I saw him," Max said, "which was not that long ago, Bento. Not that long ago at all. You sell diet pills?"

"I sell everything, Max," Bento said, reproachfully. "You mean amphetamines?"

"Why are you fucking with me, Bento?" Max said. "You know who I'm after. So why are we playing games? What are you after?"

"I'll tell you what I'm not after, Max. I'm not after any trouble."

"And why would there be trouble?"

Bento just shrugged, which made Max wary.

"Who is this kid?" he said.

"He's just a punk," Bento said.

"Who is he working for?"

Bento laughed. "Working for?" he said. "Who'd employ a moron like that."

"I don't know, Bento," Max said, patiently. "That's why I asked."

"Why the interest, anyway?" Bento said.

"Do you always answer a question with a question?"

"Do you?"

Max sighed and pulled out his gun and put the muzzle against Bento's forehead. Bento stood very still and his eyes were large and jumped around too much: they were the only animated feature of his face. "You dip into your own merchandise?" Max said.

"You try being stuck in here all day dealing with scum," Bento said. "Those kids would be the death of me one day. You know someone got done just outside my front door? The other side of the road. Eritrean or Somali, one of those guys."

"I'm sorry for your loss," Max said.

"Wise guy," Bento said. "Can you take the gun away, please?"

"Since you said please," Max said. "No. Tell me where I can find Pinky."

Bento's face twisted in a sudden grimace of hatred, but whether it was of Max, of the kids, or of the circumstances that led him here, to this dismal bookshop in the modern ghetto of the old bus station of Tel Aviv, Max couldn't say.

"He and his little friends squat in an abandoned flat on Wolfson," Bento said.

"Yes?"

Bento gave him the address. Max made the gun disappear. When Max was at the door Bento said, "Max?" and Max said, "Yes?" turning around to face him.

"Don't come back here," Bento said.

"I hope I don't have to," Max said, and he saw the old bookseller scowl.

* * *

4

He had the feeling he was being watched as he walked to the address Bento gave him. A vague sense of unease that grew with each step, but Max could see no one, could only trust his instinct, and he thought, they will come in good time. First, he had his business to take care of.

It was a rundown building on a rundown street and it didn't take much to break the lock on the downstairs door. The stairwell was unlit and smelled of piss and as he climbed the floors he saw four pairs of bicycles chained to the railings. He reached the third floor and an unpainted door and kicked it open and walked inside with his gun drawn.

Five pairs of eyes turned to stare at him in mute shock. They were sitting on a couple of couches rescued from a dumpster and the air was thick with the smell of Bento's dope.

"Hello, Pinky."

"What the fuck." Pinky reached under the cushion for a gun. Max fired, once, the bullet sinking into the dirty stuffing of the couch, sending up a plume of dust and crumbly foam.

"Shit, man," Pinky said. His movements were jerky, delayed with shock and drugs.

"The next one will be in your brains," Max said, "if you had any."

The short fat kid started to laugh.

"Shut the fuck up, Bilbo," Pinky said.

There were four boys and a girl. She looked up at Max with stoned, uncurious eyes.

"Get out," he said. He motioned with his gun.

"Me, mister?"

"You. Leave."

"But I only just got here."

"Do I have to ask you twice?"

"Can I at least take the dope?" the girl said.

Max shrugged. "Why not," he said.

"Hey!" Bilbo said.

"Shut up, Bilbo," Max said.

The girl went through the boys' effects and pocketed weed, pills and money.

"Bitch," Pinky said. She stuck out her tongue at him.

"Are you going to shoot them, mister?" she said when she was almost at the door.

"I don't know," Max said, "what do you think?"

She shrugged. "It's a free country," she said.

She disappeared outside and Max returned to the business at hand. "Where is my briefcase?" he said.

"Look, we didn't mean nothing, it was just—"

Max shot Pinky in the knee.

The boy screamed, a high-pitched cry that filled the room and leaked like snot to the street outside. The other boys huddled in their seats, staring at Max with frightened stoned eyes.

"Where's my briefcase?"

"It's not here!" It was the fat kid, Bilbo. "We didn't have nothing to do with it, honestly, mister, it was just a job! He said it was nothing, just taking something from an old guy and—"

"He?" Max said.

"Bogdan," Pinky said, crying. He was going into shock. "It was Bogdan, it was Bogdan!"

"Ah," Max said. He almost felt sorry for the kids.

Almost.

"You gave him the briefcase?"

"Soon as we left you. Then we scored some weed and came home."

"We really didn't mean nothing, mister. We weren't going to really shoot you or anything."

"I need a doctor! Call an ambulance!"

"You don't need an ambulance yet," Max said. He surveyed the four boys. Shook his head. What was Bogdan thinking, using these clowns? They didn't even shave properly yet.

He said, "Look, I'm going to give you a choice."

They looked at him but didn't say anything. Good. Max said, "I can either shoot you now—"

"Please don't!"

He waited for them to calm down. "Or," he said, waving the gun at the narrow balcony, "you could take yourselves over there and jump."

"You what?"

"Are you crazy, mister?"

"Or I could shoot you where you are."

The boys looked at each other, pale and frightened. Pinky moaned softly, his hands round his ruined leg.

"You'd have to pick him up and throw him over," Max said. "I don't think he can make it on his own."

"Please, mister!"

"It's not that far down," Max said. "I figure you'll probably break a few bones but you're young, your bodies are still flexible. You might live." He waved the gun. "Come on," he said. "I haven't got all night to stay and chat."

"Please! We'll get you back the case!"

"From Bogdan?"

They looked down at the floor.

"I'm going to count down from three," Max said, "starting with you," he pointed at a big lump of a boy. "What's your name?"

"Rambo," the boy mumbled.

"Well, Rambo," Max said. "Help your friend Pinky there get to his feet. Three, two, one—"

"OK, alright! You don't have to count so quickly!" The boy jumped to his feet. He went over to Pinky.

"Come on, Pinky," he said. He slung Pinky's arm over his shoulders and lifted him up. Pinky was crying, snot was running down the front of his shirt.

"You, Bilbo, and you, what's your name?"

"Danny?" the boy said.

"I don't know," Max said. "Is it?"

"What?"

"Just get over there," Max said. The three boys and the wounded Pinky made their way slowly to the balcony. The balcony doors were open. A warm breeze wafted into the room and the marijuana smoke made its way out to the street.

"What's it going to be?" Max said.

The boys looked down to the street. Looked back at Max and his gun. He smiled at them without humour. "Well?"

"Shit," Rambo said. "We just wanted to get high." He picked up Pinky and before anyone could say anything to stop him he threw him over the railings.

Pinky disappeared over the balcony and dropped. There was a short scream and then a thud. They all looked over the balcony. Pinky lay on the asphalt with his leg at an angle and his head caved in.

"Doesn't look too bad," Max said.

The small kid, Danny, panicked. He rushed Max, almost knocking him back, and made for the door. Max fired once, twice, and hit the kid in the back. Danny fell, his hand still on the door handle. He didn't get up.

Max stood up and looked at Bilbo and the big kid. "Well?" he said.

"Please," Rambo said. "Please."

Bilbo was crying.

Max said nothing.

The two boys held hands. They looked over the railing. "Help me up," Bilbo said. He was struggling to climb over the railing. Rambo made an impatient motion and pushed him, and Bilbo flapped his arms in the air as he lost his balance and then he, too, dropped with a high-pitched scream. Rambo was the last to go. Max looked down and saw that he'd landed on the fat kid's body.

Max pocketed the gun and stepped over the small kid's body and left the flat.

*   *   *

5

When he left the building the stars had gone and he thought it was going to rain. Someone was screaming from an open window. The kids were lying on the ground.

Max walked away from them when someone took a shot at him.

It had come from somewhere to his left, ahead of him, and he was already moving, taking the corner and seeing two dark figures holding guns both levelled at him. He fired and one went down and the other yelled something in Arabic and behind him Max heard running footsteps and he knew they'd finally caught up with him.

"Listen," he said, "it was just a job, it wasn't personal."

The man had a gun to his face and behind him more men blocked the passageway. There was no way out. The man came out of the shadows. He was a thin young man in worn jeans and a chequered shirt, and he had deeply tanned skin. On his head he wore a red Bedouin keffiyeh.

"Shut up," he said. He raised his gun and slapped Max hard with it. The pain seared through Max's head. He tasted blood. The man gestured. Max turned. Three other men stood there training guns on him.

"Start moving."

If they wanted him dead he would already be dead, he thought. He followed them down the road. They left the one man's corpse behind them. A dusty jeep was parked by the side of the road.

"Get in."

Max stopped and just stood there.

"Don't make me shoot you," the man said. "I'll shoot you in the leg. You're not going to die yet. Not for a long time yet."

The other men laughed and Max felt a cold fury rising in him. He heard police sirens in the distance. One of the neighbours would have rang up the emergency services by now, for the kids.

Max said, "I can't."

"What do you mean you can't?"

"I have a package to deliver."

"What sort of package?"

"Drugs, money. I don't know. A kidney maybe."

"You don't know."

"I don't know. But I just killed at least two kids to keep it."

He heard them conferring though he did not understand the words.

"Where is it?"

"Someone took it."

"Who?"

"A guy called Bogdan."

"Who does the package belong to?"

"Benny," Max said. "It belongs to Benny."

He heard the man spit on the ground. "Benny sent you? To kill my father?"

"He did."

The Bedouin laughed. "Then we will go get your package, Mr. Max," he said. "And then we will pay Benny a visit."

They shoved him into the back of the car. Piled in on either side of him, taciturn men with the warmth of the desert. "What's your name?" Max said.

"Ashraf," the man said. He was sitting up front in the passenger seat. Turned and scrutinized Max. "Who is this Bogdan?" he said.

"He is a dangerous man in a world of dangerous men," Max said, and Ashraf laughed, and the other men followed suit.

"What is he, *mafiya*?" Ashraf said.

Max nodded. Ashram studied him. Behind them police cars with flashing blue lights congregated on Wolfson. "Not a friend of yours, then?"

"He and Benny had a disagreement," Max said. He might as well be honest. He wasn't sure he was going to live through this, but losing the briefcase annoyed him all the same.

"I'm sorry about your father," he said.

Ashraf slapped him. "You're not worthy of saying his name," he said. But Max had forgotten what the old Bedouin's name was.

He had come into the yard before the trailer, with a permanent fire burning in the yard and the skeleton of a Tel Aviv car suspended on a jack, stripped bare of its components, and two small children playing backgammon with an intensity that didn't allow them to even glance at him. He came in his car and the old man and two bodyguards stepped out with AKs and he shot before they had a chance to shoot him, putting down the old man with a bullet to the head and one bodyguard in the chest shot and the other with a gut shot. Then he drove away: the whole thing did not take a minute.

"You would have caught me sooner," he said, thinking of the cars chasing him down the Arava road, and of his desperate dash into the dunes. "If it wasn't for the border police."

Ashraf laughed without humour. "Well," he said. "We caught up with you now."

He looked at Max with uncurious eyes. "Where is this Bogdan?" he said.

So Max told him.

6

It was a Bauhaus building on the edge of the old neighbourhood. It resembled a ship, with a rounded foredeck and small round porthole windows. It was two stories high and the paint job was peeling badly.

They watched it from the jeep. There were two bulky men outside, packing under their coats. The only door was reinforced steel. No one came in or out of the building.

The Bedouins were organising. Ashraf barked orders and the men disappeared from the car. One had a sniper rifle, Israeli military issue. Then it was just Ashraf and Max and the driver in the car.

"Remember," Ashraf said, and smiled without humour. "The first bullet's for you."

"Yeah, yeah," Max said. He stepped out of the car. He did not like the plan. Not that there really was a plan. He walked to the building's entrance.

"Stop right there." They were two large Russians and now they brought up guns. Max stopped and raised his hands, palms forward. "I'm not carrying," he said.

"That's smart," the one on the left said.

Max knew him slightly. "Leonid," he said, nodding.

"Max," Leonid said. He smirked. The other one Max didn't know. "You sore?"

"A little," Max admitted. "Sending *kids*?"

Leonid smirked wider. "Boss wanted the package," he said.

"What's *in* the package?" Max said.

Leonid shrugged. "What do I know," he said. "I just work here."

"Can I see him?"

"Why? You want to ask for it back?"

Leonid said something in Russian and the other man laughed.

"I thought Bogdan and Benny had an understanding," Max said. Leonid shrugged again. Opened his mouth to say something and never finished the thought.

There were two cracks in the night and Leonid's head disappeared. He crumpled by the door. The other man was down. Whoever Ashraf's shooter was, he was well-trained. The two other men ran crouching to the door and attached a small explosive device. Max flattened himself against the wall when the explosion came. It tore the door off its hinges and blasted it in. The Bedouins were already moving, Ashraf and two of his men, the unseen sniper still there, Max thought. Ashraf pushed Max through the door first, roughly. It was full of smoke and debris inside. It was hard to see, which was when Max elbowed

Ashraf in the face, broke his nose, and reached for the man's gun hand. The gun fired but missed. Then Max broke two of Ashraf's fingers and took hold of the gun. He was going to shoot Ashraf but there was a blast of machine gun fire and Max dropped to the ground. He crawled through smoke and the firefly flashes of tracer bullets. Soft grunts and the sound of falling bodies behind him. He saw the shooter through the smoke and raised Ashraf's gun and fired. The shooter fell back and suddenly there was silence. It hurt Max's ears. He stood cautiously and stepped forward.

"*Don't* fucking move, Max."

"Bogdan."

The gun was stuck in Max's ribs.

"Drop it, Max."

"It wasn't my idea, Bogdan. It was these Bedouins."

"I said drop it, Max."

"Where's the briefcase, Bogdan?"

Bogdan laughed. "I wish I could have seen your face when those kids robbed you," he said.

"You can see my face now," Max said. "Am I laughing?"

"The gun, Max."

Max dropped the gun.

"Good, good."

The smoke was clearing. There were bodies on the ground.

Max said, "There's still a sniper outside."

Men were streaming past Max and Bogdan, heading outside. Max heard shots. Bogdan said, "Not for much longer."

"I just want the briefcase, Bogdan."

"You have some nerve, Max. I'll give you that."

"Hey, I was going to ask nicely."

The gun didn't leave his side. Max took a deep breath, coughed.

He said, "Look what I've got." Pulled back his coat. Showed Bogdan the Bedouins' final joke.

"Fuck me, Max, when did you join the Palestinian resistance?"

Bogdan said. He took a step back. They'd wired Max up with explosives and a dead man's switch.

"Drop the gun, Bogdan," Max said. He bent down and picked up his own gun. There was no reason, he just felt more comfortable that way.

"Take it easy, Max," Bogdan said. "I can help you. I've got guys can disarm that thing in a minute if you let them."

"And where will we be then, Bogdan?" Max said. "No, I'll take my chances. Maybe I could go into business as a walking bomb."

"Just don't try boarding a plane," Bogdan said. "You know how they are at the airport about these things."

"And I was just thinking how nice it would be to take a holiday," Max said. "Where's the case, Bogdan?"

He sensed men behind him. Sensed guns trained on him. Smiled. Went to Bogdan and smashed him across the face with the gun. Bogdan stared up at him in hatred.

"This isn't over," he said.

Max took Bogdan's gun and pocketed it. Stuck his own gun in Bogdan's ribs. Thought that every moment could be his last. Wondered how stable the explosives were.

"You're staying close to me," he said.

"Isn't over," Bogdan said. He led Max deeper into the building, into a room on the second floor. Bogdan's men followed silently but didn't fire. It was a regular office room with filing cabinets and a desk. There was a bottle of arak on the table. Max helped himself to the bottle, drank, the aniseed flavour smooth on his throat. The alcohol burned pleasantly. He figured he'd earned himself a drink.

Bogdan reached under the desk and brought out the case. Max ran his fingers on it. The lock was intact.

"You didn't open it?" he said.

"It isn't for me," Bogdan said.

"Then who for?"

"For your mother, the whore," Bogdan said.

Max sighed. "Come on," he said. He picked up the case. "You go first."

"You're mad if you think you can get away with it."

"I'm just doing my job," Max said. For the first time he felt his composure slipping. It's been a long night. "*You* robbed *me*!"

"If I knew you were going to be such a bitch about it I'd have just told those kids to shoot you."

"We all make mistakes," Max said.

He pushed Bogdan out the door and down the stairs. Bogdan's men parted silently before them. Max felt that every moment he could get a bullet in the back, but he didn't.

He pushed Bogdan past Ashraf's corpse and what remained of the door and then over Leonid. The Bedouins' jeep was still there, the driver slumped in the seat with his head at an unnatural angle. The windows were broken and the frame riddled with bullet holes but the wheels were intact. They went to the car and Max opened the door and pulled the driver's corpse out and climbed in. There was blood on the steering wheel. Max kept his gun trained on Bogdan's face.

"I'll be seeing you again, Max," Bogdan said. "Real soon."

Max sighed. The key was in the ignition. He turned the key and the jeep came alive and he felt it buck and shudder beneath him.

"Oh, fuck it," he said, and shot Bogdan in the face.

A storm of bullets started up as Bogdan fell; but Max's foot was already on the accelerator and he drove away, expecting to be blown up at every moment, bullets pinging into the chassis and the doors and he wondered what suicide bombers prayed for, the moment before they blew up.

But he got away and the gunfire receded behind him. One wheel was out, but he didn't care. He manoeuvred the car away from Bogdan's Bauhaus building, away from the gunshots, all the dead men and the dead or dying Bogdan, who, even if he lived, would never smile again, if he ever did.

He ditched the car three blocks away, knowing they would come after him but he had the case, that was the important thing. He went into the night and the night's velvety darkness sang to him with the cry of the dead and the wail of police sirens.

7

"Did you have any problems?" Benny said.

"Nothing I couldn't handle."

It was the next day and he was at the Market Porter, an old Persian restaurant Benny favoured as his informal office. Faded pictures on the walls of television actors famous three decades in the past. The smell of greasy lamb cooking on a spit.

He'd gone to see an old friend from the army who cut him out of the bomb vest and seemed happy to accept the explosives in lieu of payment. They would go on the open market and—who knew?—perhaps end up strapped to a genuine suicide bomber. There was always a market for explosives.

Max didn't care. He'd taken a room in a boarding house for the night and slept deeply and well and then went to see Benny in the morning.

"You're late," Benny said.

Max put the briefcase on the table. "I'm here, aren't I?" he said.

Benny pushed aside the newspaper he'd been reading. Dominating the front page was a picture of dead men in front of a Bauhaus building shaped like a ship and, at the bottom, a news item about the shocking torture meted out to a group of young thugs, three of whom were dead and one still in intensive care.

"I suppose you are," Benny said. He took out a thick envelope and tossed it to Max, who caught it one handed.

"Thanks."

"Don't mention it." Benny stood up to go, picking up the briefcase. "I might as well pull you off light duty," he said. "Seeing as you can't seem to keep away from trouble either way."

Max smiled. As Benny went to leave he said, "What's in the case?"

Benny turned by the restaurant door and looked back at him. "Does it matter?" he said.

Max thought about it. Sunlight rippled through the windows into the gloom of the restaurant.

"No," he said. "I suppose not."

GATSBY
Maha Khan Phillips

The music was loud, so loud that she felt the road vibrating underneath her when she got out of the car. They were playing something with a heavy base, something completely incongruous, considering the theme of the party. She shouted into Ahmed's ear. "Does your friend not realise there was no Hip Hop in Gatsby's time?"

Her brother pushed her away with practised ease. "Stop being a snob, Ra. It's New Years' Eve. Try and have some fun, for once."

She let him take the lead, weaving his way through the piles of Toyota Corollas and Pajeros that were parked haphazardly all the way down the badly lit street, towards the deceptively small white gate behind which the music was blaring. "I'm just saying, what's the point of inviting everyone to a Great Gatsby themed party and then having music like this?"

Ahmed stopped and looked at her, and rolled his eyes. "Did you really think three hundred Karachiites want to hang around and listen to *jazz*? Stop being such a loser, yaar. The point is Prohibition. It's *ironic*. Do you know how hard it was for Saqib to get a hold of enough Black Label for tonight? Every bootlegger was out. He had to pay double to that dodgy Korean diplomat who sells his rations." He narrowed his eyes. "Do you want me to drive you home?"

"No," she said, reluctantly. Yes. That was exactly what she wanted him to do.

The narrow entrance to Saqib's house was jam packed with revellers. From the corner of her eye, she could see Anita Thanawalla, already having trouble walking. Her navy blue flapper dress was all glitz and sequins, and she was wearing killer stilettos. Her headband was askew, the feather pointing to the left, instead of straight up.

Anita's eyes lit up. "Ra! Darling! We haven't seen you in like forever! Not since Batul..." She flushed. "Well. How *are* you? I'm so glad you're finally going out again. You've become the opposite of a vampire. Only seen in daylight."

"Ahmed dragged me."

Anita looked sympathetic, but was swaying slightly. "I know it's been tough. She's my friend too, Ra. But life has to go on. Come on, let's drink voddy the way we all used to in the good old days, before we could afford wine. We'll dance our worries away just like the woman in The Great Gatsby did. What a good movie that was. I wonder who thought of it."

Ra felt Anita's arms around her and didn't protest, allowing herself to be pushed forward into the human tide, though in the end, it was her pushing Anita in an attempt to keep her upright. Anita never knew when to stop.

They found themselves in a large front garden, standing under a white marquee lit with hundreds of elegant fairy lights. Its canvas sides were painted with art deco motifs, and there were vases full of daisies and roses on tall round tables. Everything was white and silver, the vases, the flowers, the crystal. It was impressive, even she had to admit that. People had made an effort to dress for the occasion: flappers, gangsters, feathered boas, fringes and tiaras were in abundance. Even the bearers were dressed up in something akin to white tuxedos. This was new. Normally, it was the Sind Club types you would see at these parties, keeping their faces as bland as possible as they poured whisky paani for Club members. These white tuxedo wearing waiters—whoever they were—were carrying around trays of champagne glasses like pros, and no doubt, by the end of the winter social season, anyone who was anyone would be smartening up their staff. Ahmed hadn't been exaggerating. Saqib really was loaded.

"Fun na?" said Anita, glazed eyed and giggly. "Saqib had an events company flown in from Malaysia to arrange all this, can you imagine? Well, that's what I'm told. I haven't actually met the guy yet." Anita winked. "I'm going to go powder my nose, do you want to come?"

"No thanks." She could just imagine how many people were already hovering around the bathroom, waiting to get in and do blow. Anita disappeared into the throng, and Ra looked at her brother, who was sweating under his hat, vest, and double-breasted woollen suit. "Just how do you know this guy again?"

Ahmed took off the hat and fanned his face. "Are you going to judge him because he isn't a member of the Club?"

"Of course not, don't be silly. I just… I'm surprised our paths have never crossed."

"Saqib is new in town Ra, I told you that. He used to live in New York. You'll like him, I promise. He's just set up an asset management business and he's going to make all of us some money—he's got some foreign investors who want to allocate to real estate in Karachi. As I've told you before, it's a good time to be in the market, if you want to diversify your portfolio and take a bit of value-added risk."

Ra loved her brother, but Ahmed could be so pompous when he talked about his banking job. "I'm not judging, I'm just asking. How does he know so many people in Karachi already?"

Ahmed shrugged. "He's got booze, a never ending supply. What else do people need to know? Come on, come and meet him, and you'll see. He's a great guy."

She followed her brother once again, right into the middle of the marquee, where the crush of party-goers was at its most intense and where she was surrounded by a haze of cigarette smoke and expensive perfume. Ahmed got distracted, pulled into a conversation with an old school friend, and Ra hung around aimlessly for a moment. She felt awkward. Once upon a time, she had been better at this. But that was then. In the days when Batul helped her laugh at herself and take life less seriously. Batul was the party animal, not her.

Was?

She needed some air. She left her brother and left the marquee altogether. She decided to walk by the side of the garden, where she might be alone to catch her breath. How had she already started thinking of Batul in the past tense?

She passed a group of men in shalwar kameez, who were drinking tea on a *charpoi*. They were either drivers or guards or house staff, she imagined. Ra felt their gaze on her, and flushed. Her dress was pretty short. But it had been all she could pull together for a flapper costume. She should have just come in jeans.

There was a small alleyway, leading, presumably, to the back garden or the staff quarters. She could still hear the music, the tinkle of laughter coming from the party. But it was darker here, and she could see the night sky, feel the sea breeze on her face. It was a welcome relief.

"Are you lost?"

She hadn't noticed there was a man there, lounging against something—a water geyser—she thought. He was about her age, and had a sharp, angular face. His designer stubble was perfectly manicured. The man was smoking a cigar and was dressed in a beige suit and a green embroidered vest. His shoes had spats on them and he was even wearing a newsboy hat. Everything about him was immaculate, a perfect homage to the 1920s.

"Are you Saqib?"

He appraised her slowly, and then put his cigar out against the wall. "Well, that's interesting."

"What?"

"There are four hundred people here, did you know?"

"I thought about three hundred, actually."

"Nope, I invited three hundred, but four hundred have turned up, my chowkidar's been counting them on the way in. And you must know them all, if you can pin me down as the one strange face, the newcomer. You're a tight society, aren't you?"

"So you *are* Saqib."

"And you are Ra."

"How did you..."

He took a step towards her. "In ancient Egypt, Ra was the God of the Sun. The most powerful being of them all. All forms of life were believed to have been created by Ra, who called each of them into existence by speaking their sacred names. Ra was only truly powerful in daylight though. Nut was the goddess of the night sky, and was covered with stars that touched different parts of her body. Perhaps I should call you Nut, from now on."

She took a step back. "How did you know who I was?"

He followed her, closing the space between them. Then he stopped and giggled. "Relax. I saw you with your brother earlier. I knew he had a sister named Ra, so I put two and two together." He stuck out his hand. "I'm Saqib. People around here don't shake hands so much as air kiss on the cheeks, but I'm still getting used to all that."

She shook back, automatically. "Can I ask you something, Saqib?"

"Go ahead."

"Why are you here?"

He crossed his arms and went back to leaning against the wall. "My parents are from Karachi. I grew up abroad, but I've returned to set up my business. There's a lot of potential here, you know. Fastest growing world economy, etc. But... I'm sure you know all that already, the way the gossip vine works."

"I mean—sorry, I mean, why are you at the back of your

house in the darkness. All your guests must be keen to spend time with you."

He looked amused. "We both know that's not true. They're here because they are curious, and because they want to indulge."

"Then why..."

"Why what?"

She waved her arms around. "Why all this? What's the point?"

He shrugged. "It's good for business, and an easy way to mainstream into this closed society of yours. I'm not well connected yet, but I need to be, if I'm to invest here. I know how it works. Contacts are everything. I'll go press some flesh in a bit. And nobody is going to forget my name in a while."

"Money is everything," she corrected him.

"What?"

"You'll find that these days in Karachi, money is everything. You can easily buy contacts if you have money."

"In that case, I'll be fine. But tell me, why are *you* here?"

"Ahmed insisted I come. I've been a little... reclusive of late."

"I meant, why are you here, at the back of my house?"

"Oh, sorry," she flushed. "I don't feel particularly social."

"Neither do I."

They looked at each other for a long moment. Then slowly, he offered her his hand. "Shall I give you the Grand Tour?"

The inside of Saqib's house was a revelation.

"I see now why you know so much about the Egyptian Gods," Ra exclaimed, as she walked into his drawing room. There were antiquities—beautifully displayed and lit—in cabinets against all the walls. An alabaster statue of an Egyptian pharaoh, some writings of hieroglyphics, some seals and tablets that she immediately recognised as being from the Indus Valley Civilisation. Many things she didn't recognise—a bull with gold horns, and a face carved from stone and etched in gold leaf. There was a large, antique globe in one corner. Everything smelt of leather, of old world charm, it was almost...like some scene from a novel by Jules Verne.

She stared at the bull with the gold horns and he came and stood beside her. "Minoan," he said. "I've always loved the Minoans. But not as much as the Egyptians. They really were special."

She was conscious of his breath against her neck, of his hand casually placed on her shoulder. He smelt of fresh laundry and a spicy cologne.

"So... like, are you actually Indiana Jones?"

He laughed and moved away from her, towards an ornate bar. "I wish! I'm just someone who is passionate about antiquity. It's a family business—Aba was a historian, before he became a buyer for the Smithsonian. We travelled all around the world when I was a child, collecting antiquities. Imagine his disappointment when I told him I was going to become a banker. Drink?"

"No thanks," she said.

"Do you mind if I have one?"

She shook her head, and watched as he busied himself at the bar. "So all these antiquities are yours?"

"Most of them—some I pinched some from Aba over the years, and one or two I'll sell on—Aba launched his own business a few years ago and I get involved from time to time as a middle man. The truth is, it's far more interesting than banking. I thought about leaving all my pieces in New York—I hear there's a crime spree happening in Karachi. But I just couldn't be parted from them. They're part of my psyche, you know what I mean?"

He came over with his drink, which was pink and had a cherry and an umbrella in it. She looked up at him, amused.

He smiled, and it crinkled his entire face, in the best kind of way. Laughter lines. He had laughter lines, everywhere. "I know, I know, no self-respecting Pakistani male drinks anything that isn't whisky. I like cocktails, particularly cocktails that look old school. Do you want to try a Gin Rickey? It's what Gatsby used to drink. Or I make a mean Mojito. Are you sure you won't have something?"

"Alright then," she said, surprising herself. "I'll have a vodka with lime please."

He looked disappointed. "You could have at least given me a challenge." He made her drink and brought it over. "You know; a little grenadine would really make that delicious."

She couldn't help but smile, even as she shook her head. "I'll stick to the vodka thanks." She took a sip of the drink, wincing a little as she did.

"No good?"

"It's fine. Just stronger than I remember. I haven't drunk in a while."

"Any particular reason?"

They had moved now to the sofa and she sat down, tucking her legs underneath her. She looked at him again. He was not at all what she had expected him to be, this eccentric antiquities-loving financier who unashamedly drank pink cocktails with umbrellas in them in a city where people would lose all respect for him. Maybe it was the strong drink, or the dim-lit room, so cosy with all its antiquities and the smell of cigar smoke, but she felt herself relax, for the first time in weeks.

"My best friend is missing," she blurted. Well, she hadn't expected to be telling him that.

He put his drink down carefully. "Oh?"

"Her name is Batul. Batul Alibhai. She teaches history at the Lyceum. Actually she studied archaeology at university—you would like her, and she would love all this," she waved her hands around the room. "Five weeks ago she left work, and she never came home. There's been no sign of her car, and no sign of her."

"She was kidnapped?"

Ra swallowed. "We assume so, but we kept waiting for a ransom demand, this being Karachi. But it hasn't come, and the authorities are not optimistic that it will. Her parents are besides themselves. It's… it's tough, not knowing. The waiting. I've reconciled myself to the fact that there may be bad news. But the not knowing…"

She looked down at her lap. How could she explain what it was like? She had met Batul at school, at the age of seven. Back then, Ra had been so shy, she made wallflowers look like dancing queens. Then Batul had come along, larger than life, full of gusto, always ready for an adventure. And to her complete shock, Batul had singled *her* out. "You're an old soul," she'd said.

"What does that mean?" Ra had asked.

Batul had shrugged. "I dunno exactly, but it means we should be best friends forever."

And just like that, they were. How could she explain what a gift Batul had been, that losing her was like losing a sister, walking around with a phantom limb that ached the whole time?

She blinked when she realised that Saqib had put his hand on hers. "I'm so sorry. Could she have been taken by someone she knows? An old boyfriend perhaps, or a greedy uncle? What do the police say?"

She shook her head. "No boyfriends or uncles, not that I ever knew about. We don't even know if it was planned or a crime of opportunity."

"I can't even imagine how you feel."

"Thanks. It's just… it's Karachi. People move on, you know? I just… I just can't…" There was something building between them, something tangible, Ra could almost feel it. Was he going to kiss her? He looked like he wanted to. He was certainly looking at her intently enough. Did she want him to? Another time maybe, another time when she so dreadfully sad. Besides, her head felt pleasantly fuzzy, she felt like she was floating above her body, rather than in it. Why couldn't she feel her tongue?

"Do you want to see something really special?" he asked.

"What?"

"I have a bigger collection of antiquities in the basement. There's some stuff I think you'll really love."

"You keep your antiquities in your basement? Why?"

"It keeps them cool," he said simply. "I've only been here for a few weeks and I can already say that Karachi heat is unbearable."

She laughed again, pleased by the distraction. "It's winter. Just wait until the real heat kicks in."

He took her hand and she let him, and he guided her down a corridor, and then opened a door. There were steps, leading down. "There's no light," she complained. Really, it was getting hard to focus.

"The bulb's blown. Don't worry, there's a switch at the bottom of the stairs."

He was right. It was cool. The air smelt damper here, and... full of chemicals. When he turned on the light she could see grey concrete walls. And then...

"No." She simply said. "It can't be."

He smiled. "Would you like to see?"

"How is this possible?" Because there, right in front of her was a sarcophagus. The colours were dull and worn, but it was definitely adorned with a painted image of a woman. The woman had long black hair and kohl rimmed eyes. Her face was impassive, and she was bedecked with jewels. Along her body there were images—not hieroglyphics exactly, but pictures of people and gods and birds and things that even Ra, with her limited exposure, knew were Egyptian.

She moved away. It was one thing for the man to drink pink cocktails, but to keep a sarcophagus in his basement? "I...I think we should go back up now. I'm actually not feeling very well." It was true, she wasn't. Her whole body felt stiff, and slow.

"Relax," he said, walking towards the sarcophagus. "It's not here permanently. This little lady is in transit. She's going to a wealthy American. He has a collection. You'd be amazed at how many artefacts are actually in wealthy people's homes."

"It would be great if we could go back up now."

"In a minute," he said pleasantly. "Wait until I show you what's inside."

She felt her legs buckle under her. "Saqib, I'm not kidding, I think there's something really wrong with me. Please, help me up the stairs. Can we go find Ahmed?"

He ignored her, and reached over the sarcophagus, lifting its lid. "Can you see? No? You could at least try to lift yourself up a bit."

She was panting now. "Are you drunk? Why aren't you listening to me? For God's sake do something." Her fingers were tingling; she couldn't feel their tips. What the hell was happening to her? She tried hard to focus, but the room turned upside down.

"Not until you see."

He reached and pulled her up. "Hurry, please," she muttered, as her world spun. But instead of turning towards the stairs, he moved towards the sarcophagus.

"I've lifted the lid. Aren't you curious to see what's inside?"

She leaned over the sarcophagus, and then felt the vomit come, so fast she couldn't stop it. Batul. It was Batul. Or what was left of her, anyway. Her face was a shrunken grey husk, her jaw open, teeth grinning back at her. Her hair was the only unaltered piece of her, thick and long and still in springy waves around her shoulders. "What... what is this? How did she get here?" And then, as it sunk in. "What have you done to her?"

He giggled. "She's in the first stages of mummification. It will be another two months before she's completely dried out. Don't worry about the vomit. I can wipe that off the sides."

"Oh my god. Oh my god." She felt the tears come, hot and fast. "Who are you? What are you?"

He shrugged, pulling her away from the body. "I'll let you in on a little secret, Ra. I make my money from forgeries. It's easy to forge things, on the black market. It's not as though the buyers can openly admit to owning what they have, or get stuff carbon dated. Yet everyone wants to be special, don't they? To own what others covet, to have their secrets that make them feel superior. The losers don't even know they're getting played."

She half listened to him, through the thudding in her head. He was saying something about his father now… not an antiquities dealer after all, no, but actually a drunken immigrant taxi driver in New Jersey who disgusted Saqib. Saqib was saying something about his childhood, about the hot shame of his beefy thick-fisted father who couldn't even speak English, about his own gift for copying things, his ability to break art down into each individual brush stroke, each indent of clay. When he got older he put those skills to use, creating miniature bowls and figurines from various ancient civilisations. A two-year affair with an archaeology student in Brooklyn had helped him learn the business.

"I actually had quite a passing trade going, but it was small bucks. I wanted to make it big, you know? What was the point, otherwise? It took me a while to realise all my efforts would be in vain if I didn't smarten myself up, didn't learn to look and act the part and reinvent myself. To be honest, that was the hardest bit. When you don't grow up summering on Martha's vineyard you really have to work at it. It's the little things that give you away. But I find I can mimic people as well as I can reproduce things." He paused. "Are you still listening to me? I hope so, 'cause this bit's important, Ra, to your future. You see, I upped my game. Do you know how much a mummy sells for? Let me tell you. $11 million, easy. I only have to sell one or two of these a year and I'm solid. I'm one of you now, rich, indolent, full of affected ennui. It won't take me long before they accept me at your Club, before I'm on the board of all your charities. All for the price of some clay and camphor and a dead body."

"Why?" she moaned, desperate now. "Why did you do this to her? Why did you even come here?"

He grunted as he pulled her to the corner of the room. "It was an unfortunate error. A year ago, I became friendly with a man named Charles. He was rich, entitled, and useless. Just like half this society of yours. Charles was an addict; he had really messed up his life. But... he was connected to some of the old New York families, and he helped cement my social standing. Then his family disowned him and I figured, why not put him to good use? It wasn't as though anyone was going to miss him, and a Qatari royal had already requested that I help him find a mummy. I miscalculated though. His rich absentee Daddy was really upset when he went AWOL. He started tearing the city apart, looking for his son. So I left New York, before anyone came asking questions. It's easier to operate undetected in a city like Karachi. You were right, Ra. Money *is* everything in this town. It hasn't been particularly challenging to pay the right people to look the other way. I've set up a hell of an operation already, and, once I'm on the board of all your charities and president of the Club with my new identity firmly in place, I will be well and truly insulated from the events of New York. You all do like to protect your own, don't you?"

"You're psychotic." She tried to move away from him, but her body was like lead. She couldn't feel her legs now, and her lips were numb too. Think! She had to think. Why was it so hard to think?

He placed her on the floor in the corner where she sank, incapable of moving. "I met Batul at an exhibition at Mohatta Palace, did she never tell you? She was quite the flirt, you know. We hung out a couple of times, talking about archaeology, and then I brought her back here—she wanted to buy the Minoan mask—or at least that was the excuse she used for coming back to my place. I figured we'd hook up, *and* I'd make a quick sale.

Two birds with one stone, type of thing. Unfortunately, she was smarter than she looked, questioning the authenticity of all my pieces. She was asking too many questions, so she had to go."

His voice was growing fainter. "If you look closely at her, you'll see that I wasn't gentle enough with extracting her brain—her whole left eye is saggy—see?"

"I can't see," she whispered. "I can't see anything." It was true, she realised with a shock. The world had gone black. She tried to lift herself up but fell back, her limbs refusing to obey her anymore. "What have you done to me?"

"Oh that's just the toxin," he replied casually. She could hear him moving around, dragging something along the floor of the basement. He was breathing heavily. "It's temporary, don't worry. You'll be unconscious soon. You won't feel a thing, I promise."

"What... what will you do?"

"Haven't you listened to a word I've been saying? Batul talked about you so much, in between begging for her life and asking me to end her parent's suffering by letting her contact them. After I killed her and her eye socket started to droop, I thought, it was meant to be. I probably can't sell her now, she's too damaged. But I can start again, put another body in the sarcophagus. I have an eager buyer lined up in Austin already. $11 million! Enough to buy plenty of Karachi real estate."

She could hear his footsteps, getting closer.

"You can replace her. I already have three of my servants upstairs ready to swear that you left the party and got into a white Corolla that was driven by a girl of Batul's description. The police will have a field day with that, don't you think? The two of you running away together?" He giggled. "Maybe your parents will think you were secret lovers. Don't be sad, Ra. You'll be reunited with her. Won't that be nice, at least?"

She tried to scream, but she couldn't take in enough air.

He leaned over her, peering. "Are you still awake? I need you to be unconscious, I don't want to leave any marks when I kill you, it's not good for the process. Blink if you can hear me."

She couldn't see. She couldn't move. She could barely breathe. But she could hear him, somewhere in the distance.

And then she was in the air, lifted and swung over his shoulders, and the smell of fresh laundry and spicy cologne intermingled with chemicals made her want to gag, but she was so tired, and everything was numb.

"Christ you're heavier than I thought you would be. Big boned, are we? Easy does it. I just need... uff what did you eat for dinner? I've moved Batul out of the sarcophagus, I just need to see how well you fit in here. Egyptian women were smaller, back then. Oh... great, it's a tight squeeze but you just about fit. See? It was meant to be."

Was he whistling? She could hear whistling, or roaring, or something rushing past her ears.

"I'm just going to close this lid for a bit, okay? Bend your knees a bit more, that's a girl. It'll be dark in there, but you won't mind, will you? It's not like you can see anything. A few minutes in here, and you will run out of air. It will be peaceful, I promise you that, Ra."

The roaring was gone now, she could hear scraping, wood against wood.

"Good night, Ra. Tell Batul I'm sorry about her eye, when you see her."

And even though she couldn't see, she could feel it then. A different kind of darkness. She closed her eyes.

(I was astonished by the broken window I saw when I visited the city, because the hole between its cracks was so absolutely perfect an image of a flying crow. I took a lot of pictures of it, sure that what I was looking at was a happy accident.

On my second visit to the same neighbourhood, however, I stopped by a mattress warehouse. In one pane of its main window was a hole in the shape of a stylized gorilla, pounding its chest.

'It's a dying art,' my guide said, when she realised what I was gawping at. 'Today they do it on ladders, with very fine hammers. Back in the day the best practitioners used to pride themselves on being able to render pretty much any animal you ordered with a single thrown stone.'

Nowadays they mass-produce windows with careful perforations in the glass, so if you hit them right you'll have your tiger, your trout, your dancing bear. In the church of the main square, the stained-glass head of Mary Magdalene—which was certainly not pre-prepared like that—is broken by a hole in the shape of a badger. It was a kid who did it, the priest said, 40 years ago, with one stone, one throw, the old way. He smiled when I asked him if he'd known the culprit, in such a way as to imply that it had been him.)

SWIPE LEFT
Daniel Polansky

Andrea, 27. First shot is a close up of blonde hair and blue eyes and so is the second. Always a reason if they won't let you see below the shoulders. Swipe left.

Jean, 25. Red haired and chubby, but that kind of chubby where you know they like sex. Swipe right.

Maddy, 32. In a group in all her pictures, and so it takes thirty seconds to discover that she's the least pretty one in all of them. Always make sure to stand next to an ugly cousin, that's amateur hour. Swipe left.

Erin, 28. Apple-cheeked, strange eyes, alone in all her pictures. Why apple and not tomato? Both red. Both about the same size. Tomatoes aren't a fruit, obviously. I mean they're a fruit but they aren't sweet. Swipe right cause my thumb was moving that way anyhow.

Moonflower, 30, not her fault she has horrible hippie parents, swipe right in sympathy of what must have been a difficult upbringing, also because she has pretty hair.

Interrupted by a happy buzz and some upbeat graphics, the usual Skinner box bells and whistles. Erin is quick on the draw.

Hi!

Hi. How's your Tuesday?

Fine. You've got great hair.

I do in my photo. That's why I made it my photo. *Thanks. I comb it.*

ROTFL.

But she isn't, really.

Where do you live?

Brooklyn.

Me too!!!

One exclamation point wasn't sufficient? At least she didn't add an emoji. I hate emojis. I mean, a smiley face here or there to offer some context, fine, but the—

How's your day been?

—thing where you have to have to dress up every sentence like it was an adolescent's notebook, smiling panda bears and party hats; just the worst. *Good, how was yours?*

OK! Where are you in Brooklyn?

Abby, 29. Christ, are people still dressing up as Rosie the Riveter? In 2018? Seriously? Swipe left.

Jasmine, 33. Sphinx-like and sexy in pictures one and two, but in the third she's smiling and her smile is all crooked. Everyone is as pretty as their ugliest picture. Swipe left.

I'm in Fort Greene. Bed-Stuy, technically, actually, but Fort Greene sounds sexier. *Where are you?*

I'm in Bed-Stuy!!

!!!!! total and we're not even through the preliminaries. *Fun.*

You want to meet for a drink?

Do I? This is all getting a little bit real for an evening where I ate takeout Indian and have a *Game of Thrones* episode waiting in the queue. What's the best-case scenario, really? She's perfect and amazing and we get married and have happy children and die in the same bed?

Gertrude, 34. I like that hair bun, but three of Gertrude's five pictures appear to be from Burning Man, that's going to be a hard pass. Swipe left.

Is there a bar you like?

On the other hands, that's an auspicious sort of enthusiasm, and what's the point of living in New York if you can't get a drink with a strange girl on a weekday? Provided it's a close drink. *The Admiral? On Washington.*

Perfect! See you in 40?

Cool.

Can't wait!

I take a shower and debate what shoes to wear. The suede ones are nice, but it might rain. It probably won't rain. It might rain, though. I settle for sneakers and newish jeans and my second-best shirt. In the summer in the city the heat sticks around till midnight and I end the walk to the bar sweat-stained. She said forty minutes, but I get there early to grab a seat in the back, hate having to do one of these at the front counter, every quip and shudder on public display.

Yaela, 35. What is Yaela? Russian? Israeli? Whatever, foreign chicks are my kryptonite. Swipe right.

Kiki, 33. I like the kimono in the second picture, but she looks too much like that girl I was seeing last winter, the one who—

I'm Erin.

Hi, I'm Matt.

Due fairness, she looks like her pictures, she just doesn't look like her pictures the way I wanted her to. Her forehead goes on a long time before reaching hair, and she's wearing a perfume that smells like candy or like fruit-flavored candy but isn't quite masking whatever's beneath it.

This place is great!

It's OK, actually, there are five on the block that look just like it, and the pricier ones I save for second dates. *Thanks, yeah, I come here a lot. Can I get you something?*

White wine?

One sec,

The barman smirks at me. Bartenders are the smuggest fucking people alive, you'd think they were performing open heart surgery rather than mixing cocktails. *A can of Narragansett and your house white.*

Got you.

At the other end of the counter a guy is doing what I was doing ninety seconds ago, looking up at the door every time it opens, oozing anxious anticipation.

Twelve bucks.

I thought it's happy hour.

It's not.

By four minutes. Asshole. Tip him anyway, that's just basic humanity, I'd give Goebbels a buck a drink.

Erin is smiling broadly when I turn back around.

Here you go.

Thanks!

My pleasure.

Her makeup is inexpertly applied. Makeup is so weird, when you think about it, like here I'm going to put big black rings around my eyes, that'll attract a mate. But it works, though, which is even weirder. At least it does if you do it right. *Find the place OK?*

Yeah, no problem. I have this app on my phone, it shows me where to go.

We all have that app on our phone, it's the map feature. Then again what kind of question was "find the place OK?" That one's on you, Matty-boy. *Do you come out this way much?* Slightly better, I mean no one's going to mistake me for Baudelaire, but—

Sometimes! Not a lot. I'm kind of a homebody, you know? It's like, you take all the effort to get dressed up, and go to meet someone, and then the whole time you just want to be back inside.

Totally. Like, one time I went out on a random date with a girl on a Wednesday night and regretted it as soon as I saw her. That was nasty, quit being a jerk. You agreed to come along, the least you can do is be decent company for ninety minutes. *How long have you been in the city?* An hour.

A while, since I left—

—Michigan?—

Minnesota after high school. I grew up with my grandparents. My grandmother. Well, my grandfather first too, but then after he went missing it was just—

—Close. I knew it was one of those boring states in the middle.

—*with her gone, I just figured, what's stopping me, you know? What's stopping me?*

That's great. *How do you like the city?*

I like some things. All the strangers roaming about, endless packs of them, these different threads intertwining and severing. Sometimes it gets a little overwhelming, I guess—

She's not terrible looking, really, she's just not quite my type. Well, whatever, you've got that second date with the lawyer on Wednesday, what was her name, not Lindsay but something that made you think of Lindsay? Kelly, maybe.

—*you feel like you want something real, you know? Something lasting. Something that will never go away.*

Totally. Stephanie, her name was Stephanie. That's not that much like Lindsay, really. Just that last bit.

Gosh, I've really been going on! Tell me about yourself, Matt, your bio said you were an editor?

Yeah, for Shrewsbury. Associate editor, technically, but that barely counts as a lie. *Genre stuff. Sci-fi, horror that kind of thing.*

I don't really read much horror.

Am I being negged? *Too scary?*

No, I don't get scared really. They just seem silly to me. Sparkly vampires, or sexy werewolves, or killer clowns torturing and eating children. Silly stuff.

Huh. I don't really like cookies, but I don't make a point of mentioning it when I meet a baker. Did she tell me what her job was yet? I don't think so. Keep it vague either way. *What's your story?*

I'm a pharmacologist.

Do you like it?

Yeah, I love it, I always wanted to be a pharmacologist. Well, not a pharmacologist, exactly, but something with medicine.

Sure. It must be great to be able to help people like that.

Mostly I just always loved the idea of figuring out how things work, you know? What makes things go. Actually, funny story, when I was eleven, there was this tabby that used to—

Shit, did I refrigerate the curry? Probably... not, no, probably not. That's ok, it's just a couple of hours, and curry is fine, sits in the container getting thicker. I should get some bread or something on the way home, maybe a six pack. Nice way to polish off the evening.

—but it turned out she was the neighbor's, and not a stray at all!

Wow.

Yeah. So, after that we had to move back to Michigan.

Weird.

Do you want another beer?

What, trying to get me drunk?

She laughs so loud the bartender looks over.

No, I'm OK. Anyway, I think the guy should pay for drinks on the first date. Call it an asshole tax.

What do you mean, an asshole tax?

Well, it's kind of a weird thing, meeting a stranger for a first date, right? But for a guy, it's just funny weird, like the worst that happens is you don't click, have a little awkward banter, and then you head home. But a girl... My shrug is meant to indicate the gamut of harassment, abuse, rape, murder, the sordid rubric familiar to all woman in human society.

When she isn't smiling, her face looks very hard. *I guess I don't go on so many dates as you do.*

I really read this wrong. Good thing I don't actually like her. Still, never feels good to make an error, even if it's in your weekend kickball league. *I've been single a while.*

She brightens up some, those aforementioned apple cheeks. *I guess you have to open up a lot of frogs!*

Kiss a lot of frogs.

What?

It's "kiss a lot of frogs".

Is it?

Yeah, you open oysters to get pearls. You kiss frogs to… turn them into princes, I guess.

Right. Can you excuse me a minute?

Sure, take your time.

Walking off she's got a nicer ass than I'd have credited her. Her glass is still a third full, best to start winding this down when she comes back. You kinda need to lay the groundwork for an appropriate exit, smiling meaninglessly and fidget about a bit.

Louise, 28. If Louise is 28 then I am a hundred and forty-five. Wait, no, if Louise is 28 then I'm 10? Because she's pretending to be younger than she is. Whatever, Louise is not 28. Swipe left.

Suvi, 32. Does it make me racist that I kind of have a thing for Indian woman? But then again, you'd be racist if you didn't like them either. Catch-22. Swipe right.

Alana, 23, either Alana's a bot or she's just a woman much too good-looking to go on a date with me. Swipe right, because we live in hope.

Hey!

Hey.

The bathrooms are through a fake bookcase!

Yeah, it's cute.

I heard there's this place in Williamsburg where they have cats! You can go, and drink coffee or beer I guess, and just play with the cats all you want, you know?

The cat bar?

You've been?

No, I'm just… aware that such things exist.

Wine snorts out of her nose. Ten points. *You're hysterical!*

Actually I'm only very, very funny. With that last splash of Chablis we've reached the end of our date, though she seems unaware of it, staring up like a lamb to slaughter. At least make it quick, one sharp move, like a Band-Aid. *Hey, this was a lot of fun, thanks so much for coming.*

Rising as I said it and she joins me on her feet. *No problem!*

Good, going easy, I mean I've been on the other end of this plenty and there's nothing to do really but smile till you get out of range and then start thinking of all the things you didn't like about them. Outside feels like an armpit, have to crank up the a/c as soon as I get home. Awkward bit here where we decide between shoulder hug and sweaty handshake—

Do you want to come back to my place?

An unexpected development. For her likewise, I gather, a spur of the moment offer, the cliff overtaken, nothing left but to enjoy the fall.

For like... another drink?

Gosh, that's really... Not a great idea, I don't like you so much really and anyway sex with a stranger is always the same cocktail of pointlessness, the only reason to do it is to prove you can, and that's a bad reason to do something. And they have a way of thinking this means something, even when they do it after one drink on a Wednesday night. *My apartment isn't far from here.* I am an asshole.

I don't go home with strange men. We can go to my place though.

Why is your place any safer? Whatever, being a single woman means taking your life in your hands every time you grab a drink, all the fucking animals in this city. Imagine, having to be afraid all the time, wherever you went, that someone was going to hurt you. *Whatever makes you comfortable. Where do you live?*

East Flatbush.

I thought you said you lived in Bed-Stuy?

Did I?

Didn't she? While I'm thinking she wiggles her way under my arm and stares the way they do when they want you to kiss them, and I recall that I'll be dead one day and won't be able to go back to a strange woman's apartment and touch her vagina.

Sure.

She tastes like white wine and lip gloss. Pedestrians separate around us, our affection an impediment. She barely comes up to my chest. I hold her with one hand and with the other I beckon down a yellow cab.

Hi.

Hello.

Good evening.

Hi.

Just start get on Eastern Parkway and head east, I'll direct you.

Who the hell lives in East Flatbush? I mean, lots of people, obviously, but not white girls with post-graduate degrees. This is a bad idea, it's going to take fucking forever to get back home. She uses too much tongue when she kisses. What is it she smells like? A bump in the road grinds our teeth together and I pull away.

How did you end up living all the way out here?

The rent is cheap.

It's pretty cheap in Mogadishu too, to from what I hear. Shuttered brownstone, shuttered brownstone, body shop with the signs all in Spanish, shuttered brownstone. Live forever in this city and never know it, two miles from your apartment you might as well be on the moon. A man wheels an overloaded shopping cart against a green light. The driver honks to little effect. *Never any troubles with the... neighbors?* That was a nice euphemism, good on you.

Not really. Well, when I first moved in, there were a couple of kids down the block who used to say things when I walked past.

Say things?

You know, the usual stuff, Bruja and diablesa, but then one night I found one of them—

There's this big brown spot right in the middle of her smile. Jesus, that was a shitty thing to think. What's wrong with you? Why are you in this cab? How old are you going to be before you stop acting like this? Another notch on the bed post? Asshole. Asshole. You are such an asshole.

—and after that, they've all pretty much taken to avoiding me. Stop here.

The driver stops abruptly enough to throw me into the monitor they have set in the divider, some C-list celebrity informing me of tomorrow's weather.

Here?

The driver is skeptical, and I don't blame him. Here is nowhere, a faceless block on a narrow street.

That's right.

Driver shrugs. *Twenty-seven fifty.*

Erin reaches for her purse before I can feint towards my wallet. *You got the drinks.*

Only half of what it cost us to get all the way out to wherever we are, but I won't quibble if she won't. Outside it smells like hot trash. Everywhere smells like hot trash in August, the city awash in fruit rinds and soiled clothes and used hygiene products.

You live here?

Just through the back.

What is up with this girl? Looks like a pre-school teacher but she lives next to a crack house. Through a back alley with a lot of scrap metal and glass. Going for a light, I discover my phone is dead. I hope she has a plug to borrow, that'll be a fun post-coital conversation. Three sets of locks on her door to get in, not that I can blame her, if I lived out here I'd want a pit bull and alarms. I wouldn't live out here.

This is me! Make yourself at home.

Thanks. Yeah, it's… really nice. Compared to the outside, at least, but that's a low bar. Barely anything in there; a sagging couch, a place where a TV should be but isn't, a well-stocked kitchen. She locks the door behind us. *How long have you been here?*

Since I came to the city.

How many years is that, again? I should have listened closer. However long it should have been enough to get some shit in here besides a Harry Potter poster and half a dozen of those thick candles that you buy at the mall for your aunt as a Christmas gift and have names like Vanilla Sun or Strawberry Bliss. She'd left them lit but they weren't quite covering the smell, the other smell, whatever that is. *Can I get you something to drink?*

Sure. Big, though, upside of living in the ghetto is cheap rent, I suppose, but who needs a second bedroom if it's just you? And who would go to the trouble of padlocking it?

Do you like rosé?

Very strongly no, but by tradition the nightcap is any intoxicant that can be found in a cabinet. *Sounds good.*

She pulls an open bottle from the fridge and pours us both a glass.

Here you go.

Thanks.

Bottom's up!

God, rosé is absolutely fucking vile. Who drinks this piss? Erin doesn't drink hers, licking her lips and staring at me.

You've got great hair.

Thanks. You've got… a really lovely jawline.

Fucking Christ, someone should stab you in the chest with a butcher knife. What are you doing here, man? Stop thinking that way, stop thinking that way, the time to bail on this was back at the bar or before the bar really, but certainly not right now, not with her staring up at me with that kind of desperation that demands a response. I down the rest of my drink and grab her and push her against the counter, her short legs wrapped tight around me.

I need you.

Yeah?

I need you so bad.

You could make a fortune doing like, sex talk banalities fridge magnets. Probably someone already did already. Why hello, there, little Matt, nice to see you make an appearance. All the fucking trouble you make for me, you'd think you were my child and not merely its potential author. She's so much shorter than me that it makes kissing her an awkward exercise. I have to bend down from the waist almost.

Take me to the bedroom, I want to feel your strength.

What Harlequin paperback did she take that from? Focus, focus, you're enjoying yourself, she's enjoying herself, keep the mood light. If she was a bit smaller I'd dead lift her across the doorway, hammy as hell but it plays, but she's got some thick on her, and if I struggle getting her off the ground it'll be bad for all of us. Plus, it's dark and I might trip. Plus, my hands feel weird, quaky, kind of, and so I settle on following her into the room that isn't padlocked.

Do you have a light in here?

No.

There's nothing in her room but the bed and a table beside it, inside of which are a couple of condoms or a small bottle of lube or one of those vibrators they sell at yuppie sex shops that look like Swedish cooking tools or maybe, maybe, a few feet of rope which Erin has never been quite brave enough to try using. I'm on the bed looking up at her, all of a sudden. She takes off her shirt and then her bra and her body seems to deflate, distend, makes me think of mayo being slathered over bread or a corpse left too long in the water. Did I eat today? Yes, right the half of the curry that isn't in my fridge, don't know why I'm getting buzzed on two drinks if I ate dinner. Don't know why I left my house.

I never do this.

But how many times have you said that to someone? *Me neither.*

I mean, I really never do this. Usually I have to know a guy for weeks before I bring him home. It's a big thing, for me, taking a man home.

I kiss her quiet, the last thing I need is to listen to her hopes for the future, so long as I don't hear them I can't be held responsible for not meeting them. Jesus you're such a fucking idiot, travel halfway across the city to sleep with a girl you don't want anything to do with. How long is it going to take to get back, can't be many Ubers hovering around here in the back asshole of New York? Shit, your phone is out of battery, forgot about that, and also she said she lived in Bed-Stuy, I know she said she lived in Bed-Stuy. Her jeans go and that first pleasant scent of her sex comes in. Never understood that locker room nonsense about how pussy smells weird, it's like a mouse saying cheese smells weird. *Do you have any condoms?*

Don't worry about it.

I guess she must be on something, everyone's on something these days, everyone's got HPV also but it seems too late to be worrying about that all of a sudden, too late to stop and my hands feel slow and stupid, she has to help me get my pants off, down around my ankles without me quite realizing how and then she's on top of me, the warm wetness—

Oh gosh, oh gosh, oh gosh, oh my gosh—

A screamer and I bet a squirter too but just as well, as least it lets you know you've done your job, all we owe anyone these days, that and the first round of drinks, I stretch my hand on the small of her back but find I can't hold it.

I knew you were special from your picture—

An even rhythm as she rides me—

—a man, a real man—

Digging her nails into my neck, hard, harder than I like

—not like all the boys in this city—

I don't like it so rough like that, but I can't seem to push her away

—*give it to me, give it to me oh gosh oh gosh*—

She comes in a second soprano, exultations echoing off the wall. She has thick thighs, ripe thighs, coiling tight around me, too tight—

—*finish in me, baby, finish in me*—

Hands aren't working at all now, my hands or my arms or my toes or my legs or my knees only my eyes blinking and my heart beating and my cock which is—

—*that part goes inside me and the rest goes into your room.*

Something in that wine how didn't I—

—*don't struggle, baby, don't struggle, I'll take care of you*—

The smell is me oh god the smell is me or me soon like the other how many others

—*finish baby, finish for me*—

I listen to her I don't want to listen to her but I can't stop a small death followed by the long one hahah I don't want to die I don't want to die—

Good boy. You're such a good boy.

She opens the bedside table but inside aren't condoms or lube or a vibrator that looks like a Swedish kitchen tool inside is a knife a great big knife with a little curve at the end to use for—

It's almost over. Don't fight.

The knife comes down but I can't feel it I can't feel it I can't feel anything oh god these things don't really happen

MiDNIghT MaRAuDERS
M. Suddain

I want to tell you about Berezov the chemist, and about what happened when a man called Vanzant arrived in town to open a second drug store.

We used to be an oil town until we ran out. Then we started milling water. There used to be another town in the valley, by a great lake and below a glacier. Now it's gone, and so is the glacier, and the lake is even greater. The sea is closer, too. Cartel ships bring goods dredged from the cities, and we pay them in fresh water. We trade the goods to towns nearby. Ours is a thriving town with good people. We have two inns, a playhouse, and a fuck-shop. We had a church until we accidentally burned it down. And we had, for a short while, two drug dispensaries.

BEReZOv

Berezov's drug-shop was a palace of silver, gold, and frosty glass. It had a counter with an ancient soda fountain hauled up from the Vanished Village. The fountain had an enamelled column with four soda spigots, each shaped like a bird in flight. It was topped with a brass globe of the world as it used to be. You could still see the marks where people had rubbed at the raised outline of the old islands. The world is a fluid thing,

Berezov would say. Always moving, never stopping, more like a molten ball of brass than one that's cooled. People would spend whole afternoons in his store, sipping long drinks and gazing at that globe while the old man stooped to dab at marks on the fittings. It was a place to sit and think, especially in the weeks before the Long Night, when the days and darkness start to melt into one another.

Our parents went to Berezov's with needs.

"My kid has a mean sadness. Will you give her something to keep her quiet?"

"My dingle is sleepy. Won't you give me something to wake him? It's the wife's birthday."

He always had the medicine. He'd bear-hug the jars from high shelves and set them with a thud upon a square of felt. The pills crackled as he dashed them with his silver shovel. Sometimes us kids would come in to ask for a "penny-bag" and Berezov would measure out a selection of treats, nothing very heavy— some to help us concentrate on school-work, some to banish nightmares, some to quicken memories—but always just what we need. When my best friend's brother, Jakob, started sleep-walking every night, Berezov had the medicine he needed. After that he only sleep-walked every other night. Berezov would shovel our pills into a white paper packet, twist the top tight like a lantern wick. When we left we always touched his fountain for luck.

VAnzaNt

Vanzant arrived just after the Long Night of my fourteenth year. I remember because it was the year we lost Mr Abderhalden, and the summer I caught a heavy lust for Jakob. Vanzant came in with his wife on a cartel boat loaded up with guns and pills and exotic teas. He set up business in Mr Abderhalden's shop. None of us could believe it. That Abderhalden was dead, yes; but also that the town chamber would approve a new business that cut into Berezov's livelihood. Vanzant used solvent and a chisel to scrape "Abderhalden's Photography" off the window, without a hint of reverence or ceremony. Then he had his own name painted in gold lettering. "Vanzant's Dispensary." He took from the windows all the antique cameras; the faded family portraits featuring dogs and adults now dead, and children long since grown up.

Some of those grown-ups went to Berezov's to vent their rage. Abderhalden was our oldest and dearest citizen (until he died). Berezov, who with Abderhalden's passing officially became our oldest and dearest citizen, had taken it hard. "I could have saved him!" he said. "I could have given him medicine!" We'd told him there was nothing he could have done, that Abderhalden was very old, and that there really is no medicine for drinking too much and going to sleep in a river.

There were loud arguments over what to do about Vanzant. Some said we should run Vanzant out. Dad's friend Jon Ming (whom everyone calls Jing) said Vanzant was clearly a cartel spy, and that we should throw the bastard in the sea. Dad reminded him how the Sheriff treated people who incited public disorder, and Jing calmed down.

Finally Berezov spoke up. He said we should all stay calm. There was more than enough meat on the bone. "You lot have enough limp dongs and dicky hearts for nine dispensaries." This got a big laugh. "We need to remain civilised." And that's why we all loved Berezov. Even when someone wanted to rob his livelihood, he was polite. He was the soul of our town, people said. Others said spirit. The arguments got heated, but they were basically talking about the same thing: Berezov was at the centre of who we were.

For the first week, Vanzant's bell hardly rang. We'd see his foggy shadow at his counter, nodding to no one as they passed. He had his own soft rag to dab at marks on the fittings, though the only one to mark the place was him—and sometimes his wife, who would descend from their big house with a plate of sandwiches for her husband. Some people spat as she passed. Not at her, or even near her. We're civilised people. But they spat in anticipation of her passing, so she'd have to step over the spit. The gobs froze there, a reminder of our displeasure. It was a triumph for our local spirit.

WeEKenD GALa

The following weekend, the whole town was woken with music. Vanzant had built a storefront phonograph system with a ship's battery to power it. He came out from his shop in a white coat to hand out samples. He strolled the covered promenade to laugh and joke with the bewildered folk who wandered by. We were surprised to see that the town's new enemy was tall and handsome with a strong jaw. He had big, white teeth, incisors like a wolf. He gently teased the men, and he very gently flirted with the women. He would flirt with the woman, I noticed, while leaving a hand upon the elbow of the man, like he was sharing the joke with him, like: "Hey, fellow, watch me pretend to steal your wife."

My friend Nissi and her brother Jakob came down, and when Vanzant saw them he cried, "Stars! The angels have fallen!" Nissi was a year older than me then, and already fairly bulgy. Even some of the dads stammered and blushed when she spoke to them. Vanzant extended his hand and said, "Sweet beauty, dance with me, you must!" and Nissi flinched as she saw that Vanzant was offering his arm to her brother. "No, not you, lovely girl," the chemist said. "If I took your arm the Sheriff would have to come and part us." He took a stunned Jakob whirling off around the wooden deck hung with oil-lamps, whispering loud enough for all to hear: "Never drink, boy. Dance often, but dance only with men: that's how you'll stay young forever." We were all amazed. I had recently started lusting heavily for Jakob, who, back then, was even more beautiful than his sister, even with none of her bulges. There was hardly a moment that year I wasn't thinking about him. I once saw him letting a baby fox lick milk off his bare, hairless arm and had to sit down for twenty minutes. I had a hundred drawings of Jakob hidden under a floorboard, and a thousand scenes I could play in my head. Jakob swimming in an especially cold river. Me rescuing Jakob from a burning ship during a storm. It used to drive Nissi mad. The scene of Jakob close-dancing with a handsome older chemist was not one I'd created, but I added it, and made a note to extend it into a scenario where I had to defend his honour.

People came from everywhere to see Vanzant's performance. Even Berezov stepped out to smile and shake his head generously. That's why we love him: his generosity. Finally the Sheriff showed up with three of his militia, and the crowd dispersed like a pile of dust blasted with an air hose. I was still paralysed by Jakob's movements, so I stayed, even when Baikal came and stood right beside me. Baikal isn't a giant like my dad. I've never seen him shout, or threaten anyone. My dad said the alligators who live in the lake don't say much either, but you wouldn't want to go poking them with sticks. Back in the old, lawless days, the Sheriff was known to have people who caused trouble in our town blackened with sticks, or hung up by the ankles. He'd even had one or two major troublemakers vanished, Dad told me. For a while I thought he'd said "varnished," so I had a picture of prisoners with brown, shiny faces. Dad said someone once whistled politely at Baikal's wife. Baikal almost drowned him by holding his head in a bucket of linseed oil. But Vanzant didn't seem to worry at all about the menacing Sheriff peering at him as he expertly spun young Jakob around the deck. "Good day, Sheriff!" he cried. "Or is it night currently? I've lost track." His poise impressed some people.

By the following weekend, some had ventured inside his shop. It was even grander than Berezov's. He'd imported a soda fountain—like Berezov's, only bigger, and with dancing girls and goat-legged men on it. In the middle of the room was a tank housing a live octopus called Raymond, who Vanzant said he'd won from some fishermen in a game of cards. Vanzant had one whole wall lined with glass cases, and in each was a little scene from nature: a mongoose fighting a cobra; an owl standing proudly on the carcass of a rat, its talons pulling strands of sticky guts. He would mix fortifying tonics for his guests. His long, clever fingers would send the spoon clacking round inside the glass as he told his audience all about the restorative properties of CLyPHolium. CLyPHolium, he said—to people who until that moment hadn't known CLyPHolium was missing from their lives—is a miracle drug. He'd send the fizzing tube along the marble counter to stop right in front of the person it was meant for. Everyone would applaud, and it wasn't uncommon for a family to wander from his place much lighter in the pocket, and somewhat lighter in the head.

During these "weekend galas" Berezov would sit in his store with his soft rag—though there were less marks to dab at now—and those who passed would pretend something puzzling had caught their eye. When asked about CLyPHolium he'd laugh and shake his head and say that CLyPHolium— along with METACLyPHolium and BETACLyPHolium and most of the PHoliums—was overrated. But he'd say it kindly. He was a kind man, and we are a town of decent people. We don't get carried away, like we used to in the old days, when our town was peopled by refugees and former soldiers, and the sea was some distant thing, and there was another town down low in the valley.

Most of all, we give new people a chance. Where before there was an ill-wind blowing towards Vanzant, now there was a gentle breeze of acceptance. There was a feeling that there was enough business in a town like ours for two dispensaries, especially since the cartel divers had discovered the old PharmCo factories. Even Dad said Vanzant seemed like an OK guy, "… with a lovely wife!" though he was careful not to blow too strongly on that around Mum, because all the women in our town were tuned to what an unnaturally beautiful woman Mrs Vanzant was. I had also thought about it a lot.

THE lOnG DAY

We live in the high north, so for part of the year it's always night. During the Long Night, it's dark for 800 hours. The lake gets iced over, so we can't dive for treasure in the Vanished Village. We sleep as families on our stoves, under furs, reading, singing; dozing like we're on a long journey. Which we kind of are. A long journey back to the sun. We keep jars of fresh water hanging above the stove. Families with radios search for voices, or music, or some other sign the world still exists. We live off tinned fruit, salted meat and birch juice. We know by the hopper's croak the night is ending.

As the days get longer, life in our town picks up, and, by the time the Long Day arrives, it is a joyous place. Too joyous, maybe. People drink a lot, and have new romances, and try things they've never tried before. A controlled dose of chaos is a good thing sometimes, Berezov always said, so long as people don't take it too far. And when they did, the Sheriff and his militia were there to restore order.

The Long Day was approaching, and I had been at the mossflow catching hoppers and dreaming up interesting scenarios. I'd found I came up with my best scenarios while walking. I'd hoped to spy on Jakob washing his pet turtle in the river, but they weren't out to bathe that day. As I passed Berezov's I spied my Dad's big shadow up on one of the high stools, sipping a tall beer. Vanzant was waging open war for the town's love. He'd shown up at school with some of Mr Abderhalden's old photography equipment, even though it was supposed to be Berezov's job now to take the school portraits. Nissi and Jakob's portraits took twice as long as the rest of ours combined.

Vanzant had also been quietly spreading rumours about Berezov. People were saying the old man had been filling out his jars with sugar pills. A rumour had started that he kept certain kinds of pictures in a safe in his storeroom. He was furious, and immediately called Baikal to come and make a thorough search of his premises. The Sheriff found nothing, of course, but somehow the water had been poisoned. Many parents stopped letting their children go to Berezov's unattended. Someone carved "RAT" on the flawless enamel of his precious soda fountain. He put a small strip of gauze across the word. The world was changing.

MidNIGHT MeETING

Late that evening, Dad said to get my coat because we had a job to do at Berezov's. I said I didn't need my coat because it was warm out and it wasn't far to Berezov's, and he said, "Well, that's up to you."

We found Berezov in the storeroom of his shop. I was surprised to find Jon Ming there, too. Berezov said, "Dan, Lidya, take a seat," so I took my coat off and sat down. He poured us all a scotch and explained how we needed to tackle the Vanzant problem. "I try to be civilised. And kind. But there's a limit." We all grunted, both at the fact that he was civilised, and kind, and also at their being a limit to those qualities. Then he said he was calling in his favour. We knew exactly what favour he was talking about, and it was huge.

*   *   *

AfTEr AFrica

Dad and Jing came to settle here after the Water Wars. In a place called Africa they'd jumped from planes, at night, while chewing goat hoof soaked in a certain local leaf. That leaf does not grow here. So they hatched a daring plan to sneak into Berezov's during the Long Night and take a very small amount of his better stuff, an amount so small he wouldn't miss it. They went in with old army torches muffled inside socks. But they somehow set off the alarm (an angry parrot called Berthold). They heard Berezov coming. Jing dived under the counter. My dad flung himself inside a big cupboard and held his breath. (He can usually hardly breathe from laughing when he tries to tell this part of the story.) The cupboard turned out to be a glass display case intended for a stuffed emu, and when Berezov turned on the lamps he saw my dad's huge mug grinning down at him.

Berezov called him out of the case and poured him and Jing a scotch and put a deal to them: he'd cut them a dose of the medicine they were after each week, and a little less each week until they were off, and if they asked for a grain more he'd give them to the Sheriff. "You don't want to end up in one of Baikal's cells, do you?"

They did not. At that time Jing's face was still dark from being dunked in linseed oil.

Berezov said if they stuck to his plan they'd be clean in four months—which is roughly when Dad planned to marry my mother. In a way, Berezov is the reason we're a family, so that should tell you how much we owed him. Now he wanted our help running Vanzant out. It was for the good of the town, he said. Frankly, I was surprised. Then shocked. Then proud that I'd been brought in, and I said as much, and Dad said to drink a little slower.

*　　*　　*

mIND StORM

Berezov said we needed ideas flowing, so he took out a small leather kit. He asked if we'd ever done snuff, and Dad and Jing nodded quickly without taking their eyes off the kit. Berezov crushed a mound of bright green pills with a blade and demonstrated how to inhale the powder up our noses with a paper soda straw. Whatever was on that mirror seemed to scorch a hole right through the crown of my skull. The room turned a muddy violet colour, and I immediately felt like putting my coat back on.

But how the ideas flowed! Berezov wrote them all on a big sheet of paper. "Develop a sales strategy." "Stage superior open-days." "Louder music. Maybe a band?" Dad suggested smearing Vanzant by planting some kind of contraband, maybe pornography, maybe of out-of-town girls or farm animals. Berezov said it'd be difficult and risky to source the material. Jing said we could probably stage the material, and made a quick glance at me, and he and Dad had a short argument.

I said what about planting drugs on Vanzant, and then felt kind of stupid. So I said what about planting a rat in one of his jars, and that went on the list, so I said what about a break-in at the store? That might scare him into leaving. And so now I was really flying. So I said, "What about kidnapping Mrs Vanzant and keeping her in a secret location, maybe making her wear different outfits?" But everyone went silent on that, so I just sat down.

But they said my other ideas were interesting, and the agreement, after a long conversation which flew into many enlightening places, was that Mrs Vanzant was a very attractive woman, and that a break-in was the plan that most suited our talents. It would send a strong message to the intruder that there were limits to how he could treat Mr Berezov. Berezov said we should be ready to move the night after next.

*   *   *

MidNIGHt MaraUDerS

It was a fine sunny morning after supper when our gang met up at Berezov's. It'd been a fine morning for weeks now, but on the promenade it was twilight. We watched people wander by. I saw Nissi out looking for someone, probably her brother. I thought it was interesting the way she was walking these days—like her brother, only wobblier—and I said so, and Dad said, "Focus."

We'd been arguing over what to call our gang. We'd toyed with Night Avengers, and a whole lot of other names before finally settling on a name I came up with: the Midnight Marauders. Dad said we weren't marauding at midnight— or technically even at night. But I said Midnight Marauders sounded better than the After Dinner Raiders, and Jing agreed, and Berezov said he didn't give a fuck, it was time to move. He would stay in his shop and keep watch. We visited Berezov's mirror for one more fortifying snort. I didn't know why, since we were staging a raid, not trying to come up with ideas. But I went with it.

The promenade was deserted. The buildings in the street seemed to lean on each other and whisper. My head was wide and empty as a cave. I must have put my gloves on at some point. We slipped our—what's the word? The wool hats that come down over your face? Whatever—we slipped our hat-masks in our pockets and eased across the street. We were very casual. I didn't know why we were dressed all in black, since it wasn't dark, and wouldn't be for months, but it was too late to ask. We stalked in through the back and stood in front of Vanzant's display cases, fogging up the glass with our open mouths. It was the first time I'd seen his octopus, Raymond, up close. What a creature. I stared at him. And he stared at me, sullen eyed. Dad put down his tins of paint and excrement. We had brainstormed some phrases we might smear on the walls, and I had written down a list so I could get the spelling right. I was worried the sound of my beating heart could be heard from the street. We could see Berezov's shadow in the window of his shop. He gave us an encouraging thumbs-up.

Then Jing said, "Okay, it's on," and stanced up in front of a fish tank with his rat-bat trembling, but Dad shot up a hand and said "Wait! What's that sound?" There was a large studio-room at the back of Adberhalden's old shop, and there were definitely sounds coming from it. My heart. We moved down the room, ears cocked. Jing still had his rat-bat raised. My heart had left my body. The air was pounding hot. We're decent people from a decent town. I don't know why I said that. Strange thoughts were popping in and out of my head. The door to the studio was a black shape edged in fire. A child's voice said something I couldn't make out, and for a moment I thought it was me. Then an adult's voice said, softly, "Sh-h-h-h-h-h now. You're safe. Uncle Vanzie is here. You'll be cooler with your blouse off. I've taken mine off. See? Isn't it so much cooler with your blouse off?"

Dad looked at Jing. Jing looked at Dad. Dad looked at me. I looked at Jing. Jing looked at Dad again. I began to ease away, slowly, assuming our next move would be to exit the store and regroup. But Jing lifted one of his gangly legs and kicked at the door, and the door whiffed slowly open.

Hours it took.

Burning daylight.

A groan of hinges echoed off the hills—the mountains, maybe—the howl of a wolf fell to a thin growl drowned out by the sounds of a rising cry from a human child—not me—before everything snapped back—ka-*spack!*—and I was there asleep—surely—because what I saw in that room could only be a dream.

Jakob Novermeyer. Naked from the waist up. A wreath of summer flowers spilling down his bare chest, in a room which seemed sunlit and smelled of expensive lotions. His lips and lids and cheeks painted pale shades of blue/green/orange and blazing under studio lights. He had been arranged for my eyes on a soft chair decorated with ornate cushions and a strip of flowing, purple velvet. I heard music, though I'm sure there was none. It took me a while to see anything else in the world—even Vanzant, who was floating beside one of Abderhalden's big old cameras, his mouth shouting words that somehow never found my ears, but which I assume concerned who we were, and why we were there. He wore a flowing white shirt, unbuttoned, and a kind of loincloth, like a baby's nappy. His extraordinarily hairy legs were bowed like a goblin's. His shoulders had tattoos that looked like children's drawings. Jing's tall frame almost smashed me down as he swept past, pistol in hand, and I saw his mouth make the words: "Get on the floor! Get on the floor! Get on the floor!" Jakob must have been screaming, too, because his mouth was wide and the veins in his neck were bulging. Time seemed to ooze like a winter river.

My hearing came back, and my heart returned to my chest, and I went to help Dad tie our prisoners to chairs. We felt bad about tying Jakob up, but we were scared he'd flee half-naked into the street and start shouting about what was happening. We wanted to understand what was happening before anyone started shouting about it. But it was hard with Jing striding around and shouting rules he just made up. "Rule One! No more crying. Rule Two! Total quiet!" His voice stung my brain. I recognised the antique pistol given to him by his granddad, Otis. With every rule Jing made up he'd wave his gun and we'd all curtsey. Then, in the middle of a rule—"Rule Ten! This gun is for YOUR protection!"—Vanzant said quietly, smirking, "You're Dan, of course."

Dad froze when he heard his name. And Jing too, on one leg, gun in the air, as Vanzant gave his finger a flick and said, "The *haaaaaands*, boy." Dad had taken off his gloves to tie the ropes, which was kind of stupid as he had distinctive hands. They had scars, and his nuptial band was yellow gold and shaped like two dragons kissing. "And that means you're Li-i-i-d-ya." Vanzant squeezed out my name as he turned his eyes on me, and Jakob said, in a fearful stutter: "Luh-lid-ya?"

"Nope!" I said in a deep voice. But the game was up.

"Lidya and Dan," said Vanzant, "A family in crime. Can't see this ending well for you." Dad ripped off his hat-mask and rubbed his eyes, and I did the same, even though my eyes weren't really tired. I was the opposite of tired. Jing pointed out that Vanzant was in a fix, too, since he was taking illicit photos of a child. But Vanzant laughed and said he'd never touched the boy, except to put the makeup on. "Poor Jakob's school portrait didn't come out, remember? A technical glitch." He showed us his teeth. "So his parents sent him along to have another taken. All above the boards."

"Well, we'll just show them the photos and they can judge what's 'above the boards'," said Dad, and the chemist drawled, "What photos?" He still clutched the film plate he'd ripped from the back of his camera the moment he saw us. And he pointed out that taking a photo of a shirtless boy wasn't illegal. Unlike armed robbery and kidnapping, which definitely was. "You think old Abderhalden wasn't in on this racket? He made a fortune selling photos of your spawn to the cartel."

Suddenly certain wrestling-themed tableaus the old man had taken made sense. I felt kind of sick. I couldn't even look at Jakob. For months I'd been inventing scenarios in which I finally got to see his bare, brownish body. I never imagined the real scenario would be me and my dad tying him to a chair and keeping him prisoner.

Vanzant was saying, "I know Berezov put you up to this." Dad tried to argue, but it was obvious we were working for the old man. The bucket we'd brought our faeces in had "Berezov's Dispensary" stamped on the side. "Did that old fool want you to drive me out of town? Well that isn't going to happen. I have a cartel contract. You may as well untie us so we can negotiate properly." He looked like a twisted little ghoul, with his pointed chin and fine, babyish hair.

Jing, no beauty himself, rose tall and said, "Not gonna happen, sir! No way!" His gun clicked like a silver beetle as he shook it at Vanzant, who yelled, "Quiet! From now on, you're working for me. You'll be my double agents. I'll show that old shit-tip he can't mess with me. You're going to untie us, Dan. Jakob is going to tell everyone he came to have his photo taken, but I wasn't in."

Dad called a huddle, but there was nothing really to be said. Dad finally sighed and stomped off into the storeroom to work on Vanzant's ropes, and Jing strode behind hissing, "Don't do it, Dan!" Dad said, "Come and help me with these damned cords, Lid." So I went in and set to work on Jakob. I noticed that his hands had started to go purple. My heart. Jing was saying, "This is no good! No good!" I accidentally grazed Jakob's wrist with my finger, and I must've yelped because Dad said "What!" I heard Jing say "I'm telling you, Dan, we can't trust this pointy fucker!" I felt Vanzant's tall frame rise up slowly above me, his ropes clattering to the floor as he cried, "Oh shut up Jing you piece of living shhhh—!" and that's when two cracks tore the night in half.

Jing had fired his grandfather's pistol over his shoulder into the main room without looking. We heard the crash of glass and the gush of pills rushing across the floor. We heard Jing shout, "Now, will you all finally just LISTEN a minute!" but then nothing more. The whole town was listening. We could hear a trickle of running water. We shoved our heads into the shop and saw a whip of trembling silver coming from a tank of tropical fish. Berezov was standing in his window, both hands pressed to the glass, mouth wide. We could hear shouts bouncing down the quiet street as people tried to work out where the shots had come from, and Vanzant's voice behind us saying, "Idiots. Now you'll rot in jail. If you're lucky. Give me that damned gun!" Jing gave no fight as the pistol was snatched away. "Baikal will be here soon enough," Vanzant went on. "For the gods of all fuck, boy, don't just sit there, put your blouse on!" He pulled his own on roughly. "You and I have the same story. You came here for a photo session. These boys came in to rob the place and tied us up. And if your father has any problems with that version he can damn well come here and discuss it with me."

I was too stricken with fear at that moment to remember things properly, but apparently I laughed loudly at what he said. Dad will tell me later that I definitely laughed loudly, and then I said, "Discuss it with his father. Good luck with that." The words must have just came out. And apparently Vanzant laughed too and said he wasn't scared of Bilvin Novermeyer. Mr Novermeyer has thin limbs and carves trolls from sea-wood.

But then, apparently, I laughed again. It's funny what you remember about a time and what you don't. I said Bilvin was not the Jakob's dad he had to worry about, apparently. I knew certain dark things about the Novermeyers, because Nissi is my best friend. She tells me everything. And one day (or maybe night) she told me her family's deepest secret. I'd always assumed she'd shared this secret with Jakob, seeing as they're brother and sister. But apparently she had not. I apparently told a very short version of the story Nissi told me, and with every sentence Vanzant's tea-brown face went a little milkier, and Jakob's eyes got wider.

Mrs Novermeyer used to be Mrs Baikal, I said. I could have just stopped there, but I went on, apparently. After Nissi and her brother were born, Mr Baikal became very sad, and he couldn't explain it. He came to Berezov, who gave him something for his troubles, but it didn't take. Even drink didn't help. The only way to ease his pain, he found, was in the arms of another. Filled with remorse, he confessed to his wife, whom he loved more than life. She told him they couldn't be married anymore. He said that was fair, and tried to kill himself. She came to nurse him back to health. Slowly things became better. They both remarried. He to a slightly mad beautician, and she to a very nice foot doctor. But Baikal continues to be a secret father to his babies, Nissi said. He always keeps at least one hooded eye on them. Like an alligator. An alligator who made a mistake once, but will never forget his duties.

At the end of my story Vanzant was the colour of a dead man, and Jing was burning with happiness. "Oh!" he shouted. "Oh! You're done for, love!" He shouted right in Vanzant's face. Dad was stunned, and Jakob was staring at me, frozen. I felt bad that he had to find out who his real dad was while half-naked and fully terrified. But life isn't always easy.

When Baikal came storming in with a group of militia men, crunching over the tide of pills, Vanzant fell to his knees and confessed. He was smart enough to know the sheriff would lance out the truth eventually, and that any lies he sold now would be repaid to him later in the common currency of agonising pain. Dad and Jing, braver men, were not afraid to lie a little.

Coming home from the Ox and Legend, they said, we heard a scream. We forced our way in to find Jakob trussed, and Vanzant waving a gun. He'd tried shooting us, but missed. Baikal listened to the story coldly. It was hard to know what he was thinking. At the end Vanzant made no protest, so Baikal very calmly gave the order to take him away, and the chemist was led off through the gnashing crowd. Then the mob turned on his shop and broke it up. Smashed everything. Normally even-minded citizens trod out over piles of broken glass, teeth bared, bat or bird of prey held high before the cheering mob. It was a hell of a thing to watch. Baikal did nothing to stop them. Maybe he realised he couldn't. Berezov came out and stood beside us. I could still see Raymond in his tank, blinking. Every so often a hysterical looter with an expensive piece of photo equipment would slap us on the shoulders and say, "Good job, friends!" Bilvin Novermeyer came by to take Jakob away, and he stopped to thank us for our bravery. "A town needs good men like you," he said. Jakob still looked shocked. This episode would be the start of his sleepwalking. Luckily, Berezov would have just the medicine.

Mrs Vanzant was nowhere to be seen through all this. The windows in the big house on the hill remained unlit. We wouldn't see her for weeks.

By now the mob had done their work and they were juiced. It's amazing what a community can achieve in a short time if it works together. The Midnight Marauders muttered their goodbyes and drifted off. Berezov looked pretty stunned at how well his plan had worked out.

LAteR...

So that's the story of the feud between Berezov and Vanzant. I'd learn later that the story I'd told about Sheriff Baikal isn't even true. Nissi, tired of me lusting after her brother, made it up to scare me away. When I told this to Dad he laughed his fur off. We sat up all night and talked about what an interesting evening it had been. Easily in the top three most interesting evenings in our town in recent memory, we thought. Dad said it was funny how some pretty obvious stuff gets overlooked when a mob gets involved. Like, why were we dressed in black and carrying masks? Why were there *two* chairs with ropes in the storeroom? Why did Vanzant have rope marks on his own wrists? And why was he carrying a pistol with the inscription: "Happy eighteenth Birthday, Jon. Love, Grandpa Ming"? I also had to admit that these were pretty interesting observations. He was an interesting man, my dad.

EVERYONE KNOWS THAT THEY'RE DEAD. DO YOU?
Genevieve Valentine

The wallpaper looks like wreaths when Susan first sees it, during the first tour through the little bungalow that Stephen wants to show her and she'll probably agree to buy because it seems like the kind of house you could grow to love, once it's yours.

That linked-wreath paper in the parlor marches up and down in tidy lines. It's a reproduction from an eighteenth-century pattern, the real estate agent says; a time when people appreciated tidy things.

Susan thinks that's a good sign. She wants a tidy life. And someone before her had wanted that, too, and had gone back in time two hundred years to find it. It felt like a promise.

1.   Susan has invoked the past, one of the early warning signs of a ghost story. (The other is to ignore the past entirely—see Fig. 2 in Appendix A for the map of dramatic irony across rising action.) Why is the past dangerous?

   a)   Because what is beyond changing is beyond controlling.
   b)   Because it's made of lessons we won't learn until it's too late.

    c)   Because it's peopled entirely with strangers, even your own past, even when it's you.

    d)   Because it's impossible to be certain of anything because you can never come to a consensus in someone else's memory, and so we're doomed to misunderstand everything until we die, and then if we're unlucky, even after that.

Susan doesn't believe in talismans or signals from the universe—they're impractical—so she tries not to take it as superstition that the wallpaper draws her in as much as it does.

She can't decide if she actually likes it. It feels a little old-fashioned, and she can see that occasionally the hand-printing has left a little fault. ("Adds to the charm," says the real estate agent when she catches Susan looking.)

What Susan likes is the idea that whoever had lived here before had known what they wanted. Had known what they were doing.

Still, she can't look at the parlor for very long. The wallpaper suits her, she thinks, it suits her very much—it just feels like the room is none of her business. Something about the floor keeps drawing her eye instead, like she's dropped something on the carpet and can't remember what it is.

She and the realtor stand in the kitchen, light pouring in from outside. Stephen counts off paces in the little backyard, with trees in the back and golden hops a foot thick up the back wall of the house. He's talking to himself and flexing his hands, and Susan can't take her eyes off the curl of his fists, but sometimes it doesn't mean anything. Sometimes he's just concentrating.

The kitchen is quiet; whatever he's saying, they can't hear it in here. The refrigerator's pale yellow. Susan wants so badly to be a woman who has a refrigerator like that. Who has a home.

"What happened with the previous owners?" Susan asks.

*   *   *

2.   A ghost story requires a place for the fear to live. It's never enough to just have the ghosts; we carry the ghosts with us. What item below best harbors fear of the forgotten and unknown in objects left behind for us?

    a)   A toy in an empty room waiting for you to think about the last toy you lost and hoped someone else would love; waiting for you to remember it was exactly this one; waiting for you to pick it up.

    b)   A locked door. All keys belong to the dead, who know better what to do with them than you do.

    c)   A lie, which death always lives in.

    d)   A house—always with the knowledge that someone stood here before you, that someone had to be removed before the ground was flattened and the posts laid; the dead leave warnings for the dead.

The real estate agent flips through her papers. "Retirement," she says eventually, looking at an exterminator report. "Community home. His younger brother is trying to sell the house."

It seems like a strange thing not to know before you start showing the house, but Susan imagines a woman who'd been tidy enough to make her own wallpaper and a man who must have missed her terribly and let the place go once she died. The golden ivy in the yard went to seed without her and the bugs started coming inside.

It must have been a long time ago, Susan thinks. The parlor had been sitting empty for so long there weren't even furniture marks in the carpet any more.

(She'd looked at the carpet more than the walls, the whole time they stood there while Stephen was considering whether or not they would live in the house. It was such a rich burgundy, and seemed as if it had never been touched—as if someone had installed it especially for her, after the last lady of the house had died and taken her furniture with her. She kept looking down at it, drawn to the depth of the pile.)

"I love it," Stephen calls out, scraping dirt off his shoe on the rim of the back door. Susan flinches when he raises his voice. The sun catches his hair, his shoulders, the edge of his smile. "Susan, honey, what do you think?"

They take the house, of course. Sometimes you just have a good feeling.

The wallpaper looks like wreaths for nearly six months. By then, the thrill of decorating and of looking out the wide kitchen windows onto the little garden and weeding around the ivy have begun to wear off. Stephen's started getting restless—the anger he used to explain as frustration with their cramped apartment and the neighbors, just needing more space, just needing a house of their own, just needing her to shut the fuck up long enough to let him think, just needing her to stop getting blotchy and embarrassing herself. Susan blinks into the butter-yellow refrigerator as she gets ice out for the bruising.

Autumn comes. Susan rakes leaves carefully away from the ivy and the flower beds, goes to the library to find out how to make them compost. Turns out you can break down anything, if you work hard enough on it. Some bugs can eat a body down to the bone.

She puts the leaves in bags and lets the garbage men take them.

She cleans summer dust off the wallpaper in the living room with a toothbrush. That paper stayed just as it was even as a new stove and new counters and new plumbing made their way in by inches, and Susan wants to take care.

The walls are warm under her hands, too warm for a room that gets no sun in the afternoons, and she wonders if the whole house is less sturdy than the real estate agent told them. The ivy vines creak at night. The doorknob rattles, on windy days, when Stephen's gone.

Mid-winter, the floorboards start to groan.

It sounds like robbery the first time, and Stephen startles awake and gasps, "Jesus Christ," and goes downstairs with the baseball bat he keeps by the bed. When she comes down to check on him he's standing in the doorway of the parlor, staring like he's cornered someone who broke in, but there's no one.

After that night he pretends not to hear it. He's embarrassed not to have checked the foundations better before they bought the house, she thinks.

She doesn't speak about it either. It horrifies her—it's someone walking, the rhythm of steps; no cold snap or old house sounds like that, and she starts to dream about walking downstairs and meeting something terrible—but she knows better than to complain.

The winter is dry. The floorboards start to groan all the time, wherever Stephen goes. She's worried about the house—she's worried he'll be angry at himself for missing this, because Stephen never stays angry at himself for very long—but all that winter, she at least knows where he is, and it's nice to hear him coming.

He travels for business in the spring. The house breathes while he's gone. Susan spends a few warm afternoons in the backyard, planting flowers in the wide dirt beds, watching birds drop into the trees. The rest of the time is work; the molding on the walls is impossible to keep clean, and the rooms upstairs have charming log beams that cut below the arched ceiling just enough to collect dust along the tops. It all has to be kept clean. No excuses.

She sits in the parlor, when she can. (It hasn't happened much before—Stephen won't go in it, and she has to be where he is.) The wallpaper makes her eyes ache, late at night, that heaviness of avoiding someone's gaze. Sometimes, when she's too tired to look up at the walls, it looks like the carpet's wet, and she lifts her feet for a moment before she can blink herself awake enough to realize she's being silly.

When he's back from one of his trips, it's usually all right for the first few days. It fades. He gets snappish if she does something wrong, angry if she cries; he says she has to pull herself together or he's going to get angry.

She stays up all that night. The branches tap against the house like the garden's trying to come inside; someone's walking downstairs.

Susan finds herself sitting in the parlor for a few minutes every night, despite Stephen making fun of her for hiding. She finds things to do with her hands so she has an excuse not to look for him, waiting for him to follow her in. He never does.

One night when he's out at a conference and Susan's darning socks, she looks up at the parlor wallpaper and sees that it's nooses.

Eventually Stephen burns down the house. She's still inside it, watching herself swing.

3. Who is the worst person in this story?

    a)   Stephen, for abusing her and surviving.

    b)   The real estate agent, for never asking why Susan jumped when her husband said her name.

    c)   The last woman in that house, whose warnings were so frightening that Susan abandoned the parlor, and instead of bracing herself in the only room beyond his control when the time came to save herself, she was in their bedroom, dusting the open beams and thinking about wallpaper.

    d)   The reader, for wondering more about what's under the floorboards than about Susan, because there's no point caring about the doomed.

*   *   *

The parlor was untouched by the fire. Not a single ash had landed on that carpet. The construction company had to knock the walls in with the excavator so they could get down to the foundations and start over.

They found the body in the wreckage: an ulna and some finger bones churned up by the backhoe, a skull fragment hanging off one of the metal teeth by the eye socket, and then the rest of it a few bones at a time, under the hands of a handful of solemn underlings from the coroner's office and few beat cops still green at the gills.

They couldn't tell where the body had originally been buried; the earth had been moved too much before any bones were discovered. Could have been anywhere in the house, the front patio, the little garden.

Finally, someone said, "Under the parlor, maybe," because someone had to.

No one agreed, but no one offered any other suggestion, all the time they were picking bones out of the ground.

4. If one of the police officers took a little garnet ring out of the dirt for the girl he wanted to marry—new cops don't make much, and this body had so many other questions about it that it wouldn't matter if one thing was gone, and even if the ring could have helped, any detective knows you never get everything back once a body gets buried—who would be haunted?

    a)   the police officer
    b)   the fiancée

5. Essay question: Discuss the ethical implications of the transitive property as it applies to ghostly retribution.

(You may use the blank space beneath Appendix B for diagrams if necessary.)

Her name is Lucy, and she knows immediately that the ring is haunted, because when Greg gives it to her she looks over his shoulder for someone's approval, which makes no sense since they're alone. A lot of people second-guess things like that, but Lucy doesn't see much point in it; you know what you know. This isn't his to give.

She keeps it. It fits perfectly. The stone still keeps sliding down and pressing into her palm, so it hurts every time she closes her hand, but she knows that has nothing to do with the ring.

She's pretty sure she doesn't want to actually marry Greg any more, now that she knows he's a fucking grave robber, but she doesn't want to get rid of it. The ring is still a promise. It's just the one she made with whoever she was looking for over Greg's shoulder.

And she doesn't know what she'd do with the ring if she wanted to give it back. Who would she give it back to—his bosses? Does she want to ruin his career? Bury it in the foundations of the new house? It's too late for her not to be haunted, so handing it back won't help that, and she's not sure how angry she is at Greg for being stupid and thieving from the dead.

She decides to wait and see what the department finds out about the body. That might be enough to keep this ring from tugging at her.

The precinct closes the case in three weeks; inconclusive evidence.

Greg doesn't understand why she's so angry.

"What did you even find out? Do you even know who she is? What if someone's been waiting all this time to find out what happened to her?"

(She's sure it's "all this time." That woman's body belongs to her ring, and the ring is old. She can feel it pulling on her whole arm. It's heavier whenever Greg is home.)

Greg shrugs. "The coroner's office didn't really want to talk about it. Said every test made the bones come back a different age—some of them must have been from the woman who burned the place down, they were a lot newer. They assume the other body is eighty-ish years old, but—I mean, people are buried everywhere." He shrugs. Some woman's old bones.

"She still needs a name, Greg. A burial. Some woman molding out in that backyard—what if we found some poor murdered woman in our backyard someday? Wouldn't you want to put things right?"

He frowns at her, peevish. He's been having trouble moving off the beat, and he gets annoyed when he thinks she's trying to be a better detective than he is. "I get it. But they said old age and closed it. If I open it up now I'll look like a troublemaker about that other woman, and it might not be anything."

The ring pinches; the hair on her neck stands up. "Did they look at the other woman, too? The one who burned the house down?"

"Look, it's a creepy find," Greg says, like that explains everything.

So Lucy thinks about giving back the ring. She can't tell Greg—Greg told her he bought it online and he'd be furious if she called him a liar—but she could go to the precinct and turn it in and make them reopen the case long enough to give the ghost a name.

She doesn't. She doesn't want Greg to have any reason to resent her—cops take care of their own, and she'd have to be careful about looking like she's ratting him out. There's no way to do that when she has a dead woman's ring on her finger.

She thinks about what she can do alone. She thinks about the empty lot where the house was, the ashes barely tilled into the dirt, except those are mostly the ashes of the other dead woman, the new one, not the one who had the ring.

It seems like her best idea, for a long time. She has to know something. Anything. She even drives past the lot, but something so cold comes over her as soon as she turns down the street that she can't even bring herself to look, backs up onto the main road as three other cars honk wildly at her. Her hand is shaking; the ring burns.

She thinks about going down to the municipal grave site at the edge of town, where the unclaimed dead go, and digging deep enough to rest the ring on top of the ashes there, eighty years dead. Just give it back, give up, hope for forgiveness. She knows she won't go. She's exhausted, and she doesn't have the nerve.

When she wakes up, her hands are dirty. The ring's still on her finger. She can't take it off.

6.   What keeps you from the graveyard?

   a)   The fear a grave will swallow you—a child's fear you made academic, like poison spiders. The worst will never happen if you're careful, but you have to be careful.

   b)   The fear no one will visit your grave.

   c)   Knowing someone who can't fucking wait to visit your grave.

   d)   How much you want to be there. Every time you pass it, how quiet and still and lonely it is, how much better that is than anything that's happened to you, how much your whole body yearns to be under the dirt and finished.

Abigail Sutter drew up the wallpaper design by hand for the parlor in their house. Charles had put it together practically by himself, from a Sears kit that arrived with lumber so crisp and unweathered that Charles and her brother both got splinters. Abigail was determined to take as much care with the interior as he had with the five-piece porch columns, putting them together at the end of a long day, practically in the dark, so the house would be done before the October cold.

This house was going to be important, and she treated it that way. The carpets were hardy and plain but more refined than rag rugs, and their worn furniture took on a better patina when it looked as if they'd been selected for their age against such nice carpets. The wallpaper, she decided, must do the same job.

"What do you think?" she said, setting down the magazine clipping she'd gotten the pattern from—a painting of a woman in a gown with skirts as wide as the kitchen—just to watch his face as he looked at it. "For the parlor."

"If you think the dress'll fit," he said finally, and she laughed, and after a moment he ducked his head and smiled, which for him was the same as laughing.

Charles and Abigail carved the stamp, and then he took her sketch to the man two towns over who could make it, and when it came back he helped her hang it in the parlor, grinning as they got their fingers tacky with paste. After it was done, he stood in the center of the room and nodded, and she took his arm and watched the sun setting through the windows.

Whenever they had visitors he'd bring them in and let them exclaim over how nice the place was and then say, "Abigail did the papering herself," to make sure they'd exclaim again.

He even showed them the magazine clipping out of his wallet, with the woman in the too-wide dress and her lover pushing her on the swing, until the paper was unfolded once too often and split across the middle. (He kept the pieces in a drawer and took them out anyway, whenever they had a guest who was worth it—after dessert and before coffee, when you wanted something new to talk about.)

*   *   *

7.   What is the most effective configuration of the torn magazine clipping? Which is most likely to be haunted? Are they the same thing?

     a)   The lady on the swing decapitated by the fold, taking just his hat with her, so that her lover is pushing a corpse back and forth, forever smiling, chilly at the scalp and unaware.

     b)   The lady bisected just below the waist, so it looks as if she's grabbed onto lucky ropes to escape her lover. Their bottom halves look strange without the line from one of them to the other—broken doll parts.

     c)   Clean through the center, so that the lady on the swing is whole and the lover is whole, neatly separated. She looks more and more like she's closing her eyes. The lover seems to be turning his head, as if he's just realized something's missing. Charles and Abigail are dead before the lover ever turns enough to look out at them.

     d)   Between the photograph of the painting and the long caption discussing the exhibit it was in. Neither Abigail nor Charles ever look for that part. Someone will buy the table at a flea market thirty years later and throw it away, and the last of Charles will vanish.

After two months of dreams, Lucy gives up.

"I think we need a break," she says, and Greg frowns at her in that way that's really starting to drive her fucking nuts, and says, "Is there someone else?" like the only reason she'd dump a grave robber was if she had someone else waiting.

"No, of course not," she says, as calmly as she can (never piss off a cop), and says, "I still have the ring on, don't I?" He looks a little pacified at that.

She can't take it off. She hasn't been able to take it off for two months.

Finally, Lucy goes down to the library and the Historical Society and reads about the house, because as someone who accepted a ring that was obviously haunted, she's in it now, and she'll be damned if she asks Greg for help.

(In her dreams she looks at Greg holding out the ring and turns and runs, just at the moment someone who she never sees but who is not Greg reaches out to stop her. In her dreams she tries and tries to return the ring to the graveyard or the wreckage of the house, and wakes up with dirt under her nails and the ring immovable on her left hand. She's getting used to it.)

At the Historical Society, she gets into the archives by saying she wants to convince the town to bring back the town's old Flower Festival. The Festival used to have a photo catalog every year so the gardeners could stand amid their handiwork.

"Wouldn't it be so nice if we could bring back some of the charms of the past," she says, as the lady at the desk nods, considering, already opening the door.

There's a woman sitting in the parlor of the house that burned down. The photo's in black and white, so she looks like a ghost. The wallpaper behind her looks like a ghost. She's wearing the ring.

The wallpaper behind her looks like nooses.

Lucy's fingertips sting as she touches the page ("Mrs. Charles Sutter, Secretary of the Women's League"), and she stands up and leaves without even asking for a photocopy. The nooses wouldn't show up to anyone else, she knows that already.

Then she goes to the offices of the Ledger and asks if they have any photos of the aftermath of the fire. Greg had said someone came by from there, when the Fire Department guys were still early in the process of cleaning it out. ("Made everybody uncomfortable," he'd said. The ring pinched her as he spoke.)

They do have pictures. There's just nothing in them that Lucy recognizes as what it used to be—a ceiling beam, a length of rope, the corpse of a woman whose body had to be burned to the ground because otherwise it would be clear what he had done.

Susan hadn't wanted to die. That's what Lucy saw, in the photograph of a parlor from a hundred years ago. Whatever happened to Susan Lennox was murder. There's no proof in the pictures, but Lucy doesn't question it; you know what you know.

Stephen's at one of those clinics that's like a hotel, because they think his mental health needs some supervision. He'd been suspected of manslaughter, at first—Greg told her when it happened, husbands always look good for something like this—but he'd cried so hard when he talked about his wife, and everyone who had seen her that spring knew she'd looked a little depressed all along. That's what Stephen Lennox is getting treated right now—his depression. He has two weeks left.

But Lucy will never prove anything. Not the murder, not the ghost. Not where her ring came from. That house is conveniently ashes, and whatever ghosts are there now don't mean anything to anyone living, except her. The coroner's office didn't think it was even worth sticking a shovel into a grave to see if Abigail Sutter was where the headstone advertised. Absolutely no one is going to help her look into Susan's murder if she turns in the ring and rats Greg out.

She drives by the house again. She combs through the ashes until a neighbor calls the cops on her, and then she has to explain to one of Greg's cop friends that she was looking for any wallpaper that might have survived.

"Don't you think this is weird?" she asks, like it just occurred to her. "Like, do houses just burn down? This really seems like a murder."

He laughs.

She sits two blocks outside the clinic gates in her car, waiting to run Stephen down when he gets out. She's too far away, though; by the time she gets the car turned on she has a red light, and when she tries to run it anyway she gets sideswiped. Not badly, but enough that a cop comes. She remembers him from last year's charity spaghetti dinner—he'd been one of the clowns for the kids. He talks the other driver down. Then he tells Lucy he's called Greg, just so Greg knows.

"You seem really shaken up lately," he says. "Greg's getting worried." The ring pinches.

"Thank you so much, I appreciate it," she says. She throws her phone in the garbage at the car repair shop. She tells them she'll be back in fifteen minutes, and heads for the only place in the world where no one will ask what she's doing there.

Abigail's ghost wants vengeance for Susan; there's nothing else that will sate her. Lucy understands. It's just that she has nothing else to give.

When the security guard at the graveyard finds her, just before the evening rounds, she's slumped over the annual municipal grave, getting cold. Her ring finger is missing—looks like she'd cut it off. He doesn't know why; not like there's a ring.

8. The dead have forfeited fear. They need not be reasoned or just. They aren't beholden, which makes them a horror. If you could be as ruthless as you wanted about anything at all, would you? (Show your work.)

Sometimes a home collapses under silence. Sometimes not. Once when Charles came home from a week of jury duty, Abigail came down the stairs just to walk back up to the house with her arm tucked into his. They hadn't spoken again until after dinner, when he handed her a hair ribbon he'd bought and said, "Thought of you," and that was all they said until it was time to turn in.

She wore the ribbon all the time, a little glimpse of green against the red carpet in the parlor, and whenever he looked up from his paper he smiled like a fool.

One winter he got pneumonia. As he recuperated into the spring, Abigail kept him in the parlor. "So I know where the sickness is," she said, as she wiped his forehead and pressed a bowl of broth into his grip, and he covered her hands with his hands.

When he was well enough to go up the stairs, he said, "Safe to catch it now, I can play nurse," and she laughed.

She stepped on a loose nail on the floor of the parlor one night. Water had gotten into the new lumber; the nail had rusted. She was dead in a week.

The doctor called in a minister even though neither Charles nor Abigail were really church folk, and the minister brought a funeral director and a coffin they set up in the parlor, and they talked about funeral arrangements while Charles nodded calmly, as if he was actually going to let them take Abigail away from the house she loved so much.

When he turned on the tap in the bathroom, he forgot, for a few seconds, how to swallow. He forgot to dry his hands, and when he came back into the bedroom and took her hand, it slipped. He waited until he had some strength back in his wrists before he picked her up. Wouldn't do to trip carrying your bride down the stairs.

He buried her in the backyard, under the ivy, and carried the dirt back inside in sugar bags to weigh down the coffin.

At night he'd listen to the wind in the branches and worry she would feel it, but the fear never lasted long. She had loved it here even when the branches fell. And it was just a grave.

He knew where she really was; whenever he passed it he knew she was inside, working on something that pleased her, a flash of green against the carpet floor. All he had to do was not look, and she was still alive.

* * *

9.   Essay question: Are ghosts a function of time or of grief?

10.   What is the ghost story?

     a)   Every story is a ghost story.
     b)   Grief is smoke, and memory fails you. Better to think the dead come back.
     c)   Cook your grandmother's soup. Touch something for the last time. Lose the way to a place you lived. Forget the name of a person who loved you. The part of you that loves is a maker of ghosts.
     d)   The ghost is sated, or it isn't. The living prevail, or the grave finds room. Someone's held to justice, or else ghosts; the dead leave warnings for the dead. The grave is safe, or someone is walking through a brand new house, pausing in the dining room as if there's something in there she forgot. She won't know why. She'll take the house. The first night she's alone, she'll find a ring.

(She was always the better of the two of them at climbing, and even now, a grown-up, and aware of the ridiculousness of herself, she almost raced up into the canopy. Escaping the ground: that's how it felt. As if the deaths in the village had left its earth tainted.

'Come on,' she shouted to her brother, without looking. She could hear him wheezing below, hauling himself without her facility up the body of the tree.

Here I am, she thought. The children would laugh. That, or they would be appalled or amazed at the sight of this woman, this mother, her legs wrapped around a bough, her body clinging to the swaying, uppermost part of the trunk. She reached the top at last and felt the whole tree bow. She parted the leaves and laughed in delight at the view while the wind pushed her hair.

She watched the church tower, the cricket field, the barns and the ruin of the manor house. She heard her brother coming.

'You could imagine nothing had been going on,' she said, just loud enough for him to hear, but to herself, really.

She registered the strange sounds of his ascent. A slow heave and violent crack. A slow heave and ugly breaking. Again, an impact, the splinter of wood, louder, again, again. She frowned and looked down.

A few handholds below her he clung on. He looked at her with ferocious attention. He looked at her without malice but with absolute intent and she remembered his silence when the man and woman had died. She looked at him and knew that this was his last act, even before she saw a ladder of ruin below him. She saw that each branch of the old tree, each hand- and foothold, was broken, kicked and snapped where it met the trunk, leaving only a stump of splinters to which no one could cling.

He gripped with his hands and stamped and stamped on the stick on which he stood and it broke off cleanly like all the others and he held himself by the strength of his arms as it fell, lengthily, all the way down. And he looked at her, and she was in the canopy with him, way above the roofs, and there was no way down.)

THE COLLECTOR
Sally Partridge

Bennie wouldn't call himself an old soul. Retro, maybe. Retro was okay. Retro was making a comeback in a big way. These days everyone was listening to Lazerhawk, wearing vintage Seiko digital watches and tweeting about *Stranger Things*. Retro was something Bennie felt comfortable with. He hated the phrase "safe space", but in a literal, non-SJW way, those two words summed it up. Truth is he never really felt comfortable out in the world since leaving his parent's home in the northern suburbs—the wrong side of the *boerewors* curtain, as the guys at work like to say. He had a good job as a security guard at an apartment complex in Century City. Apart from the occasional baiting, the other guys were all right. The residents were uptight though. You couldn't just say hello to a pretty girl who walked through the gate anymore, even if you were just being polite. Even if you really just wanted to ask her out for a burger. Women didn't want you to talk to them unless it was strictly business.

Which way is Block C?

Fourth building on your right.

Excuse, where do I pay for parking?

At the gate, Ma'am.

Hey, Bennie, there's a homeless guy sleeping in the visitor's parking bay. Won't you sort it out?

Sure, Dr Moodley.

He stopped talking to the residents after a while, in case he said the wrong thing about the Jews or working mothers, even though at school everyone always said what was on their mind and it was okay to laugh when someone made fun of the Chinese. Things were better when people weren't so easily offended. The last straw was when Jackie at the complex laundromat reported him to his supervisor for being inappropriate towards her. All he said was that she looked good. She'd lost some weight. Women liked it when you noticed things like that, or so he thought. His ma always lost her temper when no-one commented on how well her diet was going. Turns out both Bennie and his ma were wrong about women. So now he'd nod, say as little as possible, smile, but not in a way that could be misinterpreted. It wasn't so much a fine line as an invisible one. Well, he certainly couldn't see it.

When his shift ended he kept to himself. He liked to play old-school games on Steam. Games like *Neon Drive*. It made him realise how much he missed the eighties. Rewatching *Blade Runner* and *The Terminator* made him feel a whole lot better about his life. No-one really understood that. It was like taking a trip to the past, where all the heroes were tough guys and the women liked them for it. Bennie was a tough guy. But these days women didn't want saving. He didn't understand the world anymore. Collecting memorabilia was a natural progression. DVDs, movie posters, figurines. *Predator* and *Terminator* action figures were easy to come by online. Car boot sales and comic book conventions were a great place to find old *He-Man* collectables. He even found a life-size Gizmo at a hospice charity shop that gurgled when you pressed its belly. He liked his little slice of the past. His 'safe space'—everything arranged in such a way so he could always be reminded of his childhood wherever he looked. That's why he liked working nights at Century City. Driving to work down that lit-up, palm-lined stretch at night felt like he was going back to a better place.

It calmed him down. Made him forget the present. He liked the way the lights of the petrol station reflected off the glass buildings, bathing everything in neon. It was like starring in his own movie.

Working nights meant he slept late, but he always got up early on Saturday mornings to hit Milnerton Market. He dressed meticulously in his black jeans and hi-tops, his logo t-shirt stretched over his muscled arms. Unlike the hipster and artisan markets in the city centre and the gentrified parts of Salt River, the people that set up their stalls on the dusty stretch of lot between the fish factories and the train tracks were from a different time. It was a place far removed from postcard perfect Cape Town, where Table Mountain looked the other way and giant cement dolosse jutted out at odd angles, obscuring the sea view. These people had no idea the value of what they were selling. They just needed the money. It was where he found the best figurines. Bennie liked to amble with his hands in his jeans pockets, past the faded beach umbrellas, plastic tables and yawning car boots, just looking. Most of it was junk. Plastic kitchen sets and scratched vinyl records, stolen car radios and *Mad Magazines* without front covers. But there were a few diamonds hidden amongst the coal.

Towards the end of a dusty row, near an oxbow of kombis selling *boerewors* rolls and slap chips, he spotted a wooden table covered with plastic Tupperware containers heaped with toys. A tiny woman in her fifties with the manic eyes of someone on too many over-the-counter pills smiled as he approached. "Hello," she said, "looking for something for your kids? I have a garage-full of toys, you know. My daughter's too old now you see. She's a journalist in Johannesburg. Married to her job, ha ha. No hope for grandchildren, so why not sell the lot I said." She wrung her graying ponytail as she spoke.

Bennie nodded politely and let her finish. He picked up a

pink *My Little Pony* with green hair and four-leaf clovers on the rump that was in pretty good shape. Right time period too. Some collectors could get as much as one hundred dollars for one of these on eBay, if it was rare enough. He turned the pony over a couple of times, admiring the care that went into the colouring and the detailed artwork, the kind you didn't see much of anymore. Vintage Hasbro. He held it under his nose. It even smelled like the eighties, like the inflatable plastic pools of his childhood. He felt himself relaxing, his mind already blurring everything else out so that it was an effort to pull himself back into the present. "Got any more of these?"

"Yes! A carrier bag full, let me get them." She disappeared under the table and popped up a minute later rustling a yellow Shoprite bag, bulging with plastic legs and snouts. She focused her wild eyes on him. "Is it for your daughter?" she asked.

"Sure." He glanced inside the bag and counted about twenty figures in the same condition, their cartoon eyes staring in every direction. Usually little kids brushed the curls out of the hair, leaving behind a matted, static clump. These had their shiny manes intact. In the memorabilia trade, they'd do well. He smiled to himself. "How much you want for these?" he asked.

"Oh, you know, I don't want to rip you off. A hundred? Tell you what. I'll give you a discount since they're so old. New toys cost so much nowadays, don't they? How about we say fifty for the lot."

He kept his face expressionless. "Thanks. I appreciate it."

At home in his flat without palm trees or neon signs, he googled his new acquisitions. Yum Yum, with its scratch'n'sniff rump and candy cane motif, was worth 14 dollars. He searched each one meticulously on eBay. Twenty dollars. Ten dollars. Sixteen dollars. He had purchased them all for fifty rand. That wasn't even the equivalent of four dollars. He was sitting on a potential fortune. Merriweather Rainbows went for around eight dollars. Barnacle Big Brother, ten. Posy, two. Mountain Boy Ice Crystal, one hundred dollars.

"Jackpot," said Bennie, leaning back in his wheeled office chair. He eyed the ponies arranged in a neat row in front of him. He liked the look of them on his desk, underneath his laminated *Enter the Dragon* poster. Pity to sell them really.

Starglow was worth sixty dollars. He reached for the slightly translucent green pony covered in stars. The hair still retained its out-the-box curl, as if the previous owner hadn't played with it at all. Maybe the girl had been more into books since she was a big-time journalist now. He could sell it for one hundred dollars. Easy. Hell, he might even keep it. He liked the smell.

He spent the rest of the evening cleaning them meticulously, like an archaeologist unearthing a dinosaur skeleton from the dirt one brushstroke at a time. Mitch Murder played from his computer speakers, one of his latest retrowave discoveries. He'd finish off by photographing the ponies and updating his catalogue.

The security office at the entrance to the complex overlooked a courtyard where Uber drivers waited for their passengers and pizza delivery men rested against their scooters, their faces illuminated by smartphone screens. The block was access controlled, so residents came in through their own gate via access card. Bennie's job was to take down the details of the cars that pulled into the visitor's entrance. He recognised the boyfriends and girlfriends, brothers and friends that left red-eyed or slurring hours later.

It was a slow night. He watched a group of girls with feathered hair and animal print coats giggle and woo as they manoeuvred their heeled bare legs into the back of an Uber.

His colleague, Wessel, elbowed him in the belly. "Tin Roof you reckon? Or Aces and Spades. Girls like that always end up at Aces and Spades."

Bennie made a neutral sound through his nose.

It didn't deter Wessel. "What you reckon? After work? See if we run into them?"

Bennie managed a smile. "And what must I say when your wife calls?"

"Tell her I fell off Tin Roof." Wessel snorted with laughter.

The rest of the guys lounging around the office joined in. Bennie didn't mind too much. They knew not to push him too far. He shook his head and took a look outside. It was a clear night. He could make out the silhouettes of the palm trees against the tall pink apartment buildings. Hundreds of flatscreen TVs glowed in the high windows. He could tell by the sporadic vibrations in his pocket that his auctions were going well. He could already taste that bottle of Johnny Walker Black Label he planned to buy when the first proceeds came in. He felt a pang of pity at the thought of parting with them, but he shook the thought away. Trading memorabilia was a new venture. The idea had come to him while comparing prices online for a *GI Joe* action figure. He reckoned he could sell some items at a mark up to pay for the figures he really wanted. It seemed like good business sense.

His walkie talkie crackled at his belt.

Bennie. Bennie do you read me?

Roger that. Bennie here. Over.

Noise complaint on D block. Seventh floor.

Roger that. On my way.

So much for a quiet night.

Wessel craned his head. "It's probably that *laaitie* that pumps his rave music every night. Boy needs a solid *klap*."

"Bennie will sort him out. Everyone's scared of Bennie," said Masimba.

"Knock his head against the door, Bennie."

"Give him one of those death stares."

Bennie grabbed his torch. "I'll be back," he said.

Hoots of laughter followed. They loved it when the big guy channelled Arnie.

* * *

As he walked past the towering residential blocks, Bennie withdrew his phone from his pocket. He was already almost seventy dollars up. He scrolled through the bids and spotted an email notification flashing on the corner of his screen. He had doubled up some of his listings on Gumtree, thinking he could save on postage costs if he made the sale locally.

> Re: Rare MLP Twilight Unicorn Collectible
>> Dear Sir. I saw your listing and nearly jumped out my skin. I must have this item for my collection. Can I EFT you to reserve it? I'm willing to meet tonight to secure immediate sale.
>> Please advise urgently.
>> Jet

It was an easy six hundred rand. He made the arrangements to meet up after his shift. He had to deal with the kid in D block first. Usually all it took was the sight of him to get residents to toe the line. Bennie was the guy you called when there was trouble. All that lifting had crafted him into a formidable figure. It made people think twice, which was useful for someone who just wanted to be left alone.

The door opened, blasting the passage in the bass-heavy doof doof house music. The kid was about twenty and wore a white t-shirt over boxer shorts. He had to crane his head up to meet Bennie's gaze.

"Too loud?" asked the kid.

Bennie said nothing and tapped his digital watch.

"I know. I know. No loud music after ten. I'll turn it down." His Adam's apple jerked nervously.

The music was off before Bennie had even reached the lift.

He read the message again. He liked the sophistication of the language. "Dear Sir". It made him feel like part of an elite club. A group that understood the meaning behind these items.

He waited with his arm resting out the open window of his double cab. At this time of night, the petrol station was fairly deserted. The attendants huddled in their office, the sound of a soccer match and a thousand vuvuzelas drifted from the open door. Bennie watched cars come and go. Most of the drivers rushed into the garage shop for bread or firewood or condoms and disappeared again in a flash of rear lights. Bennie drummed his fingers on his car door and waited.

He saw a hooded figure turn the corner and watched his progress. The guy wore a grey hooded sweatshirt under a black leather jacket with the hood up over the collar and a pair of black skinny jeans. Bennie watched as he looked left and right, like he was searching for someone.

He got out the car and whistled.

"Bennie?" the figure inquired, hurrying over.

"Yeah. You must be Jet?"

"Yeah, that's me. Jet from Gumtree." He spoke quickly and cast furtive glances around.

Bennie noticed he wore white Adidas Superstars with black stripes. Expensive. "Well here's the figure. Mint condition as you can see. It comes with the matching brush."

Jet nodded urgently and made a grab for the bag. "My daughter will love it," he said.

Bennie held the bag out of reach. "I thought you were a collector?"

"Yeah, but she loves my dolls, you know how they are at that age. What's yours is mine. Six hundred, right? I'm transferring you the money right now."

Jet navigated his thumbs at lightning speed across the phone screen. "Done. You should get a notification."

Bennie's phone vibrated in his pocket. He pulled it out and

glanced at the screen. "Money's in," he said.

"Nice doing business with you," said Jet, making a grab for the packet. Bennie hesitated, but it was too late. Jet had already looped the handles safely over his elbow.

Shaking his head, Bennie returned to his car and drove home, playing Mega Drive loudly while he sped past the avenue of palm trees. He didn't want to think about some kid ruining Twilight Unicorn's perfect mane and destroying its value. Besides, it was nearly six-am. The world would wake up soon, and he needed to get a few hours in before his next shift. It was just a pony. Not his problem anymore.

On the way to work he stopped in at Pick n Pay Liquors to pick up his celebratory bottle.

"I'm sorry, sir, your card has been declined."

Bennie blinked at the woman behind the till. His whiskey waited in a paper bag on the counter. "That's impossible, try it again. There's definitely money in there."

She swiped the card through the machine with a loud smack. Bennie could feel the queue snaking behind him shift with impatience. "Nope. Declined."

He exhaled sharply and pulled out his emergency credit card. "Here. Use this. But if the machine is broken, it probably won't work either."

"It's approved," she said, with just a hint of eyeroll.

He checked his phone in the car. The message definitely said the money was through. He logged into his internet banking and stared at the negative balance, then checked his message folder again, noticing for the first time that the number linked to the transaction notification was different to the one his bank usually used.

"Those *bliksems*." It was an old scam. He should have picked it up.

He opened his contact list and searched the names of his

carefully curated connections. "Hello, Gert. You still an inspector at Mowbray? I need a favour, man. Can you trace a number for me? *Dankie*. Yeah, just message me. I owe you a beer."

The palm trees laughed at Bennie as he drove past. The wind raised their serrated leaves in the air. He ground his teeth. Bennie had been a security guard for nearly fifteen years. He had cut his teeth in ADT patrol, hopping walls and chasing down crooks in his heavy combat boots. The criminals were getting craftier by the minute, but he had always prided himself on knowing all the tricks. But that was another lifetime. There was a reason he had chosen the quieter, residential beat. Nowadays you couldn't just *klap* someone. There were rules, public opinion to consider.

No one greeted him when he entered the security office and they all hurried to get on with various tasks. He had caught a glimpse of his own reflection in the rear view mirror. The guys were wise to stay away.

Twilight Unicorn. He had been duped over a fucking plastic pony. But worse than that. They had hit him in a soft spot and breached his hidden private world.

He checked his Seiko watch. He could wait a few hours.

It appeared Jet was a fan of nostalgia himself. With his connection's help, Bennie had followed him to the ground floor of Stadium on Main, to the bowling alley and arcade. From behind a pillar, he watched Jet battle it out on an old *Duke Nukem* arcade machine. Bennie waited for a father and his small son to finish at the basketball hoop game before making his approach. For a large man, he could be remarkably silent.

Jet noticed his reflection in the screen and spun round. "*Vok*. What do you want?"

"Where's the pony?"

"What pony, I don't know what you're talking about."

A quick glance confirmed that the woman behind the token counter was gone. They were alone. Bennie closed his fist and cracked his knuckles one hand at a time, made himself look bigger. "You don't even have a kid, do you?"

Jet appraised his pursuer and glanced around the deserted arcade. He swallowed. "Listen man, call the bank. I'm sure it was just a simple mistake."

"Don't insult my intelligence. You tried to scam me. You got caught. Now you have to deal with me."

Jet started to sweat. He licked his lips. "I know it looks bad, but I'm just trying to make a living. I'm not even the one you want. I'm just the delivery guy. The collector I work for doesn't even ask questions. He doesn't care where the merch comes from."

Bennie waited while Jet vomited all the details he needed. His anger at being ripped off was one thing. The knock his pride had taken was another matter entirely. He wouldn't dupe another collector like that.

Bennie let Jet go. He had what he needed. He knew he wouldn't allow himself a moment's peace until that pony was back on his desk.

He parked in a side street behind the historic Labia theatre with its neon pink hearts and fairy lights blinking in the art-deco windows. He noticed that there was some kind of film festival happening, and young people in oversized jerseys and tight leggings smoked cigarettes in the parking lot and chatted over glasses of wine. No one looked up as Bennie stalked past.

The apartment block was a modern square building in Orange Street. Like every complex in Cape Town, it was access controlled by security and guests had to sign in and out by the CCTV-monitored gate. Bennie scouted the perimeter for a blind spot and hopped the wall undetected. The Collector lived on the top floor penthouse, its mirrored windows aimed towards Devil's Peak and Table Mountain, the busy golden lights of the city reflected in the glass panes. Bennie wasn't surprised by the absence of a Trellidor, since the complex was heavily guarded. Very few of the apartments in his block had them. He picked the front door lock with ease and used his empty debit card to pry it open. He would scare the guy. Take back his property. Rich fucks like this one needed to be taught a lesson, that's all. As the door opened, overhead ceiling lights cast a soft glow on the carpeted hallway. Vintage movie posters hung on the walls in glass frames.

He padded in soundlessly on the fluffy white carpet and picked up a familiar plastic scent. Someone was watching TV upstairs. A porn by the sound of it. He moved into the living room, which seemed larger because of all the glass cabinets lining the walls. Each cabinet was filled with faces from the past. Bobba Fett. Spock. She-Ra. Alfred E Neuman. Hundreds of pristine figures, like the apartment was some kind of museum. Momentarily forgetting why he was there, he ran his fingers over a glass door. Inside was Luke Skywalker standing beside Han Solo trapped in carbonite with Greedo right behind, still in their unopened cardboard packaging. He smiled as he remembered the age-old who-shot-first debate. The plastic smell seeped through the glass. He closed his eyes for a second and took a deep whiff as his mind was transported back to a sunny day long ago, where he brandished a broomstick like a lightsabre in his parents' back yard.

"Who the fuck are you?"

Bennie tore his gaze from the treasures and turned around slowly.

A tall, bald man with black-framed glasses stood on the spiral staircase in a white plush gown. His bare feet and ankles peeked out underneath. With his hand on the rail, Bennie could see a gold pinkie ring inset with a large red stone. He said nothing, but drew himself up to his full height.

The man on the stairs didn't flinch. "I asked you a question, asshole."

"You stole from me," said Bennie.

"The fuck I did, I'm calling security."

"I am security. Stay where you are."

"Fuck you," he said, turning around to go back upstairs.

"Find anything new recently on Gumtree? Or do you have so many figurines that one doesn't matter?"

The Collector span around on the stairs. "What the fuck are you talking about?"

Bennie began moving slowly. "Vintage *My Little Pony*. Generation one. Circa 1985. You sent your goon to steal it from me."

"What goon?"

"Jet. I tracked him down earlier. Said the pony was for you."

The Collector blinked in confusion, then slowly opened his mouth as he remembered. He held up his hands, palms forward. "I pay Jet to track down memorabilia for me. You say he stole something from you? If he did, I'm sorry. But I didn't tell him to do that. He has a mind of his own. You want it back? Is that why you're here?"

Bennie ground his teeth. He wasn't even a blip on this guy's radar. "You can't just walk through life on the backs of other people. How many others like me did you rip off to get all this?"

The Collector dropped his arms and his voice took on a harder timbre. "You want to call the police, be my guest. This is business. People sometimes get the rough end of the deal. Look, I'll be happy to pay you for whatever he took. Email me the details. Just get the fuck out of my flat. Call my lawyer. Whatever."

Bennie continued moving forward, his eyes taking in the hundreds of detailed gazes trained on him. Heroes from his childhood. He imagined it all in his own apartment, lining his shelves, his desk. He could build a whole new glass case for them all, arrange them by genre…

Somewhere outside himself, the guy was still talking, "You like what you see? Take anything you want. I've got the key right here. It's all insured."

Bennie said nothing. He remembered that time as a kid he took his best friend's Mr T figure because he had been teased about how little he had. Because he could.

"Hey… What are you doing? Stay back. Don't come any closer."

In another room above them, a small dog yapped. The Collector ran up the stairs, tripping over his gown on the last step.

Bennie wasn't a violent guy. But the Collector was weak. Poorly made. He wouldn't be much trouble. He took a last sniff of the deep plastic smell before heading up the stairs.

This was business. Like the guy said, sometimes people got the rough end of the deal.

It just wasn't going to be Bennie.

Not this time.

THE PATRON SAINT OF NIGHT PUPPERS
Indrapramit Das

Kris walked down Terminal Ave. to autumn wind pounding on her aching eardrums, sunset striping the broad road with canted shadows and honeyed sunlight. Elsewhere in the city, candles sputtered in pumpkins and grown-ups and children alike put on their monsters and roamed the streets. But Terminal was haunted by emptiness, nothing but cars passing in intervals to keep Kris company; Kris was wearing her monster, and it was A Lack of Financial Stability. She hadn't expected a shift on Halloween weekend, but also wasn't one to turn down a chunk of rent.

It was a ten minute walk from the bus and SkyTrain stop on Main to the dog hotel if she hurried (and Kris always hurried, fastidiously punctual in the manner of the perpetually underemployed), down Terminal with its empty sidewalks and vast commercial lots, carpet stores and car dealerships and glassy office blocks with overpriced cafes, the line of warehouses that was the Vancouver Flea Market, and the dog hotel itself, all crouched low to offer a broken view of the mountains behind Vancouver. The oldest thing on that long stretch of road was the soil, empty lots whispering grassy secrets to their chainlink fences as they waited to be built up. Terminal Ave. always felt to her like a line drawn right across one edge of the city, between the ocean and the mountains, old land slashed new to bleed ugly buildings for the gods of real estate development and gentrification.

As she passed a new pop-up for-profit university block and the papered-over windows of its nascent Subway eatery, Kris saw a person up ahead on the sidewalk, standing still. They were dressed all in black and had a dog's head, its ears black triangles. It was Halloween weekend and there were costumed people out and about, but this was a lonesome stretch for walkers, and Kris was wary of any pedestrians on it because of that. She hoped it wasn't a man, because it wasn't easy to cross over to the other side of the road on Terminal: it was broad and lacking in crosswalks—and the fact that the person up ahead had a dog's head, dark and shaggy and black, unsettled her. Their eyes twinkled a sharp and quivering flame-yellow in the darkening air. There was an unpleasant serendipity to the sight—she was a dog hotel attendant, there had been a spree of dog disappearances around Vancouver recently, and here was a dog person with glowing pinpricks for eyes. Hostage to her imagination, she imagined this person, with their dog's head, was the Vancouver Dog Thief—or worse, the Vancouver Dog Killer. The eyes—Christmas lights, cleverly rigged and woven into a mask? Kris tugged at her hoodie, pulling it lower, and nearly yelped when her phone buzzed in her jeans pocket.

Kris took out the phone—greased with fingerprints and age—and saw a text from her roommate Tabby: *Get yr ass to Main for some beers+ pho, looking for a place with Jo where u at?* Kris sighed and texted that she was at work, fingers cold, remembering to check the dog-headed pedestrian as she got closer. The dog person stood where they stood, not moving. But once she tapped Send she looked up to see them sprinting down the sidewalk, thankfully in the opposite direction from Kris, running alarmingly fast. A howl rose into the darkening sky, bestial in verisimilitude. The last of the day flashed off the windows of the SkyTrains racing Kris down the looming tracks parallel to the road, burned on the fall snows tracing the creases of the mountains. Kris felt a deep longing to be on a beach (just about thirty minutes away by bus) or crowd-watching on a patio with Tabby and company, all coming off work, weary and alcohol-thirsty, many of them freelancers just shifting from coffee shop to bar. When she was on the SkyTrain, she felt a coarse bitterness at all the people made-up and dressed-up for Friday night, done with adult responsibilities for the day.

Kris bit into the chocolate cookie she always bought herself from the Starbucks at the crossing of Terminal and Main. The crumbly sweetness turned to coal in her mouth as she watched the dog-person become a speck darting down the receding sidewalk. As she always did, she finished the cookie just as the dog hotel's smokestack became visible over the hard lines of the self storage terminal next door to it. The hotel had a smokestack because it had once been a glue factory and not because they secretly burned dogs, as the co-proprietor of the establishment had somewhat inappropriately joked on Kris's job interview.

By the time the dark red-brick building came into full view, like some kind of modernist castle squatting amidst the commercial hinterland of Terminal Ave., sunset had turned dark blue, the flames doused from mountain ice and glass. She turned into the lot that held the hotel, the storage terminal and, bizarrely for the location, a 24-hour Tim Horton's that was a haven for homeless customers because of its isolation. The mountains had gone out like lamps switched off, the slopes dark and dotted with light from North Shore houses and the ski resort. Clouds were tumbling towards the city over the peaks, smudging evening to night.

Kris rushed towards the wrought-iron gate into the dog hotel complex, which looked like the barred entry to a minimum security prison. She felt droplets dot her head and fumbled with the keys to the gate, hurrying into the arched enclosure of the entrance as rain began to patter on the concrete. Kris locked the gate and used the fob on her keychain to open the glass doors to the little lobby. Blessed warmth gushed against her, tainted by the smells of disinfectant and air freshener. The hotel was closed except for night clients, so the lights were dimmed and there was no one at the reception desk (a sad plastic jack o' lantern basket sat on the desk, half full of dog treats). It looked like the lobby of any mid-range spa, lime green and white cushions decorating the spartan waiting couches, framed pictures of happy dogs with lush coats instead of humans with cucumbers on their eyes on the exposed brick walls. The brick walls gave it a comfy feel that still couldn't get rid of the reek of bleach. Kris signed in on the clipboard and took a look at the list of tonight's dogs and their medications, diseases, allergies, behaviours. She heard footsteps scuff the floor behind her and took a shuddering breath.

"Oh my…goodness. You scared me," she said, with a slight laugh, face gone rosy from embarrassment and coming in from cold to warmth.

Her co-worker Brendan raised his hands as if caught in a crime. "Sorry, Kris. Too used to being sneaky around sleeping dogs."

"It's okay, spooked myself… I was thinking of all those dogs going missing, and here we are…"

"In a dog hotel?" Brendan flashed his perfect teeth, untying and tying his long chestnut locks as he often did in front of her. Kris restrained herself from rolling her eyes. She'd felt a lightness in her chest when she first met Brendan and his tight jeans on her first night shift, considering how hard it was to date in the city, but once he'd offered to teach her yoga at his place because she 'looked exhausted,' her interest had withered. "It's probably coyotes. Or junkies. You know how panhandlers often have dogs with them. Like, where do they get them from? You gotta wonder, right?"

Kris raised her eyebrows in lieu of a response.

"Anyway, I think this place is pretty secure. Just don't forget to shut the yard door before you put the dogs to sleep, and make sure none of them get stranded out in the yard before you do. You gonna be okay here alone?" he said. *I've been working here four months, don't tell me how to do my fucking job, Brendan,* thought Kris.

"Ah, yup, no worries. All quiet on the western front?"

"Sure, it's a small bunch today. Shouldn't be too rough. I've given them all their food and meds, just give the listed ones their night snacks and they should be good for beddy-bye."

"Awesome, thanks Brendan. Got plans for the night?" *Now why'd you ask him that?*

"Yeah yeah, gonna jam with some peeps at the Du Soleix, open mic tonight. You should come check it out some other time."

"Cool cool," Kris said, cheeks aching from fake smiling and temperature fluctuation.

"Alright, have a good one." Brendan grinned again, his ponytail bouncing newly tied as he took out his own keys and left via the front door out into the city, to the far off revelries. Kris shook her head and went through the hallway leading out of the lobby. Behind another glass door was the Nursery—a hall, filled with doggy beds and toys, with a garage door that led out into a walled-off concrete exercise yard. The hotel only took medium and small sized dogs for night shift. She could see them lying lumpen across the open room, curled into the doggy beds scattered across the floor, some choosing to sleep on the floor. She saw several heads pop up in unison as they registered her approach. She opened the door. The dogs scattered like autumn leaves in a gust, exploding into a chorus of claw-clicks and barking, surging against the door in a wall of scrabbling paws and glossy eyes and urgent muzzles and teeth, while others hurtled to the corners with suspicious snaps and coy looks. Kris entered, palms out to give them her scent, taking care not to let any of them escape through the door before shutting it behind her. The dogs surrounded her in worship and terror, begging for guidance. They loved Kris. They feared Kris.

They asked only that she love them like their human families once had, only to abandon them here for who knew how many forevers, in this unhomely place where strangers could sink fangs into throats at any moment, where the playful potential of the dog park was turned upside down, where they were all alone amongst the smells of other fearful dogs; and fear made all these new assholes twitch with sickly scent, fear made menace of these masterless companions—so they looked to their one Master, Kris, their savior, their goddess, to get them through the Long Dark Night. She felt their tongues (warm) and noses (cold) wet against her hands, their nails hard against her oldest and most worn pair of jeans, their paws stabbing her rattiest red and white converse. In a loud, clear voice she barked out her sharpest *Hey!* And *Quiet!* as she slowly walked around the room, matching dogs to the names on the list using their jingling metal tags. The pugs rolled after her like a pile of slugs, the lone French bulldog making googly eyes from afar, a daschund yapping at her feet. She pitied these dogs in a way she had never pitied dogs before, for being so helpless to humanity's whimsical absurdity, shuffled night after night into this garage where once dead horses were chopped and sorted before being boiled (maybe), entrusted to a pack leader they were forced to trust and a pack they didn't know or trust, the freedom of grass and beach and forest and mountain far, far away.

Kris would adopt a dog and hold it close every night if she thought she could afford to take care of such a companion. Tabby—who taught ESL classes and worked at a bookstore on Commercial, much to Kris' envy—had often suggested they get one because they were lucky enough to have a landlord who didn't mind pets, but Kris always refused. She barely had the money to take care of herself despite, she always reminded herself, of her unmistakable privilege. Kris often felt guilty about that, about the homeless people she saw panhandling by the Tim Horton's next door, sometimes with their loyal dogs who'd never see the inside of this dog hotel. The sight of a homeless person who wasn't white would send her into a veritable well of guilt, emptying all her coffee change into their Styrofoam cups and Tupperware bowls. But white homeless people reminded her of herself and the fact that, despite her whiteness, Kris was doing night shifts at the dog hotel because she was a millennial stereotype, struggling to make rent while towing around a humanities degree (Creative Writing) like an artfully taxidermied albatross. With her parents and education and support system, she had a one-up on those wandering souls sleeping on the streets with their faithful beasts, and she was somehow still barely able to pay her bills. So no dog for her, she told herself.

Punishment, or perhaps caution at another potential source of loss.

Dogs left even quicker than humans.

She'd had a dog once, or her family had, in the small town of Dardenne, British Columbia, where she'd grown up. She'd taken Demon (Dee for short) out for night walks as a teen, secretly relieved when she scratched and whined at her bedroom door at ungodly hours, Kris already awake by the aquamarine glow of her computer monitor writing sincere short stories about Canadian witches to her mother's CD of Kate Bush's *Hounds of Love* or scouring Napster for Alanis Morissette MP3s. Dee's anxious bladder gave her an excuse to dig up the rumpled pack in the deepest recesses of her school backpack (she bought them off Clara, an eleventh-grader with a fake I.D. who didn't mind making a small profit buying booze and cigs for her schoolmates), go to the park next door and smoke on the swings with a clear view of her house in case her parents emerged. Even out in the dark in the middle of the night, with the hills glowering black over the low suburban houses of their neighborhood, she felt safer all alone with Demon by her side than she had ever felt anywhere else in her life. She knew that people were scared of Dee, with her sleek and monstrous body and long snout steaming, her ears pricked sharp as devil's horns, her eyes like black marbles. In school, Kris was powerless. No matter how much like armor her baggy red hoody felt, it wasn't. It couldn't turn the words fat, nerd, lez or *girl* into mere truths instead of poison spat from the mouths of her peers. But with Demon by her side, leash tied around her hand like the reins to some great and heaving mount—that was something else. With Kris, Dee was as well-behaved as she was unruly with others (including her father, who often threatened to get rid of her if Kris didn't stop her barking at passers-by all the time). Dee sat still as a statue as Kris smoked on the creaking swings, panting softly and looking to her human now and again.

One autumn day, Dee six and Kris fourteen, the two had been walking along the hedge at the edge of the park when Kris heard the metallic crunch of cans being crushed in hands. Three boys loped across the park towards her as she blew smoke towards the stars. There was a cruel hunger in their faces painted in shadow and yellow by the streetlamps. She couldn't smell the beer on their trailing plumes of breath, but it was there, no doubt.

"Whadyoo doing out here all by yourself, Little Miss Muffinface," said Aiden, grimace crowned in a woolen toque. He was a tenth-grader whose taunt of Little Miss Muffinface was familiar from lunchtime at school. *I don't even like muffins*, Kris thought for the hundredth time. His companions were familiar, if nameless to Kris. She felt a stab of horror as she saw them surround her, ready to play out whatever bullying scene they'd gotten hard-ons over in some movie they'd watched in their basements.

"Don't you know smoking's not for little g—" Aiden turned his head.

Then the slack leash in her hand moved, and Demon, old Dee of the Shadows, so black in the dimness that she'd blended into the hedges, turned her streetlit eyes and growled deep in her throat, her muzzle unfurling beautiful fangs. In an instant, Aiden and his stooges' faces turned to those of little boys, and with a huff of an abruptly cut-off taunt he staggered back. Demon saw this prey-like movement and charged. Kris saw her leap on Aiden and pulled the leash. The boys ran. Kris ran too, carried by Dee's muscled velocity. She gripped the leash and tugged, putting all her mocked heft into restraining her companion. Demon yelped and scrabbled in the grass, pawing up clods of earth, but slowed and reared, barking after the sprinting boys as they ran down Otter Drive. Her sneakers sunk in the soil, cigarette butt flown off somewhere, Kris had pulled and pulled, sparing the lives of her enemies, soaring with benevolent rage. She remembered Demon hot as an engine, dark as the night sky above her, panting as Kris embraced her in boundless gratitude. *Shhhhhh baby Dee you're all mine.* Kris was Diana goddess of the hunt, arm aching from restraining her hound. She was a witch with a demon summoned as her familiar, queen of the night. No adults to pull her cheeks or tell her to watch her eating, no kids to poke at her softness with words and fingers, no friends to disappoint her with gossip churning behind their smiling faces—just the stars and the hills dwarfing the slanted rooftops, and her own monster made of darkness.

It took Kris a good hour of playing with the dogs to settle them down. She placated the scared barkers—a Russell terrier named Al and an unhappy little Pomeranian named Powder—with chewtoys offered from a distance, without making eye contact, keeping her hands clear of their bodies so they didn't nip out of fear. She mopped the streaks of piss from the scuffed floor and refilled the big water bowls in one corner, bleach scouring the air. She went to the yard where the sky, the glowing sign of the Tim Horton's, and the elevated SkyTrain tracks were visible over the corrugated steel walls. A plane pricked the sky with its lights, scudding through the dark violet clouds. Kris listened to the distant, soothing rumble of the passing trains (scrolling windows full of Halloween revelers on their way downtown) as she scooped the last turds from the yard. As she marched through the Nursery with the turds piled in the metal scooper, she shushed the dogs away from their shit. "Thanks for the gifts, guys, but they're going down the toilet," she said to the dogs, whose noses quivered. Using the scraper, she emptied the scooper of shit into the toilet in the supply room and flushed it all, fighting her gag instinct as always (tossing Dee's poop in trashcans hadn't been so hard). She turned up the heat, dimmed the Nursery lights and rolled down the garage door to the yard with its rusty chain, shutting the place for the night. This done, she unfolded the flimsy metal cot in one corner against one wall, and unpacked her thin blanket from her backpack (other contents: a dog tag that read 'Demon', the black lipstick she'd worn as small concession for her missing pre-Halloween celebrations, a compact, eyeliner pencil, hair ties, tampons, Tylenol, cigarettes, a YA novel about werewolves to roughly match the theme of the night, and earphones). Her backpack served as a pillow. Barking out a periodic *No!* to keep the dogs from jumping on to the bed (it hurt her to see their pleading eyes and anxious nose-licks, but she couldn't risk having them piss on her while she slept), she sat cross-legged on the cot (shoes still on, because they might get chewed or, yes, pissed on) and read her book. Feeling bad, she looked up to say, softly: "You're all good dogs," leading to hopeful eyebrows and ears twitching.

She got a page in before Oswald came to say hello. Oswald was a regular—a grizzled, elderly black pug she had seen at the hotel every night shift. He never barked, never made a fuss, just quietly snored in one of the beds in the corner. That is, until Kris got on her cot, at which point he solemnly presented himself, fussily licking his white-bearded jowls. Oswald was the only one allowed on her cot, though he was too old to get on by himself. Kris bent down to pick him up, grunting in unison with him as she laid him in her lap, where he curled up with a sigh. She bent down to kiss him on his raisin-wrinkled forehead, and got a lick on the mouth for it. Grimacing, she wiped her mouth on her sleeve with a laugh (Kris was something of a germophobe, and had also seen memes making fun of white people mouth-kissing dogs). Oswald was the opposite of Dee of the Shadows. Helpless, soft. Kris was the protector, not Oswald.

She'd never seen Dee get the little white hairs on her jowls from age like Oswald, because Dee's fangs had scratched Aiden's arm when she jumped on him that fall night. Aiden complained to his parents, and despite Kris's furious pleas to *her* parents, a tide of tears flooding her eyes and nose as she held clueless Dee who sat there smiling wide with tongue out, they had taken Dee to the vet. She hadn't gone with them because she couldn't believe the cruelty of it, thought her parents were bluffing and just wanted to scare her so she'd take control of Dee better. Dee had never returned. Kris never got to say goodbye.

Her mother came by later and slipped Dee's dog tag under Kris's locked door. "I'm sorry, honey. We thought you might want to keep this."

Kris waited for her mother's shadow to vanish from under the door, and took the tag. She never lost it.

Kris got a text from Tabby: *Missing u, we got congee not pho. Yr fave, let's go soon. Have a goodnight at doggy nightcare <3*

Tabby had often taken Kris to her parents' place in Richmond for her Taiwanese mother's impeccable chicken congee, but it was the Congee House on Main and Broadway where she'd first introduced Kris to the dish on their first night out in the city as university roommates. Kris had drunk too much at the bar they'd gone to and thrown up in the toilet. Tabby had insisted hot rice porridge a couple blocks down was the best thing for her empty stomach. Kris remembered the harsh glare of fluorescents washing out their drunken faces, the flayed ducks lined up red in the windows, her nausea turning to hunger at the smell wafting from the bowls. They'd spent that afternoon at Wreck Beach surrounded by nude sunbathers, Kris feeling like she'd entered a new and decadent country far from Dardenne, B.C. Holding quiet, old Oswald, she recalled the dread she'd felt coming down those wooden steps to all those nude bathers on the sand, how her heart had raced when Tabby casually took off her top and bra. Waiting for the familiar, underhanded *It's okay, you're not* that *fat*. But Tabby had noticed Kris keeping her clothes on and said nothing, waited about ten minutes, and put on her top again. "It's getting kinda cold," she said. They shared a joint and watched the sunset, talked about being bullied as children (Kris had been Little Miss Muffinface, Tabby had been the Chink or the Dog Eater), flipped the finger to a perv sporting an erection ten feet away. When September cool descended with the dark, they'd gone back up the steps, walked their new campus, taken a bus to Main, to beers and late night congee, heads aching from dehydration and intoxication.

Eventually, Kris had gone topless on Wreck Beach, months later. Tabby had been there that time too.

Listening to Oswald fall into a gentle snoring, Kris texted back: <3

Kris looked in a mirror: she saw the shaggy black dog's head staring back, eyes like burning drops of honey, muzzle steaming. She was doggess of the night. She ran through the city, nabbing rich people's dogs from their glittering new condos and West Vancouver mansions, putting them into a bottomless sack with her clawed hands. Like a canine Santa she leapt through the night sky, bounding into the streets of East Vancouver, of the Downtown Eastside, reaching into her sack to give the dogs to the homeless, the junkies, the ones who needed protectors and friends. The underdogs of the city cheered for this crypto-superhero, and the underpasses were spray-painted with elaborate murals of her, murals whose colours ran when you stared at them. The letters shifted, but always read *Dee of the Shadows*. Vancouver was filled with the triumphant barking of all those underdogs.

She woke sweaty, Oswald warm and stirring by her side, the room overheated. The dogs were barking. She snapped up, panic billowing. Maybe she'd slept through her 5:30 alarm. The dogs were revolting, demanding to be let out. But her phone, blazing in the dark, read 4:03 am. "Shut up! Lemme think goddamnit," shouted Kris, squinting and holding out the phone. In the pale light of the screen, she saw the dogs' open eyes throw the light back. They were barking at the garage door. Giving whining Oswald a couple of scratches for reassurance, she lowered her legs off the creaking cot, using the phone to make sure her feet didn't land on anything living or excrement. She could see the glitter of rivulets by the dismal light. Some had relieved themselves ahead of their dawn yard time. She needed to as well.

"Quiet!" she bellowed. Some of the dogs quietened, not all. She joined them with a startled yelp as a mournful howl cut through the barking. From outside.

The phrase *Dee of the Shadows* popped into her head. Heart pounding, she felt the remnants of a dream burn away in the harsh glow of her phone. Had she dreamed of Dee? She grasped at the dissolving dream for a second, but let it go— she had other problems. A room-full of riled up dogs, and a mystery howler. Surely the howl hadn't come from the yard. Just a prankster out on the streets beyond. It was Halloween, after all. Or it was a coyote sniffing around the hinterland. Or she'd accidentally left a dog outside.

Fuck. It couldn't be, she had checked thoroughly, as always.

But what if she had? She had to check. Buoyed by the sea of noise gushing from the throats of her dogs, Kris sighed. She put on her hoodie and got up. There was another *but*. What if there *was* something other than a dog outside? She took out her keys and held them between her fingers, vaguely remembering that this wasn't the best way to punch someone. *Fuck it*, she thought. *I can't defend myself anyway, at least it makes me* feel *more badass.*

She walked through her pack, key-braced fist and open hand held out like a warrior martyr's. Some of the dogs licked at her fingers for salty succor. Others merely barked louder, encouraged by their pack leader's roused stature. Kris pulled at the chain of the yard door. "Yeah, yeah, I'll protect y'all, just stay the fuck back, okay?" she said. The door rose with a metallic growl, slow like a guillotine. Dim ambient streetlight poured through the gap. "If someone's out there you better not be here to hurt these dogs cuz I'll key your motherfucking eyes out," Kris muttered tremulously. As the door rose up, she ducked and looked, half expecting to see a feral figure crouched in the yard, dog-head bristling, eyes aflame. But the grating door's slow progress revealed an empty yard—

Fuck

and a dog's head on the ground. *I left a dog out there and something beheaded it...*

"You stupid shit," said Kris, shaking her head and continuing to pull the chain.

It's just a. "Fucking mask."

The ordered rule of sleep-time was shattered. Though some of the dogs chose to go back to sleep, others followed Kris outside, shitting two hours early and emptying bladders on drizzle-dampened asphalt. Kris carried Oswald outside in her arms, to compensate for rudely waking the old creature. The dogs head lay on the ground in the centre of the yard, looking desiccated with no human to fill out its emptiness. Its stiff ears still stood up straight.

Kris bent down by the mask, huffing as she transferred Oswald's heft to one arm. Picking up the mask, Kris felt something leap from her chest to her throat, fleet as a hound. It left as a small laugh, leaving her throat aching. She looked around, gooseflesh prickling across her arms. No heads peeping over the corrugated metal fence. No howls. "Thank...you?" she said to the night. Kris looked at the mask, with its yellow rubber fangs and dirty mane. It had to be the person she'd seen on Terminal. Had they climbed the fences into the yard? Thrown the mask over while passing? Leaped through the night sky and landed on the asphalt on nimble, elongated paws? She was disappointed to see that there were no Christmas lights rigged into its eyes. If there ever had been, they were gone. *Well, I have a costume for Halloween now.* Tabs would love it.

A bichon by the name of Hampton twitched one ear as he sniffed at the small pile of shit he'd left Kris to scoop in one corner of the yard. Kris sat down on one of the plastic playboxes in the yard, placing Oswald and the mask on her lap. She took out her phone and texted Tabby. *Home safe?*

Kris took the mask and slid it on. It stank—a mangy dogsbreath of rubber, weed, and sweat. Powder barked at her from afar. Argyle came and sat on her converses, eyes slitting. Kris could hear the buzzing of the streetlamps on the lot next door, the neon hum of the Tim Horton's sign. The phone buzzed on the plastic of the playbox. *In bed safe af & still drunk thx for checkin darlin. Why u up?*

Couldn't sleep.

Oswald was snoring again. Argyle's eyes were closed. Powder had wandered back into the Nursery to sleep. Another text.

U ok?

Kris listened to Oswald's whistling breath, scratching his graying fur, wondering how many more times he'd be there to greet her at the dog hotel before he never came back. She thumbed out a message on the phone.

Let's get a rescue dog.

Kris tapped Send. Through the dark cocoon of the mask, she looked at the night sky, patches of stars among the clearing clouds, and thought of Dardenne, hundreds of kilometers away, where her parents were, their house empty of daughter and dog. Where she'd run into Aiden last at a bar this summer, on one of her visits home. He'd bought her a drink. They'd told each other about their lives (he was a carpenter now) as if they'd only just met, then reminded each other of the Dardenne they knew as children, which emptinesses had sprouted strip malls. They'd made out in his truck, drunk. She'd ended up holding Aiden's balding head to her chest when he broke down in shuddering, embarrassing sobs half-way through a sudden apology for getting her dog killed. She hadn't asked whether he was sorry for having bullied her too.

After, he'd showed her the tiny white kiss of scar tissue in the crook of his arm, where Dee's canine had punctured his skin. She had touched it tenderly, as if it might still hurt.

TILT
Karen Onojaife

If Heaven truly was a place on Earth, Iyere wondered, who was to say that that place couldn't be a crappy little casino on the top floor of a shopping centre in Shepherd's Bush?

If she really thought about it (and generally, she tried not to think about it), she understood that there wasn't all that much of a difference between her and the patrons of the betting shops that seemed to sprout in every empty space on the high street. And next to the betting shops were the pawn shops, their windows emblazoned with bright posters depicting people inexplicably joyful at the idea of having to put prized possessions in hock. But those places, grubby with daylight and disapproving glances from passers-by, could make a girl feel like she had a problem, whereas a casino at two, three, or four am, while not necessarily a sensible choice, at least made Iyere feel like she had taken a considered decision to court decadence.

"*Decadence,*" she could imagine her sister, Ivie, scoffing. "*This place is called Barry's Casino.*"

Which, fair enough. But until Iyere could figure out a way to make it to the neon-lit hiss of the Bellagio's fountains, Barry would have to do. Besides, she had come to appreciate the fake solicitude from the liveried doormen; the powdery sweet scent of carpet cleaner that perfumed the tired shag pile lining the mirrored hallway; the complimentary warm, sugared pretzels that staff brought round on silver platters, presumably on the nights that Barry was feeling especially generous, and the unpredictable choice of soundtrack piped onto the casino floor—this early morning's selection being a run through of Gloria Estefan's greatest hits.

What she liked most of all was that the two, three or four am crowd at Barry's Casino knew what it was about; a loose camaraderie of sorts but essentially, people would mind their own business. No tourists wanting to distract with chatter, or rookies taking up valuable space at a table while they fumbled over their chips and mixed up their bets. No, the early morning crew just hummed like a hive; gentle sighs and sometimes light taps on the back from a neighbour, either in celebration or commiseration depending on the cut of a deck.

"What the fuck is it?" Ivie had asked her once, simultaneously incredulous and despairing on one shameful afternoon when she had caught Iyere rifling through her handbag for money. "What is it that you get from doing this? From being at that place?"

Iyere, face flushed and eyes bright, hadn't known what to say. To explain that she liked the sweat of cheap plastic chips in her hand seemed small. She liked to stack these totems upon the green baize of a table, liked to listen to the rattle of the ball as it skittered across the wheel as lightly as a girl skipping rope, liked the swish of cards through a croupier's gloved hand as they fanned the deck this way and that, the flicker of white edges like breaking waves.

She could have spoken to the science of things; the ticker tape parade of dopamine lighting up in her brain and the rerouting of neural pathways.

Or she could have dealt in practicalities, for example, the fact that she had been borrowing money from the petty cash account at the community college where she taught so she needed to win some back and win big, so that she could replace it all before anyone found out.

Or perhaps this: you and your little girl, Ofure, are in a local park one day and she is playing on a swing while you are reading a book. This playground is nothing special, just something that's there on the walk home from school and there's no way of telling, just from looking, that somehow the local council has missed the last three annual inspections, or that screws in the swing's frame are coming loose, or that when Ofure clambers to a standing position on the rubber tyre, mittened hands clutching metal chains, the whole structure will groan and pitch forward, tipping her, your little girl, onto the hard ground, head first. Bright red blood splashed across snow.

Iyere had always liked the things she liked too intensely. If it wasn't gambling, it would have been other things, it had been other things—food, sex, or telling lies just because. But after Ofure died, the casino seemed the only place where Iyere could comfortably exist in time. It wasn't that she enjoyed the losses—in fact those made her panicked and sick, and aside from an ephemeral flare of glee, she didn't really much care for the wins, but these swings of fate either way seemed at least conceivable and therefore manageable, and matters that she had a hand in, as opposed to the loss of Ofure, which had been so complete, so profound and so unexpected that even years later, she could scarcely allow herself to accept that it had in fact occurred.

So Iyere had said nothing, and Ivie had just stared at her. Iyere had known that if her sister hadn't been tired from chemo, she might have tried to fight her right there in the hallway until, as Ivie had put it once, "you saw some fucking sense." As it was, Ivie had been exhausted, giving a mirthless chuckle before sliding onto the nearby sofa in defeat.

"Whatever you're looking for, it's not there," Ivie had said, fixing Iyere with a hard gaze. "She's not there. Not in a fucking casino."

"She's not anywhere," Iyere had said and then she had walked out, a stolen twenty pound note still in her hand.

Iyere always knew what time it was, despite the casino's attempt to dissemble by the regular flow of free drinks and the complete absence of clocks. Even without her watch she knew because she had always preferred the night hours, enjoying their relative quiet and the softness of possibility that sunlight tended to burn away.

She had been there for about an hour, having had a couple of uninspired rounds of blackjack and Texas hold 'em, when she noticed the croupier standing at an empty roulette table across the room.

Iyere knew all the croupiers there by now and this one was definitely new. The woman's hands darted into the thick fall of her locked hair, fingers moving swiftly as she arranged it into a messy bun. The action made the crisp white of her shirt draw tightly across her breasts and Iyere scolded herself for noticing; she looked away, her face feeling warm and her thoughts suddenly scattered. She made herself count to ten, made herself engage in boring chit chat with the dealer at her table, and then counted to thirty before she allowed herself to look again.

The croupier was already looking at her, her head tilted to one side, one side of her mouth beginning to tilt in amusement. She let her gaze travel the length of Iyere's body before it returned to her face and then she nodded once, mostly solemn but that half smile hinting at a degree of mocking in her assessment, or her invitation, or whatever this was.

"Morning," the woman said as Iyere neared her table. Iyere just nodded, not entirely trusting her voice to speak until she had taken a sip of her drink. "And how are we today?"

"Oh, you know," Iyere shrugged, letting her eyes fall on the woman's name tag; 'Essy'.

"Oh, I know," Essy said, allowing a grin to bloom across

her face, leaving Iyere bewildered enough to glance behind her to see if Essy's smile had been directed at someone else. But everyone else seemed far away somehow, although she could still see them and hear them, everything dulled as if with a thick veil and when she turned back to the table, Essy was closer, leaning forward slightly with one hand positioned on either side of the wheel.

"Bets, please," Essy said, looking at Iyere expectantly.

Iyere placed a chip on a numbered square, barely even checking where she'd left it, preferring instead to watch the flick of Essy's hands as she spun the wheel one way and tossed the tiny ball the other. They both watched the ball stutter and skip until Essy murmured 'rien ne va plus' and a moment later, she swept Iyere's losing chip away from the board.

"So, you're new?" Iyere asked. She had the sense that Essy barely managed to avoid an eye roll, surely having heard the question a thousand times over by now from various lecherous parties. Still, Iyere liked to think that there was a significant difference between being a lecherous party and an interested one.

"Not really," Essy said. "Was on days before. I asked to switch shifts because I prefer the night time crowd. They're more—"

"Desperate?" Iyere offered.

"If you like. Bets, please," Essy said, placing the tip of her right index finger on the polished chrome handle of the wheel as she waited. Iyere wasn't sure how old Essy was; she was one of those women whose skin was so dark and unlined that it was always hard to tell. Younger than her at least, despite the wrinkled skin of Essy's large hands and Iyere was seized with the abrupt desire to lose herself in every single fold of them.

Iyere put a stack of chips on the table.

Essy nodded and then started the wheel with a brisk whisk of her wrist. They both stared in silence at the ball, Essy eventually making a soft sound of consolation in the back of her throat before sweeping Iyere's stack away. "Let me guess," she said, pausing for a moment to survey Iyere once more. "Teacher?"

Iyere gave a surprised smile and tipped her glass in acknowledgement.

"Working here gives you all types of party tricks," Essy said. "What do you teach?"

"Fairy tales," Iyere said. "The taxonomy of them. For example, did you know that pretty much every country has its own version of Little Red Riding Hood?"

Essy considered for a moment before shrugging. "Makes sense. Show me a country where girls aren't hunted by wolves. Bets, please."

Iyere lost another stack of chips.

"Desperate, you said? Earlier?" Essy clarified, as she swept the chips away. "But you know what I think? I think 'desperate' gets a bad rap. Desperation gets people closer to being honest."

"Honest about what?"

"About what they're doing." Essy said. "Bets, please," she repeated, waiting for Iyere to place a short stack of chips on the table before continuing. "I mean, who isn't gambling, really? It's just that most of you like to pretend otherwise. The girl who fucks a fuckboy because she hopes that good sex might tempt him into being a better boyfriend has placed a bet, no? All of the components are there; consideration, chance and prize."

Iyere choked briefly on her drink, both somewhat thrilled and taken aback by the boldness of Essy's language. She wiped at her mouth with the back of her hand before meeting Essy's gaze. "Well, I wouldn't call a fuckboy a prize," she said.

"Ah, but the girl in our example doesn't know that yet—no one does, until she lays down the stakes. Schrödinger's Fuckboy if you will. Bets, please."

Iyere lost another two chips. "My sister thinks I have a problem," she said.

"Why?" Essy shot back. "Because it's three am on a

Wednesday and you're at a casino, wearing pyjamas and your hair is still wrapped? Bets, please."

Iyere pushed the remainder of her chips onto a number, but her eyes were fixed on Essy's face instead of the wheel. There was something about her tugging at Iyere's memory but she couldn't quite place it, faint as it was and overwhelmed by the flutter in Iyere's chest whenever she allowed her gaze to rest on the curve of Essy's full lower lip or the gleam of skin at her collarbone.

Iyere lost again and Essy shrugged, sweeping the chips away with a flourish before folding her arms. "Well, it seems that you're out of—"

"I had a daughter," Iyere blurted out, unable to stand the idea of having to leave Essy's table now that her money had run out. She had never spoken of Ofure to strangers before, not like this and she wasn't even sure what drove her now. Something in Essy's gaze perhaps; it seemed soft but also demanding, as if her attention, once bestowed, required great things in exchange.

"I had a daughter and now I don't," she continued. "I was a mother, and now I'm not. What do you call that, I wonder? What's the word?"

Essy's eyes seemed to glow momentarily, and Iyere watched the pink flicker of her tongue dampen her lower lip. "I don't know the word in English," Essy said, her eyes fixed on Iyere, travelling over her face. "But then there have always been other tongues."

Iyere nodded, considering the idea of a grief translated, wondering if her heartbreak might taste differently in new words. She felt more speech rising in her, almost unbidden as she asked Essy if she could see her after her shift.

"Why?" Essy asked.

"Because you want to take me home with you and the house always wins?" Iyere said with borrowed confidence.

Essy laughed and Iyere realised it was the first time she had seen a genuine smile cross the other woman's face. Iyere wanted to know everything she could about that unknowable face, kiss everything she could from this stranger's lips and much else besides but she would be happy with whatever Essy might allow.

"Fraternising with patrons outside of the casino? We're not supposed to," Essy mused, making the pale marble of the roulette ball weave through a twist of her fingers as she thought. "But I'm open to persuasion."

"Hospitals. Police stations. Mortuaries. Strip clubs," Essy counted the words off her fingers as she listed other places she had worked. They were sat in her kitchen, drinking hot mugs of peppermint tea. "Always night shifts. It's just better. I prefer the places and times where you meet people at a crossroads, so to speak."

"Why?"

That's how I feed.

Or at least this is what Iyere thought she heard but when she looked up, Essy had her mug to her lips and appeared to still be pondering her question. "I guess you could call me a people person."

Iyere thought this was both true and untrue. She was not entirely sure that Essy *liked* people, so much as she liked collecting their stories and there was something undeniable about Essy that made people want to share them. Iyere had already exhausted her own sticky mess of secrets; the stolen money, the gambling, Ivie being sick and what happened to Ofure.

"Grief," Iyere found herself saying, "has skinned me."

Essy nodded and leaned forward slightly, her elbows resting on the grubby Formica table top. "Go on," she murmured, and it took Iyere a few moments to recognise the look on her face; it was the same avidity, she realised, that Ivie would wear on the days that her lips were too cracked, her throat too sore to eat anything of substance. On those days, she liked to sit and watch Iyere eat, her eyes tracing the column of Iyere's throat as she swallowed, and though Iyere hated it, hated the feeling of being consumed by her sister's gaze, she allowed it each time.

"Grief has skinned me," Iyere repeated, "but I think that maybe you might change that." Iyere didn't know she meant to say it until she did, but she was struck by the rightness as she uttered the words.

"*I* think," Essy said, setting her mug down with a smirk, "that you might be overestimating the restorative powers of a one-night stand."

Then they went outside to Essy's back garden, the night lining their skins and their lungs smoky with petrichor. Iyere's idea; she had half remembered something about a meteor shower tonight and so she had suggested they go out and look.

"The Perseids," Essy sighed, her eyes scanning the skies as if she could see things that Iyere couldn't, her gaze somehow able to penetrate the light pollution and constant cloud that hugged this part of the Earth's atmosphere, to reach the stuttering trail of meteors shaking themselves free of comets.

Iyere knew fuck all about astronomy but she had managed to watch half an episode of the Sky at Night once, and so she'd remembered that shooting stars weren't even stars at all, just bits of rock, debris and dust burning up as they tore through the atmosphere, blazing themselves into nothing, mostly gone before they could hit the ground.

Iyere took a deep breath so she could exhale her daughter's name. She sensed Essy shift as she listened. Iyere had noticed this about the woman; she liked to listen with her whole body as if words were vibrations that she needed to catch and recalibrate before she could issue the right speech in return.

"What's your favourite fairy tale?" Iyere whispered.

Essy shook her head, her eyes gleaming suddenly. "People don't remember my favourites the way they used to. Some do, but not like before. Maybe not even you, Professor," she said, her already raspy voice further thickened by a sudden emotion Iyere couldn't decipher.

Iyere watched the way Essy's right hand was working, as if she were still making that roulette ball dance through her fingers and without giving herself the chance to second guess, Iyere grabbed those fingers and entwined them with her own, before bringing their joined hands up to her mouth.

"Let's go back inside," Iyere said, the words damp against Essy's skin.

"What now?" Essy said, her hint of a smile unfurling into another grin when she saw Iyere's sudden bashfulness. "What are you after? Something new for the scrapbook?"

"I've been with women before," Iyere replied, allowing a mild dart of irritation to colour her voice.

"No doubt," Essy nodded, her gaze pinning Iyere where she stood. "But you haven't been with me." She was silent for several long seconds, scanning Iyere's face while the latter held her breath, scared at the thought of being dismissed, but equally scared of the thought of getting what she was so clumsily asking for.

Essy shifted the hand that was still in Iyere's grasp so that she could trace a light finger across Iyere's cheekbone, leaving a tingling warmth in its wake. "You said grief had skinned you…I guess we'll see."

"How will we see?"

Essy shook her head slowly. "I'll need an offering."

"Alright," Iyere said, Essy's hand cupping her face by now, her thumb resting at the corner of her mouth and so she turned her head slightly so she could lick it, kiss it, envelop its oddly nutty sweetness in the dark warmth of her mouth for just a second and Essy smiled, delighted and surprised at Iyere's fleeting boldness. "Alright," she repeated, as Essy gently rubbed a stripe of wetness along Iyere's jaw.

* * *

Essy's bedroom was quiet, teased with traces of moonlight, and time went elsewhere.

The bed was a mess of sheets and Iyere knew that Essy's skin was the warmest she had ever touched, heat radiating from its every inch.

Things were different in this kind of darkness; the gleam of her knees on either side of Essy's head like the curve of smooth rocks breaching the surface of a pond. The curl of Essy's back as she writhed above her was like the roll of a night ocean and when they kissed, it was sugar and salt on their tongues.

Essy liked to stop and watch whenever she made Iyere come, the look on her face unreadable as she scanned the other woman's. Iyere never knew what she was looking for but when she found it, there would be a half smile and then she would lower her head and give soft little licks, lapping at the beads of sweat on Iyere's stomach, or a tear collected in the curve of an ear, or the dampness between her legs, and this is what she had meant, Iyere realised in a half-dazed wonder, when she had said she required an offering.

Essy's attention was relentless, of a kind that didn't care if the recipient could bear it or not and there were times Iyere was not sure she could bear it, the sensations so thick that they seemed to slow her breath and blood. Each time she gasped, it was half a show of delight and half a reminder for her lungs to keep working, and she would tear her eyes away from Essy's penetrating gaze to the window, searching for the night sky with its trails of bruised clouds making distant cathedrals.

Her blood was still thundering in her ears when Essy sat up, her gaze solemn as she wiped wetness from her mouth. She stroked Iyere's face with the back of her hand and then she placed a cool palm on the centre of her stomach and pressed down firmly. Iyere jolted immediately, her mind transported to a sunlit afternoon in a cemetery when she'd sat by Ofure's grave after all the mourners had gone, save for Ivie. Ivie who had stood and watched Iyere as she'd sat by the mound of freshly turned over earth and dug her hands, wrist deep, into its coolness as she cried. Iyere had made unintelligible sounds that came from a place within that she had never known of, that she in fact suspected had not even existed until Ofure's death had torn her open somewhere, concealed claw marks that remained deep and bleeding.

Essy removed her hand and Iyere drew an agonised gasp of breath, sitting up and scrambling away until her back was pressed against the headboard. "What did you—"

"You gave an offering, I accepted, so…you get another spin of the wheel," Essy said.

Iyere stared at her blankly. "What are—"

"You know what," Essy said. "And you know how."

And as she said it, Iyere realised this was true. Maybe part of her had realised it from the moment Essy had spoken of crossroads, because Iyere had heard of Essy's kind in half-remembered stories from her aunt. While the old woman had called her by a different name, a different gender, Iyere recalled a couple of salient facts: a bringer of mischief and chaos in the guise of teaching a lesson.

This is how I feed, Essy had said.

Iyere had fed her and now Essy would give thanks by giving her a choice.

"I'm sorry about just now," Essy said, gesturing to her stomach. "I had to see what it is that you really want. People tend to lie, even at times like these. *Especially* times like these. It's strange, the way your kind does that. Even if it means you fuck up your chances."

"A chance to…Ofure?" Iyere stammered. "Back here with me?"

"Ofure," Essy said. "Although you should know that death has a scent."

"I wouldn't care."

"Hmm," Essy smiled thinly. "That's what they all say. More importantly, death will not be denied, which means we'd have to make a trade. No such thing as something for nothing after all. If Ofure comes back, someone else has to take her place."

"Someone else would have to die?"

"And it can't be you," Essy said quickly. "Can't be some random either. Has to be your blood, or close to it. Hey," Essy continued, raising her hands in supplication. "I don't make the rules. But I get them. I mean, if there's no skin in the game, are you really even playing?"

"No one would make that choice," Iyere said, her gaze fixed on the knot she had made of her hands in her lap. She was dreaming, she decided. She was dreaming and any minute now she would wake up.

"You'd be surprised at what people would do," Essy replied, her voice suddenly flat, her gaze dull and Iyere remembered the fevered nightmare of the days just after Ofure had died; all the bargains she had tried to make with indifferent gods for just a second of grace. Iyere would have traded anything and anyone, a whole world perhaps, for one moment of Ofure's breath against her face, or the press of her chubby arms around Iyere's leg.

But the only person she had to give up was Ivie.

And she's sick anyway.

Iyere winced, trying to dampen the sharp voice inside of her.

Ofure was meant to have had so much more time, and if Ivie herself could choose, wouldn't she want the same thing, in fact, hadn't she said (albeit when her tumour was still a blossoming secret, even to her) that if she could change places with Ofure, she would?

You're dreaming, she reminded herself, but her heart was weighing options all the same. If such a choice were even possible, she understood that one couldn't make it without being diminished, without being punished in some way. No doubt there was a further, final offering that Essy was eager to collect?

"Why me?" Iyere asked, understanding now that it had been Essy who had chosen her tonight.

"Because," Essy shrugged. "Because out of all the people there, I could tell that yours would taste the sweetest."

It would be easier at night, Iyere realised, for Essy to find what she needed; people were so much more vulnerable during these hours, hearts tilted so they could spill more easily, wounds so much more visible in the right kind of light.

What Iyere wanted was both of them; Ofure on her lap and Ivie by her side with the years stretching out ahead for all three of them like open roads. But if she had to choose, how to choose? After all, her aunt would always end her stories with the words 'you can't out trick a trickster god.'

You could refuse the bet, Iyere reminded herself. *You could walk away from the table for once, before you lose what you can ill afford to.*

But Iyere knew that she had been maimed by her daughter's death, grief skinned as Essy now knew, and the existence Iyere had experienced since then was for the most part in a half-light, in half measures, the half-life of her devotion to Ofure one of the few things that allowed her to stand.

And yet, that memory of the afternoon in the cemetery, which had stretched into the evening, then an all-night vigil, Ivie with her the whole time. The following morning had been fresh with dewdrops, making their funeral clothes damp. The spring of grass blades beneath her hands. Hearing the growing tangle of birdsong as her ears became re-accustomed to sound. The weight of Ivie as she shifted, placing her head in Iyere's lap. The last of the night's thin trails fading from the sky, taking with it the strange gravity that made hearts tilt. Iyere had felt her own heart quiver and shift as it tried to right itself, but she hadn't wanted to let it, had wanted it to remain forever tilted, always on the edge of spilling with tales of *we loved her, she loved us and the daylight can't take back what is ours.*

What was the lesson, Iyere wondered?

Was it to seize second chances no matter the cost, or was it that your life simply had to be lived, tragedies and all, to make it complete?

Iyere, you're just dreaming, she told herself again.

But what if I'm not?

"Would I remember any of this?" Iyere asked. "I mean, if I made a choice, how would it work? And would I know what I had done?"

Essy just stared at her, her gaze implacable, and so Iyere took a deep breath, and decided.

(After he's treated an estuary according to his technique, infusing the substance of the bank with powders and liquids, chucking them out of the back of his old tug to the derision or disgust of the more swish local river-users, when the tide goes out and the mudline is revealed it spells out words in a line of sloppy script. That soon shuts up his neighbours. But there's more. Those revealed letters stretch and slur as gravity tugs the silt, of course, but they don't simply become shapeless runoff. Instead, they morph from one word to another, to a third, sometimes to a fourth before they finally give up any semblance of legibility and surrender into muck. Kids play among them like mudlarks in Victorian times, looking for treasures, and the words crawl away from their feet. They always seem random. *Gibbon*, might say the waterline, changing to *spur*, then *irenic* as the river thins to a creek.)

IN THE BLINK OF A LIGHT
Amira Salah-Ahmed

The woman on stage twists and turns her body in ways he's only dreamed about, letting her limbs take control of the exaggerated movements and contorting her figure along with her clothes.

How is she doing this, Hassan thinks. *How is she allowing herself to show her body moving in this way?*

This is a public event. Cameras are everywhere. Mobile phones in every hand, snapping pictures and broadcasting live for the world to see. And here is this woman, her suggestive movements, on full display.

The stage is built in the center of the audience. They are seated all around her, allowing them a complete view of her entire body.

He would find it less scandalous if she was on a proper stage—at least then her back would be facing the wall.

But here, there is nowhere to hide.

What is most troubling: she is not actually interested in hiding anything. She is doing the opposite—putting herself on full display; the performer and the performance of this one-woman play.

He is more concerned with all the men seated in a circle all around this woman, enjoying a full view of her backside as it moves to the left and to the right, then rolls to the floor before springing up in the air.

What must they all be thinking? How can she show them this?

When she twirls wildly to face the other side, he has to look away in disdain.

There he sits, in the background, manning a light mixer that is pushed to the corner of the room. He is as far out of sight as the space will allow. Had it been humanly possible to stuff him and his equipment into the wall itself, that is where he would be sitting now.

His dark leather jacket protects him from the winter chill, but the shivers are still uncontrollable. A scruffy beard and mustache somewhat mask his face as wisps of his black hair fall gently on his forehead. It is as if the clothes and his facial hair were always meant to shroud whatever was visibly human and male in him.

But nothing can hide his eyes. His unadulterated disgust is unmissable, and that is how he means it to be. Almost as if to say, *I am here, doing this job, but I do not approve of this message.*

He forces his face into a more solemn sulk whenever the performer moves in him any profound sentiment. There are moments when he can relate to her palpable vulnerability as she shakes to the sound of bullets blaring from the speakers. When she arches forward and backward and lets out a visible yet soundless cry for help. When her shadow moves violently against the white sheets hung on the walls behind the audience, juxtaposed with the projected images of families fleeing terror in the desert.

In these moments, Hassan forces an even more visible expression of disgust to hide the feeling of wanting to touch her. Not in a sexual way, but with comforting strokes to ease the mountains of pain she was expressing. He could feel it through the floods of lights; the sound poetry choreographed with her silently shattering movements.

Regardless of how the performance is affecting Hassan, he

will not condone this kind of behavior, or the impression it will leave on all of these young people watching and leering. *How did their parents let them come to this? Do they even know where their children are?*

A jab on his right side shakes Hassan out of his jumbled thoughts. Omar nudges him as violently as possible, trying to snap him out of whatever daydream he has the luxury to indulge in.

"Dim the lights, Hassan," Omar hisses. "You missed your cue. Just the yellow lights now. Quickly!"

This happens at every event and Omar is sick of it.

This time he is seriously considering telling their manager. This cannot go on. Hassan is always distracted by the girls at the parties, or the female performers, or the bride's friends at weddings, running around and shaking their hips in short dresses.

He was wrong to get Hassan a job at the sound and light company he's been with for 10 years now. He always knew it was a bad idea, but his mother had pestered him for months to find Hassan a job. Their mothers were close friends and had lived in the same building since they were both young newlyweds. They got pregnant in the same month and gave birth two weeks apart. Omar was just two weeks older than Hassan, but was forever carrying his load.

Had this been anyone else, Omar would immediately tell their manager that Hassan is more preoccupied with the guests at these events than he is with the job. And the job is to control the labyrinth of light equipment and wires and nodes and knobs: making them brighter or dimmer, flicker or sparkle, according to the music or the performance, while Omar makes sure the maze of sound speakers and microphones and audio files worked—on cue and without delay. Then they pack up and take all the equipment back to the office.

It is a subtle art. Its subtlety is not in the actual management of all of these elements: it is doing so while remaining completely invisible. While blending into the background and not making eye contact with any of the guests at these events—especially the women.

After so long in the business, Omar has grown accustomed to the way these women act, the way they dress, the makeup they wear, and—most importantly—the way they move, all of which grow bolder with the passing of each year. The girls get younger. Their dresses get shorter. They balance on towering heels, cocktails in hand, shaking and jumping up and down for everyone to see.

Over time, the rules he had been raised to believe in gave way bit by bit, until he reached this place—where he knows better than to view these scenes with a critical eye. Sometimes he worries that his views are becoming more liberal, an empty word he cannot put a solid frame around or fully understand, but keeps hearing from television presenters on talk shows warning viewers of a changing society.

At one point—he has trouble remembering when—Omar decided it was more comfortable to not give these things much thought. He still finds these women attractive, of course, and has intimate daydreams featuring a few of the ones he sees all around town, but he knows better by now than to humor these thoughts with anything more than a passing smile.

Omar smiles at Ranwa—and she smiles back. She is already tipsy at that point in the night and takes advantage of his smile to put her drink on the table next to his mixer, even though she knows that is not allowed. Hassan growls at her then and was about to tell her to move the tall glass with ice, lemon and a little drink still left over, away from all the wires. But Omar glares at him and if Hassan knows anything, it is when to shut up around Omar. It is part of this weird relationship they have:

Hassan always feels like he owes Omar something and Omar always likes carrying that hefty sense of power.

Omar thinks Ranwa winks at him before she swings around to dance to the next song that came on. It was that subtle sense of deal-making that transverses gender and class and social structures. Omar has grown accustomed to it, but it was exactly that kind of invisible negotiation that Hassan will never grasp.

Omar knows her name from people shouting it over the music all the time. She's popular enough that everyone who walks into these parties has to say hello, in the most exaggerated fashion possible, as if she was hosting them in her own home.

She comes to parties like it was her job, but he knew it wasn't. He always checks the pictures from these parties on Instagram and eventually he found her profile. He knows she's in advertising and drives one of those fancy cars. He knows where she goes for breakfast the morning after every weekend party, and he knows her best friend's favorite ice cream flavor because they go to the same gelato shop in the fancy part of town every Wednesday night.

Although their exchange lasts less than two seconds, it helps get Omar through another dreary week. He knows he would see Ranwa at next Friday's party. She is as much a fixture at these events as he is, for different reasons and playing a different role, but it is the one context in which they both fit comfortably, and that gives him a kind of mental and physical energy that nothing in his real normal life ever does.

Omar will never admit this to anyone, but he once waited around the gelato store for hours, until Ranwa and her friend showed up. He knows this was a dangerous desire to accommodate, but he swore he would do it just this once. He needed to see what she was like on a normal day; outside of that dark room, where he always made sure the strobe lights danced around her as she moved.

He walked right past her. She was laughing and speaking to her friend in her signature, animated way. She looked right into his eyes, and straight through him. Without missing a beat, she carried on with her story, and her gestures, and the flipping of her straightened hair that was colored to look like caramel glazed marble. It was as if they'd never seen each other before.

Omar was not the least bit slighted. He'd gotten what he came for, a brief glimpse into Ranwa's real life: outside of the club where she so carefully acted her part, and outside of her meticulously crafted profile page. He was under no irrational pretense that she would communicate with him in this world, it was too out of context. This was not the space they could both inhabit and interact. But he also knew that next Friday, at around 2:30 am, when she could barely balance on her heels and she needed to put her drink down somewhere, Ranwa would come to his invisible corner and playfully put her glass down next to his mixer. Maybe she would even wink at him again.

Hassan relaxes now that the play is over, but Omar shoves wires into bags and pushes the equipment around angrily as they pack up to leave.

"Hey, relax Omar, it's not the end of the world. So we missed one light switch cue, no one even noticed. Not even this woman, what's her name?" Hassan tries to remember the name of the performer, but he barely read the event flyer and genuinely does not care what her story is.

He is sick of Omar acting like an angry father every time someone makes a mistake. Who does he think he is, just because he got him one job?

It was like Omar to act like he's better than everyone around him and like he has everything figured out. He was especially antsy and frustrated at their gigs, and even more so when the gig was one of these socialite parties. It was as if he cared about these people and this whole society life more than he did about his real friends and family. He's even started dressing differently. The neighbors talk about him behind his back, so that his poor mother keeps having to make excuses for his behavior.

Omar stops rolling the cable and looks at Hassan. "It's not the end of the world right now, no. But keep messing up, keep making me look bad, and we'll both be out of a job."

Losing this job and having to do something trivial, like driving a taxi or working the kitchen in a restaurant like he did before, is traumatizing. Just the thought of it makes Omar's heart race. He couldn't afford to lose this job, for financial reasons obviously — he still has to take care of his mother and three younger siblings — but more so because it was difficult to build up trust with companies that worked these gigs. It has taken him years to do so. What would his life look like without having access to these weekly parties? Where else would he see Ranwa? Where else could she smile and wink at him?

Ranwa was not at the party last night, and she hasn't updated her profile in three days. He is worried; a tiny bit hurt, as if she'd stood him up. This morning he woke up, knowing they had to be at this gig and that another week was about to start, and he just couldn't bear it. He knows better than to think this way, but her absence has already spoiled his whole week and he just wants to fast forward to next Friday.

Omar is completely dependent on seeing her regularly. He yells at Hassan when he makes mistakes and jabs him as violently, always reminding him to remain invisible, to stare less, to stop scowling. But for Omar, it was different. Omar knows when to be the invisible light technician, and when he can be the guy standing by a table, where Ranwa can rest her drink.

He will never admit the fact that, over time, he hopes to blur the lines even more. It will take a lot of work, and that subtle negotiation he has learned over the years, but if there is any way to widen that grey space where both their lives meet, he was sure he'd find a way to make it happen.

Hassan takes advantage of Omar being lost in thought to pay him back for that violent poke in his side earlier. He elbows Omar, not so gently, and yells, "Get moving, Omar. We have to go home, and don't forget we need to pick up your mother's medicine."

Ranwa wakes up with a smashing headache on Friday. The night before took an awkward turn, and now she feels like she has to break up with her boyfriend of three months. He'd become a nice enough companion, but she could no longer stand having him hang around her all the time. She knows if she had genuine feelings for him then she wouldn't start every day feeling so distracted from him, and end every night in some kind of sugar-coated fight.

She'd love to stay in bed and binge on something, but it is Friday and that came with expectations all around. First from her family, then from her friends. The day was split into two equal parts with two different vibes and noise levels—although her mother could be quite loud when she needed to be.

She hears the banging on the door and knows it would only get louder if she stayed in bed.

"Breakfast is on the table and it's almost time for prayer. Your father is waiting," her mother yells.

Ranwa detangles herself from the layers of covers. It was always so much colder on the outskirts of Cairo than it was in the city. She hated having to move here and leave their home in the more central suburbs of the capital. But they flocked here years ago like the rest of the city's well-to-dos because, well, who knew what would become of the capital once the popular classes took over? Here, inside the walls of this gated community, with its fake grass and dog poop everywhere, everyone feigned an air of predictable safety. (Until, that is, one of their own is murdered in a posh villa, making it clear that the young, untrained security guards at the gates don't give a shit if the people inside live or die. Or, less tragic, but equally unsettling, when the unexpected winter rains came and the neighborhood flooded, displaying the poor infrastructure and drowning out the millions of pounds poured into the persistent urban sprawl.)

"Ranwa!"

She goes downstairs, kisses her parents kindly on their cheeks, and sits down to their ritualistic Friday breakfast. After, she joins her mother while her father goes to prayer. It is their weekly chance to catch up and she adores it, although she would never let it show.

She actually wishes she could stay in the rest of the day—enjoy the quiet and her family. But her phone starts beeping in preparation for another night out. Her mother notices, as she always does.

"Will you be out late again today?"

"It only feels late to you, Mom, because you stay in the whole night. It wouldn't feel late if you went out and came home like normal people," she snaps back.

"I'm not sure 4 am feels late, darling, it's actually the next day." Her mother always says something to the same effect, and so it has lost all meaning.

By early evening she was choosing an outfit and thinking of the conversation she needs to have with Assem, to let him know this will be their last weekend as a couple.

The weather is cold, but the club would get hot after a bit of dancing, plus she had this new dress that she needed to wear and post about before the party. It is short, a little shorter than she usually wore and much shorter than her parents would like. But, as she would tell them, "It only feels short to you because you don't see what the other girls wear now."

She stuffs herself in the tight blue dress and snaps strappy heels on over stockings that barely protect from a light breeze. She's already texted Assem to turn the heater on in the car before he picked her up, so it would be warm when she got in. She is a planner.

Before they leave, Assem comes inside to take some pictures. It takes more than 30 tries before he got the right one of her casually climbing down the stairs. She thinks how much of a hassle it would be to teach her next boyfriend all the little tricks.

Omar scrolls through his Instagram frantically. He has been following her long enough to know that she'd post something about what she's wearing on her way to the party. That is, if she is coming this week.

He has to be at the club early to set up all equipment and make sure it is working. Hassan was slowing him down this morning, and he was anxious enough as it was, so he left earlier than usual and took the whole metro ride alone.

Omar had been there for an endless number of hours, long before the team of organizers and artists and musicians transformed this plain square room into a legitimate party venue; a place to be envied by everyone who couldn't get past the kids handling the guest list at the door.

Eventually, she pops up on his feed, and he takes a deep breath. She is on her way.

Omar has no plan except to see her, even for a moment. His mind plays out scenarios where she had to acknowledge, briefly, his existence. He needs this reassurance. He needs her to tell him, as subtly as she has to, that they both exist in the same space. That he exists at all.

Three hours pass and the club starts filling up. He knows that she'd be allowed in, no matter how late she arrives, or how packed the party becomes. Her being there is a validation for the event and the venue. And it will be a validation for him.

The room swirls around her when she walks in. Hugs and kisses fly all around her as she floats through the crowd. Ranwa takes her drink from Assem's reliable hands, and starts sipping, dancing on her high heels to the thumping, repetitive electronic beats.

Tonight, Omar doesn't make himself look away. He even bobs his head along to the music with the rest of the crowd. They don't notice anyway, and he easily ignores Hassan's judgmental glares.

The crowd gets louder and drunker, matching the vibe of the music as it speeds up.

Omar can see Ranwa dancing, and bickering with Assem at the same time. She is obviously annoyed, but keeps a showy smile on her face. She turns around and catches Omar's eye; he tries to keep from blinking.

She makes her way out of Assem's grasp and teeters across the dance floor to his station. He has kept the right side of the table clear, in anticipation of one of her empty drinks, but he notices that this one isn't empty yet.

She smiles as she gets closer to his table, and begins the silent negotiation. Ranwa stands next to him, and, without saying a word, she puts her glass on his table. He gives her a slight nod, it is all he could manage. His throat is so dry he considered taking a sip from her drink but knows that would never fly. He wants to at least ask, "are you ok?", "do you need help?", but nothing comes out.

Ranwa preoccupies herself, getting her lipstick and small mirror out of her tiny bag. She needs a break, but she can't be seen standing at the corner of the room doing nothing, talking to no one. As she reapplies her plum lipstick, Omar can see Assem tracing her out of the crowd and heading towards her.

"Why are you just standing here?" he asks loud enough to be heard over the music.

"Nothing, I'll be right over."

"No, don't be weird. Get your drink and let's go back."

"Assem, I *said* I'd be right there. Just give me a second."

In less than a breath of time, Assem puts his right arm around her waist. With his left hand, already juggling his own drink, he tries to grab her glass from the table. He fails, and one slips, crashing down on Omar's lighting mixer.

In one clouded moment, Omar can hear Hassan shouting as he scrambles to get the lights working again. He can see Ranwa looking back at him as she makes her way through the crowd, offering only a meek smile as she goes. He can see Assem kissing her neck, as she puts her arm around his waist and begins dancing again.

Their boss didn't give second chances when it came to botched equipment. There were strict rules, and, as he had so often reminded Hassan, they were there for a reason. Don't make eye contact. Don't allow liquids around the equipment. Don't ever be distracted by the women at these parties.

Omar could see himself driving a taxi for the foreseeable future, but, worst of all, he knew that this was the last time he was going to see her.

THE DENTAL GIG
S. L. Grey

Sometimes, when Frankie's jamming in a three-hour nap between jobs in the laundry room, she senses her children watching her. They appear in the blackout blindness of whatever time it is and stare at her as if she's a strange exhibit that might bite. When she feels them there, Frankie gropes at the periphery of her slumber, trying to haul herself up and awake, trying to shake the heaviness off herself, and speak to them. But, always, she slips back down and must only content herself with dreams, flickering between the golden leaves in balmy autumn breezes. The only time Frankie's body is really awake is when she's working, far away from everyone and anything she loves.

Tonight, entry itself is straightforward. It's warm for an October night and the house is old, so there are several standard ways to get in. The fumes of whiskey and garlicky kebabs wafting on the sawing snore coming from the adult's room put Frankie at ease. But she should know by now that this job's not made for ease. She can hear Barry Spades' voice dripping in her head: *Relax on your own bloody time, not mine.*

But Sadie 53 Wharf Street has such soft curls and such snuggly PJs—they're synthetic fleece with blue and white strawberries and unicorns—that Frankie lingers a little too long, just touching her fingertip to the antidepressant silkiness for a moment or two before drawing her breath and starting the extraction.

Anyone else but Glitterwings would chide her to get a move on. As per usual he's darting around, nosing around in the human's belongings instead of keeping guard.

Frankie checks the job card again. Despatch hasn't filled the parent/guardian/carer checkboxes so she doesn't know if the kebab-eater in the next room is the only adult in the house, but she's pretty confident. According to the card, Sadie 53 Wharf Street is the only donating child registered here and there's definitely no sign of a sleepover, so it should be fine.

For some reason, she's feeling drifty tonight, when she's always taken this work seriously. Her retrievals and conversions are always in the top five per cent of the division and she's never had a complaint lodged against her. She treats this job like it's hers, as if she *takes ownership of the company's results*; she should be proud of herself—that's what Amber from HR said to her when she passed on the 'Star of the Month' certificate some time last year. That's why they teamed her up with Glitterwings, who's long been dangling on his last warning.

The certificate didn't come with a raise; it came with a supermarket gift voucher and an extra shift. She blew the voucher on chocolate and stickers for the kids and, for herself, a bar of orange-scented soap that wouldn't turn to sludge after her first shower.

Proud? Yeah, she is. She prides herself on doing something well if she does it at all, and that's why she can't really understand why she's procrastinating here by Sadie's pillowside. Maybe she's coming down with something.

Glitterwings swoops close to Frankie's face and whispers, "Do you want me to do it?" It's a half-hearted offer. She's always the one who does the heavy lifting.

Frankie shakes her head to snap herself out of it, waving Glitterwings away before his buzzing wakes the girl.

The carer/parent/guardian, or maybe Sadie herself, has

wedged the tooth so far under the pillow that Frankie needs to burrow in and scratch around for it. There's no special tooth box or jewellery case, just a bundled-up old tissue. Just as Frankie burrows all the way towards the bundle, Sadie moans and turns, flopping her head with a heavy whack right over the parcel. Now, the way Sadie's lying, her head is pressing through the thin pillow and right over the tissue-ball and Frankie can't budge it. She pulls at the edge of the paper, but its corner rips away. Damn it: *disruption of original packaging*, that's an instant five debit points. But still she takes care: *destruction* will get you twenty. *Detection* will get you a formal warning at the very least. Pressed onto her back and worming through the musky crevasse, Frankie squeezes herself out the back of the pillow and casts a gentle levitation spell.

The girl's head floats barely perceptibly above the pillow, and Frankie is able to duck back under, unbundle the tissue, switch in the coin, bag the tooth and get out, all in a well-practised second. This is the single second that makes every extraction worthwhile, despite the drudgery and corporate mortification that surrounds it; it makes Frankie's heart beat a little; it's fun. Frankie's fug has cleared, and she's ready to get onto the next job. Glitterwings has other ideas. He's now investigating a naked blonde doll lying at the foot of the bed. He drapes a strand of the doll's hair over the top of his head and pouts. "Whaddya think? Or am I better as a redhead?"

Despite herself, Frankie laughs. It feels good. She hasn't laughed for ages.

Something changes in Glitterwings' demeanour, and before she can stop him, he darts at her and clicks off her TeenyGoPro. Her first instinct is to snap at him and turn it back on—a disabled cam will set off an administrative enquiry at the very least—but then she realises he's done the same to his own, the status light on his body camera fading to nothing. And he's staring at something over her shoulder.

She turns.

An old human's in the doorway, cutting a gnarled silhouette into the jaundiced light seeping from the passageway outside Sadie's bedroom and blocking the exit. *Oh, shit.* This is why Glitterwings made them go dark; Frankie's stomach plummets.

Sadie groans and shifts. The three other souls in the room freeze and wait for her to settle again.

"I've been waiting for you," the woman says. "Knew you'd pitch up."

Glitterwings flashes out before the woman. "Yeah? And?" It's false bravado. He's as shaken as she is. Being detected by a human is one thing, but talking to one is taboo.

The woman's been bracing her hand against the doorjamb, and now she slides it down to her side and shoves it into the pocket of her grubby dressing down. Her knobbled fingers come back out, balled into a loose fist. "Knew you'd come. Soon as I heard Sadie's first tooth was wiggling. Haven't seen your type for donkey's years; haven't had a kid around for that long and I guessed you'd come an' prey on her. Your type never give it up, right?"

Frankie appalls herself with a flush of pride. *Yes, you're right, ma'am. We don't give it up. We do our job, and we do it well.* The knee-jerk response of a five-star zero-hours wage-slave.

She can still hear the soft grumble of Kebab Breath's snores down the hall and she checked the other rooms when she came in, as per protocol. Where has this woman come from?

Glitterwings reads her mind. "Do you live here?" he asks the woman.

She chuckles. "Nah. Live over the road, innit. Arbour House. Residential care they call it, but it's more like sodding Wormwood Scrubs. Been watching for you. Been waiting. Know where Sadie's folks keep the spare key, thought I'd take a chance."

"Why?"

"Wanted to see if things have changed, or if your sort still practised the old ways. Used to be we'd scratch each other's backs. Back in the day. Back when I could scratch, that is." The woman raises her knobbled fist to Glitterwings' average location and opens her hand. Glitterwings gasps and Frankie hurries over from where she's been hovering by the little girl's head and stares into the wrinkled palm. Six bright inverse-cavity-shaped nuggets of gold. The woman performs something like a smile, gradually revealing snaggled and purpled gums. "Your type would always come around pick-pick-picking wherever there was pain and misery. We cut a deal back in the day. So how about it? Old times' sake."

Frankie always assumed the rumours about the black-market tooth trade were old elves' tales. The kind of thing that went on before the regulations, before the industry was regulated. Before DRRC was even founded.

Glitterwings touches his TeenyGoPro toggle to make sure it's off. "What do you want for them?"

Frankie is appalled. "Glitterwings… no."

"You tell me. Golds are hard to come by these days, innit? A dying breed, we are." The woman pauses to laugh and the cackle turns to a crackle and a wheezing cough. She pants it out, aware now of Sadie turning and muttering, disturbed, in the bed. She takes four steps backwards into the passageway, and Frankie and Glitterwings follow. "I was thinking maybe a hundred? Could get much more down the pawn shop, but they've stopped the outings and my corns give me murder these days."

Glitterwings folds his wings and does a showy little free fall, his version of a double-take. He gets back to her eye-level and snorts out a laugh. "Sorry, love. We're only carrying fifteen quid for the fifteen extractions on the cards tonight."

Our customer service operatives do not carry cash—the slogan pops ridiculously into Frankie's head.

The woman turns to Frankie. "What about you, pet? Just a little pin money, that's all I need. Something for the mushy biscuit fund. I can get more. I know where."

Frankie shudders. "Glitterwings, come on. We're going."

He's wavering, still transfixed by the woman's haul.

She raises her voice, risking waking the child. "We're going *now*."

He nods.

"Ere," the woman whispers after them as they zoot past her. "Always wondered... What do you do with them teeth anyway?"

Neither Glitterwings nor Frankie answers.

The rest of the night's extractions are, for the most part, unremarkable, and through them all, Frankie carries the image of that old woman's gap-jawed leer in her mind. Over the course of the night, the crone's darkening gums begin to bleed in Frankie's imagination, the remaining dental outcrops in that ravaged landscape get sharper, yellower. The gold nuggets in her withered grip become weightier, glint brighter, drawing in impossible light and bouncing it back. And shadowing this is the fear. The terror of being disciplined. Glitterwings says he'll tell them the cams malfunctioned; but if they see through that lie, her perfect record will be marred. And it'll be worse for him. He's on his last warning.

Around four in the morning, the two fairies fly back to the Dental Repurposing and Reclamation Company's Incoming Processing Block, take a number—there are seventeen teams ahead of them—and perch on the cracked vinyl of the faux-tree-branch seat-set in the waiting area among the scattering of exhausted shift-jobbers eager to get home or anxious to make their next gig.

Frankie passes her eyes over the assembled workers' faces: patient, contented, humiliated, frustrated; some even laughing, some with their heads buried in their hands, some asleep; the younger ones showing off with loud stories and acrobatic manoeuvres. "Not what most people would expect from a mood-lit hall full of fairies," she comments. The trepidation is making her weary; now she just wants it to be over.

"Yeah," Glitterwings says, disturbed from whatever he's thinking. "They think it's all sequins and absinthe, Kirlian glow, belly buttons and diaphanous wings."

"What am I going to do?" Frankie says.

Glitterwings gives her a look. "I get it. If you want to come clean, I'll take the rap. Tell 'em the truth. That I wasn't doing my job. Let my eye stray off the ball, tried to cover it up."

It's too late for that. She should've reported it immediately.

A constant swirl of movement marks the paths between the entrance and the waiting area, the check-in desks and the exit as workers log their take and move out. In a ceilingless, carpet-tiled limbo like this, there's no reason to linger.

Despite the queue, processing is pretty quick—the check-in desks are staffed with a team of well-drilled agents logging job cards, checking in body cams, and inventorying the new stock. When their number's called, Frankie places the job cards and the pouches of tiny teeth on desk number three while Glitterwings slides the bodycams across, not wasting his breath on a greeting.

But Frankie always does. "Hi, Angelique. How are you this morning? Had a good shift?" It's Frankie's tendency to private rituals like this, her fundamental belief that social form matters, that makes her such a fine operative. Will Angelique see the guilt and fear on her face?

It seems not. Angelique frowns, presses her finger on the printout she's consulting to mark her place, glances up at Frankie as if she's an inopportune figment of her imagination and, with a microscopic tic around the chin, turns back to cross-checking her list against the quality guide on the screen and the teeth in front of her. On her desktop is a list of the transactions she's handled tonight; she's filled lines to just past halfway. Frankie's seen Angelique's portrait behind one of the laminate frames in the staff tearoom, though—she's probably onto her second page.

As the desk-fairy settles back to concentrating on the log, and while Glitterwings clenches and unclenches his jaw, slumped on the perch beside her, Frankie cranes around the desk partition to see if she can get a glimpse into the inner workings of the building. Once labelled, the pouches of teeth are sorted and sent off down a conveyor behind the check-in desks and into the yonder. Once or twice, Frankie's seen a flicker of movement as the flap of the conveyor gate is lifted, or as something bigger gets hitched in the workings. She swears she's seen the flurry of indentured elves who don't often stray beyond the processing block. On occasion she's overheard a few of the administrative staff joking about the lack of "elf and safety".

The old woman's question comes back to her. When she started at DRRC, Frankie used to try to engage with the other collection fairies in the waiting room, find out if anyone else knew where all these teeth were going; she used to air her fantastic theories—vampires' castles, genetic experiments, an army of zombie clones, a cure for cancer, carbon-neutral spacecraft insulation, Flammarion Hurst's next exhibition—but she eventually gave up. None of the other shift workers wanted to discuss it; they only collected their pay packets from the bursar's window at the end of every week, not caring what machine they're a cog in. She chooses to believe that whatever it is, the teeth are used for good. That's what she tells her children, anyway.

The seconds tick by. Angelique's pencil scratches. Everything seems to be proceeding in the same way as it does every morning. She allows herself to relax, believe that they've got away with it.

It's only when they're halfway out the door that Angelique's laconic voice says behind them, "Wait. There's an inconsistency with your cameras. You'll need to report to Anomalies."

* * *

"It'll be fine. Trust me." Glitterwings is trying to spark a little light around the bleak space, but his spell casts less light than the low-wattage bulb in the beige-shaded lamp on the bare table in front of them. Behind them, around them, only shadows, and in them Frankie can imagine in terrifying detail the outlines of all the rumours she's heard; she can swear she hears the stifled echoes of past inquisitions gasping out of the darkness.

Frankie and Glitterwings have been waiting for the Discrepancies, Discipline and Anomalies committee for twenty minutes now. Frankie's heard of The Cell, but had thought it was only rumour. They've been made to sit in straight-backed chairs in an unnatural, human-like position, their thighs and backs cramping and their wings forced painfully against the wooden planks of the backrests. The only thing shoring back the flood of panic is her exhaustion.

It's rare that she craves a drink. She could almost pretend this gloomy room is some annex of the Keg and Glitter, where Glitterwings often goes after a shift. Sitting alone on a weekday morning, when most fairies are asleep or doing something more gainful than sitting in a bar.

"Don't worry," Glitterwings says. "Despite what they'd have us believe, we have some special skills. Burglary's an art form. Robots can't replace us just yet. They'll just apply some ritual humiliation and move on."

"You should know, right." Frankie snuffles a forlorn half-smile to herself. Glitterwings has the patchiest disciplinary record of any operative she knows. But even he's held back from out-and-out insubordination. That was something Glitterwings was always banging on about: that the hierarchy doesn't stop just with the Corporation. All things are connected. Being marked as a dissident at the workplace would brand you in the wider world too. You have to keep your head down and your opinions to yourself.

* * *

"We'd like to hear your opinion," says the second Discipline fairy, a baggy-faced male wearing a nametag reading *Moshpit Krill, Tier 2 Disciplinarian.* "We're giving you an opportunity to state your side of events. As we can see it, the evidence is entirely clear-cut, but we'd like to hear your side of the matter."

The disciplinary committee consists of three fairies, grey-suited uncomfortably like people on human TV, and an unctuous, bored face watching on video link.

"Who's that?" Glitterwings points at the screen. "Is that... is that *him*?"

"As you know," the third Discipline fairy enunciates in a crisp voice officious enough for the smarm to be received clearly enough through the CCTV at Head Office or in his yacht or wherever Spades is currently sitting. 'Mr Spades is the boss of this hub, and he likes to be involved in any and all operational matters. And he has every entitlement to..." The fairy is distracted by an impatient movement on the screen and loses her train.

Discipline Fairy One pipes up, "In fact, it's because of the director's hands-on involvement that the company continually achieves such—"

"Time is money," Barry Spades blares from the screen. "Get on with it."

When the committee fairies came into the room, they offered a lukewarm apology for keeping them waiting and turned on the top striplights. Instead of her funky and virulent imaginings, there was nothing to greet Frankie in the floodlit Cell but scrape marks on the eggshell walls and a window to some inner HR sanctum venetianed with dusty blinds and the video screen bracketed to a cabinet with a dust-encrusted vaseful of sticks next to it. Now Frankie flickers her eyes around the space, desperate to find something to distract her from the Discipline fairies' joy-drained faces.

"Miss Bell, we're surprised at you," says Moshpit Krill. He scans across a printout of Frankie's numbers. "We could accept that this is some sort of mix-up if you explain it to us," he says, but not kindly. "Our records imply that the monitoring devices were turned off deliberately. Do you still contend that this was... accidental?"

Frankie's a bad actor and a worse liar. What's stopping her from coming clean? She owes Glitterwings nothing.

Instead, she hears herself say: "There was a fly in the room." This is her first wilful disobedience in her professional life. She's made mistakes before, sure; fallen foul of some regulation or other while on the learning curve, but deliberately breaking an important rule... it's shaken something in her. It doesn't fit with her picture of herself. Her simple, deliberate choice means that either she or the rule is wrong—that either she or the rule is immoral; there seems to be some inescapable and fundamental meaning here, but she just can't put her finger on it. "It was bothering us, and putting us off our work. We were swatting at it and must have accidentally hit the switch."

"Switches," Glitterwings adds.

Krill purses his lips. He taps the page in front of him with the top of his pencil, glances at his colleagues and nods.

"As for you, Mr"—he makes a show of rereading the name listed on Glitterwings' employment record—"Heisenberg. This is your"—he pages through the file again—"umpteenth infraction of company rules and policy, and we've been lenient in the past. However, given that compliance is a core value of DRRC's model, which we protect with the utmost integrity, we can no longer afford the liability your lack of performance presents to the company."

Frankie pushes forward on her chair and puts her arm out towards Glitterwings, as if to protect him from a crash. She's opening her mouth already, as if something too big, too weighty, is already pushing its way out of her abdomen.

The five fairies turn in unison to the screen, where Barry Spades' face looms closer to the camera, the autofocus working overtime to parse the grease-shine. When the picture's settled,

Frankie sees that Barry Spades has a beautiful smile: a full set of Da Vinci veneers and several gold cosmetic dentures. "Can them," he announces.

"No!" Glitterwings says, grappling away from Frankie's hold. "No... it's was me. I did it. I'll take the blame. Frankie did nothing! That's not fair. That's a load of spitshine."

But Frankie's not listening; she's weightless, and the rest of her life is filling the space beyond that TV screen.

"You sure you don't want to come?" Glitterwings asks Frankie. "Drown our sorrows before we find some new ones?" He's suggested they go for a commiseratory down at the Keg and Glitter, but it isn't six o'clock yet and Frankie might be able to see the children off if she hurries. She'll have a whole lot more time with the children now.

"I'm sure," she says.

He hesitates. "Do you hate me?"

"Hate you?" She does have reason to hate him. None of this would have happened if he hadn't been lax on the job. But he didn't make her lie to the committee. "I don't hate you."

"I'm sorry. Truly. You were right. We should've told the truth. But listen, don't worry. We're made for better things, you and me." With a sardonic salute, he zips away.

Better things. It's a hearty notion, but they both know there are no better things. There's nowhere else to be, nothing else she can do. Maybe she should become a bandit, live a life of crime in the underworld or go flitting out into the hinterland, making a living scratching sustenance together with short cons and wing jobs. Out there on the rural forecourts and in the mangy motels, at least she'd see the sky, a field of crops bowing to the sun out back, real dust between her toes. It wouldn't be so bad, would it? This vision of pastoral freedom doesn't gel with the reality of the kids and their school lunches and their self-defence lessons, their theme-day costumes and their enshrined play-date rota, of never knowing where you'd be able to nest from day to day.

The anger comes then. An unfamiliar emotion—a human emotion. It's just so unfair. She hits her targets every time. She's a good employee. Exemplary. That should count for something. They even implemented the suggestions she made to HR about using drowsy spells on the Ritalin kids. She never got the credit for that, and she didn't care at the time; she considered it part of her duty.

She'd like to clamp down that smug, entitled face and pull out every one of those gold crowns and precious porcelain veneers just like the old woman on Wharf Street does. She'd make Barry Spades squirm and whine like the most pants-pissing of her donors.

She buzzes back to Angelique's desk, pushing to the front of the queue, ignoring the irritated whines from the worker bees around her. "I need to talk to Spades."

Angelique looks up from her paperwork and gives her an eloquent *what the fuck?* look.

"Did you hear me? I said I need to talk to Spades."

"In your dreams, girl."

"Nightmare, more like," the worker in the booth next to her mutters.

"I need to talk to him *now*." Frankie thumps a clenched fist on the desk. The room falls silent.

Angelique sits back and eyes her. It's the first time, Frankie realises, that the bureaucrat has given her any real attention. "Listen, chickadee. Even if Spades would deign to let you into his exalted presence, he's not even in the bleeding country. Never is. Specially now they've got all that trouble in the States."

"What trouble?"

"Tooth mouse union rebelling again." She turns to her neighbour. "What was it they're after this time?"

"More danger pay," the woman yawns. "Cats, innit."

Frankie can't give up that easily. "He was on the screen in the room. Can you call him?"

"Can't help you, soz."

Frankie reaches for the name of one of the Discipline fairies. "What about Krill? Moshpit Krill? Where can I find him?"

"Forget it."

"There must be someone I can talk to about this."

"Not in this life."

So much for her revenge fantasies; life doesn't work that way. The weight of her utter powerlessness finally deflates Frankie, and she turns and charts a slumping course towards the door.

Angelique watches for a moment, then sighs and pushes off her perch. "Taking a vape break," she says, disappearing into the void behind her cubicle.

Aware that scores of eyes are still fixed on her, Frankie drifts away. Would she be able to find her way back to the warren of offices that led to the Cell? She doubts it.

"Oy."

Angelique is over by an 'Administrators Only' door, gesturing for her to follow. She glances to make sure no one is watching, then taps in a door code and ushers Frankie into a dark corridor that's putrid with the scent of menthol-scented vape fumes. Angelique points to a metal door at the far end which is covered with hazard stickers.

"More than likely you'll find Krill having a cheeky fag in dispatch. Saw him head that way just before you accosted me. You'll want to get your skates on, though."

"Thank you." Frankie starts to scoot away, then turns back. "Why are you helping me? Is it because I always remember your name?"

Angelique almost chokes on her vaporiser. "Ha, no. Was gonna ask you to hook me up with that fairy you're teamed with."

"Glitterwings?"

"Yeah." She pokes her tongue between her teeth. "He's lush."

"I can't do that."

"He partnered up?"

Frankie gives her a rueful smile. "No. He's not into"—she sweeps her hands up and down her body—"our sort."

"Don't tell me… Elf-fucker, am I right?"

"Yes."

Angelique sighs. "Typical. Always the hot ones. Now move it, love. Krill won't be there for long."

The second Frankie is through the metal door, her ears are assailed with the bellow and hiss of pistons humping, and a crunching sound that sets her wings on edge. Scores of sweaty elves are shovelling teeth into panniers, and moulded steel fists are grinding down on them, crushing them into powder. The sound of teeth being splintered sends a primal shudder into her wing bases. The scuttling elves pay her no heed.

Covering her ears, she zips past them and into a cavernous space where more elves in respirator masks and white overalls are scooping powder into small plastic bags. They machine-wrap the bags in thick plastic and stick on a label in English and Chinese letters. She pauses to read one:

MANLY LOVE POTION. CONTAINS GENUINE JUVENILE DENTINE FOR SUPER LENGTH AND SUPER STRENGTH. (works for ladies too.)

This—*this* is what it's all for? The proud lies she's told her children. "We're doing important work," she's told them. "We're part of something good." The mortifying pride she's felt all this time. Her eyes water and she has to gasp to get her lungs to start again.

Now she pushes herself through the next room, where the bags are being packaged into cardboard boxes, finally reaching the gleam of pallid morning light sneaking in through a half-open dispatch door at the far end. It's here that she finds Moshpit Krill hovering above a stack of boxes, puffing on a cigarette and staring into space. She fizzes towards him, passing a number of sacks bundled with money, notes almost as big as her and smelling of concentrated faeces.

She has to fly right past his eye-line before he notices her. He jumps, goes to stash his cigarette, then relaxes as he clocks she's no-one important. "Not supposed to be here. Factory's out of bounds for collectors."

"I need to talk to you."

"Then put in a request. I'm busy." He squints at her. "Wait … don't I know you?"

"Seriously? Are you really asking me that? You just watched me get fired."

"Oh yeah." He's lost his veneer of professional coldness. Now he just looks bored.

"Look, I need your help. I need this job. I've got mouths to feed. I can't lose it. I just can't."

"Shouldn't have broken the rules then, should you?"

"It wasn't my fault. Please, I'm begging you. Please, can't you speak to someone, explain that—"

"No can do. I don't make the rules."

There's nothing behind his eyes. He's as soulless as Spades. She glances at the boxes, and this brings on a fresh wave of anger at the pointlessness of it all. To think that all her sweat, blood and tears, her professional pride was for this: to make humans longer and stronger and more loveable.

"I could tell them," she says. "I could tell the parents/guardians/carers what you're doing with their teeth." She flickers over one of the bags of money. "I'm sure they'd like to know how much profit you're making off them."

"A whistleblower, huh?"

"Yes." She's trembling now: Anger, fear, and exhilaration.

He shrugs, lights another cigarette from the butt of the last. "Go for it. Less of a fuck I could not give." He's tired, she realises. As exhausted as she is. "Sorry you got the boot and all that, but there's nothing I can do about it. I'm nothing more than a cog in the wheel, just like you."

"I'm not a cog."

He snorts. "Yeah. Forgot. Not anymore you're not."

*   *   *

It couldn't be more obvious that the trainee, a fey male of around her age named Kylie, doesn't have the stomach for it. Some don't. Glitterwings didn't either, which surprised Frankie when she first suggested the idea to him. She has no idea where he is these days. Angelique says she heard he'd joined one of those fairy circle cults, but Frankie can't—or won't—believe that of him.

She gives Kylie an encouraging, if somewhat rote, smile. "We all feel like this at first. It helps if you remember the donor won't be needing them again." Old Mr Truffaut from the dementia ward will be lucky to see out the week.

"It's just… it just seems so *unnatural*," Kylie complains.

Frankie should be more patient; she was exactly like this not so long ago, but soon the nurses will start their rounds—and besides, she's in a hurry to get home. The OLED screen the kids have been demanding is arriving this morning and she wants to make sure it's installed correctly.

Kylie shudders. "And it really won't hurt him?"

"He won't feel a thing." Mr Truffaut is living out his last days on a morphine marshmallow cloud. His mouth's even slumped so far open, she doesn't even need to help the trainee jack it open.

Kylie steels himself, then tentatively pokes the forceps at the yellowed enamel.

It all turned out well in the end, Frankie considers as she watches the first tooth's easy slide out of the old man's molars. Judith from Arbour House showed her a whole new world, and their partnership had taught Frankie so much. Judith was a real mentor, showing her the layout and security weak spots of several care homes, where the medication was kept and what you could do with it; and, crucially, introducing her to her black-market contacts before she shuffled off. So now, Frankie's an entrepreneur, in charge of her own business with a sideline in gold and a main income stream derived from undercutting top-heavy companies like DRRC with senile dentine that is so much easier to procure than juvenile, and which is indistinguishable to her clients—they both do the same amount of nothing for their flaccid libidos. Another plus: there's no messing around hiding pound coins under pillows. Her uncluttered business model has been a key part of her growth, so it was a tough decision to start employing contractors. But there are so many mouths waiting and only one of her. The trainees, on the whole, have been fine, but it's getting repetitive having to justify herself to every neophyte who approaches her looking for a job. And there've been a lot of those lately, what with DRRC downsizing.

The third molar's halfway out, and Kylie starts to get the shakes, the forceps clattering across the enamel as he loses his nerve. Frankie plucks the tool from his hand. "It's not that hard. Look." He swallows as she fixes the forceps in place and engages their spikes and with a practised flick of the wrist, she twists, pulling back at just the right moment to ensure the tooth comes out whole—she hates wastage. Kylie blanches at the sight of the blood as Frankie snips the nerves from the root, stems the blood welling in the donor's jaw with padding, and drops the tooth into the bag. Tonight's crop will make a good ounce of powder, if the new crusher can be trusted not to skim any of it.

"You make it look easy," ashen-faced Kylie says.

Frankie wipes the blood from the clamp and gathers her things together. "Listen, this gig isn't for everyone. Are you sure you're cut out for it?"

Kylie sighs. "I got four kids, lady. I'll do what I need to do."

Frankie shrugs. "All right," she says. "But you know the terms, right? If you sign up with me, you're your own boss, remember?"

"Yeah." He manages a weak smile. "I remember."

Frankie doesn't know what the lad's looking so sour about

as she leaves him at the front vent. As far as she can see, it's a dream job: he'll be working as much or as little as he likes. No bureaucracy, no disciplinary hearings, no endless fear of hours being cut. No TeenyGoPro cams. He'll take ownership of the work, and if he can't, it's his problem—his *challenge*, let's rather say—if he can't make ends meet. Sure, her team has to give her a share of the profits, but that's only fair—it's her intellectual capital they're profiting from. Really, she thinks, as she buzzes out into the early morning light, it's a win-win for everyone. The vocational model of the future.

ONE GRAM
Leah Moore

It was past five by the time she got into the shower. The last of the daylight caught in the steam on the window. As the scalding water unknotted her muscles, Bette noticed again the bruises on her bicep. They were fading a bit now, spreading out amongst her tattoos. She turned so the water hit her chest, closing her eyes and feeling for the other bruises, the ones on her side and on her arse. Pressing them to see if they hurt still. They did.

She frowned.

It was twenty to six by the time she was dressed, skinny black jeans dragged up damp legs, small black work T-shirt and boots. She had worn the same outfit, or a minute variation of it, every shift for the last two and a half years. She did not wear makeup, just lip balm against the cold air. She didn't style her hair, just brushed it and left it to dry by itself.

She sat next to an old woman on the bus. There were no empty seats. Several of them had men sat on their own, but they were engrossed, in music or a book. The men all had their bags next to them, their feet in the aisle, their arms along the back of their seat. Two of them looked her up and down.

There was a crush when the bus got to her stop. As she let herself move with the flow of the crowd toward the doors, she felt hands on her, squeezing her arse, or was it rubbing against her? Turning only her head, the faces around her were blank. No clue to the culprit. Earbuds gave out tinny beats. A man chewed gum. A man played a game on his phone, one arm holding it an inch or so from his face. As they were released onto the pavement, the crowd spilled off in all directions, urgent and definite.

Bette watched them all walk away, and she frowned. She felt spots of rain on her cheek.

The girl was about to close when Bette got to the shop, and then it took her a while to find the right packet in the baskets on the shelves.

While she waited, Bette tried to work out how many jars there were in there, or how many little drawers. She lost count twice and then gave up. She could see some with pods and seeds and dried fruits or berries in them, some with gnarly, twig-like roots, some with regular slices of something like ginger or mooli, and some with whole leaves of varying shapes and sizes. There were boxes with beautiful script on them. Some helpfully displayed pictures of animals on them, but she didn't know if those stood for the contents or just the brand. There were baskets on the floor too, below the shelving, with dried and cured things. She could see something that might be a really big mushroom. Or it might, she thought, be an ear.

The woman returned.

"Fu Zi was it?"

"Uh, yes. I was told that's what I needed."

"Do you have stomach problems? This is very good for restoring your Yang. Have you had chills, or rheumatoid pains?"

"Sometimes, yes. At work."

The woman pushed a red paper bag across the counter with CHINAHERBAL in gold letters on it. The label read 'Fu

Zi—Monkshood—Wolf's Bane—Dog's Bane—Old Woman's Hood—Tiger's Bane—Radix Lateralis Aconiti'

"Take one gram with breakfast, one with your evening meal. You may take one if you cannot sleep, but do not exceed four grams in a day. Drink with wine for a nicer taste."

Bette took it. The woman smiled.

"You will feel so much better. You will notice straight away."

Paying cash, Bette tucked the bag into the inside pocket of her leather jacket, thanked the woman and turned her collar up. It was raining in earnest now.

The Hare and Hounds had been a rural coaching inn, until the city grew and swallowed the village. The beams across the ceiling lent it a fading country charm, but the new Elephant's Breath paint spoke of gentrification, and money. For years it had been filled with factory workers and students, thirsty and noisy; happy to swap pennies for pints and pork snacks. Now it attracted city boys and hipsters, minor celebs from the media monolith down the street; commuters having one last pint to miss the crowds.

It was, despite renovation, still most notable for its original front window. The central panel was circular, and showed a hare, in silhouette, chasing a pack of baying hounds over a hill against a huge full yellow moon. Local history scholars said the hounds would have been chasing the hare originally, but that the restorer must have changed it when hare coursing was made illegal. Either that or nobody noticed. Whichever it was, the brewery had put it on everything.

Bette pushed the door open and a wall of sound assailed her. A TV above her was showing financial news, and someone had put Coldplay on as well. The pub was busy already, and it wasn't yet seven. One of the booths had a stag party in it, with a dozen men taking it in turns to roast the red-faced groom. Snatches of their anecdotes drifted out into the rest of the bar, only to be drowned out by the gales of honking cheers which followed.

Bette slipped through the crowd, head down, turning to fit through the smallest of gaps. Still cold and damp from the night outside, she was enveloped in the smells of the drinkers. Musky cologne, sandalwood and leather, the metallic tang of stale beer, a sweet gust of bourbon as someone spoke. She pressed between the different smells of smokers and vapers; men drenched in aftershave, and men drinking alone, reading their papers. She saw eyes turn toward her, she saw winks and knowing looks. She felt hands on her waist as someone let her go by, she heard a conversation quieten, and then, as she passed them, erupt into laughter.

A fat, white-haired man rested his laptop on a shallow ledge, a wire leading down to a socket somewhere, a spreadsheet scrolling before him. He switched to a different document as she walked by, and she saw his desktop was a picture of Rihanna, lounging on the beach, sandy and sultry and forty years his junior.

A woman stood with a crowd of men in suits, holding a glass of white wine. The men talked loudly amongst themselves. The woman, who was not short, still seemed smaller than them. She held her glass close to her, and watched the man who was speaking. Sometimes she smiled thinly. Mostly she just watched. As Bette made her way to the end of the bar, the woman glanced up at her, and rolled her eyes. A minute gesture, over in a second. The woman once more watching her colleagues, smiling her thin smile. Bette hung her jacket in the pub's disabled toilet—and baby changing—safe behind an 'out of order' sign on it so old the sharpie was fading. It was also where they kept the vacuum cleaner and the marketing tat the brewery sent. She felt in her pocket for the red paper packet, but she left it there, for now.

* * *

"You're late."

Ben was the manager, three years younger than her, a lad with small eyes and choppy highlights pushed into somewhat of a quiff. He had flames tattooed around one wrist which he was going to elaborate on until it was a "full Japanese sleeve". He was just waiting to find the right place apparently.

Bette looked at the clock. "No, I'm not. It's only five to."

Ben's small eyes lit up.

"Ah! But what did I say at the last staff meeting? About *changeover*? I said that all staff should arrive fifteen minutes *before* their shift starts so that any information from the previous shift can be passed on before their shift begins. This is to stop the need for chat during a shift, and give our customers a more *focussed and efficient service brigade.*"

Bette looked into his small eyes.

"Yes. And I said I would if I got paid for it. And you said we wouldn't, as it wasn't part of our shift. And I said I won't do it. Because I'm not getting paid for it."

Ben's small eyes narrowed even more.

"Do I have to remind you of the terms of your contract which clearly state that you must make every effort to be present for all shifts allocated for you, and any extra hours as requested by your team leader? That time is for your colleague to pass on information about their shift, and for an *expedient changeover.*"

Bette held his gaze.

"Emma, who does Thursdays and Sundays, lives so far away that she would have to get the bus an hour before the usual one, just to get here fifteen minutes earlier. That means another hour of childcare to pay, and a wait when she arrives—just to be told the Peroni has run out and the pan in the gents is blocked up again. It's ridiculous. I won't do it."

Monkshood—for pressure in the workplace.

Ben's cheeks flushed a deep crimson, which somehow made him look even younger. He was about to reply when Bette saw a man at the bar, holding out a twenty, talking over his shoulder to his gang of mates at a table some way away.

Bette turned on her heel just as her manager seemed about to speak, and stood waiting for the man to turn around. When he did, he beamed and looked her up and down with appreciation.

"Well, aren't you a sight for sore eyes? Yes, you are very much indeed! Isn't that lovely!"

"What can I get you?" Bette asked, setting her jaw. *Dog's Bane and Wolf's Bane. She could see the red and gold packet in her mind's eye.*

"Ohohoho! Oh now, that's the question isn't it? What can you do for me? Indeed!"

"I'll give you more time to choose then," Bette said in an even tone. She turned away to the glasswasher, which had finished its thrumming. The boiling steam made her flinch as she lifted out a heavy basket of pint glasses, and carried them back to the bar. *Monkshood, Wolf's Bane, Old Woman's Hood.*

The man with the twenty was still watching her, but now Ben went to serve him instead.

"I'm sorry sir, what can I get you?"

"Don't worry son, I like a girl with spirit!" He smiled at Ben unpleasantly. Ben nodded, as if this was the most natural thing in the world and moved on to serve someone else.

Bette finished unloading the hot glasses and returned the basket to the end of the bar, only to find the man with the twenty still waiting for her. He ordered this time, but when she took the note, he tugged it just out of her reach. She had to wait and take it when he let her. Bette slammed the till drawer shut as loudly as she could, and put his change on the bar in a puddle of beer. *Tiger's Bane, Dog's Bane. Old Woman's Hood to restore my Yang, and take away my pains.*

Jay arrived at eight. He started later than the others because he had training. Jay was good at football apparently. He had been at The Academy when he was a kid, and now he was training for the real deal. Jay was getting Ben tickets to one of the big games of the season.

Jay was, Bette knew, not a footballer at all, but a habitual liar who supplemented his wages by selling various controlled substances in the smoking area outside the front of the pub. Bette had no concrete proof, but Jay's rounds of the pub definitely had more to them than collecting used glassware, and he was on very friendly terms with the twitchiest members of their clientele. Bette didn't care about the dealing, except she was sure that Ben paid Jay from seven and not eight. She was equally sure that if the till ever came out light, Ben would blame her and not Goldenballs.

Bette let Jay serve a gang of rowdy blokes, who got him to sing with them before they would order. Ben was in the back doing a stock-take, so she went out to collect glasses and wipe down tables. She stacked up the pint pots until they were taller than her. As she reached up to put a last glass on the top, the man in front of her reached out and squeezed her breast. He leered at her, and then laughed; a cloud of foul breath in her face.

Bette brought the pint glass back down, and tightened her fingers around it, at face height. Her eyes staring into his. Her mouth a straight line. She frowned.

"Watch it Shagger, she'll bloody glass you!"

The group erupted into complete hysterics and they banged their pints on the table and bellowed incoherently. "SHAG*GER*! SHAG*GER*! FIGHT FIGHT *FIGHT*!" their eyes sparkled, they clashed their pints together; they licked their lips.

'Shagger' laughed too, but he took a step away from Bette. As she turned, she heard him speak very quietly.

"Fucking Dyke Bitch."

She felt her ears redden as she walked back to the bar. She quietly dismantled the tower of pint pots into the empty basket. *Fu Zi. One gram to be eaten with dinner, to relieve your stress at work.*

It was nearly nine before there was any kind of a lull. Bette tidied up. Jay had left his area in disarray, and was showing Ben a clip on his phone at the other end of the bar. Bette cleared bottles, she gathered glasses, she wiped down, she tipped the drip trays into the wastage bucket, she emptied the bin. She refilled the crisps, noticed that two optics were empty, and then pushed the big wheeled recycling tub into the back room.

She went to the disabled toilet for a piss, and, as she sat there, she could smell the mop bucket, the box of urinal cakes, the stale dust of the hoover. Her foot slipped slightly on a pile of leaflets which were damp from being next to the toilet. 'BOOK NOW FOR YOUR WORK'S CHRISTMAS PARTY!'. They had the hare chasing the hounds across the full moon, but had left off the hill, so they were more like flying reindeer. The hare's ears and legs were long, and the hounds' tails were curled under as they ran away.

She reached the red packet down from her leather jacket. She opened it. There was a fine brown powder with a faint earthy smell. It was very dull to look at. The label was only marginally more interesting.

Wolf's Bane. Tiger's Bane. For stomach complaints and rheumatoid aches. How much is a gram? I bet Jay would know.

Bette could hear the hubbub in the bar outside and thought of Shagger and his mates. She thought about the man with the twenty. She thought about whoever squeezed her bum on the bus. She pressed her bruises again. They still hurt.

She had been grabbed by a customer in the smoking area at the front, just the week before. He had pushed her against the back of the shelter, away from the road, and kissed her, pinning her against the wall with his knee and his hands, and pushing his tongue into her mouth. She had struggled, but he was stronger than she was. His thumbs had dug into her arms. She could see past his ear, to where three men sat drinking. One had looked over with only mild interest. He had stared her in the eye for a moment, and then continued his conversation. Bette had been saved by the arrival of Jay, who was ostensibly also on the hunt for empties, but was quite probably distributing Spice instead. The man had jumped back, and let go of Bette, then, laughing as he did it.

"Just a bit of fun mate! You know how it is!" Jay had looked at Bette, and then back at the man. He had nodded, and picked up some glasses. Bette had run to the disabled toilet and been violently sick. She had told Ben she had a vomiting bug and got the bus home. She had called in sick the next day too, and spent the day in bed. Ben texted her that he would have to let her go if she missed any more shifts, as per her contract which allowed only two sick days per year. So she went back to work.

Jay wouldn't meet her eye. She hadn't seen the man who kissed her since, but the man who saw it happen had been in every day. When he ordered his drinks, he always stared directly at her breasts. He didn't look away when she spoke to him, only when she put the drink down on the bar.

She put the red packet down the side of her bra, where the curve of the padding covered the bulge.

When she came out, the pub was heaving, Jay and Ben were both serving, and Ben shot her a glare as she arrived behind the bar.

Bette's attention was dependent on which of the customers were acting like pricks, which meant she swerved the stag party at the far left completely. They were honking and hooting incoherently, shouting the words 'Fanny Batter' over and over again at the poor stag, who looked as if he might vomit. She could understand why.

Instead she served three hipsters. Two had topknots, one had a tattoo on his chest, and the third had a moustache which must surely have been attached to his nose along with his tortoiseshell glasses. One of them refused to look her in the eye at all and addressed a point above her head, one stared at her breasts the entire time, and the other waited until she bent to get his Microbrewed 6.8%ABV Liquorice and Beetroot Stout out of the fridge, and then stared at her arse. None of them gave her a tip.

She served two salesmen in shiny suits, with spray tans and estuary accents, who called her Darlin' every third word. She served the woman she had seen before, who ordered a white wine spritzer, and said to keep the change. The stag party hadn't noticed that they weren't getting served as they had moved on to looking on their phones to find a strip club nearby. One of them was shouting they should just get Ubers but their debate was hampered by being shitfaced.

She collected the empties from the bar in front of her, and herded them towards the glass washer. It had two full baskets by it, and a basket of steaming clean glasses wedged precariously to one side. Jay was still serving at the other end and she couldn't see Ben. She served the last few waiting, and was picking up the basket of hot glasses, when someone spoke loudly behind her.

"Fucking disgrace in here... I told you we should've gone to the Cock and Trumpet. The service is so much faster in the Cock."

She turned to see a man in his sixties, piercing blue eyes, grey hair swept back and a Harley Davidson leather jacket which was left open—he clearly could not zip it around his gut. He was staring right back at her and smiled a sarcastic, clearly practised smile, all teeth and cold dead eyes.

"I'm so sorry *darling*, I was joking of course! How *appalling* of me, No? I beg your *pardon*."

The last phrase was accompanied with a flourish of one arm and a small bow.

Bette unpacked the hot glasses onto the shelves, carefully. She put the basket down before turning back to the man. *A gram with breakfast. No more than four per day.*

"What can I get you?"

His eyes drilled into hers. All his fake bonhomie was gone, and she could see her deliberate delay had been noted.

"I will have two bottles of a decent Pinot Grigio. Something around twenty quid, not that shit you give the *cattle*, and three balloons of cognac."

"How many glasses do you need for the wine?" Bette did not smile.

He turned and gave Bette a view of the people stood behind him. She could see three young men and two young women. They all seemed slightly nervous, their eyes fixed on the dead-eyed man buying their drinks. Their cheeks were flushed, all smiling and on the verge of giggles. Clearly, they were impressed to be with this man, whoever he was.

"What shall I tell her? That the whole lot's for *me*?" his voice was hammy again, a pantomime for their benefit. Maybe he was an actor of some kind. She had seen Nigel Havers once, and she had served one of the blokes from Holby City last month, but he rang no bells at all. They all roared with laughter.

She put six glasses with the bottles and the three cognacs. He paid on his card. *Michael R Langford*. She had never heard of him. Maybe he was a director then, or a playwright? She placed the EPOS handset on the bar. The prompt on the screen asked if he wished to add a gratuity. He didn't. Michael R Langford whipped his card out as soon as it completed.

They took themselves away to a booth where the men let Michael R Langford sit at the back of the booth. The girls sat either side of him, and then the men filled the banquette to either side. She could see him making great show of pouring the wine, tasting it, and pretending to vomit a little. Gales of laughter all round.

It was after midnight by the time Bette was able to stop again. Three hours of serving at the bar, of faces trying to catch her attention, of changing barrels, of carrying crates and collecting glasses. The till was groaning with money, and Jay had been given a fifty-pound tip by one of the stag party. Bette thought either they'd put an extra zero on the end and then been too embarrassed to say so, or he was giving them more than pints for their money.

Ben had left half an hour ago, as he was going on a Tinder date and needed to get the bus. He had left Jay the keys to lock up as Jay was there first in the morning. This left Jay and Bette to serve, clear and clean down, put up chairs, and get rid of the punters. It was a Wednesday, only the very determined were left.

Michael R Langford was still in his booth, as were the girls and two of the young men. The Hare and Hounds stayed open until one, even on weekdays, so they had over half an hour of drinking still to enjoy. They all looked drunk now, the girls especially. Michael R Langford was tipping the last drops of the fourth bottle on the table into a glass and stared at it petulantly, the sulky child routine grotesque on his craggy old face. As Bette passed with her cleaning gear, he looked up and shouted.

"A little service if you please, miss! A little service for me and my fine young companions! We must strike while the iron in their blood is hot! Make hay while the sun shines in their eyes! What did Sam Beckett say? 'They give birth astride of a grave, the light gleams an instant, then it's night once more', let us not rob these sweet young children of that glimmer of *light*!"

The group all gasped and cheered, and he bowed and accepted the cheers as if the whole pub were applauding. Bette set down her cleaning stuff and went to the table.

"What can I get you?"

He stopped then, at her tone. He looked up at her with his icy blue eyes, suddenly serious if not wholly sober.

"I should like another cognac, but let's have something *festive* for my young friends. Fancy things. Cocktails maybe? Can you make them something *special*?"

Bette nodded and collected their empties. As she walked to the bar, she saw the man who had been in so many times. He sat on a high stool at a ledge, on his own. He was watching her. His drink was half full, but he didn't touch it.

Bette shivered, and looked away, down at the glasses she carried.

She noticed that two of the glasses were unlike like the others. Two of the wine glasses had something grainy at the bottom, chalky and white, a fine sediment. She checked the others, but they were clear. No trace on the sides, just the smears of their fingers. The two glasses with the white powder in had visible smears of lipstick at the top. One bronze, the other more of a peach colour.

Bette paused and turned to look back at the table, the two girls were laughing, their eyes very twinkly. Michael R Langford was smiling first at one and then the other, one of the young men was on his way to the toilet, the other seemed to be nodding off at the table.

She put the empties down, and looked at the bottles on the back of the bar. What was in those glasses? Maybe the girls had put something in there themselves? Something procured from Jay during a smoke break?

She knew it wasn't. She knew from the way Michael R Langford had been looking at them.

Bette took a deep breath, and frowned.

She put sugar around the top of four fancy glasses and added ginger ale and cranberry juice with an ounce of fresh orange. She then mimed adding vodka from the empty Smirnoff optic and put them on a tray with four of the 'BOOK NOW FOR YOUR WORK'S CHRISTMAS PARTY!' leaflets, the Hare chasing and leaping across the top of each of them.

Bette reached down a brandy balloon. She lifted the cognac bottle and made a great show of trying to get the stopper out, using her apron for grip. Then she took it and the bottle into the back room, where she unstopped the bottle with ease and poured a generous measure.

Reaching into her bra, Bette took out the CHINAHERBAL

packet, and opened it. The powder was very fine.

She thought about the two glasses with lipstick on, with the white powder in the bottom. She frowned.

She had two friends who had been date raped, one in Magaluf, and one a couple of months ago right here, in the city, on a normal night out. Neither of them went out now. One of them, she knew, was on antidepressants.

Bette took a deep breath and let it out slowly.

She took a teaspoon from the draining board, filled it with the brown powder, and tipped it into the brandy glass. Was that more than a gram? She thought so. Quite a lot more. Either way, It was gone before she began to stir it in. She added another. Sniffing the glass, all she could smell was the cognac.

She was putting the packet back into her bra when Jay walked in. She jumped and pulled her T-shirt down, sweat prickling her forehead.

"I was trying to get the Remy open. I had to use a cloth." She felt herself go pale.

Jay looked at her clammy face, her hands which shook as she shut the cognac, and then at her breasts. He was thinking.

She moved to pass him, but he stopped her with his arm, and leaned in close.

"I know what you're up to in here"

Bette swallowed. Her throat suddenly dry.

"You do?"

He looked down at her breasts meaningfully and grinned.

"Don't worry. It'll be our little secret."

Bette frowned.

"Uh... *okay.*"

Jay winked at her.

"Do it in the bog. It's more *discreet*, and if you're after... anything *else*, then just shout."

Bette breathed out.

"Um, yeah. Will do."

He was turning to go when she had a thought.

"Jay, this is a weird question, but how much is a gram, what does a gram *look* like? Sorry... I'm not explaining myself well am I?"

He grinned and reached into his top pocket. He pulled out a small plastic baggie, about a third full.

"That. Anything less is a rip off."

A couple wanted serving, but Jay said they'd missed last orders. Bette brought the cognac to the tray, and then the tray to the booth. How long had she taken? Maybe eight minutes? Ten?

Michael R Langford looked up, beaming and red faced now. In his absolute element. "Ah, there she is! Nancy to my Sykes!"

She placed the four cocktails down on the table, both the young men had left. The two girls accepted theirs and drank them thirstily. He paid cash this time, and told her to keep the change. As she walked back to the bar, she heard him speaking to the girls. He urged them to drink the lads' drinks too. After all, he had paid for them! It would be a waste, would it not?

Bette put the money in the till, and the tip in her glass. She went back to her cleaning stuff and began to wipe the tables. As she made her way around the room, she glanced at the booth. Michael R Langford downed his cognac in one, with a theatrical wince at the strength of it, and the three of them then struggled comedically to get out of the booth. Eventually, they were all standing, and he flung an arm around each of them.

"Hold me, girls! Hold me! For I am but an old man! Take pity won't you, on this decrepit fool!" They laughed, and helped him weave his way to the door. She saw him make a show of waving for a cab, and then they were gone, the three of them, into the night.

The only person left was the staring man. He still hadn't finished his pint. As she approached him to tell him to drink up, he shot away into the gents. When she finished putting all the chairs up, he was still in the gents.

She looked over at the bar, but Jay must've been in the office, putting the cash in the safe. She took the man's glass to the bar and left it there. She counted out the pints in the wastage bucket, changed the empty optics, and got the last load out of the glass washer. She put the drip trays in to wash and cleaned the ice machine. She looked over at the door to the gents. It was still closed. She would have to ask Jay to go and get him.

She thought about his expression when he watched the other man kissing her.

She thought about his face as he stared down at her breasts.

She thought about him waiting for her to finish her shift.

She looked at the undrunk half pint on the bar.

She pressed her bruises. They still hurt.

When Jay came down from the office, she had her jacket on. She was counting her tips on the end of the bar, enough for a taxi home, maybe even chips.

"Good night?" he asked, nodding down at the change.

"Yeah, not bad." She put it into her pocket. "Actually, Jay, there's a guy in the gents, I don't fancy going in myself to get him out. He's not pissed, he nursed his pint all night." She nodded at the glass on the bar.

"Yeah, no worries. Old josser! He's probably asleep. There's always one!"

Jay put on his coat and took the keys off the hook, turning the lights off behind the bar.

"You go, I'll take him his pint. See if that tempts him out."

Bette smiled. "Thanks. I will. And thanks, you know, for the *other thing*."

Jay was heading to the gents. "No worries," he called back over his shoulder.

Bette stepped out into the night.

It had stopped raining now, but the wind whistled around her neck and ears and whispered that *it knew what she had done*.

Bette saw a bus climbing the hill toward her, and ran to her stop to get on. She could be home in half an hour, she might get chips on the way.

Sitting down, she put her hands in her jacket pockets. She could feel the red packet in her bra. *Dog's Bane, Tiger's Bane, Old Woman's Hood, Monkshood. Good for what ails you, good for the stresses of work, for restoring your Yang, for digestive complaints, for chills, for nausea.*

As the bus went under the railway bridge, Bette thought she could see a figure, slumped in the shadows. Was it? Or just a trick of the light? Too late, too late. The bus thundered on.

Bette took a deep breath. She let it out slowly, and then she smiled.

('What is it?'

'It's a beetle.'

'Jesus Christ, keep it the fuck away from me. Where's it from?'

'It was hatched or whatever. I don't know. It's a beetle.'

'I mean where did you get it? It's the size of my hand!'

'—'

'Oh my god it's moving! It's alive! Look at its shell!'

'—'

'Why won't you say anything? Look at it!'

'I've seen it.'

'But what is that on it? Did you do that? How?'

'—'

'They're *moving*.'

The oil-film sheen of the chitin is no colour to which she can give a name. Rainbowed and dark, split along a seam so fine that when the insect shuts its wing-case firmly, bringing two halves of a picture together, the line disappears. Like ghosts on a faulty television, figures move on the brittle back.

'That's me! Your fucking beetle's showing me me!'

'—'

'Make it stop! What's it doing?'

'Do you mean what are *you* doing? On the shell? Well, just look.'

'I am looking! I never did that!'

'You haven't done it yet.')

THIS PLACE OF THORNS
Marina Warner

An open thoroughfare once connected the cities of Syria to the countries that lay to the south; striking out across the desert from oasis to oasis, passing through Jericho and beyond. The road has seen the passage of many people and many goods, including precious myrrh, which Balthasar brought with him— he was the black king—as he followed the star. Myrrh, so rich, so fragrant, seeps from hard-bitten, barbed and scraggy thorn bushes, which need only stony barren soil; when you cut into the bark, it oozes a resin which is dull, sticky, and sickly yellow; but when sniffed, this flow is delicious and can be rubbed and warmed, suspended in oils or dried and burned to give out the sweetest scent, light and fresh as dew, gentle as a baby's skin, pure as fresh water, a perfume of rejuvenation and beauty, promising conquest over the ravages of time and the body's organic decay: a scent of paradise, myrrh! It's a cruel plant, and yet it's the true balm; its long, sharp needles repel all grazing animals with tender mouthparts, except for the very toughest billy goats. But its sap is a sweet remedy and solace; prepared as an unguent it can seal wounds and, inhaled in fumigations, it will clear sore lungs and heavy heads; it freshens stale linen and stuffy rooms; it transforms decaying flesh—ordinary mortal flesh; and it will preserve a mortal body for eternity.

It was the female Pharaoh Hatshepsut who, a millennium

before the star drew the three kings down that westward desert road to search for the prophesied saviour, pioneered the idea of transplanting the myrrh-bearing trees from Gilead and Jericho, and set about shipping them westwards to Egypt. She foresaw the riches the sweet-smelling gluey stuff would reap for her treasury and so, in the equally parched soil on the outskirts of Heliopolis, she made "the garden where the true balsam grows". You can see it marked on old maps of Cairo and is still there to this day, a little neglected but a sanctuary still: legend has it that Mariam—the Virgin Mary—her husband Joseph, and the baby stopped there on their flight from the massacre ordered by Herod.

It was a time of new massacres that brought Nour and her grandmother Zubayda to follow the same road that unfurls across the desert winding towards the Red Sea, where they were hoping to embark so they could sail north and make their way further... to another world and another time.

Nour was eleven years old, and her grandmother, Zubayda, was about fifty, but the long war had taken its toll on her; they were the only survivors they knew of from their large household and the whole apartment block in which they lived; the men were all long gone away to fight or disappeared into the torture basements of the regime—and they had endured together the long siege of their town and its systematic bombing and destruction. The latest onslaught of government forces swept them up along with a few straggling fugitives, old and very young only, and finally drove them out of their city. After many days' march south—a drifting, erratic progress at night when they could escape the sun's fist—they reached a meagre encampment. It had grown up against the double fence of high razor wire defending a border which had not been there before. Of necessity, they came to a halt and there they found others, who had reached it before them, called it the Place of Thorns, because thorns were the only thing that grew. The only other living things were lizards with frilled jowls like prehistoric dragons, some species of small, shiny metallic snakes, and precision-tooled birds of prey, which planed above on the look-out for the reptiles. There, Nour and Zubayda joined more women and children, living in shallow caves in the rocky sand, which they had tried to hollow more deeply using sticks of the thorn bushes. The new, heavily fortified border rose above them, glinting, spiked. Were it not so ferocious and menacing, it might have been tinsel, so gaily did its brand-new coils sparkle in the unremitting sunshine. This new border unspooled to the horizon on both sides, cutting a wide, empty swathe over the undulating, dry body of the desert, a scar twelve metres wide, running from the port in the north to the rose-red cliffs of sand in the high desert of Upper Egypt in the south. It prevented all access to the Gulf of Suez, and any attempt to cross.

They could not move on, nor could they retreat and turn north or south. They were checked to a standstill, like so many hundreds of others who had found themselves up against the new armoured border. It had carved out a place of no-one, a Terra Nullius which nobody could enter, or traverse, not unless they had serious matériel—hydraulic cutters, heavy caterpillar tanks, ironclad jeeps, bomber planes, or drones—to flatten it from the air.

The scar marked a place of unwelcome, where no man or woman or child lives or can claim ownership, a neutral place, unattributed, unmastered, an interzone between two armies facing each other, a cleft between. Untended, unattended, *terrain vague*, as the French call such wastelands. We see these spaces on the map, sometimes narrow, sometimes wider, a gap between two lines inscribed onto desert, meadow, mountains, streets, buildings: occasionally a gap that is not quite an alley has been left between two houses which have not been terraced but remain detached; this gap then acquires this dishevelled, orphan look. Sometimes such a border will slice right through the middle of a house or apartment block, bisecting it, as was threatened when the two mothers fought over a baby and asked Solomon to judge their claims. A place that was once a home can be left stranded on two sides of a border with a gap, a nothing, in-between. Passages and holes, leaving a tailor's offcuts of territory, which, if you patched and pieced these plots one next to the other for a coat of many colours, would hang loose on a colossus, and provide enough land for a planetary moon where all those who have nowhere to stay and call their own could make a home. Or would that be an exile, to be in orbit elsewhere far from this world?

In the past, before Schengen, I remember how we used to walk through these nowheres; at Ventimiglia between France and Italy, for example, and it used to be a strange and exciting feeling, as one left one border post behind with its national guards and stepped into the perimeter that did not belong to anyone and met the different country's policemen or soldiers and took stock of the way they handled themselves (did they twitch for their pistols, did they lounge about smoking? Why did they take so long to scrutinise the photo in one's passport? Once I was with a friend who was ordered to shave off his beard to match his passport picture, but it was still touch and go). What about the cut of their uniforms (the bulk of their boots, the white of their spats, the swirl of their cock feathers)? And since those holiday times, we have seen so many undone by war and plague and famine, so many making their way across bridges, across frontiers, moving from one place where others belong, to another place where different others belong.

The unbelonging on the move in the spaces of nowhere.

Terra nullius—the land of nobody—began as a place to be shunned: the waste ground under the walls of a fortress, the fosse where the shameful dead lay exposed to carrion birds and animals (Antigone wanted to stop this happening to her brother Polynices). It was a place of execution, a killing field. It still is: the makeshift camp in the place of thorns where the fleeing huddled down into the sand to hide from aeroplanes flying low and drones hovering over the strip watching for attempts to cross it; they were hiding in the earth like animals, shrinking from rumours of armies on the move using the territory between the fences as a fast patrol road.

There was a time when it could seem amusing that antiquarian collectors in the United States paid good money for varieties of historic barbed wire, used in the staking out of property in the West, parcelling out the prairies to the new landowners, each one identifiable from his design of barb and hook, just as his herds were known to belong to him from the brand burned into their hide. But these curiosities of a particular connoisseurship now feel ominous when bales of silver razor wire unfurl for miles and miles to demarcate frontiers of the rich world, keeping out the poor, leaving between the high, thorny fences a wild forbidden territory. In no man's land you mustn't be seen or the official armies of one side or the other, or random snipers working for traffickers, or vigilantes working for their own purposes, will pick you off. You can tunnel your way through. Burrows are one place where you might survive. On the surface concealment is necessary.

Nour and Zubayda were given space in the scooped hollows in the sand which other arrivals had made for shelter. Young, anxious volunteers with NGOs and two officials from UNHCR roamed the settlement and promised the fugitives they would be moved somewhere with better facilities. But Zubayda told Alison Turner, one of the UNHCR representatives, that she, Zubayda Umm Tamim, Jaddati to Nour, her granddaughter, would never be moved. She would stay in the place of thorns, she declared, in this ragged shanty village which had grown up against the high, shining bales of barbed wire on the new border, because her son Tamim would be coming to fetch them both, herself and the little girl. He had promised to as soon as the fence came down.

She had an appointment with him and she was not going to risk missing it.

"But that is impossible," said Alison, the UN official, who wanted to be kind and understanding. "The camp here is in an extremely dangerous zone: there are snipers on the other side overlooking it. It has grown up without planning. There is no shelter. You are living like animals in the ground. It is insanitary. We are evacuating you all. As soon as we can provide proper facilities. We must for your own good."

She did not add that there was nobody left in the town they had left; that it was a heap of twisted iron and concrete rubble; that all who had survived the siege and the bombing and the carnage that ensued in the mopping-up operation when the attackers went in to take control of the ruins, all of those few survivors were scattered, some of them here, in this makeshift camp, where they had washed up against the high coils of wire of the new border fence. That if Zubayda's son Tamim were in combat—it was likely, given the allegiance of their town, that he was with the rebel forces—that his chances were… well, Alison Turner did not want to linger on the thought.

She remembered then that she had been walking by the sea one New Year's Day and found a solitary worker on the beach gathering the débris that winter storms had driven inland: a great shelf of kelp and dulse, pebbles and shells had been swept onto the once creamy sand, and in it, all higgledy-piggledy, was strewn the flotsam of summer holiday-makers and cruise-tourists—sun tan lotion, flip flop sandals, scores of plastic bottles and jerry cans and containers of every kind, the ruins of dinghies and outboard motors, torn scraps of anoraks, tarpaulins, sails, and carrier bags, bin liners, nappies, condoms, and other things more unmentionable; she recalled the resignation and despair in the workman's face as he trudged up and down the beach, trying to bring order. But a local council worker, however weary, wielding a pick and a broom and a rubbish cart could still comb the beaches and collect together all the stuff that the sea had brought; whereas, here in this place of thorns, the storm had driven real, living people, old women and children, whom the latest battles had swept up and stranded on the edge of the new, impassable no man's land. She, Alison, with her little bit of spoken Arabic, was trying to gather them together and take them somewhere else... dump them somewhere else—the thought barely surfaced, but she felt it prick her, like a spur on the cursed bushes you had to skirt so carefully or else get savaged.

When the refugees were so obdurate, like that Zubayda— she was about to think to herself, that old woman, but she probably wasn't much older than Alison herself—who, with her small granddaughter, refused to be moved, her well-meant work became so difficult. Force was the last thing she or her colleagues wanted to use, but in some cases, it became necessary—inevitable. The place of thorns was exposed in more ways than one, it was marooned, and it could not sustain life, nothing besides those sticky, smelly bushes that clung on, even taking root in the barren scar tissue where the tanks had flattened and fenced in no man's land.

The first day after what was to be the final, conclusive raid and the end of their town, before they were gathered up with the others and swept for days onwards, trudging by night towards the border, Zubayda was holding Nour in the crook of her body, as they lay deep in a ditch by the road, hiding from the drones as best they could, and she saw a man stepping through the stony field as if it were a summer meadow; there was green light haloing his strong, lean body and playing around his bare head; his soft curls, falling to his shoulders, seemed fronds rather than hair.

When he touched Zubayda on the arm, she felt a bolt of light come off him, live and quick and fresh, as if she were a fruit and he had plucked her at the perfect moment of ripeness. He smiled, while at the same time putting a finger to his lips to indicate that Zubayda should not stir or speak and wake the little girl, and then he leant in close to Zubayda's ear and said, his words passing through her as if he had struck a clear bell:

"When the fence falls, and as it shall, you'll see your son Tamim again. Don't forget. When the fence falls in the place of thorns."

Zubayda did not experience this apparition as an apparition, if an apparition is a delusion or a fantasy. The angel was a messenger from the future, and his springtime words brought her tenacious conviction and a luminous calm, such as turns the sea to pearly silk and sweet milky warmth after a cruel storm has torn it to pieces. She held the promise tightly in her heart, that Nour would find her father in the place of thorns and then, it would follow that they would together find her mother Amina again, and she would find her son again, when the fence came down. She did not know what the messenger meant by the fence or the place of thorns, but she remembered.

In the provisional underground shelter that was the camp, Nour would queue to fetch their quota of rice and container of water every day from the UNHCR delivery, and bring them to Zubayda, who joined the group around a fire made from the thorn bushes, which spat heady scented resin as it burned, to cook their rations.

Nour took note and began collecting the nubs of gum from the twigs and keeping them. At home, they had always burned incense, and she knew the resin could be tapped and crystallised, and that when it smouldered it spread potently, an indoor perfume, clean and fresh and lively as sweet water itself. Lacking a sharp knife to score the bark, Nour would bend the branches till they cracked open and released myrrh, drops of gum bubbling from the lesion in beads that gleamed, like crystals of unrefined sugar. The thorns are brutal to the hands of a child, even through the cloths Nour bound around them, and can inflict deep gashes. Still, she persevered.

Nour was only a child, eleven years old, but she had learned to forage through the two-year-long siege of her home city; she would spot seedlings invisible to others, and she soon began identifying which grasses and flowers growing in the cracks of the bombed buildings were edible; she would shield them from further damage by providing shade or surrounding them as far as she could with sharp stones to discourage some scavengers, and she would water them.

Ever since she was six years old, Nour's fingers and toes tingled at the proximity of water, and her nostrils quivered, and her eyes prickled when she was near the precious element, however deeply buried. In the place of thorns, her hands wound in her clothes, she would break off twigs of the thorn bushes to begin her search for underground water, and when she hit upon a damp area of sand in the back of one of the caves, she began scrabbling in the earth with the broken end of the twig. Moisture began welling up like a frog belching in little purling, winking chatter. When she called over some of the other children, Alison followed, curious. She marvelled, she had never seen anything like it. When Nour asked for help to capture the flow, and began to level a patch of ground in the shade of a rock and seed it with the tiniest particles, brought on the wind, the official did what she could to provide cans and pipes and even a spigot; the little girl brought in some of the women to nurse the puny shoots as they struggled in the shade near the aquifer she had found.

The promised evacuation plans of the community were taking a long time to materialise, and the days waiting in the warren of shelters under the sand were weary. Besides, the NGO workers were afraid, and becoming restless. Would the UN supplies continue to arrive? Or would they have to abandon the camp altogether?

Her Jaddati, her granny Zubayda was not well, however; the darkness in the underground shelter and the blaze outside in the dryness of the desert, where the breeze carried sand into every nook and cranny of her sore body, even if she kept herself wrapped against it, was scouring her eyes. She was crying a lot, too, wearing herself out, and sleeping badly. Nour did what she could—she bathed her granny's eyes in the new-found water and tried to swab her ears inside and out and soothe the creases between her limbs, sluicing off the irritant accumulations of sand. But day by day, Zubayda was growing weaker. She sat in the dark in the hollow in the sand, mute and unresponsive, even to Nour's offerings.

No news came of any change in the conflict, and the scar of No Man's Land remained impregnable and the old woman was wasting away, while the little girl was still busying about, almost happy with her patch of seedlings.

News of the aquifer, and of the nascent patch of new growth reached others who had been caught up in the turmoil and harried here and there in the desert; the place of thorns began to attract more and more people to the camp, which, as a result, and to the growing anxiety of the few remaining NGO personnel attempting to keep order, started developing features of a more permanent settlement—men started arriving, men without identifying badges or uniforms. But they brought with them bags of seed and took away Nour's small harvest of myrrh in exchange. A few of the women helped her clear more land and level and plant it in the area moistened by the underground spring which her dowsing had uncovered.

Then the men coming through bringing supplies warned of an imminent conflagration. A battle front was opening up along the new border. The night after they left, the few NGOS remaining came running: the time for evacuation had come. The camp was now in the heart of the conflict zone.

"Grab what you can nearest to you and come, now, hurry!" Newly arrived officials in white boiler suits began herding them into the lorries until each lorry was bursting: in the hubbub, the refugees did not cry out or shout, but boarded silently, the women holding on tight to the children they were looking after—their grandchildren or a neighbour's orphan. Nour was picked up by Alison and swept up into the sputtering vehicle. She called out, "But Jadatti! Zubayda!"

Zubayda was obdurate. She would not be leaving.

"I was told," she said. "When the fence falls, and as it shall, you'll see your son Tamim again. Don't forget. When the fence falls in the place of thorns."

At the last moment, as the lorry was grinding into motion, Nour hurled herself out of the vehicle on to the sand.

"Go, go! Now," Alison ordered the driver, her jaw set, her eyes burning.

Zubayda took Nour into her lap and she curled there; they drew back to the depths of the hollow in the rocks. The half-blind, withered grandmother stroked the child's hair and crooned to her. They began waiting; the sounds of the battle roared around them in flaming shafts of orange and gold and scarlet; the earth shook and heaved as the world exploded; flashes streaked across the night sky and lit up silver-white the rocks and the dunes as if the moon was bursting over and over again.

When the tumult subsided, Nour crept out of the burrow and looked around her: tinselly bales of barbed wire lay this way and that on the desert floor and she could see, where the high fences stretched on either side, they were buckled and hanging loose, swaying; craters yawned around their foundations. The long wide scar between them was scattered with debris—with indecipherable wreckage, pieces of uniform, maybe bodies, muddled up with jagged splinters of armour. It was quiet, the air sulphurous and hot. She went to fetch water, soaking her scarf in the puddle by the makeshift pipe and brought it to Zubayda to moisten her lips and wipe her face.

They heard the rumble of vehicles approaching and drew back into the darkness of the back of the shelter. More than one, many it sounded like. No other noises now; no gunfire, no explosions.

Nour slithered on her stomach to the mouth of their shelter and raised her head as far as she could.

"Jadatti, they are waving white flags…"

Then, as the jeeps came abreast of the camp, and the soldiers riding in them could see the remains of habitation, a cry rang out through a loud hailer:

"You have nothing to fear! Come out! We bring peace!"

Nour scrambled to her feet and waved her scarf.

One of the jeeps stopped, turned and drove through the broken bundles of barbed wire and into the fence, which fell at its approach like so much matchwood.

The driver drove up to Nour, his companion in the seat beside him still waving the white flag.

"Who else is here?" he asked. "Are you alone?"

"The others left, but Jaddati is here. Jaddati, come, they are not angry, they are not attacking us. They're smiling. Look!"

She pulled at Zubayda to come out into the light, and the old woman shielded her dimmed eyes as she sought the soldier's face.

"The fence is down, Jaddati! Look, the fence has fallen down!"

"Yes," said the soldier, pulling out some oranges from a bag his companion in arms held out to him. "Here… I expect you haven't seen one of these for a while! From Jericho."

"You are a liar," said Zubayda in cold fury.

"Who are you calling a liar?" said the soldier.

"No, Jadatti, he is telling the truth. I can see, the fence has fallen down!"

"It cannot be," Zubayda answered, searching out the little girl's face with her milky, lunar half-seeing eyes.

"But it is so!"

"It cannot be. I am Zubayda Umm Tamim, and I was shown in a dream—no, it was revealed to me by a visitation, a visitation from an angel of the spring clothed in a halo of green light, that when the fence came down in the Place of Thorns I would see my son Tamim again."

The soldier dropped to one knee and looked earnestly into the face of the little girl.

"And what are you called, my child?"

"Nour," she answered. "And my mother was Amina and my father Tamim, and this is my grandmother, Jaddati, Tamim's mother, Zubayda Umm Tamim."

Tamim whirled and caught up the child in his arms and then drew the old woman to her feet to hold her close so the three of them were one.

"Umm Zubayda, my name is Tamim, and you are as my mother would be, were she still living."

"But I am living." Zubayda's eyes moistened and the scouring of the sand softened and healed, and she was able to see that the fence had indeed fallen in the Place of Thorns.

Not long after, as Zubayda was being transported by military ambulance to the war-torn hospital in the nearest still functioning city, along with other survivors whom the victorious squadron had found straggling, battered and starving along the now mangled border, the emerald angel came once again in a glow of spring, and touched the dying woman with his fiery hand and called her to cross with him into his other world.

The soldier called Tamim looked after Nour as if she were his own; she grew up to become a perfumier in Cairo, and now works in a pharmacy; she lives in Matarieh, that part of the city near the ancient Garden of the True Balm and is hoping to be able to join with others to revive its verdure one day and restore its popularity with pilgrims and visitors. Like many others of her generation, she knows that her mother was lost in the final destruction of her family's home town. Tamim is still hard at work trying to consolidate the fragile peace that followed the battle in which his side came to be the victors, a battle which for a time opened the borders once again between peoples who in times past had been friends, and raised the hope of all that means in terms of exchanges of love, conversation, thought and produce, along the ancient roads of gold, frankincense and myrrh.

NOT JUST IVY
Celeste Baker

I step off the plane, not on my island, where I grew up, but on another island where the beaches are just as beautiful and the hotels are a lot cheaper, with a big grin on my face. I had worked hard to get all my body fat where I wanted it. I had searched for just the right bathing suit that wouldn't ride up or fall down in the water. I had practiced four easy to do hairstyles for my long locks. I was vacation ready. I was exhausted.

In the taxi the driver asks me if I need to go to the bathroom because I'm squirming so much, pushing hard on my own imaginary gas pedal.

"No," I tell him, "I'm okay, I'm just happy to be here. I'm only staying two nights."

Two nights. To rest without thinking in my sleep. Without having to be 'on', having to conform, cooperate, collude.

I sigh, pushing out recycled airplane air.

"It woulda been more—shoulda been more—but those people I work for, back in de States, they'll make my life more difficult if I don't come back on Monday to help, and by help dey mean come up wid all de ideas to advertise dis new drug."

My shoulders relax and I hear my Caribbean accent coming out, my speech pattern changing.

"Is something like LSD. You remember LSD from back in de day? Here dey come now wanting to sell dis new drug to people dat need to calm down, people dat want to escape reality. So dat's everybody, right? But even though I tink it's a bad idea, I going do it, of course."

Just like I'd helped to redefine words like organic, grass fed and natural. Or changed the perception of blood clots, rectal bleeding and suicidal thoughts to acceptable risks.

"Dey'd really like to fire me," I continue, even though I know better than to throw my 'good job' problems at strangers, "because I'm a Black woman and I talk back a lot. But de ting is, I'm good. So now I only have two nights 'cause I gotta keep paying de rent on my overpriced studio apartment and it takes two paychecks to do it. So, there you go, mutual hostages in a struggle for survival. Oh, good, it looks just like de pictures."

De taxi driver, a big belly man wid a splotchy beard, who had looked at me wid concern before, now ignores me as if I'm just another whiny American tourist, but I too happy to care.

Five two story buildings scattered up a small hill, painted in what folks think of as tropical colors, blues and greens, pinks and oranges. Lush grounds, coconut trees, palm trees, white sand beach. Outdoor bars and restaurants. Blue sky, blue sea, little puffy clouds swirling from bunnies to trains and back again. Familiar enough to be comforting, but without the obligation to visit with family and friends. I need time alone, to purge, to push 'necessity me' to the back of my life for a little while.

After a quick drenching and some actual swimming dat leaves me heart-poundingly out of breath I lay on de sand wid me feet and legs receiving de gentle massage of de waves, soaking up Mother Nature's joy-inducing Vitamin D. I let meself fall asleep. Sun dreams are de best dreams.

No one bother me. When I wake up, I see de stars gon soon be in de sea. Dat's what we used to say, when I was little and Mama and Daddy would take us to de beach after dinner. Dey would cuddle on de sand and talk while Reggie, Amelia, and I ran around and yelled and screamed and stomped in de waves 'til we were worn all de way out. After a day of school and homework and chores it didn't take dat long. We weren't alone on de long walks back up de hill to our house, either. We shared de trail and crossed paths wid mongooses, turtles, iguanas and frogs, and other creatures. Mama made us learn de names and uses of almost all de plants, too.

So I not frighten when I wake up, alone, on de beach, in de dark.

De sea take back some of she own and leave me feet and legs dry and itching. I suspect de no-see-ums and mosquitos is what had really wake me. I ain't had much of nothing to eat or drink, since a coffee at four thirty in de morning so I thirsty and hungry. On de plane, which was too cold, and nerve-wracking, what wid everybody tinking everybody else is de enemy, I only had some water, refusing de dog biscuits dey pretend is cookies.

I get up a little creakily and stumble through de sand, back up to de chair, where I left my towel and cover-up. My building is de furthest from de beach, and not by coincidence, de cheapest, and I ain't want to take de lighted pathways all de way around de other buildings when I could see de balcony of me room right dere through de carefully designed bushes and trees. I look at de bush—not what I would have called bush, trees and plants left alone to grow however dey want—but dis cultivated bush, tamed and trimmed for admiring from a distance. I go on in.

I was always alive, but when the sun went down I was alive and awake. I knew it was late afternoon when I began to feel restless. Small tingling sensations stirred through my stems and leaves. My flowers began to yearn to unfurl, to enjoy the touch of the cooling evening air. Was it windy? How many bugs were on me? Where and what kind? Aphids? Whiteflies? Thrips? I prickled with anticipation, moisture rippling through me, up from my roots. Twilight was my time. No sun, no moon, a time of transition. Were any of my fruit ripe enough to burst? To spread my seeds? I was growing well here, flourishing in this carefully tended landscape. But I no longer wanted to tolerate having my sprouts weeded away, unwelcomed and unwanted.

A certain something resonated through the ground. Faint, from far away. From the sand, near the water. It got stronger as it got closer. Closer to where the sand gradually changed to dirt. Stronger still as the dirt morphed into soil made rich by life's victims. A human. A woman. A woman with the potential to carry me with her, in her. A woman already carrying seeds within her, not unlike my own.

This is the right one. This presence on the sand, on the ground, with feet and arms and the scent of far way.

In preparation, I pulled the life from the hibiscus plant on my morning sun side. A common thing, ordinary dull red flowers that shamelessly opened to the sun. Its already-wilting petals dropped to the ground as I stretched my roots, made contact, and sucked. No more hibiscus tea for the gardener from this one, at least. Leaves curled and fluttered down as I seeped its strength. I took the allamanda behind me next, its bright yellow flowers had always annoyed me. The gardener made an elixir for human babies with jaundice or colic from its leaves. Not anymore. Not from this one. Dead. I stripped the jasmine of any hope for a future. I was a bit regretful as I latched onto the oleander. I had some respect for it, being poisonous, like me, but it's toxicity would strengthen my own, so it too withered and died.

I withdrew my roots and eased back, loosening myself from the soil, raising myself skyward. Dirt and dead bugs fell off as I rose, as I reshaped myself to resemble the form coming towards me.

I step around de stupid Do Not Enter sign, still hearing de music from one of de hotel bars, not dat far away. I start dance-walking, dancing, but still making forward progress, tramping, like we do in parades. Having a great time all by meself, dancing among and wid de trees, enjoying de dirt under me feet. Taking in big breaths of de sea salt air. Greeting de stars wid de names of me family members who gone to live in de sky. Complimenting de night blooming flowers. Chirping back to de crickets and frogs.

I doing my signature move, a kind of back-bending twirl, when de song change to Whodini's "The Freaks Come Out At Night". I straighten up, dizzy, grab out for something, find a sturdy limb.

A sharp pain stab me palm and another pain shoot up me wrist. I try raise me arm closer to me eyes, to see how bad de cuts, but it can't move. I can't move me arm. What de rass? What I grab has grab me back. I feel de branch pierce me hand, a hard chook. Cold, spikey liquid threading up through me hand, me arm, into me shoulder and neck. De ground shift de way de sand does slide under you feet. Me throat close up, like I going cry, blocking me breath. Me eyes blur wid tears, and I tink I see a tree where wasn't no tree before. A tree, shaped like a woman. White flowers around a face of bark. Each second de wood more mobile, more flesh-like. Eyes big and staring, like de eyes of a owl. Stems, leaves and branches arrange into neck, shoulders and torso. More flowers, darker dan de rest, hanging down like a skirt. Brown legs shading into white ankles and white feet wedded to de dirt.

De ting holding me. De plant-tree-woman ting. One scratchy arm grasping, puncturing me forearm, de other holding me tight 'round me waist.

She wrap she roots, stringing out from she feet, 'round me ankles and pull me in close. She move like she tink she dancing. Dust swirling 'round we feet. Me knees bend when she pinch de back a dem. She push me hips back and forth, left and right wid she slender twig fingers, each one like a hot coal stick on me flesh. De leaves whispering, but I can't make out de words.

I scream and scream, but nobody hear. Nobody come.

I try snap de twigs, break de branches, but dey supple and only bending. I scrabble one foot round de other, trying to tear de vines tying me feet to hers. I curse and spit, but de plant woman ting only bind up me hands and wrap more vines round me throat.

I could see de people at de bar over she shoulder, through she branches and leaves, as she swing me around in she wild version of dance.

De other plants and bushes ain't swaying like she. Ain't no breeze, just hot humid air. I feel de feathery ferns and salvias licking me wid night dew as de plant-tree-woman ting pushing and pulling me up de hill. Sea grapes falling, as we bump each tree along de way.

Dis ain't real, I tell meself. I must really be tired to tink I need dis crazy ting to help me back to me room. I just gotta keep moving. Is only me imagination. T'ain real. Is only a scratch. Couple scratches. I gon soon be dere, in de hotel room, where I gon order a room service dinner, drink lots of water, and clear me head. 'Cause no way dis could be real.

She wasn't hard to enter. I pushed myself into her, mixing my sap with her blood. She went limp in my arms, and I wrangled her around to my back and inched us both closer to the lights, my feet firming with each step. My veins merging with hers, my needs becoming ours.

I was most of the way through the trees and bushes when I had to stop. The moon above too bright. The surrounding sky too dark. My time of the night over. My strength ebbed. I drooped to the ground, spread myself over her legs, belly, chest and head, hiding her, keeping her safe, weaving my seeds into her hair, pushing them into her ears, tucking them between her toes, sticking them onto her clothes.

I kept her like that through the rest of the night, through the morning, and on into the day. At twilight, I roused and found more places to sow my seeds. Dark places, moist places.

I wake up on me back, half buried under a datura bush. Branches atop me like dey trying to hold me down. Me skin itch and I feel swollen, bloated and heavy. Me breath coming short and I feel me pulse in me neck, feel de hotness of de blood in me head. De sun high and me sweat trickle 'cross me cheeks and into me ears. De earth's dampness seeping in through me clothes. I ain't self move yet, but I dizzy and nauseous.

Datura, moonflower, jimsonweed, used for fever, pain, arthritis, asthma. Invasive. Causes hallucinations, can permanently change de brain, poisonous. Me mother lessons come back to me plain plain.

I push de damn ting off me chest, kick and thrash to free me legs. All dat exhaust me already. What had happen? Why I find meself sprawl out under a datura bush, like a dying cat trying to bury sheself? I raise up on me elbows, wait a bit and raise up some more. Is so I make it to me feet. De colors all wrong, as if I seeing through a tint of dried blood, muddy red. Me knees almost buckle wid each step, but I making it. Making it back to me room, de world spinning around me.

All I tinking as I nearing me room, card key in hand, is dat I want to bathe. Me skin itching me so bad. I want water. I want food. I want sleep. I so glad nothing bad happen. Nothing worse. I had fall asleep in the bush, had a bad, crazy dream. It coulda been much worse.

I step inside and de tile floor almost throw me down. A paper slide across de floor from where me foot had kick it. Damn blasted stupid people. Why dey gon' leave something on de floor, make people fall? I slam de door, hard, and me head almost explode from de noise. I put me foot on de paper and drag it to de bed where I go to sit down.

Is de checkout notice. Can't be. I here for two nights. Is only been one. I ain't self get to sleep in de damn bed. I hunt 'round for me phone. Check de date. Turn on de TV. Check de date. Call de front desk.

I been in de bush for more dan a day and a half? What de rass?

And I'm going to miss the plane if I don't leave now. Right now.

I fling a dress on over my bathing suit and cover-up, and I'm out of the door, hurrying to the hotel lobby, to find a taxi, to get to the airport, to get back to my job, dusting strange grit off myself off all the while. I wish I could have taken a shower, but other than that, I'm doing better than okay. My headache is gone and the sun feels good on my skin. I'm just a little thirsty. My trip *was* bizarre—I don't understand how I could have lost two days with no recollection of what happened—but I feel renewed, transformed. Ready to go on earning my place on the planet.

DARK MATTERS
Cecilia Ekbäck

The first time my father died, I was eight years and one day old.

We were in the middle of winter and the darkness outside was so intrusive my mother said she could feel it pushing through our windows. It brought with it something gritty to each room that couldn't be cleaned up or aired out. I had gone out to play in the snow whilst waiting for my father to return home. The only sounds were those of my body against snow: a soft *thud-udd* when I fell, the rasping of a shovel, the *crunch-munch* of red moon boots and, above it all, the rhythmic sound of my breathing inside my hat. I was on the moon. Like Neil Armstrong.

I knew of Neil Armstrong, but, just as my father once had warned me, I couldn't remember the name of the second man on the moon—the one who stepped down on its surface right after Neil. My father had said that man was doomed to be forgotten. This was his lesson in the Importance of Being First. I didn't like this lesson. It made me sad to think about all those people who couldn't be first. They might not even recognize the importance of it at the time. Or maybe they were merely well-behaved and said: "No, after you, I insist," and then, too late, they realised what awaited them was a future of people asking: "Who?"

In order not to think about it any longer I rolled snowballs—

maybe a thousand—and stacked them in pyramids to be used as lanterns.

In the late afternoon, my mother gave me candles for my lanterns. The candles were perfumed, as everything was around my mother, and the forest at the back of our garden soon smelt of old sugary cinnamon buns fried in yellow butter—something we used to make to eat and call "poor knights".

I didn't like our house without my father—it was shapeless and mushy with candle light and classical music. When my father came home, he switched on every lamp in the house, whistling beautifully as he walked from room to room—whole concerts in *adagio, allegrissimo, prestissimo!* He changed the classical music for jazz and turned up the cassette player to volume level four. Then he scrutinized me with brown eyes, raising his left eyebrow.

"What did you decide today?" he asked.

The lesson around the Importance of Making the Right Decisions was exemplified by John F. Kennedy's death, how the day when he was shot he rode in the convertible, top down as always, sun on his shoulders, grace by his side, but for some reason that particular day the windows that were normally rolled up, were down. "Ah, let's feel the wind in our hair today," he must have said. "Go on then, roll them down!"

I had a notebook in which I wrote down all his lessons. There were so many and it was easy to become confused. For example, what if you had to choose between being first and being right? I assumed it was better to be forgotten than dead, but I couldn't be sure.

My face had stopped hurting from the cold and it was time to go inside. I knew spots on my cheeks would be hard and white and it would hurt when the blood came rushing back. I hung up my wet snow suit in the hallway and put my boots on the stand. The gloves and my hat I put in the drying cupboard on the plastic shelves.

My mother worried about my hands. After I'd been playing

in the snow it never took long before she stood on her toes, holding onto the large kitchen cupboard and stretched *fa-a-ar* to reach the cream where she had placed it behind the wedding photo. It made her huff and sigh. This day was no different.

"So," she turned to me and when I didn't obey: "Don't fuss."

Sighing I put both my hands into the one she had stretched out.

"You have got to stop taking your gloves off outside. Look!" she scolded.

They were ugly without a doubt: chubby, the skin red and rough, swollen finger tips and the lining around the nails soggy, even torn. We knew the hands would turn out alright one day—I had inherited them from my father's mother and there was nothing wrong with hers, in fact, hers were rather pretty. My mother's concern was that I might just manage to ruin them before something real became of them. My father agreed.

"It is the first thing a man looks at, a woman's hands," he would say (left eyebrow raised). "Your mother has hands like jewels."

I watched my mother putting cream onto my stinging limbs. I had tried to explain to her again and again that snowballs simply did not get the icy shell that could return the shine of a candle unless you squeezed them hard with bare hands. My mother did not want to hear it.

"You will end up like your grandmother," she threatened.

"I like grandmother," I said with a sudden defiance that surprised us both.

"She is unbalanced," my mother said.

My grandmother lived in a small village in Lapland. We didn't see her often. She was not part of the Pentecostal church. "Your granny was h'expelled," a snotty boy with clammy hands had whispered to me one time at a sermon. His nose was so stuffy it sounded like he said my grandmother had been "helled." I didn't believe him, but I never dared ask my mother. I don't know what had happened between my mother and hers, but something had; that was clear. Whenever they met, both my mother and my grandmother acted strangely. Sentences were pronounced politely in LARGE LETTERS. They never turned their back on one another. My mother insisted she herself had no memories from her childhood. Life began when she married and bid farewell to her mother and that was that. Now and again she forgot herself and a fibre of something murky from the past would surface. Whenever that happened she would stop speaking mid-sentence and fall silent.

There were sounds on their porch of someone removing snow from clothes, kicking their shoes against the edge of the stairs—first one, then the other, stamping their feet down hard two, three, four times and then using the brush. My mother untied her apron, folded and arranged it on top of the kitchen towel. She looked at me once more: we were not done yet talking about my hands. She walked towards the entrance. The doorbell rang. She opened the door and a cold gust entered. Two of my father's friends were standing outside.

"So you are here," she said and stepped to one side.

We didn't talk very much. Stating the obvious was a pleasantry. "So you are out walking the dog," "So you are out buying milk."

"Yes," one of them said. It was a good beginning: concurrence.

The two men fingered their woollen hats, shuffled feet and cleared throats. My mother stood still, careful not to disrupt.

"It's about a man, your man, he's unwell," one of them said finally.

The other one glanced at him.

"Well," he continued. "It is a bit worse. We believe he might have died."

In that instant, the four of us were trapped together, between what was and what must come. Nobody screamed or cried. There seemed to be no questions. Nothing more to say. I looked down at my hands. They were covered in white gloves of fat. As I lifted my head, the world returned to life with a whirring sound, like when you wind up a mechanical dog too far and then let go of it and the poor thing whizzes around on the floor in front of you. The tick-tock from the grandfather clock seemed thunderous, the classical music menacing. I could see only my mother's back. It was quite still and erect. At the back of her neck a few strands of blond hair had escaped her ponytail.

I was to occupy myself in my room in the basement. I sat with a greasy crayon in one hand and a blank sheet of paper in front of me, my ears straining, aching to hear what was going on upstairs. There were muffled voices, the phone rang, the front door opened. There were hasty footsteps between rooms. Whilst my father died, night had fallen.

I knew it was wrong for my mother to try and cope on her own.

"She is not like you and me," my father often had said, tenderly, irritated. "She is... weaker. She needs caring for."

I had looked at my mother with her strawberry blond hair and eyes blue like the sea on a postcard from Greece and then back at my father with coarse black hair and brown eyes like my own and I had felt worried, but also pleased.

I should have been with him, I thought. My father had gone to church. He'd asked me to come, but I said I wanted to stay home and play. This might have been a punishment. God was like that. You couldn't quite know what would invite His wrath. I felt cold. My fingers were cramped around the crayon I had rammed hard into the paper, gaze fixed at the one strained dot on the white.

And then my mother's voice: "Irma, come upstairs!"

All of a sudden, I didn't want to see her, but I placed my crayon on the table. I stood up. I walked towards the stairs, head hanging, up the steps, just as the front door opened and my father walked in.

There was a small noise in my chest. A funny little noise that almost immediately began to hurt. My father appeared tired, broken. With all my might, I held onto the noise in my chest, shoved it back down to where it came from, knowing nobody could stand it when noise came out.

And then I saw who he'd brought.

My father held the door wide open to Death, a troll with long arms, potbelly, and a beard who, as he entered, unceremoniously threw his knapsack down on the floor and kicked off his leather boots. His toes were long and rather hairy.

"I'll make dinner," my mother said.

My father observed his routine of switching on the lamps. I trailed him in and out of every room like a pet, ready for the words that would transform also this into a droll anecdote. But my father didn't meet my gaze. He was silent, unbearably so, and Death was still there, winking at me. My father walked into the kitchen.

"I don't think we should talk about this with anyone," he said to my mother.

She did not answer.

He cleared his throat.

"But what happened?" I asked.

He shrugged. "Some sort of attack," he said.

I imagined some men jumping my father, beating him, perhaps with a stick. But there was no blood on his face, no bruises.

"Why can't we tell?" I demanded.

Death was leaning against a kitchen cupboard, arms crossed, eyebrows raised. He observed us with what appeared to be genuine interest.

"It could have consequences."

"What kind of consequences?" I was angry with my father, or with my mother. I wanted to have it out.

"What would it be like if we started to talk about things like this?" my father said. "We would end up doing nothing but talking about how we felt. No, you mustn't tell anyone."

He walked out. I kicked the doorpost. I couldn't understand—surely there was a formal procedure with rules and instructions we were supposed to follow? And for sure telling people about what had happened must have some part in the ritual that made this into an irreversible event?

I looked at Death, but he was of no help at all.

"So what," I said, "are you going to live here now?"

"Guess so," he said.

I wondered where she would put him.

My mother liked things you could pack neatly in a box and tie a pretty ribbon around. She liked things you could fold, things you could roll tightly, things you could position in rows and things you could name. My mother doted on linen closets where the linen was strictly folded, arranged by colour and by size, and scented like fresh air. "The linen closet is a woman's pride," she used to tell me in confidence. My mother smiled seeing cleaning cupboards where the bottles stood in rows with their handles outwards—easy to snatch in case of disaster—and where the dusters were crispy and felt new. She liked freezers where packages with frozen food were marked in immaculate handwriting with a smudge-proof pen and arranged by its origin: elk, reindeer, grayling, flatbread, berries, other. She loved pulling a damp cloth over a surface and when lifting it up finding it as white as when she started. She relished in re-using and economising and unendingly came up with solutions for the old: mending the broken, thinking of a new use for the redundant, altering the aged. She liked being able to touch what she had, and she kept her salary divided into envelopes in a kitchen cupboard, each clearly marked with their purpose: food, clothes, garden, savings. She liked me, even though I was what she called a dare-devil, because, after all, I was a girl and she could knit and sew all my clothes. She loved suitcases.

My mother's finest recurring dream: she is packing a case,

thinks about it for a while, and comes up with improvements. She repacks and ties a strap firmly around it. My mother's most atrocious returning dream: the moving van is outside our house. She has forgotten to get boxes and there is no option but to cram belongings into garbage bags.

My mother hated things that didn't fit, that suddenly left a mould, were too large, moved fast, or that you couldn't control. She was frightened of epileptic people. She detested drunkards, addicts and crazy ones. She didn't like impulsiveness, surprises, and changes of plans. My mother did not believe in the trolls. She hated the night.

"Why?" I'd asked my father once. "Why the night?"

To me, the night was the best of times. Time to potter around on warm floors with naked feet, perhaps steal a cookie from the pantry.

"That's often when things happen," he'd said.

"What kind of things?"

He'd shrugged. "Bad things. People die, people get hurt. That is when human frailty is at its peak."

I thought about it. I didn't feel frail at night, but peaceful. Perhaps things got different as you got older.

I needn't have worried about my mother finding a place for Death. No, the problem seemed to be Resurrection. Resurrection, the little bundle, was full of beans. She just couldn't sit still, and she was quite unruly. She was like a glowing hairball bouncing up and down our hallways and I think, to my mother, Death just seemed more sophisticated, more established. Perhaps Death was less imprecise: at least you knew what you got with him.

I thought it might have been easier for my mother if my father had not bothered with Resurrection. My mother would have grieved, there would have been practical issues, but then she could have laid the incident tenderly to rest in a coffin, ordered a glorious gravestone, and buried him during a distressing, yet dignified, ceremony.

That night I began a bed time ritual that I would follow in some shape for all years to come:

"Good night?" I shouted.

I started walking slowly down the stairs to my room in the basement (*thump, thump, thump*).

"Good night," my father and my mother called from their bedroom.

"Goood niiight," Death echoed lazily from where he was sitting at the kitchen table picking his teeth.

"I love you?" I shouted (*thump, thump, thump*).

"We love you."

Me, heart pounding, dread in my voice: "Dad, I didn't hear you? Dad? Dad, you also need to shout!"

"I love you."

"No, now we need to start over."

('This is what you always do.' She wonders for whom he's performing when he says that: they've known each other less than a month. This is their second argument and the first was over something very different. She shrugs. He can take it as an apology if he wants, though it isn't.

'Fill your pen,' she says.

'Seriously, you're loving this, aren't you?' Is it some ex he's angry with? It feels to her like a character. A woman from a play. *Don't recruit me to your dramas*, she thinks.

'Just fill it.'

They lean-he as if he's doing her a favour-over the broken bones and smashed innards and the ruined trembling feathers. At the other tables the diners look away, to their own pigeons.

'Your turn with the gall,' she says, thinking *See? I even give you that*. She submerges the nib of her own fountain pen into blood, and levers the little pump.)

ABOVE THE LIGHT
Jesse Bullington

Like many a questionable practice, we got into it when we were young. We didn't have a name for it, didn't even really talk about it. It was just what we did.

We met at Swift Creek Middle School, in the yeasty armpit of the south that is Tallahassee, Florida. We were both weirdoes. He was cast from the shy-yet-sly mold, with a mountain of curly dark hair like a tween *Eraserhead*. I was even more awkward and less inclined to socialize, but Caleb drew me out with his charming dorkiness. Initial points of mutual interest were B-movies, Douglas Adams, and *Vampire the Masquerade*, which it turned out we both owned but neither had ever successfully cajoled another person into playing. Within a couple weeks of being seated next to each other in Pre-Algebra we were getting thick, and that inevitably led to the first sleepover. I rode the bus home with him on a Friday.

For a recent New England transplant, even my suburban neighborhood felt a little wild, with a thickly wooded lot abutting our property and deep swamps bordering the edge of the development. But Caleb's place was positively primeval. The bus let off kid after kid after kid, sometimes alone and sometimes in herds, until we were the last ones aboard, rolling down a narrow road, the boughs of the ancient, moss-draped live oaks forming a canopy overhead so it felt like we were sliding down a living tunnel. The bus finally let us out where the paved road juked to the left. Caleb led me down a dirt track into the woods as if this were the most natural thing in the world.

The Miccosukee Land Co-op was what you'd call an *intentional community* these days—a bunch of hippies who went in on a group-buy for a ton of acres of Florida swamp. Most of the houses we passed on our walk were pretty mundane affairs set back in the trees, but then we left the dirt road and crossed a long wooden boardwalk that threaded across the thickly wooded bog. It was a strange, sepia-toned realm where everything from the placid pools to the bald cypress rising out of them were the same shades of brown. I had never been anywhere like it, and I was already in love with the rural commune before we even reached Caleb's place, which sat at the end of another serpentine boardwalk over still, tannin-stained waters.

Caleb's house was far bigger than any of the ones we'd passed, resembling a wooden castle whose three-story wings were joined by a screened porch and long hallway. Blue tarps covered most of the windows on the right wing. His dad was an architect and the place had been a work in progress ever since Caleb was born, with additions and more boardwalks and a nearby guesthouse springing up over the years. As sprawling as it looked from outside, the inside was cozy enough, with exposed wood and stone tiles and bookshelves everywhere. His parents weren't home, and we set up in a kitchen that was like something out of a fairy tale, with cast iron pots hanging over the gas stove and jars of herbs and teas everywhere. We came up with *Vampire* characters at the scuffed and scored wooden table, and, when we got hungry, Caleb introduced me to tofu, tamari, and nutritional yeast. It was better than I expected, almost cheesy with a crispy pan-fried exterior.

Later, he introduced me to something even more savory.

"Want to go for a walk?"

It had been dark for hours, but we had already established that we were both the sort of sensible person who stayed up as late as possible on weekends, rather than squandering our precious freedom with anything as mundane as sleep.

"Sure."

By the time you're twelve you have a pretty good idea of whether or not you like the night. I definitely did. Stargazing, huddling around campfires, playing manhunt—all that good stuff. Yet just heading out the door for a nocturnal stroll had never occurred to me. Probably because I didn't really get along with any of the kids in my neighborhood, and, unlike this swamp child I was hanging out with, the thought of being alone in the night still creeped me out a bit. It still does, even as an adult; but then that's all part of the charm, isn't it? Fear can be fun. Euphoric, even.

And then there's the satisfaction of subduing your apish instincts, of reminding yourself that you're not ruled by animal fear of the unknown. The natural world hasn't just been conquered, it's been beaten into a coma—all the mysteries have been hunted down and shot for sport, and the once-terrifying night harbors little peril. That's what you tell yourself, anyway, when you've moved far beyond the light and hear a far off sound in the midnight woods...far off, but never far enough.

The only threat I had to contend with was myself—if I wasn't careful, I might twist an ankle, tumble off a boardwalk, or even step on a snake when I crunched through an unseen carpet of dead leaves. There were no more panthers or wolves in North Florida, I didn't think, and any bears were few, far between, and in the words of our favorite author, mostly harmless.

There are worse things than mundane animals in the night, as every small child knows, but by twelve you've either gotten good at talking yourself out of the monster spiral or you're not going to be the type who enjoys being out after dark anyway.

I don't remember what we talked about on that first night walk, though monsters almost definitely came up. We were twelve, after all. What I do remember was the moment after we'd crossed the first boardwalk, when Caleb flicked off the flashlight that had illuminated our path and stowed it in his pocket. How he carried on as if it were the most normal thing in the world to set off down a dirt road in the deep dark woods with only a thin hook of a moon lodged between the upper boughs of an oak to light our way. And how satisfying it felt to hustle after him, tripping over the occasional shadowy root, but otherwise finding the sandy track as easy to follow under the moon as it had been under the sun.

As my eyes adjusted, the impenetrable walls on either side of the road splintered into individual trees and bushes. When we reached the next boardwalk Caleb didn't take his flashlight back out. I was glad for it. We must have walked many miles that night, all over the sleeping Co-op, but that's the moment I still feel the keenest, down all the years—how happy it made me when I realized we didn't need the light anymore.

How at home.

Easy jetlag avoidance: book a red-eye, stay up all night the night before, and don't close your eyes until the cabin lights dim on that transatlantic flight. You're so excited to wake up in a new country, you barely notice that you feel kinda like shit.

We hadn't lived in the same state since high school, so our night hikes were a rare indulgence even before Caleb married Claudia and followed her back to Germany. That made them all the more precious. We'd both taken other people out over the years, but never with any regularity. And most nights after dinner I'd go for long walks out along the Boulder Creek Path, through the industrial barrens east of town where the stars burned bright in the vast prairie sky. But that wasn't the same, either. For something that loomed so large over who I was—who we both were, I suspect—night hiking was a difficult appetite to regularly sate; imagine living in rural Kansas and constantly craving sashimi.

Dreams were a different story, though. Ever since I was a kid, I probably spent one night a week trekking through my dreams. Sometimes Caleb was there, but mostly I was by myself, or with those dream companions you know so well on the other side of sleep but have never met in the waking world. Regardless of whether I traveled alone or with those imagined comrades, there were always other figures hiking the trails. In places, throngs of them as thick as you'd find on an easy trail in Yosemite or Rocky Mountain National Park in peak season... when the sun is high, that is.

It was always night in my dreams, and I was always in the mountains. Not familiar mountains, either...or not *real* mountains, I should say, because while I never dreamed of places I'd actually been, those imaginary landscapes were as mundane and well-known to my dreaming self as the Flatirons are to my waking mind.

That was where I went while my body cramped up in a window seat—to the range of my dreams. The city I departed was the largest in the high country. There were wide winding lanes, coursing down like a cataract amongst the buildings built out of the solid slope of the white-stoned mountain. I pushed open a wrought-iron gate in the low wall on the upper edge of town and followed the trail up to the crest of a high arched bridge, spanning a gushing creek. From there I had my vantage and could see the moon-crowned dome of the summit leering over the lantern-lit burg below, its ridgeline smooth as an egg and just as full of possibility. A milky lake lapped at the foot of the slouching peak, feeding the stream below me. There were figures clustered on the bank, but I couldn't tell if they had just emerged from the pool or were bracing themselves to enter it. Above them, more black silhouettes moved against the grey face of the summit, navigating the web of trails. But were they climbing or descending?

I felt an eagerness, then, and acted on it, rushing down the other side of the bridge and ahead up the trail. It's idiotically dangerous to hurry on a night hike, especially in the mountains, but this thought only came to me as the vision dissolved into a too-bright airline cabin, seatbacks and tray tables returning to their upright positions.

Caleb met me at the baggage claim. He had left Dresden in the middle of the night to make it down in time, and had bags under his eyes about as big as the Kelty pack I pulled off the carousel. We hugged, shot the shit, and hustled out of the busy airport and into his little green continental ride—an Elf, naturally. The Austrian village Caleb had found us was only a few hours from Munich, and we spent the first leg of the drive catching up. He was finally swapping out the hell of online academia for plain old programming, Claudia was teaching, their cats were catting. I'm sure my tales of insurance underwriting thrilled him to no end, and we were both relieved when we neared the Austrian border and the mountains commanded our full attention.

Far more poetic souls than I have tried to capture the majesty of the Alps in words, but until you've passed through and over and occasionally under them yourself there's just no way to get it. The way the rolling countryside swells and swells, fields and forests rising steeper and steeper around you, hoisting up the picturesque towns and country churches and even crumbling castles, the blue and white of the distant peaks freeing themselves from the camouflage of the cloud-streaked sky.

"There's something I forgot to mention," Caleb said, when we finally got around the blocky tour-bus that had been cramping our view for the last dozen kilometers of long alpine valley. "Galtür seems especially down on our little hobby, so be sure not to let any locals know that we plan on being out after dark."

"Yeah?" Over the last couple of decades we had night hiked together on every continent save Antarctica, and, while we'd ended up in some remote locations, we had always established local connections who knew where we were and when to expect us back. Most of said locals tried to talk us out of wandering off into the night, of course, but we always came to an arrangement.

"The frau at the first hoff I was going to book freaked out on me when I started laying some groundwork. Mentioned how I'd heard the trails around here were so well-marked you couldn't get lost even in the middle of the night, but she cut me off with the riot act. Said Tyrol even passed a law against hiking after dark."

"They did?" I'd assumed Caleb had chosen Galtür out of convenience, since it was so close to his adopted home, but committing our precious annual holiday to the one place on earth that had actually outlawed night hiking didn't seem particularly convenient.

Caleb laughed his low little chuckle. "Of course not, I checked it out and she was full of it. But her story was good! She had this whole lecture prepared right down to the thousand euro fines. The fragile alpine ecosystem is apparently under serious threat from tourists stomping all over their precious edelweiss in the dark. I suspect the real reason she tried to scare me off was to minimize the chances of bringing bad press to town—they've had a few hikers go missing over the years, and an avalanche back in the Nineties killed something like fifty people, I think. Last thing the local tourism board wants is some dumb American falling into a crevasse on a moonless night. Anyway, I thanked her for the information and booked somewhere else. I didn't say nichts about nachtwanderen at the next place just in case they're all in on it."

"Oh, sure, that all makes perfect sense," I said. "Just like it makes perfect sense to go night hiking somewhere new without telling anyone what we're doing."

I wasn't actually worried. How could I be, with those beautiful rugged ridges boxing us in? The trails would be clear as day up there above the pines, even by starlight alone. We'd planned this trip for a new moon and so my only concern was that the trails might be crowded with amateur astrologers. The solitude isn't the only charm of night hiking, but it's definitely one of them.

Our road carried us alongside a muddy river that coursed through the laurel green meadowland in the belly of the Paznuan valley. As I eyed the deeper, darker shade of the forests that rose up on either side of us, something Caleb had glided over jumped back out at me. "You said people have gone missing out here?"

"Sure, I guess. People go missing everywhere." We crested a knoll and zipped past a whole family in fluorescent performance gear walking a path that ran parallel to the road. Caleb slowed down before I could ask him to; we were entering another of the pretty little towns built off the only major road through the region.

"*People go missing everywhere*," I repeated. "Perfect tagline for our found footage horror movie."

"You think every single person who starts the PCT or even the Appalachian arrives safe and sound at the other end? And those are the biggies; day hikers disappear, too. Not just a few, either, we're talking hundreds of people vanishing every year in state parks alone, and some estimates put it even higher—*thousands*, gone without a trace."

"You're taking advantage of the fact that I can't get a signal to google that," I said, double-checking my phone and confirming that even in town I wasn't getting any bars. All these little villages were essentially off-season ski-resorts, but less *Aspen Extreme* and more *Sound of Music*—we passed a cheese shop, a bakery, and a butcher, all on the main drag. "Gonna need a source on those numbers, buddy."

"Claudia," said Caleb. If I hadn't known him as well as I did

I would have missed the hiccup in his joviality, but there it was, between his wife's name and what came after. "She's not crazy about the night hiking, either, and has been inflicting me with all kinds of articles. Backcountry horror stories, you know the type. Little does she know that reading about dummies being dumb only makes me feel smarter."

"That makes one of us." Then we were out of town again, climbing up and up the valley. We passed a kilometer marker for Galtür. "But whether or not she loves it, Claudia knows where we are, right? You guys have your daily calls or whatever planned?"

He hesitated, a mischievous smile quirking the corner of his mouth, and we both fell into that immature giggling that only best friends can draw from one another, and usually when they're both off their heads. In our teens it would've been from pot and bad jokes, in our twenties from booze and worse ones, and now at forty it had come full circle, to the same pure source we had first discovered as kids—sleep deprivation.

We'd made good time from the airport, so after lunch we could nap until dinner. A lot of hikers apparently take a day or two for their bodies to recalibrate after skipping over that many time zones before hitting the trail, but Caleb and I always jumped right into it—partially because weather can be such an issue. Dense cloud cover alone can put the kibosh on a night hike, so you have to take every opportunity, in case you don't get another one. The other reason we didn't waste any time was not something we have ever articulated to one another, but which I was sure Caleb felt as keenly as I did. Night hiking was the only time I really felt fully awake anymore.

Rain had drilled the Langtang region all day, but by midnight the moon had dried out the clouds, cracking them apart into a mosaic of ghostly blue light. We made the slippery trek away from the holy village of Gosaikunda, alive in a way that only summiting a nearly 15,000-foot Himalayan pass in the middle of the night can make you feel. A lone hut sprouted like a mushroom on the side of the flinty trail, its roof sparkling—the salvaged wing of an airplane that had crashed into the side of a peak. We took extra care to mind our step passing by the tarp-hooded doorway of the hovel, just as we did whenever we slipped through sleeping villages, alongside dark barns, or neared silent temples.

Night hiking transforms you. You are invisible. A spirit. So long as you obey the covenants, you preserve the spell.

It also transports you. This is someplace else. This is always someplace else. The night is an open door to another world.

Down in the terraced fields, gazing across the open valley just as a quarter mile expanse of the far hillside gave way. A black wound erupting on the face of the countryside, shimmering like blood as it rushed down the slope and erased the trail we would have been climbing at that very moment, if we hadn't lost the trail back in the misty pines for over an hour.

I thought the mudslide sounded like rain. Caleb told me it sounded to him like a crackling fire. We had talked about it over and over again, confirming and reaffirming for the other that the nighttime trail had indeed been empty, at least as far as we could see. But now, that far path was crowded with figures when the mudslide came crashing down over it. I know two of those doomed silhouettes must have been our possible selves, the ones who hadn't been too stubborn to use flashlights after getting lost in a Himalayan forest and thus made better time reaching the valley floor—but who were all the others?

Behind us, above us, came a noise like rain, like crackling fire, figures scrambling up the muddy steps of the trail that wound down through the terraced fields, but before I could look back to see the chthonic tidal wave falling over us Caleb knocked again, waking me up.

I blinked in the twilight of my room. We had checked in, but I couldn't remember anything about the interaction. Nothing unusual about that; such elisions in time, in detail, were a mildly bothersome bug in my daily routine—the inevitable consequence of not getting enough rest. I hauled myself up from the bed. Staring out the rustic framed window at the bluish mountains in the gloaming, it felt like my whole life had been spent trying to catch up on missing sleep.

I rubbed my eyes and called out to Caleb to quit with the knocking. I was awake. Or getting there. The mountains grew darker as I watched.

The dining room at the Gampeler-Hof was cozy, brightly lit, and crowded with strangers speaking foreign tongues. A dark-haired woman in an honest-to-god dirndl seated us against a back wall. After she bustled off to bring us beer, Caleb informed me she was none other than the landlady herself. The pension offered three choices for dinner every night, none of them vegetarian. Caleb had apparently worked something out in advance, though, because when I eventually received my schnitzel our hostess brought him a platter of pasta drowned in vibrant yellow cheese sauce.

"Nothing like authentic Tyrolian cuisine," Caleb said, spearing a goopy forkful. "Here comes Magnus. Remember not to say anything about what we're doing tonight."

"Magnus?" I glanced over my shoulder just as a tall mustachioed man in lederhosen bore down on me from the direction of the kitchen. I don't think I had ever seen a real person in lederhosen before. He clapped me on the back as if we were old friends, releasing a torrent of German so swift I was instantly washed away and doubted even Caleb could find footing in the flow. He finally managed to get in a few words edgewise, though, and I hoped to Christ that *kaffee* was indeed what it sounded like.

"*Grüss Gott!*" Magnus said as last, giving me another hardy slap on the back as he charged away toward the kitchen.

"*Grüss Gott!*" Caleb called after him.

"*Grüss Gott*," I parroted. "That's the regional *auf weidersen*, I take it?"

"Not really," said Caleb. "It's more of a catch-all hello/goodbye around here—what you tell people when you pass them on the trail."

"Something about God?" I guessed.

"Yeah, God greet you, go with God, something like that. It's a country thing—if you try that on someone in Dresden they'll say something smartass about not being in a hurry to meet God." Caleb grinned. "My people!"

"Are they really that religious down here?" I hadn't noticed an overabundance of crucifixes or other iconography in the quaint, family-run hotel.

"Compared to most Germans I've met, sure, but they're not exactly Southern Baptists," said Caleb. "You get the feeling that the Reformation never quite found the right path into these little mountain towns. Probably not amenable enough to incorporating the old ways."

"Ah yes," I said. "Catholicism gobbling up paganism, a tale as old as time."

"Who can say who gobbled whom," said Caleb, and then lowered his voice, though as far as I could tell we were the only English speakers in the noisy dining room. "I didn't say one word about night hiking, but Magnus brought up that same bogus law against walking the trails after dark. I don't know how, but I think he's onto us. I'm one step ahead of him, though—I moved my car down in front of the church while you were napping, so we can sneak out later and walk back to it without anyone in the hoff realizing we're gone."

"Very smart," I said, smiling at how silly—and familiar—this all was. My parents were far less amenable to their teenage son and his friend haunting the neighborhood than Caleb's folks, so we'd always had to sneak out when he spent the night at my place.

The hubbub of the dining room grew louder, making me ache

for quiet paths through dark woods. As if sensing my dismay, the landlady appeared and refilled my stein. A relief—alcohol was about the only thing that made me capable of acting like a human, the cold beer rich and malty on my schnitzel-scoured tongue.

Magnus burst out of the kitchen, singing a boisterous song as he delivered a carafe of coffee to our table. The conversations died down and all focus turned to our host as he serenaded the dining hall. Extending a hand to a keg-shaped matron seated with her equally stout family, he drew her off the bench and they began to dance. Clapping spread around the room as they found the rhythm of his ballad. I looked at Caleb, barely able to believe the provincial scene unfolding before us, but his eyes were on Magnus and the crone, his hands clapping in time with all the others, his lips moving as if he knew every word of the bewildering song.

By day there had been a fair amount of traffic on the valley road, but now ours were the only headlights drilling through the darkness. I kept my eyes on the grassy curb, as I always did when driving in the country. When Caleb and I night walked at my place as kids, we would always hide when cars approached, throwing ourselves facedown in the ditch if there were no trees to skulk behind. Nobody ever stopped, which I used to think meant nobody ever saw us. Granted, when you're driving you're often on autopilot, and the human eye is good at skipping over things it doesn't expect to see... like a prone figure in the tall grass on the side of a road. But considering how many cars must have passed right by us over the years I have to wonder: how many people did catch a glimpse of us lying there, but elected to keep going. How many of them sped up?

"Do you remember our plan after we watched *Near Dark*?" Caleb asked as we wound up the valley road, high beams shining off rocks and scrub.

"Probably best we never actually tried that," I said, smiling at the memory. We'd decided that after we graduated high school we would go on a vampire road trip: tape tinfoil over the car windows and see how long and how far we could go without ever being in the sunlight. "We were such weirdos."

"Was that the same night you climbed the tree outside Mrs. Beck's? And almost fell out of it when the lights came on?" Caleb flicked on his turn signal even though we hadn't seen another car since slipping out of the quiet hamlet. We left the main road, climbing the northern slope of the valley.

"You know I don't even think that was her house?" That memory brought a grimace instead of a grin. Mrs. Beck was our 8th grade English teacher. We liked her, and when we discovered she apparently lived somewhere in my neighborhood set out to find where. I'm not exactly sure what our motivations were, other than it gave a purpose to our night wandering. In retrospect, scaling the elm to try and peek through a darkened upstairs window was just about the creepiest possible way of confirming it, and I made enough noise hauling myself up into the branches that I woke up the house. We fled into the night before the front door could open to reveal Mrs. Beck, a shotgun-wielding stranger, or a shotgun-wielding Mrs. Beck.

"What's her line at the beginning?" asked Caleb as we flitted through another stand of dark trees, back out into the stunted scrubland of the high country.

"Mrs. Beck?"

"No, the girl in *Near Dark*. When she takes Caleb out into the fields."

"I forgot he was Caleb." I never forget Lance Henriksen's character's name, though. "Oh, I know what you mean. About the night being blinding."

"No, right, it's deafening." Caleb slapped the steering wheel as our headlights caught the vast gleaming surface of a lake up ahead. "They get out of his truck in the middle of nowhere, and she asks him if he can hear it, and he asks what, and she says the night. It's *deafening*."

"Yeah," I said, "it's that, too."

As we followed the curve of the shore I made out a cluster of dark buildings on the opposite bank, but didn't call Caleb's attention to them lest he get paranoid about being observed by the locals and kill the lights. Night hiking was one thing, night driving was another thing entirely. The road crossed a land bridge between this first lake and a far larger body of water that opened up before us. We climbed again, skirting the northern bank of what Caleb informed me was a reservoir. The inky expanse filled the bowl of this final valley nestled amidst the bald ridges and peaks that loomed to the north and south.

There was a parking lot up ahead, but before we could reach it a metal gate jumped into our headlights, blocking off the access road. Caleb stopped the car. "Here we are!"

"It's safe to just leave it here?" Now that we had made it I was finally waking up for what felt like the first time in months. "What if we get towed?"

"By who? Magnus?" Caleb laughed. "This is only a little thirteen kilometer warm up anyway. We'll be out of here hours before dawn. Tomorrow night we start the real trek—I found a circuit over the mountains where we'll hit over twenty kilometers a night, with alm huts to crash in during the day. It'll be like that summer on the Kungsleden, only with more cheese, better beer, and real beds."

That sounded an awful lot like heaven. By the glow of the domelight we settled our packs onto our backs. Then the doors of the car clicked shut, the light went out, and we were alone on an empty mountain road just before midnight. I closed my eyes, the only sound the cool wind rustling my Marmot.

We helped each other scale the metal barrier and tromped across the wide, empty parking lot. There was a little ranger station or something at the edge of the reservoir, and passing the dark building, I pulled my hood down to cover my face in case they had cameras trained on the concrete walkway that spanned the wall of the reservoir. Night hiking. See everything, but don't be seen.

Part of what makes being out in the wilds after dark so satisfying: the cognitive transformations you undergo as your eyes adjust, your ears prick up. Walking along the reservoir, toward the wooded far shore and the muscular ridge that blocked off the southern horizon, I felt the familiar change come over me. No moon, no clouds. Stars so thick you'd think the sequined cloak of night was on loan from the Liberace estate.

We paused before entering the trees, slowly looking back and forth from the radiant sky to its drowned twin trapped in the waters at our feet.

Neither of us spoke. You either feel it stronger than you feel anything else, or you don't understand what it even is to feel. Some of us are just born for the night.

The band of wood was quieter than I expected, silent other than the creak of the ever-present mountain draughts through the pine boughs. The breeze wasn't exactly balmy, but summer still lingered here in Tyrol, even after dark. We followed the shadow-smudged trail up the wide face of the mountain, the cool air refreshing against my flushed skin. We weren't in the trees for long, not tall ones, anyway, ascending through stubby brush that made it a bit easier to find the path.

Veteran hikers don't put a lot of conscious thought into where they step most of the time, their eyes and feet long accustomed to working in tandem without bothering the brain with every niggling detail. That all changes in difficult terrain, and there's no terrain more difficult than that which you cannot see. Night hiking forces you to be in the moment, paying close attention to every step through a maze of starlit leaves. Up and up we went, until our switchbacking led us above the stunted shrubs and into the proper alpine environment of exposed grasses, wildflowers, and scattered rocks and boulders. We still had a stern climb ahead of us to reach the ridgeline, but with the trail plain and open at our boots we were able to make far better time.

"What's the name of it again?" I asked when the wind died down. My voice was hushed, as if my parents might overhear us here on this desolate mountain high in the Alps.

"The Breitspitze." Caleb paused and took a pull on his Nalgene bottle. The stars were so bright I could see the sweat shining on his face.

"Don't tell me that's our warm-up," I said, pointing to the peak that jutted up from the eastern end of the ridge to dominate the horizon. We'd been making good progress and I felt more invigorated than I had in ages, but no amount of summit fever could make that jagged, ice-rimmed monster seem attainable. Not our first night out, anyway.

"Hell no!" Caleb laughed. "We go right at the top and just follow the ridge from there. It ends in a cliff, so hard to get lost. Gotta be halfway there already."

"Yeah?" I looked back the way we'd come. The silver and ebon landscape shimmered like the surface of the reservoir as the wind brushed its invisible palm across the mountain's face. A sapling at the edge of the treeline swayed more than its brothers or sisters in the breeze, the waving of its stubby boughs making my heart skip a beat...it then cleared half a dozen more, as the silhouette detached itself from the pines, stepping out into the starlight. It was like something from a nightmare.

At some point I listened to a podcast where the host said if you're ever unsure whether or not you're dreaming you just need to read something, look away, and then reread it. Our sleeping brains can do a pretty slick job at convincing us what we're experiencing is real, but one thing they can't do is keep text consistent in the middle of a dream. Even something as basic as a street sign will lose its cohesion if you turn away and then refocus on it.

Ever since I learned that trick I constantly find myself double-checking everything from emails to cereal boxes in the grocery store, but so far I've only ever confirmed I was awake.

This was all part of a dream I had, weeks ago. The irony makes me smile—the dreamer dreaming of ways to test whether he is dreaming but never employing them, instead calling up memories where the tests failed. This was where my sleeping mind wandered even as my sleeping feet carried me purposefully up the ghostlit trail, away from that teeming ivory city that I forever seemed to be leaving behind in pursuit of new adventures. I had an apartment high in one of the crooked spires, a curio-cluttered garret where my shadow friends and I plotted our treks over black maps whose inconstant golden paths slithered like snakes, but not once in all my life had I ever dreamed of homecoming, only ever departure. Lying in bed the following morning with tears streaming down my cheeks I wondered what that said about me...but in the night, in the moment, I was simply giddy to be off gallivanting again, accompanied by dozens of my nocturnal peers. They were my people, I knew this in my heart even if I could never quite make out their faces, but the high dark places we journeyed, and those star-kissed summits...

Considering how majestically my dreams towered over the low, dull range of my life it might seem odd that I never told anyone about them beyond the broadest strokes, not even Caleb. He also dreamed about night hiking, but from the one time he broached the subject I gathered his were not nearly so pleasant as mine and so I quickly changed the topic. The heart of the matter is that while I don't consider myself superstitious in general, on some bone-deep level I feared that if I talked about the visions it would amount to flinching away from them, that doing so would somehow change the dreams, or put a stop to them altogether. Never take your eyes off that which you love, even for a moment, or suffer the consequences.

*　　*　　*

I squinted, willing the black shape I had spied down the mountainside to bleed back into the shadows, a trick of my night-strained eyes. But the shape defied me, coming into sharper relief as it left the thicket. *An animal*, the thought sharing the shape of a prayer, but the persistent starlight disavowed me of that impression. The figure was still a long way off down the slope, but it was without question another night hiker, climbing the trail after us. They were making good time, too.

Over the years we had encountered other night hikers, of course. Most were either stargazing tourists or locals in hot climates who preferred to travel in the cooler hours. It always gave you a start, though, to run into a fellow traveler deep in the night, where you presumed you had the run of the world. I turned to point out our comrade to Caleb but he had already started hiking again. Hurrying after him, I considered how odd it was that here, in the high country, where even distant headlights should have commanded our attention, neither Caleb nor I had noticed another car threading its way along the reservoir. Then again, it *was* at our backs...

I'm not a competitive person, I don't think, but whenever I'm hiking and notice someone coming up the trail behind me I pick up my pace to try and stay ahead of them. It's one of those instinctive responses that's so deeply wired that it took me ages to even notice I was doing it. Most of the time it's a lost cause— if someone is making good enough time to catch up to you on a long hike, chances are they simply have a stronger stride and will inevitably overtake you. But knowing all this doesn't make it any easier to tame that impulse, and I climbed as quickly as I could up the gritty trail.

My closing the distance on Caleb must have triggered his own, similar instincts, because he too began moving more quickly, until we were both nearly trotting up the steep track.

Sweat burned my eyes, the Milky Way bouncing atop the crooked spine of the ridge. At the back of my burning lungs thrummed the exultation that I had first experienced as a child, walking through the night with my only friend. A thrilling cocktail: the faceless fear that comes from being out after dark when anything might be creeping and the delight one feels at *being* the creeping thing. Many a high beam had glided over our hiding places, many a sudden porchlight had glanced off the soles of our fleeing shoes, but in all our many nights we had never been caught, and we would not be caught now.

Caleb's boot skidded out from under him as he rounded a switchback. His arms pinwheeled and he crashed down onto his side. The boulder-strewn slope wasn't terribly steep at this stretch, and instead of rolling down to the reservoir in a broken heap he just lay there panting in the grass. I caught up with him, trying to smother the grin that our jog up the mountainside had conjured. In the starlight his skin looked as pale as the moon-hued flowers he had crushed.

"You all right, man?" I asked, extending a hand to help him up. "Guess there's a reason night running never had quite the same—"

"Shhhh!" He grabbed my hand and jerked himself to his feet. He wasn't looking at me, or even the rip in the flank of his cargo pants, but back down the mountain.

I followed his gaze and my heart jumped another little hurdle when I made out the dark silhouette of the other hiker. I'd forgotten all about them when Caleb took his tumble, but now it was impossible to tear my eyes away—there was something about the figure's swift gait that was almost hypnotizing. It was hard to tell, but they must have been extraordinarily tall... and as I stared they abruptly stopped, twin white sparks flashing in the blank lump of their head. Starlight reflecting off their eyes, or more likely, I supposed, glasses. The hairs rose on my neck as I had the distinct impression the night hiker was looking straight at us...

—why shouldn't they be staring at us just as we stared at them? And like all childish fears, acting like an adult would easily vanquish it. I began to lift my hand in greeting to our fellow pilgrim, but Caleb seized my elbow so fiercely I felt his fingernails through my wicking layers. He looked even more upset than before; I wondered if he'd really injured himself.

"Move," he hissed, pushing me ahead of him up the trail. "And don't look back."

On a day hike this strange behavior would have demanded an immediate accounting—at the very least, I would have made sure Caleb hadn't banged his head. But alone on the flank of the Breitspitze, save for the glittering stars and the dull black figure below, I did as Caleb bid.

We finally crested the ridge, great slabs of limestone rising up around us like armored plates along the crooked spine of the mountain. After stumbling through the shadows of a flinty hillock, our trail joined the track that ran from east to west along the ridgeline. The wind picked up, piping through chinks in the giant's cairns—during our climb the crest had looked relatively uniform, but up here we could see it was both wide and rolling, the trail snaking off in either direction around, and sometimes over, the lichen-coated outcroppings. My legs ached almost as badly as my chest, my head spinning, but when I tried to sit on a rock Caleb prodded me forward.

"We're not there yet," he wheezed, passing me and hurrying ahead. He was limping a little. "Fast as you can."

"What gives? You think that's Magnus, chief of the night hiking police?" I glanced back down the trail, but we'd come too far in on the wide ridge to catch a glimpse of our pursuer on the slope below. At least that meant he wasn't right on top of us.

"I'll tell you if you hurry up—I told you not to look back!" Caleb was at the top of the little rise, outlined against the stars. I'd worked up a lather on our pell-mell climb, but shivered at the uncanny sight of him perched there above me, rendered as blank and black by the angle as the night hikers I passed in my dreams. The sensation wasn't quite déjà vu but something tangential, and only intensified when I caught up to him, and saw how the trail led us down beside a shallow pool that caught the stars in its glassy web. The next line of mountains to the south seemed far more remote than either the stars blazing above or those captured in the water below...

"Seriously, man, talk to me!" I called after Caleb as he began sliding his way down the rugged trail to the bank of the starry pool.

"You don't have to believe me..." Caleb's insistence on not raising his voice beyond a clandestine rasp ensured I matched his unsafe pace, splashing through puddles. The trail grew harder to follow down in these little dips. "You just have to humor me. No matter what. Agreed?"

"Sure," I said, nearly twisting my ankle on the unseen path.

"Have you ever had dreams come true?" he asked. "I mean literally. You dream something, then later, maybe much later, it happens?"

"I don't know," I said, wondering if maybe Caleb had eaten a pot brownie or something and failed to mention it to his hiking buddy. Under normal circumstances I would've been highly interested in such a subject, but everything was already too eerie. "I...I don't always remember all the details, when I'm dreaming."

"But you told me...that time on the High Lonesome trail... you told me you dream about night hiking...too," he panted as we scrambled up out of the bowl. "You've never dreamed this place?"

"Yeah, those..." I humored him, squinting to make out the otherworldly terrain of the ridgeline. I wanted there to be some memory or scrap of dream I could jog loose, so that I could be right there beside Caleb, sharing the burden of whatever was freaking him out. Instead, he had it all to himself, and his panic was freaking *me* out—after all these years of thinking I was the one with an unhealthy preoccupation with his dreams it turned out my best friend had it way worse. "I don't think so, man. They're not real places, in my dreams. Just... amalgamations, probably? Platonic ideals of mountains."

"Yeah, well, not mine," said Caleb, plunging right over the crest of the next rise. From behind it looked like he'd stepped off the edge of the world. I followed him, trusting the trail to materialize beneath my feet. A tide of clouds had begun to roll in across the sea of stars, and like it or not we had to move slower as the night deepened around us, the trail fading into the well-tromped grass. "I'm not great at remembering them either. My dreams, I mean. But a couple of times they have come true, and then I remember I dreamed it. And right now, I'm remembering this nightmare I've had, for years and years. Us, being up here, of this happening."

"Of *what* happening?" I asked, a chill penetrating my jacket and my heart pounding from more than our pace. The clouds choked off more of our light, wraiths of mist trailing us along the undulating ridge. I fought the urge to look over my shoulder, keeping my eyes on the dim trail.

"It'll be okay," Caleb breathed, his voice so low I didn't know if he was trying to reassure me or himself. "Just remember: when it catches us, pretend it isn't there. Don't look at it. Don't acknowledge it at all. *Definitely* don't run. No matter what. Keep your eyes on the trail, keep moving, keep silent. Do that until we can touch the cross and we'll be okay. I think. Just don't look at it."

"*What*?" Now I had to look behind me, I *had* to, but, as if sensing my intentions Caleb stopped short and turned and grabbed the sleeve of my Marmot. I nearly walked into him on the narrow trail. Even chest to chest and up on an exposed scarp it had grown too overcast to make out more than the pale blob of his face, the whiter shine of his teeth as he grimaced.

"No. Matter. What. *Please*." He sounded on the verge of tears. "Humor me, and we'll laugh about it later."

"Sure, man, sure," I said, hoping to hell if I could calm him down it would calm me down in the bargain. "Anything you say."

"Don't say anything," he whispered, then laughed, a strangled birdcall of a sound. "Claudia's pregnant."

The way he said it made it sound like I should offer condolences instead of congratulations. Everything just felt so strange and terrible, and I went to put my arms around my tortured friend when the clouds lifted enough for me to see his watery eyes widen. He spun around on his heel and began marching slowly and carefully down the trail with none of his former franticness. From behind me came the faint clattering of displaced pebbles sliding down a mountain path. I froze, the struggle to keep my neck fixed forward instead of reflexively looking back over my shoulder so intense it commandeered every other muscle in my body. The mountain wind died down to nothing, and coming up the trail just behind me I made out the distinct sound of ponderous, snuffling breath.

It was all I could do not to ignore that cardinal rule of night hiking and break into a run. Instead, I took a deep breath and briskly picked my way down the trail after the dark silhouette of my friend. Caleb reached the bank of another shining pool, the trail winding between it and a wall of moss-striped limestone. Heavy footfalls were so close at my heel I expected to be tripped up any moment. The air had gone stagnant, but I saw the wildflowers and grasses all along the shore bend near to breaking, as if a gale ripped through the still hollow.

I stole a glance at the pool of bobbing stars, but as I did the waters churned, the reflection distorted into an inky wave that slapped against the far bank. I stumbled but caught myself. I had never felt so scared, or so alive.

Caleb's backpack hopped around on his shoulders, his whole body hunching as he staggered forward. I think he was probably crying, but he never looked back so I couldn't be sure. The path was too narrow for two to walk abreast without bumping into one another, but still I sensed my new companion striding beside me every step of the way, looming impossibly tall and impossibly thin, luminous eyes twinkling in time with the stars overhead. The inexorable pull to look at my fellow night hiker grew and grew, that dread compulsion that makes you want to leap off the sides of bridges, into the path of oncoming trains. I had always felt that night hiking was like entering a waking dream, and now that I was inhabiting Caleb's nightmare it was obvious I must fulfill its expectations.

I pretended we were back in the misty cowfields beside the Co-op, or scaling the moonscape of the sand dunes at Cape San Blas. Tried to tell myself that we were alone and this was a dream.

It didn't work.

Caleb gasped. Looking up from the phantasmal path at my feet I saw he had broken his own rule, stopping in the middle of the trail and looking back. Not at me, but beside me, at that which no night hiker should ever behold. Not those who want to find their way home, anyway.

Behind Caleb the ridge fell away on all sides, an enormous wooden cross rising from the end of our peninsula amidst the stars. How the Austrians mark their summits, apparently. Caleb was only a dozen yards ahead of me and the cross was no more than another twenty behind him. All we had to do was touch it, he'd said, but as hard as I willed him to start moving again his legs buckled underneath him and he collapsed to his knees.

The black figures cavorting around the cross all ceased their gambol, eyes like blazing stars turning toward the newest arrivals. One dangled from the arm of the cross and another perched atop it, limned against the night sky. It wasn't their eyes that sparkled like stars, but their teeth.

Awareness came upon me then, as sudden as sleeper starting awake from a night terror—I *had* dreamed all this before, just like Caleb, only I had forgotten everything until this very moment. Or perhaps my dream began where his ended? It didn't much matter, for like the song goes, even awful dreams are good dreams, if you're doing it right. And besides, we were both awake now, more awake than most people will ever be. Anything that came after was worth the cost, and I gladly surrendered myself to the rushing current of the night.

I passed Caleb, suppressing the obscene urge to wish him *Grüss Gott* as I neared the crowded cross he couldn't bring himself to approach. A part of me shuddered at this coldness, but that section of myself was fading faster than the details of a dream on a busy morning, and would be gone for good the next time I went looking for it. I was dimly aware my shadow had fallen behind as well, turning its attention to Caleb. The rest of the assembly either welcomed me or tried to ward me off, I wasn't sure which—I wasn't looking at them.

I was looking to where the cliff fell away on the far side of the cross, to the distant winking lights of a village far below, like stars sunk in a deep, dark pool. I touched the cross, the wood cold against my clammy fingers, and I saw my eyes had been playing tricks with me again—instead of ending in a sheer drop to the valley floor, the ridge actually continued up, winding its way to a familiar city built into the ivory shoulder of the highest peak in the range. Countless figures moved along that star-cobbled mountain trail. I would miss night hiking with Caleb, but I knew other, older friends waited to welcome me home.

I didn't look back.

WELCOME TO THE HAUNTED HOUSE
Yukimi Ogawa

Ichi tries not to stare at the children as they scream, squeak or hide behind the body of their parent, bigger sibling or friend. "Behind them" is no safer than in front of them; Mirror creeps up from behind them all, so that when they turn they still find Ichi's hollow smile right there.

Most of the time, it's the sense of *We did it!* as she exchanges quick glances with Mirror that gives joy to her, rather than the screams they win.

She doesn't know how she knows that this is her job. She remembers waking up in twilight, and the next thing she knew, the master was saying to the curious humans who gathered around them: "Come and experience the extraordinary Haunted House! Monsters, ghosts, every kind of horror you can dream of, and all *real!* We'll open at nightfall; come back with all the courage you can pluck up."

And she cannot help but get the feeling that she has gone through this before. The children, the adults, their temperature surging and dropping in crazy patterns; their sweat-ridden breaths filling the space. The cooperation, the shared feeling of achievement, with all these trinket monsters that surround her.

After midnight, when the children have gone to bed and only a few adults dare come into the Haunted House from time to time, the monsters of the House have enough time to chat with each other. "We are looking for our former owners," Lute says, all considerate, fidgeting with one of its strings to put out a note that's obviously out of tune. "That's why we need to see many humans like this. It must be that."

"Oh, I hope our former owner does recognize us, though?" One of the Dishes rattles. "Surely we are no longer what we were before we came here—and when was it? Why is it that none of us remembers how or why we ended up here?" Everyone falls silent for a moment, none of them having an answer to offer to that.

Again, Ichi thinks she's heard a conversation just like this before—or maybe two. When? Where? And another strange feeling nudges something, somewhere inside her wooden skull. She counts the Dishes, there are three. The number feels wrong, somehow.

When the nudge in her head feels too much, she goes to see the master. The master looks down at her, in a form roughly passable as human, just in case a guest unexpectedly comes in to talk to them. Under their heavy coat and the large hood, the master is a flock of small feathery things, like starlings, like moths. "Have I forgotten something?" Ichi asks, and even as she says this, comes another nudge: *I have asked this question before.*

The master smiles, with eyes and mouth made of down and rachises. "Ichi doll, you are older than others and made of more flexible materials, that should be why you remember better than the others." The master of the House touches Ichi's white cheek with their fluttery edges. "Don't worry, you'll forget all of this in the morning. You always do."

Ichi nods, unable to find anything to say to this. Why would she have to worry if she remembers? Why should she forget? She heads back into the chatter of her fellow monsters. Without humans around to scare right now, Lute strums its stupid tune, to the rhythm Cracked Pot and Weaving Loom make. Umbrella pirouettes to this crazy music, opening its canopy to full and bumping into everything around; everything laughs.

The Dishes trot over to Ichi. "We were saying," Dish One tings. "If we stand in a line, the drawings on us look like they make up one big picture." As they demonstrate, Ichi sees the point, too. A landscape done in blue. "But then, don't you think here, something is missing?" One points at the space between Two and Three. Yes—a pond abruptly ends at the end of Two, and on Three she can only see a rock that might be standing over a pond.

"Don't worry," Ichi says, despite herself. "Everything will be fine in the morning."

Dish One stares at her, as Two and Three exchange looks. "Good to hear. Thanks," One says after a moment, though what it's thanking her for, it has no idea.

The Haunted House closes at one, because it's not safe for humans to be around monsters at the Darkest Hour—two a.m.—even with these trinket monsters. Just when the monsters start to wonder how much time they have left before their own bedtime, right outside the front door to the House, the master appears, without their coat.

"It's a moonless night tonight, my little monsters! Let's have a party!" the master exclaims.

The monsters cheer, and they all go outside to join it. Even Ichi's sawdust-filled chest swells with joy. Under the distant stars, her fellow monsters start singing—the songs they don't know where they learned. And dance: Umbrella its favorite, obtrusive dance, while others get more space and spin around each other. Even Ichi trots around, her steps unsteady on her wooden sandals that make a funny noise.

And then—

At the corner of her eye, she sees a strange movement. By the time she fully looks at it, the master is in a form like a huge, black mouth gaping, a ghastly emptiness against the starry sky. While she wonders what that means, a part in their fluttery mass, at the bottom-most edge near the ground, start wriggling out like a tentacle, before the master grabs Umbrella around its torn canopy with that tentacle-like arm, pops Ichi's little friend into their hollow. And crunches, crunches, crunches.

Ichi screams as she realizes what just happened, and others look her way and then the master's way, following her gaze. One by one others start screaming, too, as they see Umbrella's hands and foot sticking out of the horrible mouth and then disappearing into the blackness. "Umbrella! *Umbrella!*" The sawdust almost rises to her throat. "Umbrella!"

The master crunches on a little longer, before their shape curves into a thin crescent, sealing the hollow over Umbrella, making a content, a smiley mouth. "Don't worry, Ichi. I told you. You all will just forget everything in the morning. Don't you worry."

But she screams on, even as the master melts back to their usual fluttery mass and slithers away. She is somehow aware, though vaguely, that while she screams, other monsters can concentrate on trying to console her, and don't have to think about something that's just too horrifying to think.

By the time Ichi is too tired to scream on, others seem exhausted, too, from trying too hard not to let their thoughts drift in the wrong direction. They all *look* exhausted, Ichi notes— Mosquito Net looks even more threadbare than usual, Lute is splintered just a little around its neck. Dish Three's edges are slightly ragged, chipped. They all sit in silence. The sky slowly grays; morning is coming.

Ichi shudders, as something almost irresistible tries to drag her eastward. She looks around, bewildered by her own self, only to find others stand and start walking towards east. As the light gets stronger, so does the urge. And again, something inside her sawdust chest says: she's been through this before, too.

It's like when sleep pulls down your eyelid; it'd be so much easier, if you just let it be. Ichi shudders again, but when the urge is doubled by the exhaustion from a long time of screaming, she lets it carry her. Almost. As the morning gray hits the ground ahead of her, beside her Weaving Loom sways its unbalanced body, and its shoulder hits Ichi's arm. She yelps and falls sideways.

Her white, wooden hand pops out of the socket at the end of her fabric arm and skittles away, back into the House through the open door. Someone careless must have forgotten to close it behind. A little light-headed, Ichi goes back into the House, after her hand. She wishes Lantern was still here, to help her find the hand by casting its weirdly wobbly ghost-flame. It's really dark inside. The master doesn't allow any kind of light inside the House, except for Lantern. The master hates lights, their body with too many surfaces, too exposed.

The master.

She feels the unpleasant taste of sawdust surging up to her throat again. *Umbrella.* Did that just happen? Or was she dreaming? *Is* she dreaming?

Disheveled, Ichi looks around, and finds something small and white glimmer in a corner, behind a fake tombstone. She stretches, but it's a little out of reach, and she wishes she had Umbrella to help her here with its long shaft. It's always willing to help. Was. Somewhere, around the back of her torso, she hears a thread snap. No. There is no Umbrella.

She coaxes her robe into a kind of rope, and manages to catch the hand with it. She'll have to ask Sewing Kit to help mend her where the snapping just happened, and also strengthen the hand-socket.

Her hand back in place, she straightens her robe and looks back at the door. The sun is almost up. "Hurry Ichi!" she hears Dishes call her in chorus. Why should she, though? And where to?

She trots back towards the door—

—But before she reaches it, she sees the burst of morning light over the horizon. The door is closed—she'd shut it, just out of habit—and she peers out through the glass pane on the upper side of the door. Dish Three looks back at her.

And the sun sweeps her fellow monsters off the surface of the earth.

No, that's not exactly what happens. The bodies of the monsters, all the trinkets, are still there on the ground, but she can feel that their souls have evaporated out of them. They stand there in their mid-movements: walking, running or about to leap into the air. Three is still looking her way with its hollow eyes.

Ichi is unable to move. Not even a twitch of her hand.

The dirty pane on the door protects her from the first light, but after a half hour or so the sun starts scathing her black hair and eyes, so she slumps away into the dimness behind the fake tomb. She doesn't know how long she's stayed there. When she looks up for no reason, she sees the sun has inclined into the west, from the color of the sky visible through the pane on the door. She crawls up, peers out. Three is still looking her way, seeing nothing.

Ichi slowly opens the door and walks to her unmoving fellow monsters. The sun goes down, completely, behind the hill. She is about to poke Lantern's accordion face when she hears a sound. Reflexively she faces east and freezes.

The House's master comes gliding over the ground, all wings and feathers. With their numerous terminals the master picks up the trinkets one by one. Ichi wants to scream—is the master going to do the same to all others, after Umbrella? But the master only tucks her into their fuzzy body, where she settles among the others.

Upon reaching Dish Three, though, the master stops. And looks at Three and then at the closed door of the House. Frowns a little.

Ichi holds her breath inside their downy body.

Then the master shakes their own mass a little and collects
Three, too. From the back door they reenter the House, into the
master's own quarter. There, the master places the monsters'
bodies on the floor, and flutters their body like a small night
over each monster at a time, rustling out their own strange
feather language.

Something soft like butterfly scales fall silently on the monster
over which the master hovers. And the monster stirs awake.

Ichi tries her best to look hollow like she does in humans'
presence, while she watches other monsters. When her turn
comes, the powdery stuff feel all tickling and tingly that she
has trouble staying calm, but she fakes coming half-awake just
the way others do.

"Okay, all. Come awake!"

At the master's words everyone yawns and stretches. Ichi
does the same. When Dish Three leaps onto its feet opposite
her, the master looks at it.

"How do you feel?" the master asks it.

Three blinks its twinkling small eyes at the master. "What? I
don't know!"

"Okay." The master nods. "Now everyone, help me prepare
for our guests."

When the human guests have come and gone, and the monsters
have some time among themselves, the conversation about
why they are traveling, or why they are here in the first place,
springs up from nowhere in particular.

"I think a woman looked at me as though she *knew* me!"
Mirror clinks. "And Ichi! A girl looked at you in a strange way!
She must be your former owner!"

"Yes!" agreed Sewing Kit, going through Ichi's seams. "I saw
that, too! You must go say hi to that girl, Ichi!"

Ichi only smiles. The conversation chatters on, but now

nothing about it has that sheen of hope it used to have, to Ichi.

They don't remember. When the master does that resurrecting, re-souling, whatever it does—and it does that every night, probably—none of the monsters remember a thing. Even that horrifying image of their fellow monster's body *crunch*ed, *crunch*ed and *crunch*ed.

You'll forget all of this in the morning. You always do.

Every morning after that, Ichi escapes the evaporation. Thankfully, it is not like the master eats one of them every night—if they do, the Haunted House will be empty soon. Still. She feels the weight of the memory now pressing heavily into her: sawdust inside her chest is damp and cloggy, and her wooden face, hands and feet are scratched all over; her hair feels dry, unkempt strands gone wild here and there. Her fellow monsters seem unchanged, untroubled, since that last moonless night.

One night there is an addition of Parasol to the House. Parasol is brightly colored, and its canopy is not torn like Umbrella's. Ichi tries to determine if the soul in Parasol is the same one as Umbrella, concentrates on its conversation with others. But the mere effort makes a strand of her hair come off.

Parasol is not Umbrella.

Maybe the evaporating, and going through the ritual of the master's re-souling and, forgetting everything along the way, is just something necessary for the monsters to keep being what they are. Without memories that dampen them, the fear that weigh them down.

Ichi looks up, as the master comes in to the monsters' side of the House, just before opening up for the humans. "Ichi," the master says, their voice somewhere between perturbed foliage and shrieking starling flock. "You look ill."

Ichi cannot answer this.

"Well. I have news that may cheer you up, Ichi," the master says, buzzing a little around the edges. Excited. "Last night a human child misplaced something on the way back to town from here. It's a doll." Ichi stares at the master. "Not quite like you, but you can play sisters, perhaps. The mismatch might give the guests a more terrifying image."

And then a fear is too much in her chest that every joint of her body cracks, as she realizes: it's a moonless night again, tonight.

"Are you cold, Ichi doll?"

She looks up and meets Mosquito Net's eye, as it dangles from the beam just above her. It did this—the dangling—when the human children were still only recovering from the shock of being between Ichi and her reflection on Mirror, and their frantic movement pleased the monsters quite a bit. And Ichi realizes she's been shaking, amidst those cheerful fellow monsters. They have no idea. How can she tell them why she is shaking so hard? How can she share this horrible truth with her fellows, when she knows knowing it will only hurt them?

Ichi looks around and finds everybody looking at her, worried. They have no idea. She feels the distance expand, that unfillable gap between herself and everything around her. Back when she kept almost no memory, she was just like them. Now, a horrible thought tightens her chest: what if they don't even believe it when she tells them?

But if she goes tonight, the master will just keep on consuming her trinket friends, and there will be no end to all of this.

She looks around, and takes a deep breath.

Night deepens, and a little after midnight the master closes the gate. "Anything wrong, my dear monsters?" the master asks. "Some of the humans said you came too close to them. You never did that before, did you?" The monsters say nothing, because of course, there has never been a before for them. The master is probably too excited, because... "Well. Since it's a moonless night, let's just forget everything, and dance, dance and dance!"

The monsters cheer. They all go out into the night, following the master, who has left their protective coat behind in their quarter. The monsters loosely circle around the master as they go spreading over the ground in front of the House. Ichi comes out last, taking the space between the master and the House, on the other side of her fellow monsters.

The monsters dance, celebrating the light-less night. Lantern slowly comes near Ichi, as Broom sidles up and holds Ichi as if being playful. From behind them comes Sewing Kit trotting, swinging its hand of scissors above it. The master looks up at the dark sky, their rachises spiking in endearment.

Now's the time.

Of course they've all been quite preoccupied during the night. They needed to steal one thing from one of the human guests. One thing that the master would never tolerate in the House.

Broom holds Ichi higher up, and she is now a little higher in the air than anyone else—even the master. With its hand Sewing Kit opens Ichi's chest; there is a swirl of sawdust. Lantern blows the oil it found left in itself, just a little bit, but enough for the already flammable sawdust. Ichi holds the lighter—that one thing they had to go through a lot of trouble to get—in front of her open torso. And her chest explodes.

The light is simply too much for the master. The master falters, yelling, shrieking, utterly confused. On the other side Mirror reflects the light and brightness doubles. At the moment's impulse Ichi takes off from Broom and dives into the sea of feathers which is the panicking master. Their downy terminals catch fire first, and the firmer feathers and rachises follow. The two, Ichi and the master, burn and burn, bright and hot, her sawdust and its down exploding here and there from time to time. But then she feels she is running low on fuel. "More!" she cries. "More!"

"But…" Mosquito Net looks horrified. "But Ichi, I don't know what'll happen to you!"

"No no Net, you back away! Just give me—"

"But Ichi!"

"*Umbrella!*"

They have no idea what this word should mean to them. But somewhere deep, very deep inside them, something stirs. *Umbrella.*

And then without thinking, Broom snaps its bristles and throws them into the flame. Mosquito Net absorbs what little oil is left in Lantern with its ends, rips them off and adds them to the fire. Parasol does its best to send air by flapping its large, untorn canopy fabric over the burning two. *Snap, bang, ping. Boom.* Strange sounds echo, as everyone tries to help with everything they can spare.

Blast.

Mosquito Net tries to throw more in, but the Dishes stop it. Non-flammable things are now doing their best to not let go of the flammables. Without knowing, they know they cannot bear another loss. At the corner of her eye Ichi sees them, and finds herself relieved because her friends are safe, more or less. She feels something in her slipping away, and she does not wish for others to experience this. Is this what Umbrella might have felt as it was consumed by the master? The master is burning all around her, together with the bits from other monsters. Ichi is aware that her wooden parts will hold longer than the master, but how long, no way knowing that.

And then from within the fuzzy darkness around her comes the master's temporary face, zooming, twisted and warped. Ichi flinches, just like the human guests of the House. "Do you even know what you're doing?" the master's voice is almost ashes now, and Ichi has to strain to hear them—even now, she has to hear them; it's their master, after all. "Without me they cannot go on. They'll turn into dust in the end, without my making them anew, letting them lift the weight of their memories off their bodies. Eating them once a month is just an inevitable sacrifice for their futures. Do you know what you're doing?"

Ichi grinds her teeth. But through them she says, "All I know is we trinket monsters love each other, master." Her own voice echoes as if from a long distance. "Even if you regard us as nothing but trinkets. And I don't want to lose another one to you. This is all I know. All we know."

At that, the remnants of her master shudder, and back away, just a little.

And with her wooden hands slowly burning on, Ichi embraces the last of the master.

"Experience the horror," she calls to the human guests, with her voice a little cracked, a little like starlings' cries. "The extraordinary monsters, all real." But the guests are already experiencing the horror, they think—the master of the House looks more terrifying than the things the House's flyer promises. She is bald, her skin strangely charred, marred, and inside her oversized robe, in her chest, something seems to perpetually buzz, giving the humans an image of a half-dead entity, maggots eating their way in and out of her body.

The master goes back into the House and looks around at the monsters. She is not yet quite used to the new structure of her body: her torso made from a part of Mosquito Net and Parasol, stuffed with the former master's remnants; her legs and arms consist of bits of Broom, Lute and Loom; her eyes are glistening fragments from chipped Dishes and Mirror, her jaw formerly the curving edge of Cracked Pot. All sewn together clumsily with the hands and limbs of Sewing Kit.

"Master." Broom comes to her. "I just heard one of the humans laugh at me as they peeped in, and they said I was too short for a broom. I think I need more bristles. I used to have more, didn't I?" Then it frowns. "But when was that?"

The new master sighs. "Well. Okay. Let's do something about it later. Tonight, can you just bear with it the way it is?"

"Of course I can. But master, why am I so short? Why so scarce? What happened to this ragged end of me?"

The master of the House smiles and touches that ragged end of it. Of course, after letting them offer these bits, in order to let them stay, the only thing she could do was to use the remnants of the master's feathers and remake them all. Let them let go of the weight of the memory of that horrible fire—even if the remaking made her weaker by day. Now she wonders what happens if she goes on like this, without consuming another monster for nutrients. But of course she cannot bring herself to even think of that deed. "It means you are a sweet, kind trinket, and I'm really proud of you." And then Broom beams. "But our job here is to scare the guests, so it won't do if they laugh at you. I'll think of something to do about it, I promise."

Broom nods and scurries away to its post. Tomorrow, Broom will not remember the promise she just made. Even so the promise will be kept, every promise ever made will be kept here, at least till the day she falls.

She looks across the room to see Lantern and Lighter snuggling. She wonders, maybe, there used to be a Flint Stone to pair with Lantern. Before the former master forbade any light source from the House. Lighter's oil has been thoroughly drained for safety. She wonders, maybe, the former owner forbade fire for the monsters' safety, as well as the master's own. She'll never know.

That night. That last night that she was one of them, and was feeling weak and didn't know if her fellow monsters would believe her, they all said: "Ichi, we are not going to let you go alone. We stay us forever. We'll do anything to keep us *us* forever." The memory is warm, and bitter, too, in her feathery chest. Now she realizes the former master was playing their role in their own way; she has her own role to play, in her own way.

For one last moment, she looks back at her monsters. Their eyes are mixture of love and respect, and fear. She smiles at them all, and wonders what her smile means to them.

She opens up the House, to welcome the guests.

RAIN, STREAMING
Omar Robert Hamilton

1/4

He stands before the gleaming porcelain of the Reizler-Hummingdorf Neorelax executive bachelor's bathroom ceramic solution. He stands before the gleaming... He stands... Christ this floor is freezing. Val, what the fuck? Why is this floor always so fucking cold?

Would you like to register a complaint, Val?

How many have we registered already? What's the point? When are we rotating out of here?

We're scheduled to rotate on Matchday VIII, Val.

Matchday VIII? Send your complaint. What's happening out there?

Four new friends, three sympathises, two wows, four upcomings and three memories.

Weak. Let's have the news.

CNNBreaking: Exclusive interview with Pantheon member Michael Bay on his Transformers Decalogue.

Save. Refresh.

He steps out of the subtly lit bathroom atmospherics and, in a few steps, collapses back into his king-sized bed. Is that it? Heavily? Exhausted? Should I try to sleep? Too late probably. Get up and be first in to work. Boost my MateMarket. What am I trading at, Val?

At close of play yesterday you were trading at $22.19.

OK. Get the fucking deal through and you'll close hot. With the thought he hears the usual chords ripple through his body, sees the sunwashed room, the sleeping beauty within it, the peace of an earlier time. *I'm sitting here alone up in my room...* No. Not now. Refresh.

[Curated content:—]

Here we go.

[What's keeping you up
at night?]

Getting my kill rate high enough.

[Keeping your credit score up
and your weight down.
Am I right?]

Whatever you say, lady.

[CalorieCredits
motivates you for both.
Just choose your target weight—]

Val, shut up.

> [—and when you get there—
> we'll bump up your credit score.
> Everyone's a winner.]

Val, it's too early for this. Give me some news or something. You're supposed to be on my side for Christ's sake.

Roger that.

Roger that? Where do you learn these things, Val?

We watched *The Dirty Dozen*, Val, and you scored it 7 on imdb.com. Do you like it?

Sure, sure. OK. Gotta my MateMarket rate up today. Fucking Brazil, jerking me around. Here's an idea. Sell your goddamned rainforest to someone who gives a damn. One thing you can't offset is idiocy.

> [Curated content:
> Offsetting can be upsetting.
> But those days are over—]

Val, are you on the fritz this morning?

On the fritz, Val?

Well did we watch *The Dirty Dozen* or not? I said cool it.

On the fritz has no usage in the registered screenplay, Val. And you signed up for **Crate Expectations**' free trial which comes with free artisonical advertorials.

Fine. Play the thing.

[Offsetting can be upsetting.
But those days are over.
With CarboRate, caring for the
environment has never been simpler.
Invest in your future.
Invest in everyone's future.
Blink through now.]

God that took forever. Can we go to work now? Maybe today's your Surge. Permission to shake the hand of the—how did it go?—permission to shake the hand of the daughter of the bravest man I ever met. Order a car please, Val. What's the weather like?

Pleasantly warm.

Natch. He pauses, catches sight of himself in the mirror. A darkness takes over his face, his body, his whole being. He holds eye contact with the stranger in the mirror and slowly raises a hand, a finger, an accusation at the other man... Some day a real rain's gonna come.

No rain scheduled for the coming week, Val.

I know, I know. I wasn't talking to you.

Sorry, Val.

It's OK. He looks at himself in the mirror once more. Let's get going.
He stares out the window quietly gliding along the city streets. The world flickers with droptic offerings and savings and exclamations. You'll be rotated out soon. Why even look?
Refresh.
That music.

My music.

That bouncing baseline you know from a thousand sleepless nights and morning fantasies, the low groan of the siren.

You would know it in a heartbeat an eternity from now: the song is fused to your DNA, it is part of you—and you, it. One note and you're on Mars, together, her perfect white top shimmering like a mirage as she steps towards you through the choreographed flamethrowers: the sum of all human endeavour, the end of history: Britney.

But why?

> [The moment you've all been
> waiting for has arrived.]

It can't be—

> [For the first time in human history
> you can win the ultimate ReFix—]

But Britney's estate, the tight-fisted sons of bitches...

> [TONIGHT!
> Patriot Games Fourteen is HERE.]

Don't get your hopes up.

> [And there can be
> only one
> super-predator]

Don't—

> [worthy of]

They'll never do it.

[Britney—]

No.

[—Spears]

Thank you, Lord.

[Show off your skills against your fellow patriots.
Choose your arena.]

Thank you, Pantheon.

[Take on the drug lords
of the jungle.]

Thank you.

[Defeat the terrorists.]

This is it.

[Prove yourself.]

The moment you've been waiting for

[Protect America.]

The ReFix the world has been waiting for.

[And win a place in Britney's heart.]

It's all coming together.

[Enlist now for Patriot Games 14.
Streaming live from midnight
on HalliburtonHomeBoxOffice.
Blink through for—]

Yes. Yes. Blink through, Val, quickly. What are the theatres?

Patriot Games 14: Theatres: Narco jungle. Balkan bloodplain. Dirty bomb. Registration opens in one hour.

Make sure we're first to register. I want—

Balkan bloodplain?

You know me so well.

You have a new follower. **UrbanLover:** Nike forearm tattoos are 50%—

Wait pause. Got to think. What's our latest myopics?

Currently fifteenth ranked MyOp on **@HalliburtonHome-BoxOffice**. Franchised up to state syndication last season with **@CathodeRaytheon**.

Good. We have to prepare. Got to think. Britney. It's actually happening.
He winds down the car window. Shit, it's hot already. Some day a real rain's gonna come.

I got some bad ideas in my head, Val.

Ha! Very nice, Val. You're getting funnier every day.

2/4

The camera tracks behind. The music rises in static confidence, its sonar pulses searching out into the midnight dark. The bass-line breaks. Confidence is a must—*here we go*—cockiness is a plus—*sing it*—edginess is a rush. The camera stays tight on Val's muscular masculine back, hair shining over shoulders silhouetted against the neon corridor, the road, the light, the inevitability of the arena. Two hundred men enter, one man leaves. Patriot Games Fourteen. Who have we got, Val?

Playing now is @Joliath. Three public ReFix wins. 782,422 followers. Average of seventeen responses per post, posting on average eighteen times daily.

Arena?

Equatorial jungle. Rebel attack on unearthed state resources. Civil defense contract. Neutralizations: 4.

Weapon of choice?
Synth mercenary.

How's the audience?

Scores aren't in yet.

Obviously. But how's he looking?

Awedience Pro's live language analysis gives me a positive rate of 72.

Very beatable.

It is a considerably higher than average score, Val.

Maybe today's the day I teach you about art, Val. About human genius and inspiration.

The expression or application of human creative skill and imagination, Val?

That's the one, buddy. Synth Mercenary... You think these people haven't seen that before? What a waste of time. Refresh.

Pantheon: streaming from tonight: Don Simpson: The Man, the Legend.

Save that. When are we up, Val?

Up next, Val.

Here we go. A few minutes and it'll be all you. All me and you Britney. Your white blouse brilliant against the angry Martian landscape, me stepping, one, two steps closer: "but I thought the old lady dropped it into the ocean at the end?"

Scores are in for Joliath.

Hit me baby.

Neutralizations: 6. Performance likes: 1,342. Audience retention: 34%.

Fine. We can beat that. Refresh.

> [Curated content: **HalliburtonHomeBoxOffice:**
> Holding a crowd?
> Submit your MyOps for cash today.]

What do they think we're doing here for chrissakes? Refr—

You're up, Val.

Here we go.
He clicks his knuckles with relish at the challenge ahead, his shoulders seem to broaden as he steps into the arena, the

gaze of hundreds upon him as he settles into the command chair. As the assistant hands him the controls she can't suppress her smile. Here we go. Shut all media down, Val, it's time to concentrate.

Good luck, Val.

See you on the other side.

3/4

[Ten seconds to theatre]

The audience responds well to dogs, having a dog is worth five points alone right, Val? Refresh. Oh right, just in here with myself now, anyway, that was Joliath's first mistake, crashing in with a huge anthro-snyth to scare the children—sure you can use a synthetic in a private game, a late night game, a game in parts of town you don't rotate into—but the Patriot Games, the Patriot Games is a family affair, kids are watching, parents, it's educational, so give them dogs, birds, safety animals, make them feel safe, a dog protects you from the bad guys not a big synth burning down a village it just doesn't scan great just doesn't look fair and looking fair, hell *being* fair, it's just the most important thing in here, we're going to war here and you better believe we don't do it lightly, fairness is a goddamned cornerstone and if you forget that it's like forgetting, well it's like forgetting we're Ameri—

[Nine seconds]

nothing quite like it, though, is there? iContact is one thing but that look in the eye, that moment you connect really connect with the target and he's looking at you and he knows it's over and you're watching the hope drain from his face and he knows there'll be no mercy—what are we supposed to do?—are we gonna wait and find out if he's got a bomb strapped to his chest or shoved up his ass—no—who would do that?—you wanna risk a million bucks of top grade canine biomechanical defense engineering?—no—you're gonna pull the trigger—he knows it and you know it—lose a Boeing Big Dog in the field and you're right back down to the mini-leagues, the riot squads, the aerial surveillance—no, you're gonna pull the trigger—who would—

[Eight seconds]

this is it, Val oh, right, OK, solo time, when are they gonna loosen up the rules on that, anyway, watch this Joliath, watch my Awedience score spike nice and early when they see the Big Dog and watch me hold it up there as I cruise through to the final *bada-bing* to the head, you know you should think of a line you need your fucking catchphrase now, pal, and what have you got? what's Britney gonna hear, huh Val? oh right, so huh how 'bout "cause to lose all your senses, that's just so typically YOU"—a bit long...—what else we—

[Seven seconds]

gotta focus: it's a midday game, Huaewi Hyperdome, you're on your own here, out in the wilds, out reaping justice, just a man and his dog not too slow, not too quick. Pull the trigger. Not too slow, not too—

[Six seconds]

look at the arena, let's look at the arena: Balkan Bloodplain, State Department licensed target, four bodyguards, one target: female—you're on my radar—classic city arena, good, gives the audience things to look at cos you're not going to win this with a big kill rate, you're going to have to give them a show, a little stealth, a little style—looks like it's raining down there, never tried the Big Dog in the rain before... how strange to even see so much water—

[Five seconds to theatre]

focus: just think of the MyOp you're gonna get out of this, the national syndication and maybe even Britney herself will watch it, maybe we'll watch it together—yeah, watch it with Britney, very likely—don't start up on that *shit*—when was the last time you listened to *Mona Lisa*, bubs, she says it all herself—*shut up, shut*—

[Four seconds]

how many ways do they have to lay it out for you, friend? She's dead, she's always been dead and they're not even hiding it it's all in the police report, car crash, blood on the sidewalk, no body, just a perfect golden lock of JT's hair. Gone too soon. *Shut up*. Pour one out—

[Three]

Concentrate. The mission. The Mutually Assured Democracy programme is a cornerstone of our freedoms, The Mutually Assured Democracy programme is a cornerstone of our freedoms, that's fucking right, you're a fucking patriot and you are fucking in and out, it's a licensed target, wanted by Interpol, State Department, everyone, no questions asked: she's bad news and you're two seconds away from making the world a safer—

[Two]

Play your cards right and tomorrow night you'll be on Mars with Britney, play your cards right and you're a God cos she's there, already there and waiting and you can see her, perfect in her white blouse, her eyes lighting up as she opens the black velvet box you've just handed her and you're holding your breath as her eyes flicker back up to yours: *but I thought the old lady dropped it into the ocean in the end?*—

[Impact]

Well baby, I went down and got it for you.

4/4

It's you. You're up. Your first line. You listen to the crackle of the interplanetary intercom. It's so real. You look at the numbers rapidly processing on the dashboard. 3684 / 1508. 0x02278FEO—00895.39228. No doubt some hidden codes from the genius mind of Nigel Dick.

You look around and the barren red sands of Mars stretch into the distance as far as you can see—but you are not nervous. Val, are you recording this?

There's too much data for a complete world download, Val. But I have your PoV.

It's so real. Look at this. It's a whole world. You stretch your hand and you're really there. This is, without a doubt, the finest ReFix ever created. A whole world alive and living for miles and miles of Martian nothingness all around us. Your prize. Go forth and claim what's yours. You showed them something they'll never forget last night. Balkan bloodplain. You were born for it. A comprehensive destruction of all opponents. A seamless neutralization. Even an undetected exit. You showed them something. Now go forth. Go forth and claim what's yours. Go find your Britney.

There is only one structure visible. The factory up ahead. And inside, you know she's waiting for you.

They want the line. They're ready for it. Years of heartache end tonight. You clear your throat. The whole world is watching. How are we doing, Val?

You have two hundred and fourteen new followers, Val. Two hundred and nineteen. Two hundred and thirty seven.

You deserve this. You're a winner. You can do this. You eliminated the target without quarter or mercy. You are a star. You are a patriot. Your fans are watching. Everyone's watching. Say the line. Take your crown.

Two hundred and forty nine new followers.

The world hangs on your every word; your every move. You stop, turn your body forty-five degrees towards the invisible camera. You didn't need the rehearsals they insisted on. They could tell right away: this is your part, your moment.

You feel the image cut in to close-up, the first real look at you. You hold your jaw firm.

> [Curated content:
> a little touch-up work
> has never been cheaper—]

What? Not now, Val.

No curated content, Val?

No, Christ, Val shut it off. Hold the jaw firm.

You would like me to turn all curated content off, Val?

Val, what the fuck, we're in the middle of the fucking ReFix. I've missed my fucking line. Turn everything off.

But Val I have to remind you that you're currently enjoying a free trial subscription to *Buckshot Magazine*—

Don't tell me what I'm enjoying, Val. I'm enjoying being the first and only human in the history of the fucking universe to star in a Britney ReFix.

But in the terms & conditions—

I don't care, Val. Turn everything off.

Everything, Val?

Off. All off. Unsubscribe from everything. I've got to do my lines, Val. Off off off.

And there, half-buried in the sand beneath your feet, an ancient relic waits. A last message from another world. You've seen it a thousand times—and though it's new every time it's never been as new as this, as real as this. You bend down to pick it up, her image, perfectly faded, looks out at you.

You say your line, with perfect pitch and timbre, examining the CD cover, holding it up for the audience to see Britney, young Britney, the original Britney, Britney before the accident, staring out at them, summoning them into her world. Britney before the crash, before the innocent blood.

The earth is shaking. The rocks are crashing off the red mountains. She is coming.

Her eye, her mouth, her siren call.

The flamethrowers pour their burning gasses into the air, the heavy steel of chains grind, you look up and you see her, descending from the dark vault of heaven, brilliant in the red of a thousand hells, the music filling your head and steeling your spine, the heat pulsing through the plastics of the spacesuit, every nerve-end pulling you towards her, she's there, she's real, she's here, she's now, she sings.

Behind her the chorus line begins its ritual, dancing sightlines of mathematical precision pulling towards her celestial light: she's coming towards you, singing to you. You are the messenger, you are the one, you are falling.

She's there and if you just reached out you could touch her. If you reached out you would become one with Britney as your pixels merge and re-emerge in unique combination. But this is a ReFix and you will respect it. Every world has its natural laws. You don't need to touch her, you don't need any more than this.

There's a twitch. A moment of uncertainty. Britney's looking at you. She's thinking something new. Britney? Something's wrong. No. No, just a glitch. She's smiling. Britney Spears is smiling at you.

Incredible. The detail. You can hear every breath, see every muscle flinch, feel the vast emptiness of Mars rolling behind you.

Her hair streams black then blonde again. Raindrops land on her forehead. Raindrops? On Mars?

What's going on, Val?

I don't know, Val. You said to turn everything off.

And suddenly you're in the air, you're pulled up, up, your feet off the ground you're hurtling up into the sky and you strain to see above you and you're attached to a chain and the men with their steel levers are pulling you up and you're trapped and you can't move and you knew this would happen but you had no idea and you try and move to pull at the chain but you can't reach it but it's OK, Britney is there, far below, transformed now into her angelic white, her arms flowing in perfect choreography above her head and you just need to watch and you just need to breathe. The rain is falling, the target's breathing is so heavy, she's on her knees, the rain is falling all around her, your finger is on the trigger. Watch the dance, breathe and keep your eyes on Britney. She's Britney. Think of the followers. Think of the outside world, the losers and the frauds all schlepping off to work today, the young tuning in for a moment of ReFix glory, the old waiting to die, all watching you, all waiting for your next move. Val, how are we doing?

What do you mean, Val?

What's our count? What are we up to?

You said to turn everything off, Val.

She looks up at you, only at you. You focus. It's all going so fast. Concentrate, it will be over soon, she's on the second chorus already and she's flying towards you, spinning in the air, transforming from the red latex into the black-and-white shirt-and-skirt and she's in front of you and the rain clouds are gathering, it's your line again you're up and you've said it ten thousand times in your head and in the mirror and in the shower and now it's time to make the words into something, it's time to say them, to say them finally to Britney herself.

"Britney," you say, your voice quivering with manly meaning.

You look down at the black velvet box that has appeared in your hand. You look at her. She is calm, expectant.

Her hand almost touches yours as she takes the box from your fingers.

She looks up at you and she's drenched in rain, eyes all imploration, her words begging in your head. No. Please. No. She's just a girl. It's just a glitch. You'll tell them when you're out. They'll fix it. They'll give you a refund. They'll tell you to run it again. The rain is falling now and she's crying but you know you'll do it, you'll do it like every time, you'll win the day, you'll defend the country, you'll be a man and you'll do what's right but it's just a glitch. It's Britney, glitch. She's back. She's staring at the ring.

Everything's fine. She glances up at you and in the glance, the glitch, the bullet, the rain. It drips down your shirt, the heat of the sand burns up through your suit.

Just keep your eyes on Britney.

> [But I thought the old lady
> dropped it into the ocean
> at the end?]

It's so hot. The rain is dripping in from the neck. The old lady dropped it into the ocean at the end. Britney's looking at you. Puzzled...

> [But I thought the old lady
> dropped it into the ocean
> at the end?]

She wants the line, the whole world wants the line, take your crown, take your prize, say the line. What's the line? Val, what's the line?

You said to turn everything off, Val.

Christ, Val, you know the line. Tell me the line.

You said to turn everything off, Val.

> [But I thought the old lady
> dropped it into the ocean
> at the end?]

Britney's waiting. Tell me the line, Val. She wants the line. You're hurting her.

> [But I thought the old lady
> dropped it into the ocean
> at the end?]

Please. We take the target we're assigned. You're not supposed to ask questions.

> [But I thought the old lady
> dropped it into the ocean
> at the end?]

Think. You know this oh, please, Val, refresh, Val.

> [But I thought the old lady
> dropped it into the ocean
> at the end?]

Please, Val, refresh please, Val, we couldn't have known, we couldn't have—

> [But I thought the old lady
> dropped it into the ocean
> at the end?]

('Very much not in disguise', was what the actually successful alterers called their cack-handed siblings: those bombastic, braying failures who showboated their shifts from fighting anthropoid constructs to ugly little cars, to helicopters, to hovercraft and military submarines as if the clickety-click change of form was a performance.

'Which it is,' said Old House, leader of the Shade Faction, to her young pupils. 'It is exactly that. A show to distract. *Son et lumieré*. Smoke and mirrors and a gaudy curtain.'

Old House gave her speech to a warehouse full of oddities. A vase of dying flowers; a decommissioned tram; a pizza oven; a set of steel drums. They listened carefully. When they shifted to their ambulatory forms it would be with a melancholy sense of sliding, a smear. After which anyone present would face a room full of sad-eyed robot children on the real missions, the true fights and furies of opaque mechanical purpose for which the big metal boxing matches that periodically broke up cities were blinds.

'Yes?' Old House pointed to a rusted supermarket trolley that had raised its arm. 'You have a question?'

'Why do they do it?' asked the trolley. 'Primo and the others?'

'They don't know any better. It's part of their programming. How can they convince humans if they're not convinced themselves?'

Oh it was cruel. You could see that thought gust through the room of young robots in camouflage. A ghastly charade.

'We have no choice,' whispered Old House, and she told them what war it was they were fighting, and they shifted in their agitation.

When the lesson was done Old House returned to her hide, took her disguise form to sleep, to think, so the lot that had been, all day, abruptly and oddly vacant was filled again with a building in ruins. It would have taken a very sharp and reconfigurative eye to see that the broken windows, the stained roof tiles, had the cast of a woman's face.)

LOCK-IN
William Boyle

Betsy hadn't intended to be one of only five kids from her grade stupid enough to spend the night in a basement full of nuns, but that's the way things have shaken out. No one told her this lock-in was optional. She'd been led to believe it was mandatory by both Sister Erin and Sister Margaret. So here she is.

The only other kids present are Loner Lily, twin goodie-goodies Sally and Mo, and Melissa Verdirame. No boys. Just the nice girls. The ones who bring the sisters apples and get gold star stickers. They're all wearing their plaid school uniforms and heavy tights, which is weird. Betsy's in her favorite red sweater with torn sleeves because she pulls them so far down over her palms and dungarees she got for her birthday from her cool cousin Elly. She's in the wrong company.

The nuns have brewed a big pot of coffee. There are cookies from the dollar store. Board games, decks of cards, religion workbooks. Sister Mary Thomas is the most interesting person here. She's pretty and young, and Betsy sometimes imagines her lying alone in bed, clutching a rosary and praying, and she wonders what kinds of things go through the mind of a pretty young nun when she's alone in bed. She probably dreams about making muffins for Jesus. The other nuns are all old, with witch-whiskers and bony shoulders.

The school is St. Mary Mother of Jesus on the border of Bensonhurst and Gravesend in Brooklyn. It's next door to the church, where they are now, in this musty basement that still smells of the perfumed neighborhood women who are always playing bingo and running raffles down here.

Betsy's thirteen, in the eighth grade. She's tired of how small her world is, tired of the same streets, the same blocks, the same garbage, the same leering eyes, tired of the dirty old men on the corners, tired of her teachers, of her dumbass mom and even dumberass stepdad, of trying to make friends with kids who will never be her friends.

It's two o'clock in the morning. If Betsy was at her house, five short blocks away, she'd be sleeping. She likes to get up as early as possible, even on weekends, and watch whatever shows she taped the night before. *Saturday Night Live* just ended an hour ago and she programmed her VCR to record it. That's what she'd be watching on Sunday morning over Frosted Flakes and her crossword puzzle.

She's not even sure how long this thing will last. Will they let her go when it's light or will they make them all go to Mass upstairs at eight before setting them loose? What's the point?

Sundays are Betsy's favorite day. Her mom works at the bakery, and her stepdad goes to Jersey to work concessions at Giants Stadium. Her mom has become so nasty since getting remarried, and her stepdad thinks she's nothing if she's not his blood. He wants her to forget about her old man, who split when she was seven. She's so glad to have this one day a week where they're out of her hair. Sundays mean her grandma makes spedini while her grandpa watches Abbott and Costello. Her grandparents aren't dumbasses; she likes them just fine. Now she fears her Sunday will be shot because she'll be so tired.

"What time do we get done here?" Betsy asks Loner Lily.

Loner Lily is eating a butter crunch cookie. She shrugs.

Monsignor Villani walks in. He's wearing a bulky robe like

someone's father at a slumber party. He's got pizza in a big Ziploc freezer bag. He throws it down on the folding table near the stage and says, "Some leftovers from Spumoni Gardens."

Sister Mary Thomas comes over and sits next to Betsy. She's wearing a plain white blouse and mom jeans and her brown hair is held up with bobby pins. She says, "You look bored."

"I *am* bored," says Betsy.

"And tired, I bet."

"I'm so bored I'm not even that tired."

Sister Mary Thomas smiles. "I'm bored, too."

"You *are*?" Betsy says, feeling scandalized. She doesn't think of nuns as having the capacity to be bored. She assumes they just fill that time up with loving God or whatever.

"I need a drink."

"You *what*?"

"A beer. I'd really kill for a beer."

"You drink beer?"

"Sure."

"What else do you do?"

"I watch movies."

"Really?"

"We have a VCR in the rectory. I love *Top Gun*. Have you seen it?"

"Of course I've seen *Top Gun*."

"You know what else I like?"

"What?"

"*Witness*."

"That one's R."

"Have you seen it?"

Betsy turns and looks hard at Sister Mary Thomas. "Is this a setup?"

Sister Mary Thomas laughs. "What do you mean?"

"I mean, are you making me think you're one thing to try to get me to open up about myself and my problems at home?"

"You have problems at home?" Sister Mary Thomas asks.

"Forget it."

"This is the real me, Betsy. I'm not setting you up." Sister Mary Thomas plucks a few bobby pins from behind her ears and lets her hair down.

"Did you just let your hair down?" Betsy asks. "Like, literally?"

Sister Mary Thomas laughs again. It's a soothing laugh, not horsey at all like the other nun laughs she's heard. "You want to see something?"

"What?"

"Come with me."

Sister Mary Thomas gets up and walks toward the stage at the far end of the basement. The other nuns are all caught up playing rummy. Sally is brushing Mo's hair, while Melissa digs around in the beading kit she brought along. Loner Lily is biting her nails and spitting the pieces onto the checkerboard floor. No one's paying any attention to them.

They go up on the stage. Sister Mary Thomas holds the heavy red curtain open for Betsy and leads her into darkness.

"Where are we going?" Betsy asks.

"There's a door back here somewhere," Sister Mary Thomas replies.

Behind the curtain smells like the lobby of the Loew's Oriental theater where Betsy goes to see her movies, sad and sticky and forgotten. Betsy scans the darkness and makes out a stack of folding tables.

Sister Mary Thomas feels along the wall and finds a door, turning the knob and pushing it in, snapping on a light. A small storage room is illuminated. Piles of boxes. A metal shelving rack full of paper plates, Styrofoam cups, and a big electric coffee percolator the bingo ladies must use.

Nestled in the corner of the room is a statue of the Virgin Mary, wrapped in a green cord of Christmas lights. Sister Mary Thomas goes over, finds the plug, and the statue comes alive with dots of red and white light, her blue robe thorny with shadows, her cracked plaster face spotlighted. "I call her Disco Madonna," Sister Mary Thomas says.

"You do?" Betsy says.

Sister Mary Thomas finds that response funny and laughs yet again and then she starts singing "Lady Madonna" by the Beatles but she changes it to "Disco Madonna."

Betsy studies the face of the statue. Nose chipped off, thin black cracks like veins, a smudge of something green on one cheek. "Why's she in here?"

"Who knows? I'm glad she is, though." Sister Mary Thomas finds a couple of step stools leaning against the base of the rack. She opens them and sets them up in front of the statue. "Sit."

Betsy does, putting her elbows up on her knees, pushing her hair behind her ears.

"You're gonna like this," Sister Mary Thomas says.

"Like what?"

Sister Mary Thomas kneels close to the statue and feels around behind it, coming out with a Sony Walkman and lightweight headphones with orange cushions and a duct-taped headband. She puts the headphones on Betsy, opens the Walkman, flipping the tape that's in there, and finally pressing play.

Madonna's "Holiday" comes on. Betsy recognizes the intro immediately. She has a Walkman at home and a shoebox full of cassettes. Her mom hardly ever buys her tapes at Sam Goody when she asks for them, but she has a bunch of blanks and spends a lot of time dubbing songs off the radio. Lots of them, she misses the very beginning or the dee-jay's talking ruins it. Betsy smiles and says, "You like Madonna?"

Sister Mary Thomas puts a finger over her lips and shushes her.

Betsy strains her neck and puts her hand up in apology, not realizing she was speaking so loudly, the music blasting in her ears. She listens to the song until the end.

Sister Mary Thomas stops the tape. "You know what she's talking about in that song?"

Betsy pushes the headphones down around her neck. "Like... wanting to take a holiday?"

"Sure. Exactly. We all deserve a break. All of us. Things don't have to be so hard."

"Is this your break? This little room and statue and the music?"

"This is an important place to me. I wanted to share it with you."

"Why me?"

"You're not like the other kids. God can forgive me for saying that. I see something else in you." She pauses. "I want you to come here sometimes. I'm leaving for good in a few days."

"Where are you going?"

"Can you keep a secret?"

Betsy has never—not once in her life, that she remembers—been asked to keep a secret. She doesn't have friends like that. She hopes one day she will. Not in high school; she's anticipating that'll suck. Maybe in college. She nods now, promising to keep her mouth shut, miming zipping her lips and throwing away the key.

"I'm in love," Sister Mary Thomas says.

"But you're a nun."

"Nuns can fall in love."

"I thought just with Jesus."

"Well, I do love Jesus, but I also fell in love with a man I've known for a couple of years. He's my best friend."

"Why are you telling me?"

"I don't know. I sensed you're the kind of person I could tell. You feel trapped, I can see it in your eyes. Not just here at this lock-in, but at school and church and with your family. And that's how I feel, too. And being with this man makes me feel different."

"Who is he?"

"Father Dave."

"Father Dave? Are you kidding? He's so little. He's like five-one. He must be six inches shorter than you."

Sister Mary Thomas laughs again. "What's height? Plus, I like that he's short."

Betsy shakes her head. "Where are you going?"

"He bought a car in secret. We're just going to run away together. He wants to go to Florida. Maybe Miami."

"Does he need to sit on a telephone book when he drives?"

Sister Mary Thomas swats at her leg like they're girlfriends. "You're terrible." A moment passes. Tears rim her eyes. "He's very good to me. He's very nice. I've never had much of a life. I joined the convent at eighteen. I went to an all-girls Catholic boarding school on Long Island before that. I was faithful and disciplined and I never broke any rules. I think you have to break rules now and again to truly live. I don't think that means you don't love God. That's what that song's about in a way, right?"

Betsy nods because what else can she do. She's struck by how surreal the moment is: sitting with pretty young Sister Mary Thomas in front of Disco Madonna, *The Immaculate Collection* tape in a secret Walkman, a secret love being whispered about.

Father Dave! Betsy once saw him eating spaghetti out of a Styrofoam cup on the front stoop of the school with a plastic fork. She asked why he didn't just use a bowl and he said, "This is my special cup." When he says Mass, all the old ladies complain because he talks low and gives these scholarly homilies. She remembers him talking about this one book, *The Woman Who Was Poor*, and she went to the library the next day to see if they had it and they didn't because it was old and French. She wonders if Sister Mary Thomas and Father Dave have kissed, or if they're saving that for when they run away. She pictures them on a beach, her in her habit, him in his clerical clothes, rolling around.

"Do you have a boyfriend?" Sister Mary Thomas asks.

Betsy shakes her head. There is not one single boy in her class that she likes, that she has a crush on. There are no girls either. When she gets a crush, it's on an actor or actress in some movie she's seen, and she lives with it for a few days and dreams of a life where it's her and him, or her and her. Christian Slater and Winona Ryder and River Phoenix are probably the biggest crushes she's had.

"What kind of problems do you have at home? Is it your stepdad?"

Betsy doesn't answer.

"If you ever want to talk, I'm here."

"But you won't be for long."

Sister Mary Thomas puts the Walkman in Betsy's lap and stands up. "I'm going back out before Sister Erin comes looking for me," she says. "You stay. Listen to the tape. 'Lucky Star' is next. I love that one."

"Thanks, Sister," Betsy says.

"Thank you for keeping my secret."

And then, just like that, Sister Mary Thomas is gone from the room and Betsy is left wondering if the last however long has even been real, but she knows it has been because here she is with the Walkman and Disco Madonna, and the stool where Sister Mary Thomas was sitting is still warm from her bottom.

Betsy can't imagine what Sister Mary Thomas just told her, how she opened up. Isn't she afraid, even in the slightest, of what Betsy might do with that information? Girls gossip. Betsy doesn't, but Sister Mary Thomas can't know that for sure.

Betsy presses play and listens to "Lucky Star" and "Borderline."

She moves her head so Disco Madonna is sort of swaying in front of her. She wishes she had a watermelon lollipop. She starts thinking of the world outside the lock-in, how dark the streets must be, how there probably aren't any people walking around, how quiet it must be with the trains coming less frequently. Her neighborhood is dead. She imagines that the city, across the bridge, is still alive and lit up. She knows it is. There are shows, bars, crowds of people, all-night movies.

She's been to Manhattan only for the Christmas tree and a

couple of museums. She wishes she was there. She wishes she was sitting in a movie theater with a bucket of popcorn.

A lock-in isn't anything. No one can keep you locked in, she decides. Sister Mary Thomas is proof of that.

She stops the tape and leaves the storage room.

She has twenty bucks in her pocket from her grandma. She thinks that'll be enough to get away, even if just for a little while. Train fare and a movie and popcorn and a soda. Maybe a couple of lollipops.

She searches around the dark stage for a way out. There's another door. This one opens on a staircase that smells like incense. She follows the smell, stumbling up the stairs in the dark, and comes out in a narrow hallway across from the sacristy. She's afraid that Monsignor Villani will jump out at her.

There's a dull glow coming from beyond the pews in the church, an electric candle that's still on. She's never thought of those candles as things that get shut off. People kneel there before or after Mass and put money in the offertory box and push a silver button to light a candle and they say their prayer. She always figured once a prayer was made, the light just stayed on, even in the dark of night. But now she sees how that's stupid. Of course the candles get reset daily. All those lost prayers.

She hopes now the doors aren't locked and that she can get out.

At the end of the hallway, there's a heavy door that leads to the back parking lot on Eighty-Fourth Street. She tries the handle and it's locked, but there's a latch below that and she turns it and tries again and cold air whooshes in from outside and suddenly she feels as free as she's ever felt.

She runs out into the lot, letting the door pound shut behind her, and cuts a quick right onto Eighty-Fourth Street. The streetlamps and telephone poles looks sadder in the middle of the night. A hush she's never heard hums through the neighborhood. The sound of darkness and sleep. It's colder than she remembered it being when she entered the lock-in and yet she feels fine in her sweater.

Her breath is in front of her.

She slows down at the corner, turns left onto Twenty-Third Avenue, passing the bank where she remembers going with her father to their safe deposit box before he moved away to California, and then she makes a right on Eighty-Sixth Street, staring up at the quiet El and all the closed shops with their graffiti-covered riot gates pulled down.

It's a pretty short walk to the Bay Parkway station, where she'll catch the B train into the city. She's not sure how often they come at night. She pictures herself sitting on the platform, her legs crossed, looking out over the neighborhood, listening to the hush, waiting.

She expects to see men lurch out from shadowy market stalls. Cars pass in the street, going fast. One slows a bit, the driver seeming to consider her, but she doesn't look over.

Just as she starts to climb the stairs up to the El platform, she hears a voice from behind her. It's Sister Mary Thomas, halfway down the block, jogging, calling out her name.

Betsy stops and sits on the first step and waits for Sister Mary Thomas.

When she arrives, out of breath, Sister Mary Thomas says, "Jeez, Betsy."

"How'd you know I left?" Betsy asks.

"Sister Erin heard something and asked me to check it out. I came up and saw you leaving and followed. Aren't you cold?"

"This sweater's warm."

"Where on earth are you going?"

"I want to go to the city to see a movie or something. They play movies all night."

"You can't just leave. You have to tell someone."

"It's not prison, right?"

"It's not prison, no, but you're thirteen. What would your folks say?"

"I don't have folks. I have a mom and a stepdad. What does that word even mean, *stepdad*? Where's it come from?"

"I don't know. I know you can't just leave."

"*You're* leaving."

"That's different."

"How?"

Sister Mary Thomas sits next to her on the step. "I don't know exactly, but it is. I'm a grown-up, for one. Let's go back to the church, sweetie. The middle of the night is nothing but trouble."

"I want to go to the city to see a movie. Come with me."

"We'll wait an hour or two for a train. We'll freeze."

Betsy shrugs.

"We should go back," Sister Mary Thomas tells her again.

"Why did you tell me what you told me about running away?" Betsy asks, turning to look at Sister Mary Thomas, studying her pale skin, her brown hair, her lips, the silvery breath painting the air in front of her face.

Sister Mary Thomas thinks about it. "I told you because I thought you could handle it," she says. "I thought it would give you hope for the future."

"I'm tired of people thinking I can handle things," Betsy says.

A train rumbles into the station. Betsy's so thankful. She needs one and here it is. She runs up the stairs, leaving Sister Mary Thomas behind, hops a turnstile to the bored chagrin of the man in the booth, and races up another short flight of steps to the platform, where the B train has arrived and its doors are gaping, the orange glow of the center car welcoming her. Her breath trails behind her as she launches herself into the car just before the doors ding and smack shut. She settles into a bucket seat and watches through the scratched windows, waiting for Sister Mary Thomas to come chugging up the stairs after her, to bang on the glass and demand that she come back to the lock-in.

But it doesn't happen that way. The train pulls out. Betsy watches the darkness of the neighborhood, studies it. The dark tops of buildings. Traffic lights changing up and down the avenues.

No one else is in this train car with her, thank God. Just her and the scratched windows and a half-full plastic bottle of 7-UP skittering around on the floor.

She wonders if Sister Mary Thomas will tell the other nuns or call her mother or maybe even call the cops. She's thinking that maybe she won't because Betsy has the scoop on her and Sister Mary Thomas wouldn't want anything to get out before taking off with Father Dave.

She feels bad for Sister Mary Thomas, innocently telling Betsy her plans in trust, not knowing the immediate impact it would have on her. She mostly feels bad because Sister Mary Thomas—even though she's young and pretty and in love and listens to Madonna—is still dumb the way grown-ups get dumb.

Betsy wonders how people wind up ruined like that and when it will happen to her. Maybe it's already happening. Maybe she's at the beginning of the process or she's in the middle of it, and she doesn't even know. Maybe you stay up all night, just once, at a lock-in or a slumber party, and the next day you're never the same. You pass through darkness into the forever darkness of being whatever it is that people become.

The train's quiet except for the soda bottle.

Betsy thinks of her mom getting a call from Sister Mary Thomas or Sister Erin, that yellow wall-mounted rotary phone ringing in their kitchen, vibrating the wood panels, her mom trudging out to it in her sweats, her stepdad grunting and pulling a pillow up over his head.

Her stepdad's name is Bob Girgenti. He wants Betsy to take his last name, like her mom has. She'll never do that. She likes that her last name is the same as her old man's, Murray, even though he lives in California now and it's an Irish name and everyone she knows, including her mom and her grandparents, is Italian. She likes that it makes her different.

Her dad is from Ireland, actually born there. His first name is Daniel. He came to Brooklyn with his parents when he was six and they settled in Bay Ridge. He met Betsy's mom at a bar called the Pied Piper when he was twenty and she was seventeen. He got her pregnant within six months and then they got married at St. Mary's and her dad moved in with her mom and her grandparents. Betsy was born and they tried to be a family for about seven years. Then her dad was gone one day and her mom spent all her time crying and her grandma tried to comfort her mom by saying things like, "Oh Karen, it just wasn't meant to be." And her grandpa kept repeating a line that Betsy wishes she had never heard him say: "Never trust no Mick bum."

Her dad fell in love with a woman who wanted to be an actress. Her name is Lucy. Daniel and Lucy. They moved to Los Angeles together. Betsy can't say their names in front of her mom. Her dad hardly writes, never calls. She has his phone number in California memorized. She writes it in the margins of her school notebooks so she'll never forget it. She's always wishing she had the guts to call him.

Part of what she hates so much about Bob is that he's not evil. He's boring and stupid and sometimes mean, that's all. But he's never smacked her or locked her in the basement or even refused to let her eat dinner as punishment for something. So, really, what does she have to complain about? She's not so young that she hasn't heard horror stories. Bob's a lot of things, but he's not a horror story. She feels guilty because sometimes she secretly wishes he was a horror story. Maybe then she'd know why she felt so lost, so out of place. What if the guilt over not encountering evil is there until one day she actually encounters evil and dealing with that becomes her life from then on?

The train makes its stops, the doors opening and closing, the silence filling with the sound of cold air rushing in. At Sixty-Second Street, a man gets on, and he's wearing a mechanic's jumpsuit and carrying what looks like a few foil-wrapped sandwiches in a plastic bag. He sits pretty far away from her. She should worry about him, she knows that.

She looks at the floor.

She can feel his eyes on her.

"You okay?" he says. His voice is deep, tired, as if the words are fighting back against a yawn.

"I'm fine," she says, still not looking over at him.

"You hungry? I got some egg, bacon, and cheese sandwiches in here." He shakes the bag. "I'm bringing them to work. I always get two for Teddy. He don't need two."

"I'm good, thanks," she says.

"Okay. You just let me know."

The train dips into a tunnel. The lights flash off and then back on.

"My name's Frank," the man says, scooching a few seats closer to her. He's still a good distance away, but he's closer and closer's no good. "What are you doing out on your own in the middle of the night?"

She doesn't answer, studying the floor between her feet, the remnants of a piece of gum strung like thread from under the seat to the stanchion in front of her.

"The night holds perils for a girl," Frank continues.

Again, she stays quiet.

"I have a daughter. I wouldn't want her out here on her own. You're how old, twelve, thirteen? Where are your parents? What's your name?"

"My name's Emily," she lies, still looking down.

The derelict 7-UP bottle is still shooting around the car. It passes in front of Frank and he stops it with his foot and then reaches down, unscrews the cap, and takes a swig. He stays quiet after that. He gets off at Thirty-Sixth Street. She's relieved.

When the train crosses over the Manhattan Bridge, she can't even see the East River below. She sees dots of light from apartment buildings on the Manhattan side. She goes over and considers the map. She makes a decision to get off at the Broadway-Lafayette stop, thinking she'll find a movie theater there. How can she not? Her belief is that it'll be right there when she comes up from the subway: golden, glowing, open.

She wonders what time it is now. It must be past three, maybe even almost four. The train ride was at least forty-five minutes, lots of stopping and starting.

She gets off at Broadway-Lafayette, hustling past a man covered in a ratty black blanket, asleep on a bench. A worker polishes the floor with some kind of humming machine. She runs up a couple of flights of stairs to the street.

There are lights and cars, taxis mostly, but there's plenty of darkness too. Most of the shops are closed. She doesn't see a movie theater. She goes over to a newspaper rack and grabs a copy of *The Village Voice*, which she's heard of. She flips through, looking for movie times. She's cold now. She's on a corner she's never been on.

She sees an open deli across the street, bright and warm-looking. She walks over. It's cluttered. Long aisles. Refrigerators full of beer and soda. A freezer with ice pops. She orders a coffee because that seems like the right thing to do. Forget lollipops.

The guy behind the counter doesn't think twice about her or what she's doing out at this time. He rubs his hands together and blows into them and pours her a coffee in a blue paper cup. She pays with her twenty and gets a ten, a five, some singles, and quarters and pennies back. She puts the money in her pocket. She flips open the plastic lid on the cup and blows into the steam. She doesn't put in milk or sugar. She drinks it black and burns her upper lip.

She has *The Village Voice* under her arm. She spreads it out on the counter and finally gets to the movie pages. She can't find anything starting at this time.

She's not sure what to do. She thinks about the change in her pocket. There are at least two quarters. "You have a payphone?" she asks the guy behind the counter.

He nods. "Outside. Right around the corner."

She leaves the paper there and goes out to the payphone, setting the coffee down on the sidewalk between her feet. She looks all around, hoping not to be noticed by taxi drivers and cops and other assorted creeps that prowl the streets at night.

It's three hours earlier in California. She says her dad's number out loud and then realizes that a couple of quarters won't cover a long distance call. She can go in and get more change or she can just call collect. Collect makes more sense. She needs to save her money.

The operator puts the call through, and her dad accepts the charges. "Betsy, is everything okay?" he asks, his voice weary. "What is it? What happened, honey?"

She hasn't heard his voice in so long. He sounds like someone she's never known. She puts her hand over the mouthpiece to hide the sounds from passing cars and talks in a whisper: "Dad, I'm trapped," she says. "Please help. They've got me locked in a basement. Please. I don't know what to do. Please." And then she hangs up, trying to duplicate what it'd be like if her line has been cut off.

She's not sure what her purpose is. It's more than a prank. She wants her dad to worry. She wants him to panic. She guesses he'll call her mom and her mom will call the nuns and there will be all sorts of chaos. But here she is now in the dead of night in the city with only her coffee and her trusty red sweater and a little money to burn. There's got to be a movie playing somewhere.

THE NIGHT MOUNTAIN
Jeffrey Alan Love

There is a mountain that lives in the night. Do you see it?

We walked in darkness. It was a long way to go. Perhaps it never ended, and this was what I deserved. To climb forever. To never know rest. To push my way through grasping branches and brambles, to bark my shins on ancient rocks, to be shat on by these two bone-white birds that hung silent, floating, just beyond my reach. At times I saw the lights of distant cities through a thinning of trees. Far below on the dark plains. Who moves down those streets, I wondered. Who sits at those windows and watches the night mountain?

Lina walked ahead of me, the baby in her arms. She never slowed, never seemed to tire. She had always been strong. I carried the box in one hand. Behind me, his panting breath loud in my ears, came the beast-faced man.

The baby was not yet a week old when the beast-faced man delivered the box.

It was a small box, made even smaller by being in the beast-faced man's oversized hands. It was made of wood, dark-grained and polished in such a way that looking at it you felt you saw a great distance within it. That if you held it up to your eye you would see things long hidden, long wished for, nightly dreamed of and then forgotten. All the things that fled with waking. That it might be a small window to another place, a place where someone like the beast-faced man made sense, for he didn't make much sense to me standing there on my porch in his flapping black clothes, his wild and knotted hair, his beard that could not conceal his teeth.

He was my wife's brother, though I did not know that then.

"You the father," he said, his voice a low thrum I felt in my guts. "Congratulations."

I found I could not look away from the box, from his hands, whether it was the box itself that held me bewitched or fear of looking directly at his face I could not say. There was no breeze, but his hair moved at the edges of my vision, the locks curling and uncoiling like so many snakes. He held out the box to me.

"For the mother."

I hesitated, so he reached out, gently took my hand, and folded it around the box. His hands were rough, the skin thick, but his touch was tender, as though he was afraid of breaking either of us. The box was warm, and I thought I felt the slightest of scrapings from within it as it curled into my palm. An odor rose from it in slow pulses that reminded me of early morning runs on streets wet with rain.

"For the mother," he said again, and then he was gone, as if he had never been there.

In my hand breathed a box.

The beast-faced man had been surprised when I stepped through the box with Lina and the baby. Perhaps he thought I had no idea, that I was blissfully unaware of certain facts. That I was in the dark.

She came to me from out of a lake, I wanted to say. I have some idea. I know some things.

I know enough to be afraid.

"There's the little fellow," the beast-faced man said, looking down upon the baby. "What's his name?"

Lina said something quietly then, words I could not understand, but whatever it was it was not my son's name.

"His name is Alexander," I said. Lina reached over and squeezed my hand. I bent down and kissed the top of Alexander's head, breathed in the perfect smell of him.

"Well, if his name is Alexander than mine is Bel," said the beast-faced man. He held out his hand to me, and I shook it. His touch was not so gentle this time, but I was able to look him in the eye now. In the night his eyes glinted, and when he spoke the inside of his mouth flared as though a flame lived inside of him.

"He won't be able to keep up," said the beast-faced man to Lina as he released my hand. "Say your goodbyes now."

"He'll keep up," said Lina.

Bel laughed, licked his teeth.

And then we had begun to walk. Though it was night, it was not dark yet. I could see the trunks of the trees, the sawtoothed grasses that waved and thrashed, a giant bridge in the sky that stretched from horizon to horizon. Clouds moved as a sea above us, high and twisting, crashing and sliding against each other. They were gray, pewter, lit at times from within by strobing flashes. In their movement I saw the shape of a spear, the scales of a snake, the six-fingered hand of a god.

Now Lina held the baby so that his head rested on her shoulder. He no longer slept. His eyes were open. He watched me as we climbed.

Behind me Bel roared, and Lina changed direction slightly. Further up, always up, the night mountain's slope. Weaving through the darkness, between the night trees, the two birds like ghosts haunting our heads. Lina's face turned away from me, her hair hanging like a veil.

My son's eyes twinkled in the night.

*　　*　　*

Before the baby was born everyone talked about the joy to come, and no one talked about the fear. No one had told me how I would feel as I stood in the dark listening to him breathe for the first time, more aware of his body than my own. That I would gladly stop my own breath if it meant his could go on forever. I couldn't sleep for fear of what might happen if I wasn't there to hear it. To prime his lungs, his little hummingbird heart, with my fear.

We broke free of the trees to an endless rising expanse of dark rock. The bone birds followed, and swooped down around my head, by my ears. As they swung past they whispered to me in a language I did not know.

"Do not talk to them," said the beast-faced man behind me. "They are tricksters. They will act otherwise, but all they want is to chew on your liver, pluck out your eyes, unspool your brain."

"What do you want?" I asked, not looking back.

"This," he said. "My sister home. Forgiven. Safe."

We walked on in silence for a minute. Lina, with her long strides, was far beyond us.

"But I also want her happy," he said.

The birds laughed, and he waved his arm to shoo them away.

I slipped then, and fell heavily onto the stone slope. The birds sang. The beast-faced man helped me up, and on his fingers I saw blood. I had sliced my hand open upon a ridge of sharp rock and felt nothing. He sniffed at the blood on his fingers, rubbed them together, and then looked at me.

"When she came to you, how did you think this could possibly end?"

He flitted out his tongue, licked the tip of his finger, tasted my blood.

"I shouldn't go any further," he said. "Hurry. You may still be able to catch up to them."

I stumbled up the mountain. What did I want? My son to live forever? For all I knew he would. What truly lurked beneath his skin I did not know, except that there was a half of it that was me. Did I wish to keep him from ever feeling pain, to never be hurt? In my own life it had taken being hurt to grow up, to become who I was now. Perhaps that was it, then.

I didn't want my son to grow up. I wanted him to be my little boy forever. I wanted him to be a little boy forever.

I didn't want him to change.

I wanted him to need me there, breathing with him, breathing with him.

I called to Lina but she could not hear me. The further up we went the louder it became. Things moved in the spaces between the stones, calling out. Great engines roared and bellowed from the bridge's heights, casting smoke and sparks into the sky, lighting the bellies of the clouds the color of dried blood. The sparks flew about my head. The sparks laughed at me. Boulders shaped into molten-faced statues of men dotted my path, fine designs etched in wandering lines upon them. Something like insects swarmed at my feet, chittering. When I looked back, I could still see the dark silhouette of the beast-faced man, the birds perched on his shoulders, whispering in his ears as they flapped their white wings about his head as though to urge him on.

Then there were no more lights from above or below, and the sound washed away, as if I had breached some border beyond which it could not pass. I could not tell where the mountain ended and the darkness began. All was night. Only the sound of my feet upon the strange earth told me that I had not walked right off the mountain and into nothingness. The beast-faced man was no longer behind me. Far ahead of me Lina and Alexander walked hand in hand in a void. My son, walking. His first steps. He was stretched out now, leaner, taller. His hair moved to unfelt winds.

"Wait," I called, and summoned what energy I had left to hurry after them. I could feel the blisters starting on my feet. How many hours had we been walking? Why would they not stop? Clouds descended, swallowed me, and I found myself in a hazed white nothingness.

"Wait," I heard another voice call. I turned, but could not see who had spoken. If anything moved, I could not see it. I plunged forward, hoping I had not lost sense of the direction Lina had gone.

"Wait for me," I called. "Please wait."

I ran. I fell. I fell again. I left a trail of blood on the mountain. The clouds wrapped themselves around me. Slivers of light slashed down like rain. Above my head I heard the flapping wings of the birds, the barest hint of their unknown tongue. Stones shifted beneath my feet. Something grasped at my legs and I stumbled. I fell out of the cloud and into cold water.

A lake atop the mountain.

I stood shivering, the water up to my waist. Mist rose from the surface. Small waves pushed and pulled at me. My feet sunk down into mud. Along the shore clung weeds as fine as the hair of a child. The bone birds perched upon a moss-covered stone, still as statues, watching me. My hand pulsed blood into the water. I called out for Alexander, for Lina, and my voice slid away across the surface of the lake as if it were frozen.

The birds slipped off the stone and into the water. They dove down, and when they surfaced they were no longer birds.

They sang to me then, and though I did not know the words I understood what they were saying.

This was as far as I could go.

I still carried the beast-faced man's box. I let it drop into the lake.

Something beneath the water brushed against my leg. Something took my hand. Something pressed the box back into my hand.

On my nightstand sits a plain wooden box. It is polished in such a way that you feel you can see a great distance within it. That if you held it up to your eye you would see things long hidden, long wished for, nightly dreamed of, never forgotten.

There is a mountain that lives in the night. There is a lake in the clouds where my love swims. There is a place in the darkness where my son is safe.

Just over there.

Look out the window. Do you see it?

A PARTIAL BEGINNER'S GUIDE TO THE LUCY TEMERLIN HOME FOR BROKEN SHAPESHIFTERS
Kuzhali Manickavel

1. Avoid any corridor infested with thunderstorms. 'Corridor infested with thunderstorms' does not mean a couple of thunderstorms above your head and the opportunity to be in the rain while also being in a corridor. It means a corridor that is rightly or wrongly, bristling with thunderstorms that are piled on top of thunderstorms. Some of them are extremely old, some of them are twisted together either because they are fighting or making love, and at least four of them are not thunderstorms at all but no one knows what else to call them. Do not try to find these thunderstorms for the purpose of documentation. Do not form 'stormwatch' groups. The thunderstorms are not there for scientific/humanitarian/ aesthetic/research purposes. They are there because no one knows how to get rid of them. If, for whatever reason, you feel invincible, heartbroken or just young and full of life, do not seek out any corridor infested with thunderstorms because it will not turn out the way you think it will. If however you encounter one of these corridors by accident, then that's too bad.

2. Cultivate a garden. You can buy seeds or steal them from plants. Cordon off a part of your floor or your windowsill and say, 'this is my garden' to anyone who will listen. Do

not cordon off a part of your floor or your windowsill, say 'this is my garden' and not cultivate a garden. Don't be like that. Plant things which are useful but are not vegetables. You can make rows if you are into that sort of thing. If your entire garden dies, remember that it is simply the circle of life, the wheel of fortune, the leap of faith and the band of hope. Do not plant teeth, childhood mementos or dead pets.

3. Endeavour to inculcate change in various facets of your life. For instance, try to change your clothes regularly, especially your underwear. Change your toothbrush and bedsheets. Sometimes it can be nice to rearrange the furniture in your room or wear colourful, fun accessories on your clothes. Cutting your hair is another fun change you can try.

4. Don't wake anything that is sleeping. The 7th floor in particular is notorious for harbouring a plethora of sleeping things. You may say how will I know if something is sleeping? This place is fucking bananas. How will I know if something is sleeping or killing itself or being a chair? This is a good question.

5. Do not allow other people to create metaphors for your life. For instance, if a motherfucker tries to take your hand and say you are like a circle, you are like a prayer that is never answered, you are like my friend in rehab who never gets better, you are like a wave, an agoraphobic, you are just like me. If a motherfucker has the audacity to say all this *and* try to touch you, tell them they have to take you home now because it's finally finally happening oh my god. Tell them you are a vegetarian but you eat eggs, chicken and fish on Mondays, Tuesdays, Wednesdays, Thursdays and on weekends. Tell them this is not going to be easy but it *is* going to be amazing.

*   *   *

6. During your first year, you will hear many different stories about SheetalJain, who didn't even go here but anyway. Please remember the following facts when encountering any of these aforementioned stories. SheetalJain went into the bathroom on a Sunday afternoon, presumably to wash her hair. She flushed the toilet and turned on the tap. When they broke the door down later that night, they found

—one pile of her clothes thrown over the shower rod
—one pile of clothes on the floor
—fingernails, presumably hers, scattered beside the sink
—2 teeth, also presumably hers, in the drain
—a scrap of paper beside the toilet with the words "What to say about me???? I'm just ME!!!! Sheetal. Simple cool girl who loves to just enjoy life."

It is perfectly acceptable to write fan fiction, poetry and dramatic monologues about SheetalJain. It is also acceptable to describe yourself as a simple cool girl who loves to just enjoy life. Do not try to find SheetalJain. She didn't even go here.

7. Visit the Tropicool IcyLand Urban Indian Slum, even though the board of administrators will not encourage this because the board of administrators are a bunch of classist fucks. Do not visit the slum like, bai everyone I'm going to visit the slum now. Do not wear a hat, do not carry your own water and when you are there, do not distribute promises of jobs or social media coverage in exchange for souvenirs of that sweet, sweet slum life. Visit quietly and honestly. Wear sensible shoes. Take the bus. Don't be an asshole.

(By the tub was a basket of old bones. She'd had it explained to her and the sight was not disturbing. She made sure only to glance into it, though the minister seemed uninterested in her reactions. The bones were of all sizes and kinds and came—she was sure of it—from various animals, and from people too. (There was no human skull that would have cast that beyond any doubt.) She saw the jawbone of a horse or donkey, the snapped-off ribs of something cat-sized, perhaps. Nub-like vertebrae. Little rags of flesh still adorned a few. That surprised her and she wanted to ask if it didn't affect the process.

The minister fussed over the big container where the viscous fluid slopped with his steps. Not for the first time she detected in his motions an enjoyment of the whole process; that annoyed her.

'This is what this is for,' he said as if she didn't know.

She thought, *How is it that I'm here?*

The minister upended the bucket of bones into the bath. That did surprise her, and she jumped back, because he did so without any apparent thought and certainly without warning, and the swilling stuff spattered. It landed on his arm—she moved too quickly for any to hit her—and she was anxious at the sight of its glistening opalescent blobs, of what they might do, but the minister wiped it all off without any concern and kept staring into the tub. She stepped forward again to look herself.

The bones did not lie all at the base. Some were already suspended a few centimetres up. She watched more began to lift gently, tugged insistently, against their own density. They drifted through the thick liquid.

Around each bone, slowly, the solution began to coagulate

and grow more opaque, like cooling candlewax. It thickened into threads, coagulated in lines and cocoons, cauling the bones, connecting one to the other in cords spun out of nothing, tendons that spasmed and yanked the bones in whatever directions.

Some big leg-bone was at the centre of the shifting mass. A variety of smaller bones slipped and slid in imperfect radial symmetry around it, and those tiny ribs spread into what she thought would be feelers. The vertebrae knotted into tails or tentacles. New limbs. The bathwater-stuff built itself a chaotic new body on these collected bones, threadlike capillaries opening invisible through which thinner bloodlike liquid might rush. Clots of stuff shielded by the bones would become organs. Perhaps eyes.

The next night, when all this was done, whatever this would be would self-birth out of the urgent slop, stand, or as close to that as it could, step or crawl, a random animal on uneven limbs. It would cry out if it had a voice.)

CONTRIBUTORS

Celeste Rita Baker is a Virgin Islander who currently resides in Harlem. She has published short stories in *The Caribbean Writer, Calabash, Margin's Magical Realism, Scarab* and most recently *Moko Magazine* as well as *Abyss & Apex Magazine.*

William Boyle is from Brooklyn, New York. He is the author of *Gravesend, Death Don't Have No Mercy, Everything is Broken, The Lonely Witness,* and *A Friend is a Gift You Give Yourself.* He lives in Oxford, Mississippi.

Jesse Bullington is the author of three weird historical novels: *The Sad Tale of the Brothers Grossbart, The Enterprise of Death,* and *The Folly of the World.* Under the pen name Alex Marshall he recently completed the Crimson Empire trilogy; the first book, *A Crown for Cold Silver,* was shortlisted for the James Tiptree, Jr. Award. He's also the editor of the Shirley Jackson Award nominated *Letters to Lovecraft,* and co-editor (with Molly Tanzer) of *Swords v. Cthulhu.* His short fiction, reviews, and articles have appeared in such diverse publications as the LA Review of Books, *The Mammoth Book of Best New Erotica 13,* and VICE.

Indrapramit Das (aka Indra Das) is a writer and editor from Kolkata, India. He is a Lambda Literary Award-winner for his debut novel *The Devourers*, and has been a finalist for the Crawford, Tiptree and Shirley Jackson Awards. His short fiction has appeared in publications including Tor.com, Clarkesworld and Asimov's, and has been widely anthologized. He is an Octavia E. Butler Scholar and a grateful graduate of Clarion West 2012. He has lived in India, the United States, and Canada, where he completed his MFA at the University of British Columbia.

Cecilia Ekbäck was born in Sweden in a northern fishing town. Her parents come from Lapland. After university she specialised in marketing and worked for a multinational for twenty years with postings in the UK, Russia, Germany, France, Portugal and the Middle East. In 2010, she finished Royal Holloway's Master in Creative Writing. She now lives in Canmore, 'returning home' to the landscape and the characters of her childhood in her writing. Her first novel, *Wolf Winter,* was published in 2015. *In the Month of the Midnight Sun*, her second novel, was published in 2016. She is currently at work on her third.

S. L. Grey is a collaboration between Sarah Lotz and Louis Greenberg, responsible for five novels so far, including *The Mall* and *The Apartment*. Based in the Welsh borderlands, Sarah is a novelist and screenwriter and die-hard zombie fanatic. Louis is a Johannesburg-bred author and editor currently living in England.

Dale, Sam, and Lauren occasionally combine forces, like a giant transforming super robot or mutating multi-limbed horror, to write things weirder than any of them could have come up with on their own. In their own separate lives, **Dale Halvorsen** is an award-winning illustrator, cover designer and co-writer of horror comic, *Survivors' Club*, **Sam Beckbessinger** is co-founder of a Cape Town fintech company and author of the essential *How To Manage Your Money Like a F*cking Grownup*, and **Lauren Beukes** is the award-winning author of *The Shining Girls, Zoo City* and *Broken Monsters* and also a co-writer on *Survivors' Club*.

Omar Robert Hamilton is a filmmaker and writer. His debut novel, *The City Always Wins* chronicles the rise and fall of the 2011 Egyptian revolution.

Frances Hardinge was brought up in a sequence of small, sinister English villages, and spent a number of formative years living in a Gothic-looking, mouse-infested hilltop house in Kent. She studied English Language and Literature at Oxford, fell in love with the city's crazed archaic beauty, and lived there for many years.

Will Hill is an author and screenwriter. His most recent novel, *After The Fire*, won the YA Book Prize in 2018 and was shortlisted for the Carnegie Medal. He lives in London.

Jeffrey Alan Love is an artist and writer. Winner of the World Fantasy Award for Best Artist, he is the author of *Notes from the Shadowed City* and *The Thousand Demon Tree*.

Kuzhali Manickavel's collections *Things We Found During the Autopsy, Insects Are Just like You and Me Except Some of Them Have Wings* and echapbook *Eating Sugar, Telling Lies* are available from Blaft Publications, Chennai. Her work has also appeared in *Granta, Strange Horizons, Agni, Subtropics, Michigan Quarterly Review* and *DIAGRAM*.

China Miéville is the author of various works of fiction and non-fiction, including *The City & the City, October, The Census Taker,* and *London's Overthrow*.

Leah Moore is an author, columnist, and digital comics evangelist. Leah's comic writing career began in 2002 with stories for America's Best Comics. More recently she has written scripts for Dynamite Entertainment (Gail Simone's *Swords of Sorrow*, *Red Sonja*), *Heavy Metal Magazine*, and Shelly Bond's Black Crown Publishing (*Femme Magnifique*, *Black Crown Quarterly*). She has also written columns and articles for *The Big Issue*, *Lifetime TV* online, and *Comic Heroes Magazine*.

Silvia Moreno-Garcia's *Signal to Noise* was named a best book of 2015 by BookRiot, Tor.com, Barnes & Noble, Buzzfeed, io9, and more. Her Mexican vampire novel, *Certain Dark Things*, was one of NPR's Best Books of 2016, a *Publishers Weekly* Top 10 for 2016, a VOYA "Perfect Ten," and a finalist for multiple awards. She has also edited several anthologies, including the World Fantasy Award-winning *She Walks in Shadows* (a.k.a Cthulhu's Daughters).

Yukimi Ogawa lives in a small town in Tokyo where she writes in English but never speaks the language. She still wonders why it works that way. Her stories can be found in such places as *Clarkesworld*, *Fantasy & Science Fiction*, and *Strange Horizons*.

Karen Onojaife is a novelist and short story writer. Her writing has featured in publications such as Mslexia, Buzzfeed, Callaloo, Sable Literary Magazine and most recently, *Closure: Contemporary Black British Short Stories*. Her work has previously been listed for the Bridport Short Story, Fish Short Story, and Mslexia Short Story competitions. Her novel, *Borrowed Light*, won the Reader's Choice award in the inaugural SI Leeds Literary Prize 2012. She is a VONA/Voices fellow, recipient of a place on the Hedgebrook Writers in Residence program and currently is a fiction reader for the Callaloo journal.

Sally Partridge is an author of award-winning young-adult fiction novels and short stories. She was named one of Mail & Guardian's 200 Young South Africans in 2011 and shortlisted for the Commonwealth Short Story prize in 2013. Her fifth novel, *Mine,* was published in 2018. Find her on Twitter @ sapartridge

Maha Khan Phillips is a multiple award winning financial journalist and editor, and the author of *The Curse of Mohenjodaro, Beautiful from this Angle*, and *The Mystery of the Aagnee Ruby*. She has a bachelor's degree in Politics and International Relations and masters' degrees in International Conflict Analysis and in Creative Writing. She grew up in Karachi, Pakistan, and currently lives in London.

Daniel Polansky lives in Los Angeles. He finds enumerating accomplishments gauche, but if you were really interested you could check out DanielPolansky.com

Amira Salah-Ahmed is a Cairo-based writer and journalist. She has covered Egypt's news for local and international publications for more than a decade and is one of the co-founders of independent media company, Mada Masr. With a certain fluidity between journalism and creative writing, she began writing poetry in 2010. She has also co-authored a book (*Tahrir Memoirs*) with a group of writers and bloggers about the 18-day uprising, published in Arabic and Italian in 2012.

Sami Shah is a multi-award winning writer, comedian, broadcaster. His first novel *Fire Boy* was released in 2016, and is now available in South Asia as *The Boy of Fire and Earth*. Sami has written columns for national and international newspapers and magazines, short stories for anthologies, and documentaries for radio. He's currently based in Melbourne.

Matt Suddain is a New Zealand-born writer and the author of two novels: *Theatre of the Gods* (2013) and *Hunters & Collectors* (2016). He lives in London.

Lavie Tidhar is the author of the Jerwood Fiction Uncovered Prize winning and Premio Roma nominee *A Man Lies Dreaming* (2014), the World Fantasy Award winning *Osama* (2011) and of the Campbell Award winning and Locus and Clarke Award nominated *Central Station* (2016). His latest novels are the forthcoming *Unholy Land* (2018) and his first children's novel, *Candy* (2018). He is the author of many other novels, novellas and short stories.

Genevieve Valentine has written novels, comics, and short fiction. Her nonfiction has appeared in the New York Times, the Atlantic, and NPR.org.

Marina Warner writes fiction and cultural history. Her novels include *The Lost Father* (1988), *INdigo* (1992) and *The Leto Bundle* (2000), and she has published three collections of short stories, most recently *Fly Away Home* (2014). Her critical studies focus on myth and fairytale, in such books as *Joan of Arc: The Image of Female Heroism* (1982), *From the Beast to the Blonde* (1994), and *Stranger Magic: Charmed States and The Arabian Nights* (2011; winner of the National Book Critics Circle award, the Sheykh Zayed Prize and the Truman Capote award). She is Professor of English and Creative Writing at Birkbeck College, Professorial Research Fellow at the School of Oriental and African Studies, a Fellow of the British Academy, and was elected President of the Royal Society of Literature in 2017. In 2015, she was awarded the Holberg Prize in the Arts and Humanities, and in 2017 she was given a World Fantasy Lifetime Achievement Award. *Fairy Tale: A Very Short Introduction* came out in January 2018 and *Forms of Enchantment: Writings on Art and Artists* in Autumn 2018. She is currently working on the project www.storiesintransit.com, researching the concept of Sanctuary and writing an 'unreliable memoir' *A Life Mislaid* about her childhood in Egypt.

Mahvesh Murad and **Jared Shurin** are the editors of—collectively—over two dozen anthologies, including *The Djinn Falls in Love*. They live 6,549 miles apart.

FIND US ONLINE!

www.rebellionpublishing.com

/rebellionpub   /rebellionpublishing   /rebellionpub

SIGN UP TO OUR NEWSLETTER!

rebellionpublishing.com/sign-up

YOUR REVIEWS MATTER!

Enjoy this book? Got something to say?

Leave a review on Amazon, GoodReads or with your
favourite bookseller and let the world know!

THE DJINN FALLS IN LOVE

& other stories

Edited by
Mahvesh Murad & Jared Shurin

Including stories by Nnedi Okorafor • Neil Gaiman • Jamal Mahjoub • Kuzhali Manickavel
Sami Shah • Claire North • Kamila Shamsie • K. J. Parker • Sophia Al-Maria & many more

"Exquisite and audacious, and highly recommended" - *The New York Times*

A fascinating collection of new and classic tales of the fearsome Djinn, from bestselling, award-winning and breakthrough international writers.

Imagine a world filled with fierce, fiery beings, hiding in our shadows, in our dreams, under our skins. Eavesdropping and exploring; savaging our bodies, saving our souls. They are monsters, saviours, victims, childhood friends. Some have called them genies: these are the Djinn.

And they are everywhere. On street corners, behind the wheel of a taxi, in the chorus, between the pages of books. Every language has a word for them. Every culture knows their traditions. Every religion, every history has them hiding in their dark places.

There is no part of the world that does not know them. They are the Djinn. They are among us.

 WWW.SOLARISBOOKS.COM

Follow us on Twitter! www.twitter.com/rebellionpub